Correct But Wish to Explain

Grant Hall

Self-published, Richmond, Virginia

Printed in the United States of America

ISBN 979-8-2696-7649-4

A Note to Readers

This book uses the language and traditions of the Southern Military Institute (SMI) to tell a true-to-setting story. Institute jargon appears for accuracy—terms like Rat, Ratline, Brother Rat, and Dyke are used in their SMI-specific sense. Outside the Institute, some of these words carry different meanings or can be offensive. Where they appear, they are presented descriptively and with context, not as value judgments. Claims are limited to the people, places, and time described; readers should avoid overgeneralizing beyond that scope. When discussing sensitive topics (discipline, culture, identity, and tradition), the goal is clarity and respect. Feedback from readers—especially those with lived experience in Corps life— is welcome.

About This Series

This trilogy follows Ethan from the forces that shaped him in childhood, through the crucible of the Southern Military Institute, into middle life, and toward a steadier stride.

• **Book One — Correct But Wish to Explain**: Childhood pressures, the decision to matriculate, and the Ratline's demands—how Post forges and tests him.
• **Book Two — *The Long March Home***: Careers, commitments, and course corrections as Ethan navigates work, love, and identity after SMI.
• **Book Three — *At Ease***: Confidence without the armor— integrating discipline with grace, purpose, and balance.

Table of Contents

Chapter 1 — The Beginning 7

Chapter 2 – Shattered Illusions 15

Chapter 3 — The Boots 34

Chapter 4 — A New Divide 52

Chapter 5 — The Challenge 72

Chapter 6 – The Road to Virginia Tech 92

Chapter 7 – Across the Parade Deck 110

Chapter 8 – Skunk 132

Chapter 9 — The Boots 148

Chapter 10 – Moonshine 161

Chapter 11 — Hell Week 174

Chapter 12 — Stripped 191

Chapter 13 — Sweat Parties 206

Chapter 14 — Jimmy Buffett 219

Chapter 15 — Specials 230

Chapter 16 — Drumout 241

Chapter 17 — The Forced March 252

Chapter 18 — Breakout 266

Chapter 19 — Natty Bo 279

Chapter 20 — Sophomore Year: Broken Hands & Broken Hearts 291

Chapter 21 — Detour: Army Green 306

Chapter 22 – The Buffett Escape 319

Chapter 23 – Back to The Institute 327

Chapter 24 – Jack's New Game 336

Chapter 25 – The Barber Townee 348

Chapter 26 – The Last Hurrah 356

Chapter 27 – One Hundred Fifty-Four Specials 364

Definitions & Qualifications — SMI (Southern Military Institute)

Definitions (Jargon & Acronyms)

Rat: First-year cadet in training status during the Ratline.

Ratline: Structured first-year training emphasizing discipline, customs, and teamwork; ends with Breakout.

Brother Rat (BR): Member of one's entering class; class bond and mutual support.

Breakout: Milestone event marking completion of the Ratline and transition to full cadet status.

Dyke: Upper-class mentor assigned to a Rat. Context note: Institute jargon; potentially offensive outside this context—define on first use.

The Corps: Collective term for all enrolled cadets.

Post: Institute grounds/campus.

Matriculation: Formal entry of new cadets; start of Ratline.

Parade: Formal drill/review of the Corps.

Mess: Dining hall; also refers to formations for meals.

ROTC: Reserve Officers' Training Corps; military-science instruction affiliated with the Institute.

Blue Book: Cadet regulations/manual of conduct (use the manuscript's canonical title).

Penalty Tours / PT: Disciplinary marching ("tours") or physical training assigned as corrective action.

General Committee (GC): Cadet leadership/disciplinary body; structure varies by year.

Honor Code: Cadet-led system covering lying, cheating, stealing, with reporting/adjudication.

Furlough: Authorized leave from Post.

Taps / Lights Out: End-of-day signal and quiet hours.

Old Corps: Colloquial for previous-era cadets/alumni; used in tradition comparisons.

Chapter 1 — The Beginning

In the early 1970s, on a quiet cul-de-sac outside Richmond, Virginia, Ethan believed in the American dream because nobody had told him not to. He was five, small for his age, and fast on his feet. In his drawings, the houses all had square windows and smiling stick people; the sun wore sunglasses; the grass was always the color of green crayons.

The house was a modest brick ranch, one story, three bedrooms, maybe 1,200 square feet. Ethan's room was the first off the hallway—close to the living room, too close, as it would turn out. He liked hearing the TV from bed at night, the laugh tracks of sitcoms and the low drone of the evening news. It made him feel tucked in by the world. What he didn't like— what he learned to dread—was how the living room could turn from harbor to storm without warning.

At first it was a tone, a thread pulled too tight in his father's voice. A "What did you say?" followed by his mother's "I didn't mean it like that." Voices rose and fell like a seesaw. Plates still clinked in the sink, the dog still thumped her tail. But sometimes everything else went quiet except the words.

The house smelled like dog. In Ethan's earliest memories it was a dachshund, a hot-dog dog who tolerated cowboy hats and capes. Later it was Brandy, a chocolate lab his mom's boss had bought as a hunting dog. She had been sent away to training but flunked out—she was terrified of gunshots. What she lacked in field skill she made up for in loyalty. For more than a decade Brandy was Ethan's best friend. No matter what was going on in the house, no matter how sharp the voices or how loud the crashes, she was always happy to see him, always ready with licks and tail wags that seemed to say: you're safe with me.

Dinner came every night at six o'clock sharp, a neighborhood ritual. Parents all up and down the street stepped onto their porches like clockwork, calling their kids in unison. Inside Ethan's house, though, dinner was a trial. The rule was iron: no one left the table until their plate was clean. Ethan's palate was limited, and more nights than not he sat staring at cold food long after everyone else had gone to bed.

Bored and angry one night, he moved his placemat and began carving into the table with his knife. He etched out a Pac-Man, open mouth chasing dots, the maze crawling to life beneath his hand. When he finished, he slid the placemat back over the carving and crept off to bed, smug with the secret. The next night, when he found himself still stuck at the table with untouched food, he added to the scene—ghosts, another path, another bite of rebellion hidden under the cover of cloth. He kept at it until Saturday morning, when his mother lifted the placemats to wash them.

"Ethan! Get in here right now!" Her voice cracked like a whip. She read him the riot act and promised punishment when Dad got home.

Ethan hid in his closet, trembling as he heard his father's car crunch into the driveway. He heard the front door slam, then the two of them talking in low tones. Then footsteps, heavy, deliberate, down the hall. The sound of leather snapping as his father pulled his belt free and began snapping it together in his hands; it was a terrifying sound.

The closet door flew open. Ethan was yanked out, bent over a knee, pants yanked down to bare his backside. His father's voice was hard and flat: "This is going to hurt me more than it hurts you."

Ethan shook with fear, his small body quaking. Crack. Crack. Crack. Each strike raised red welts across his skin until he couldn't breathe for the pain. When it was over, he curled into a ball on the floor, crying, wishing he could vanish into the shadows of his room.

The violence wasn't reserved for him. Sometimes it was his mother who bore the brunt. The worst nights were punctuated by her screams as his father slammed her head against the olive-green push-button phone mounted on the kitchen wall. The phone had gray keys that clicked under your finger, and beneath them a clear strip where the family number was scrawled in uneven block letters. Ethan had even replaced the six-foot cord with a fifteen-foot one so he could pull it into his bedroom and pretend it connected him to the world.

But when his father wrapped that same cord around his mother's hair and the hard plastic handset cracked against her skull, the phone was no longer a lifeline. It was a weapon.

Ethan's reaction was always the same: his body shook uncontrollably, teeth chattering as though he were freezing. Rage surged inside him—he wanted to bite, to claw, to hurl himself at his father's hand. Shame followed, shame that he didn't, shame that he couldn't protect her. He didn't see other families like this. Why his?

The next mornings were the worst. The kitchen table set as if nothing had happened. His mother in sunglasses, saying brightly, "Big day at school, boys." His father sipping coffee. Evan staring at the wood grain. Ethan pushing his cereal around in silence, bargaining with himself: If I get straight checkmarks…if I score two goals…if I just behave, maybe it will fix things.

One Sunday, it all ended. His father packed his navy-blue hardshell suitcase, not carefully as for business trips, but angrily, hurling clothes in, slamming shirts down, yanking photographs off walls and shoving them inside. The suitcase clicked shut like a slammed door. He said he'd be gone "just a little while." Ethan asked, "Friday?" His father said, "Friday."

But Friday came and went.

When the car finally backed out for good, Ethan and Evan exploded out the door barefoot, first over the gravel of the driveway, sharp stones biting, then onto the blistering asphalt of the road. The sun had baked it hot enough to sear, but Ethan felt nothing. It was like a dream where you run and run, but what you're chasing slips further and further away. His arms pumped, his chest burned, but the taillights only shrank until the car turned the corner and was gone.

Only then did Ethan stop, bent over with hands on his knees, gasping for air as tears rolled down his face. His feet were blistered and torn when he finally trudged back to the house. Inside, silence swallowed him whole. The kind of silence that presses against your ears until it hums. Heavy. Suffocating. Final.

The police came once to Grandma's house. Ethan and Evan were halfway into pajamas when the knock rattled the glass. They crept to the top of the stairs. Through the frosted pane, two blue uniforms blurred into shape.

"Evening, ma'am," one said when Grandma opened the door. "We're looking for—"

"Lord have mercy," Grandma whispered, hand flying to her chest. "Boys, stay upstairs."

They didn't. They perched on the steps, peering through the railing. Their father stepped into view from the living room, calm as if greeting dinner guests.

"Sir, we had a call regarding threatening statements," the taller officer said.

Grandma bustled around the coffee table, opening drawers, muttering. "Where is that deed? Where did your grandfather put that deed?"

Then, in the glow of red-blue light through the window, Ethan saw his father cuffed. It looked wrong — his dad, who could lift both boys at once and gallop around the yard like a horse, suddenly small between two strangers. Ethan's stomach clenched. He didn't know who to be angry at.

Hours later, Grandma found the house deed in a manila envelope under a stack of Sears catalogs and drove the boys to the jail to post bond. The fluorescent lights buzzed in the lobby. A man slept across three plastic chairs. Evan gripped Ethan's hand hard enough to hurt, and Ethan didn't pull away.

When their father finally walked out, eyes bloodshot, he hugged them too long. The next morning he was pacing the kitchen, voice sharp and words aimed like knives at their mother, though she wasn't there to hear them. Ethan and Evan stared at the table's grain and measured their breaths until they could escape to Grandma's garden, picking tomatoes under a heavy sun.

Divorce wasn't a word spoken out loud in their neighborhood. People whispered it like a diagnosis. On the school bus, Ethan felt the stares, like kids were checking whether the condition was contagious. He wanted to say, My dad just works far away, but the lie was heavier than the truth.

Weekends belonged to their father now—when he wasn't angry. More often than not, the three of them ended up at The Quarterdeck, a family bar and restaurant. Gordon, the owner, a big man with a booming voice, always greeted them at the door. For Ethan and Evan, the shuffleboard table in the back was the draw. For their father, it was the jukebox.

Without fail, he played his song: "Take It on the Run" by REO Speedwagon. Ethan and Evan didn't miss the message. The lyrics about betrayal, about a woman "messin' around," felt like a weapon aimed at their mother. While the boys flicked shuffleboard pucks down the table, their father sat staring into the distance, nursing a beer, the music telling a story he wanted them to believe.

Dinner always followed a pattern: pleasantries with Gordon, food ordered, burgers or fried shrimp. Their father asked about school, about friends, and always, inevitably, about Mom. Was she dating? Who was the man? What kind of car did he drive?

If the beers had been flowing, his voice dropped lower, conspiratorial. "Remember, boys, you only have one dad, and that's me. You don't have to listen to these guys." And then came the missions.

Their mother worked constantly now—secretary by day, cashier by night—so the boys were on their own. She tried hiring a babysitter once, a teenage girl from down the street. But Ethan wanted no part of it. He heated up the iron until it was scorching, yanked the cord out, and brandished it at her. "Get out." She did, fifteen minutes into her first shift.

After that, Ethan and Evan managed themselves. They experimented with the stove, scorched pans, and learned how to make boxed macaroni and grilled cheese. Other kids weren't even allowed near burners; the brothers mastered them. At night, when the house creaked, they built forts of couch cushions and blankets, whispering plans about how to get their parents back together. Dreams that never came true. When words failed, they leaned on a vow: I am my brother's keeper.

The neighborhood itself was divided. An invisible line marked their property as the start of "lesser." Some neighbors treated them with pity, invitations out of obligation. But next door lived a family who never turned away—a Navy man, his nurse wife, two kids. They pulled Ethan into their fold, even bringing him on vacations to their beach house, trips he otherwise never would have known.

Soccer opened other doors. One teammate's house sat behind a guard gate, acres of manicured lawns and four-car garages filled with exotic cars. Ethan arrived with his mom in their purple Chevrolet Citation, which promptly stalled. Embarrassed but practiced, Ethan popped the hood, loosened the wingnut, jammed a screwdriver into the butterfly valve, and told her to crank it. The engine roared to life, but shame clung to him. His friend never mentioned it, but Ethan thought about it often—how hard his mom worked, how little support she got.

So he and Evan cleaned the house, cooked dinners, mowed lawns, delivered papers. They started working years before their peers, determined to ease her burden, even just a little.

Soccer became Ethan's escape. At five, in a rec league championship, his coach handed him the goalie jersey for a shootout. Ethan stared down five shooters and stopped them all, then buried the winning kick himself. His father told the story for years, always adding the line from his godfather: "That boy's leg is golden. Teach him to kick field goals."

As he grew, soccer became his second family. Tournaments meant motel pools, ice machines, socks drying on shower rods, teammates roughhousing in hallways. In Baltimore, age twelve, he met Thomas Kirkland, a retired professor who invited the team into his room, poured whiskey for himself, and told stories of his travels. At one point he leaned close, eyes glinting: "Boys, there's one thing you need to know. The golden hole—you'll kill your own mother for it." Ethan didn't understand, but he filed it away. If a man who had seen the world said it mattered, it must.

On the field, no one cared about hand-me-down cleats or whether his mom's car would start. The ball only cared if you could play, and Ethan could. He was faster, sharper, hungrier. For ninety minutes at a time, he wasn't the poor kid from the wrong side of the line. He was somebody.

That winter, Ethan learned silence by its shapes. The big silence when his mother was too tired to speak. The sharp silence when the phone rang and went unanswered. The comforting silence of falling asleep to a TV laugh track.

He also learned mercy's sound: the thud of a soccer ball against the side of the house, Brandy's tail beating the floor, the squeak of sneakers on the gym floor.

At night, he made bargains with the ceiling: If I score two goals, Dad comes back. If I get straight checkmarks, Mom won't be sad. If I sleep with the covers over my head, the world can't find me.

But he knew better. He could still see the phone cord wrapped in his father's fist, the suitcase slammed shut, the taillights vanishing around the corner. He could still feel the hot pavement blistering his feet.

Those were the images that branded him. Yet in the morning, there was toast, cut grass, and the certainty of chalked lines. Rules, order, a whistle that meant what it said. For a while, that was enough.

Chapter 2 – Shattered Illusions

Everything in Ethan's young life seemed to unravel, piece by piece, like a sweater pulled at the hem. The threads didn't snap all at once — they frayed slowly, unraveling into a tangled mess that a boy of his age could never hope to mend.

The divorce had already left deep cracks in his sense of security, but as time marched forward, so did his parents. Both began dating, as if the family that once was could be swapped out, rearranged, replaced. For Ethan, it was a world he hadn't asked to enter.

The first time he saw his mom across a restaurant table, smiling at a man who wasn't his father, it hit him like a punch to the gut. She laughed — the kind of laugh that used to belong to their family dinners. Ethan wanted to shout: That's not his laugh. That belongs to us.

Seeing his father with another woman wasn't much better. Love, in Ethan's young mind, was supposed to be forever. The vows, the bedtime stories, the family outings — weren't those promises? Weren't they ironclad? Now they seemed written in chalk, washed away with the first rain.

His father wasn't just dating. He was angry, bitter. That bitterness spilled onto Ethan and his older brother Evan like oil on water.

Weekend visits became interrogations.

"So who was at the house this week?" Dad would ask, gripping the steering wheel tighter than he needed to. "What's his name? What kind of car does he drive?"

Ethan and Evan squirmed in the backseat. They were just kids. They didn't want to answer, but Dad pressed.

"Remember — I'm your father. Nobody else is. Don't you forget that."

Sometimes it went darker. If Mom had been seeing someone steadily, Dad's voice would drop low, conspiratorial, as though he were giving orders in a war zone.

"You know what to do, boys. He doesn't belong there. If you see his car outside, take care of it."

The words chilled Ethan. But he and Evan knew exactly what he meant.

Late one summer evening, Ethan climbed out his bedroom window as if he were heading to war. He crouched low behind the bushes, heart hammering. Every sound felt magnified — the chirp of crickets, the hum of streetlights, his own uneven breathing. Sweat slid down his forehead in the muggy night air.

At the end of the row of bushes, he froze, checked the street, then low-crawled to the driveway where his mom's boyfriend's car sat waiting. He fumbled with his pocketknife, hands slick. When he finally snapped it open, he shut his eyes and whispered to himself: No turning back now.

He stabbed down hard. Clang! The blade skittered off the rubber like water off glass. Confused, he tried again, even harder. This time the knife flew from his hand, spinning end over end, and clattered into the neighbor's gravel. To Ethan it sounded like a cymbal crash. Panic surged — he was exposed. He grabbed the knife and sprinted back behind the bushes, lungs burning, chest heaving.

Back in his room, he cracked the door and called for Evan. His brother appeared, grinning like he'd been waiting for the report. Ethan, still gasping, told him what had happened. Evan thought for a moment, then grinned wider.

"Don't worry, little brother. I got this."

Evan slipped out, screwdriver in hand. Minutes later, he was back, triumphant. "Mission accomplished."

The two crouched by the window, hiding behind the curtain, and watched as their mom walked her boyfriend out.

The man frowned at the sagging tire, sweated and cursed as he swapped it for the spare. Ethan and Evan laughed — nervous, giddy, as if they'd pulled off a prank.

But later, lying in bed, Ethan felt only shame. The image of his mom's smile at dinner pressed against the picture of her boyfriend wrestling with the jack. Deep down, he knew they hadn't protected her. They had hurt her. And that realization sat in his chest like a stone.

At school, Ethan's world was marked by small humiliations. Each fall, classmates strutted in wearing brand-new jeans and spotless sneakers. Ethan shuffled in with hand-me-downs from Evan, knees already thinning, shoes scuffed and faded.

At first, it barely mattered. Clothes were clothes. But whispers, side glances, and his own growing self-consciousness burrowed under his skin. What do they think of me? Do they notice?

The divide showed itself everywhere, but nowhere more sharply than in the cafeteria.

For most kids, lunchtime was a highlight. They lined up with lunch money in hand, came back to the table with square slices of pizza, french fries piled high, chocolate milk cartons balanced precariously. On rare occasions, when Mom had a little extra cash, Ethan and Evan joined them. But most days, they carried brown paper bags from home.

A "good" day meant peanut butter and jelly, or maybe bologna. More often, it was just bread with mayonnaise, or a single slice of cheese between two pieces of white bread.

Kids didn't mean to be cruel — not really. They were just blunt in the way children are. At Ethan's table, food was currency. The first kid to snag one of the few pepperoni pizzas might barter it for a plain slice plus someone's fries. Deals were struck with the gravity of stock trades.

One day, caught up in the barter, a boy turned to Ethan. "What you got?"

Ethan's stomach sank. He knew what sat in his bag. Just bread with mayonnaise. His face flushed red.

"Oh, just a sandwich," he muttered. "Nothing you'd want."

The boy grinned. "What kind of sandwich? Let me see — I might be feeling like a sandwich today."

Ethan hesitated, then slowly pulled it out. Before he could react, the boy snatched it, opened the bag, and burst out laughing.

"Bread and mayo? That's it? Man, couldn't even afford the meat!"

The table erupted. Ethan's ears burned crimson. Desperate, he blurted out, "I was in a rush this morning, must've forgotten it!"

The laughter died down. The other kids shrugged and went back to bartering. Crisis over.

But not for Ethan. He sat there, staring at his hands, drowning in the same old shame. He wasn't just hungry. He was branded again — the poor kid.

Soccer was his escape hatch, the one place where none of it mattered. The field didn't care about lunch money or hand-me-downs. It only cared how fast you ran, how hard you kicked, how long you could keep fighting when your lungs were on fire.

His travel team wasn't just a roster. They were brothers — sweat-soaked, grass-stained, rowdy, unbreakable. They practiced together, traveled together, and turned hotel hallways into racetracks of laughter and pranks.

And they were good. Tournament after tournament, they brought home trophies. They didn't just move up one age bracket but two. Ethan, wiry and undersized, played against boys taller, stronger, older — and often walked away the better player.

The game gave him a place where the poverty, the divorce, the whispered rumors, all fell away. On the field, there were rules and whistles that meant what they said. For a boy living in chaos, that was salvation.

The new coach arrived like a storm from another world. He wasn't just another parent-turned-volunteer with a whistle; he was Italian, from California, and he carried himself like he had fire stitched into his veins. He wore blue shirts with Italia emblazoned across the chest, and when he talked about the game he spoke of poetry and passion, of the great Azzurri who played with heart that could outlast talent.

He was older, heavier, past his playing days, but when he joined scrimmages he still had a magician's touch. One flick of his instep, one curling ball from the outside of his foot, and the boys stared in awe. You could tell he had once been great.

The first day of summer, before practice even began, he gathered all the players and parents together on the field. He didn't sugarcoat it.

"If you're here to play casually," he said, "this isn't your team. We will train harder than anyone. Two-a-day practices, every day, for the entire summer. Every session begins with a five-mile run. Some of you will want to quit. Many of you will think I'm crazy. But in the fall, when league play starts, the team that stays will be unstoppable."

Parents exchanged wary glances. The boys looked at each other, wide-eyed. But Ethan felt a jolt of excitement in his chest. This is it. This is what I need.

The coach wasn't bluffing. Day one, he was on a bicycle, pedaling alongside them in the July heat as the boys pounded pavement, shirts soaked with sweat before practice even began. Kids groaned, cursed under their breath, thought about quitting.

Ethan wasn't immune — his legs burned, his chest ached — but somewhere inside he found another gear. Out here, he wasn't the poor kid with mayo sandwiches. He was just a runner, a worker, a competitor. And he wanted to be first.

By the end of the summer, he almost always was.

When fall came and the league season began, the coach called a team meeting after practice. The boys sprawled in the grass, exhausted but buzzing, sweat cooling on their necks.

"I've been watching all summer," the coach said. "You've suffered together. You've pushed each other. But I need leaders — captains who will set the tone."

He named two boys. One was the goalkeeper, steady and loud, the kind of kid who could organize a defense like a drill sergeant. The other was Ethan.

For a moment, Ethan thought he'd misheard. Him? Captain? He turned red as the team clapped and slapped him on the back, but inside he was soaring. That night at dinner, he couldn't stop talking about it. He even picked up the phone and called his dad, eager to share the news.

The response wasn't what he'd hoped for.

"Soccer, huh?" his dad said flatly. "You know that's not a real sport, right? You can't get a scholarship for that. You'd be better off with football. Kick field goals or something. Now that's a future."

The words cut deep. Ethan hung up, pretending he didn't care. He did care. But he also knew something else: his coach believed in him, and that mattered more than his father's dismissal.

The first big test of their new conditioning came in late summer at a tournament in Virginia Beach. The air was thick with heat, the kind that clings to your skin even in the morning. By warmups, the boys were drenched in sweat.

But the coach had a plan. "We will not only outplay them," he told the team, "we will intimidate them. Show them who you are before the whistle even blows."

So instead of stretches or passing drills, they practiced diving headers. Boys flung themselves across the grass, jerseys streaked green, knees scraped and bleeding before the game even began. Parents shook their heads in disbelief. Opponents stared wide-eyed.

The coach called them in. "Hands in. On three: Mud, blood, guts. Win, win, win!"

The chant was raw, primal. Ethan's pulse raced. This wasn't just soccer anymore. This was war.

They steamrolled their first opponents, winning 2–0. But late in the second half, Ethan went up for a header near the sideline. The other boy missed the ball and slammed into Ethan's face. Pain flared like fire across his eyebrow, but Ethan stayed on his feet, still chasing the ball.

It was the assistant coach who saw the blood. He sprinted onto the field, grabbed Ethan by the shoulders, and steered him off. Only when the sweat cleared did Ethan realize his eyebrow had split wide open. Blood poured down his cheek, staining his jersey.

Paramedics were called. In minutes, Ethan was lying under hospital lights, the doctor stitching him up — seventeen neat black knots across his brow. They patched his eye, and he went back to the hotel with a bandage that made him look like a pirate.

That night, the team treated him like a hero. They crowded around him, peppered him with questions, laughed and joked. For the first time, Ethan felt like a legend in the making.

The next day was the championship match. The coach pulled Ethan aside beforehand. "Are you up for this?"

"I'm playing," Ethan said without hesitation.

The game was brutal. Their opponents were big, fast, and strong. By halftime, the score was still 0–0. The coach gathered them in the huddle, voice thunderous.

"You've worked harder than them! You've bled more than them! They didn't run five miles twice a day all summer! This is your time. All hands in — Mud, blood, guts!"

"Win, win, win!" the boys roared.

Early in the second half, a through ball split the defense. Ethan sprinted after it, his patched eye throbbing, his stitches pulling with every stride. The goalkeeper charged out, massive and quick, determined to smother the ball. It was a collision course.

Neither slowed.

They met with a bone-crunching crash. Ethan flew one way, the keeper another. The ball squirted free and trickled toward the goal line. For a split second, time froze. Then it rolled in. Goal.

Ethan leapt to his feet, ready to celebrate — but the referee's whistle cut through the air. He reached into his pocket, pulled out a red card, and held it high.

Ethan was stunned. Ejected. The goal disallowed. His team would have to play down a man.

The coach erupted on the sideline, shouting at the referee, but it was useless. Ethan walked off the field, fury and despair churning inside him. He felt like he had just let everyone down.

But the team rose to the challenge. Fueled by anger, they played harder, faster, fiercer. By the final whistle, they had won 2–0.

That night, at the pizza party, the coach stood to make a speech. He praised the team's grit, their conditioning, their willpower. Then he singled Ethan out.

"This boy," he said, pointing to Ethan, "played with seventeen stitches and an eye patch. He threw himself at a goalkeeper twice his size, not for himself but for all of you. That courage — that heart — inspired this victory."

He handed Ethan the MVP award. The room erupted in applause. Ethan turned red, embarrassed but glowing inside. For once, he wasn't just good. He was indispensable.

By the time fall season ended, the team wasn't just good — they were feared. They had beaten boys older, bigger, stronger. They had run miles until their lungs burned, and now they stood taller for it.

Then the coach called another meeting. Parents and players circled up, curious. The coach wore his trademark Italia shirt, arms crossed, eyes shining.

"You're ready," he said. "In California, there's a team called the Cerritos Giants. Number one in the nation. People say they can't be beaten. I say we're going to Anaheim to prove them wrong."

The words dropped like fireworks. The boys erupted with cheers, high fives, fists in the air. Ethan's heart pounded with excitement — and fear. California? It sounded expensive.

That night at home, he overheard his mom on the phone with Grandma. Money was tight, tighter than ever, but Mom wasn't going to let Ethan miss this. She promised him they'd find a way. Grandma agreed to help.

"We're going," his mom told him later. "You've earned this, Ethan. I'm proud of you."

Ethan nodded, overwhelmed. He hustled for extra spending money, mowing grass, washing cars, any odd job he could land. By the time the trip rolled around, he had saved three hundred dollars — the most money he'd ever had at once.

The first day in Anaheim was a dream. The team hit Disneyland, racing from ride to ride like a pack of wild animals. Parents trailed behind, exhausted but smiling. For a day, they were just kids in the happiest place on earth, screaming down roller coasters, buying cotton candy, laughing until their sides hurt.

That night, most collapsed into bed without mischief. But the next day was free — no games, no curfew.

Ethan and a few teammates wandered the streets near the hotel, ducking into shops. In one store, a pair of shorts caught Ethan's eye: Jimmy'Z, with velcro for a waistband. They were the thing every cool kid back home wanted. Ethan had never owned anything like them.

He bought them with his own money, ripped off the tags, and changed right there in the store. Walking out in those shorts, he felt lighter, cooler, like maybe he finally belonged.

That night the whole group — players, parents, and coaches — ate dinner together in the hotel restaurant. Afterward, the boys went tearing through hallways, pranking each other, pounding on doors. Parents drifted toward the pool, a sparkling blue oasis surrounded by palm trees and fountains.

The boys were mid-chase when someone shouted, "Let's go ask our parents if we can hit the shops again!" They rounded the corner, breathless, laughter echoing. Ethan led the pack toward the pool, expecting to see his mom with the other adults, sipping drinks, laughing in the glow of string lights.

He scanned the crowd once. Twice. Then his eyes snagged on something that made his stomach twist.

There was his coach, leaning back in a chair. And in his lap — not his wife, but Ethan's mother.

They weren't just sitting close. They were kissing.

The world seemed to tilt. The sounds of splashing water, of boys talking, of palm fronds rustling — all of it faded into a ringing in his ears. His chest went tight. His face flushed hot, ears burning red.

No. No, that can't be right.

He blinked hard, hoping the image would dissolve like a bad dream. It didn't.

One of his teammates smacked him on the back. "Dude… is that your mom? With the coach?"

The words stabbed deeper than the sight itself. Ethan couldn't answer. He couldn't breathe. All he could feel was rage and shame boiling together. His body trembled; his legs felt heavy, like he was trapped in quicksand.

He turned and walked away without a word, each step slower, heavier, as if the air itself were pressing against him.

Back in his room, he lay on the bed staring at the ceiling, motionless. When his mom returned later that night, she stood in the doorway for a moment, then asked softly, "Do you want to talk about it?"

There was nothing to say.

He rolled onto his side, back to her, silent. She didn't push. The silence stretched between them like a canyon.

The next day was the game they had been waiting for — Cerritos Giants, the best in the country. For every other boy, it was the chance of a lifetime. For Ethan, it was a nightmare.

He couldn't look at his mom. He couldn't look at his coach. He couldn't even look at his teammates without wondering if they knew, if they were laughing behind his back.

He played, but halfheartedly. His passes lacked bite. His runs lacked fire. He wasn't the captain who had led them all summer. He was a boy whose safe place had been poisoned.

The Giants beat them, 2–1. Ethan hardly remembered the final whistle. The loss didn't even sting compared to the wound already lodged inside him.

On the flight back to Richmond, Ethan sat by the window, forehead pressed against the cool glass. The world below looked peaceful, orderly, like a map. Nothing like the storm inside him.

Nobody talked about what had happened. Not his mom. Not his coach. Not even his teammates. But silence doesn't erase. It festers.

By the time the plane landed, Ethan had recoiled into himself, retreating into a place where he didn't have to rely on anyone. If the people he trusted most could betray him, then maybe trust itself was a mistake.

Back home, the world looked the same—same street, same mailbox leaning a little left, same cracks in the front walk—but the air felt different, like the house had shifted on its foundation. Ethan moved through rooms as if the furniture had teeth.

On the second evening after they returned, the coach's car slid into the driveway. Ethan was at the front window with Brandy's chin in his lap when he heard the engine cut and the soft thunk of a door. His stomach clenched. He didn't need to look to know the coach's silhouette: the thick torso, the forward lean, the confident stride. Mom came down the hall, smoothing her blouse in a way she didn't know he noticed.

"Back by ten," she said, then paused, eyes searching his face. "Do you need anything?"

He shook his head without meeting her eyes. Brandy's tail thumped. The door closed gently, the lock clicked, and their laughter floated once through the glass as they crossed the porch. Ethan pressed his forehead to the cool pane. Brandy whined, licking his wrist. He whispered, "It's okay, girl," though nothing felt okay.

He didn't turn the TV on. He listened to the clock in the kitchen, to the old house settling, to the distant hum of tires on the main road. When the porch light finally flared again, he slipped deeper into the couch, eyes on the dark corner of the ceiling. Mom's key scratched at the lock. She stepped in quietly, shoes dangling from one hand. She started to speak, stopped, then kissed the top of his head as if he were still five. He kept still. When her bedroom door shut, he pressed a palm over his sternum, the ache there like a bruise he couldn't show anyone.

At the first practice after California, heat lay over the field like a sheet of glass. The boys jogged in, tossing balls and jeers. Ethan felt their glances skate off him and return, the way fish circle something in the water they don't recognize.

The coach blew his whistle. "Let's go! Five miles—move!" He mounted the bike and pedaled alongside, the chain clicking, his voice hitting that same singsong rhythm Ethan used to find reassuring.

"Dig in! Think of September! Think of trophies!"

Ethan ran, shoes drumming the trail, sweat gathering at his temples. He used to fight for the front, used to feel righteous fire when the coach rolled up beside him and barked, "Good, Ethan! Set the pace!" Now, when the coach edged his wheel into Ethan's peripheral vision, Ethan drifted back a step, then two, until spokes and breath and praise fell behind him.

After the run, they scrimmaged. Ethan took the left flank, the sun in his face. Twice he received the ball in space—his old favorite picture, grass yawning open and the goal like a magnet—and twice he hesitated, the pass arriving from the coach's voice in his ear instead of his teammate's foot. His first touch skittered. A defender pounced. The moment was gone. He heard a boy—maybe the center mid—mutter, "What was that?" Not mean. Just tired.

Water break. The coach approached, hands on hips. "You okay?"

Ethan nodded without looking up.

"You're playing tight," the coach said, voice lowered. "You don't have to prove anything to anybody."

That almost made Ethan laugh. Prove what? To who? He kept his eyes on his cleats. He didn't notice his fists were balled until his nails bit his palms.

"Hey," the coach said softly.

Ethan took a long drink, then jogged back out without answering. He could feel the coach watching him, like sunlight he couldn't step out of.

At the next tournament, the air in the hotel was thick with chlorine and whispers. Boys raced up and down the hall, towels snapping. Ethan heard his name drift with the laughter, then die when he turned the corner. In the elevator, two parents stopped talking mid-sentence and smiled too brightly at him.

On the sideline, a cluster of dads and moms stood with arms folded, voices low. Ethan's mom was there, sunglasses on, her smile tighter than usual. The coach joined late, clapped a father on the shoulder, and the circle opened to admit him.

Ethan ran sprints along the touchline to get away from the picture of them together, but the picture followed, a negative burned into the film of his mind. When the ball came to him in the game, he played it safe—one-touch layoff, sideways passes, never the old cut-and-run that had been his signature. His teammates covered for him. No one said a word afterward. The silence made him feel smaller than if they'd yelled.

In the hotel that night, he lay on his back and stared at the stippled ceiling until the dots became constellations. He whispered the names he'd learned in science class—Orion, Cassiopeia, Scorpius—trying to conjure order. He could hear laughter through the wall, a television down the hall, the ice machine grinding. All the sounds of a road-trip family he no longer trusted.

He told himself he wouldn't tell his father. He didn't want to hand the man more weapons. But the next Quarterdeck visit, with shuffleboard wax dusting their sleeves and Gordon booming hello from behind the bar, Dad put three quarters on the table and said, "Music or food first?"

Ethan shrugged. Evan grabbed the quarters and headed for the jukebox. Dad watched him go, then leaned across the table toward Ethan.

"So," he said. "Anything new with your… coach?"

The word hung there. Ethan looked away. The jukebox clicked to life—REO Speedwagon, of course, the opening riff like a reflex. Dad's jaw flexed, a smile that wasn't a smile.

"Boys like you need men who teach them right," Dad said. "Not men who take what's not theirs."

Ethan stared at his water glass, the ice fracturing faintly. He felt an old panic rising—the sense that he was being drafted again, that missions would be assigned the way they had been after dinners in this very booth. He pictured a screwdriver, a tire valve, the tightness in his chest afterward. He set the glass down carefully and said, "I don't want to talk about it."

Dad's eyes sharpened. For a second Ethan thought he'd push, the way he always pushed. Instead, Dad leaned back, folded his arms, and nodded once. "Okay," he said. He turned to Evan returning from the jukebox, slapped him on the shoulder, and said too loudly, "Shuffleboard?"

They played. Dad knocked pucks with unnecessary force. When the song hit the line—You take it on the run, baby— Ethan's stomach turned. He wanted to walk outside and keep walking, past the Quarterdeck, past the dark strip malls, past the neighborhood boundary line that always felt like a fence even when it was just air.

Fall shaded into winter. Ethan still strapped on shin guards, still laced his cleats, still ran drills until the sweat streaked salt-white when it dried. From the sideline, Mom cheered at the right times. The coach barked and praised and corrected the way he always had. On paper, nothing had changed.

But inside the white lines, Ethan stopped trying to be the first runner, the daring dribbler, the kid who crashed into giants without blinking. He learned new habits: the safe outlet pass, the near-post run he could abandon early without being noticed, the way to jog hard enough to look busy while never getting the ball. Survival skills, learned from a boy who had already became an expert at reading rooms.

Teammates adapted around him, subtly. The center mid looked off the pass he used to send Ethan in behind. The right back overlapped less, unwilling to gamble without Ethan's old cover speed. No one said a word—it wasn't that kind of team—but the pattern changed like a tide you only notice by the line of kelp left behind.

After one game, a mom—sweet and clueless—patted Ethan's shoulder and said, "You must be so proud to have a coach who believes in you so much!" Her smile was genuine. Ethan managed a nod that felt like swallowing glass.

It happened once—almost—on a Tuesday night in the kitchen, the olive-green push-button phone glinting on the wall like some relic of a world that had made different promises. Mom was rinsing lettuce. The coach's car lights flashed across the window as he backed out of the driveway. Ethan had sat at the table long after dinner, the fork lines still etched in the gravy on his plate, heart thudding the way it did before penalty kicks.

"Mom," he said.

She turned, wiping her hands on a towel. "Mm?"

He opened his mouth and found no words. Everything he wanted to say loosened into fragments—you knew he was my coach / you knew / why him—and none of the pieces fit together without exploding. He watched her face, saw worry and hope and a tired kind of joy that had become an unfamiliar visitor in their house.

"It's late," he said finally. "I'm gonna take Brandy out."

She studied him for a second, then nodded. "Okay, honey."

Outside, the air was cold enough to sting. Brandy trotted ahead, steam puffing from her mouth. Ethan followed the sidewalk to the corner and back, hands shoved deep in his pockets, the leash slack between them like a question he couldn't ask.

At the winter indoor league, the coach wrote lineups on a whiteboard. Under "Captain" he still scrawled ETHAN. The words meant less now. Leadership used to feel like a job—rally the boys, set the pace, run through the wall first. Now it felt like a costume he'd outgrown. He shook hands with referees, won the coin toss, said "Let's go" in a voice that sounded like his, and played a game of keep-away with his own heart.

Evan saw it before anyone else. They were in their room one night, both homework books open but neither reading. Evan tossed a foam ball up and down, catching it with a soft thump.

"You don't have to carry everybody, you know," Evan said finally.

"I'm not carrying anybody," Ethan said, flipping a page he hadn't read.

"That's kinda my point," Evan said gently. "You don't have to carry yourself alone, either."

Ethan stared at the same paragraph until the words blurred. He nodded, the smallest dip of his chin, and that was the end of it. Evan had a way of saying enough and not too much. It was a skill Ethan envied, the same way he envied how Evan could make a plan, execute it, and keep his soul intact.

There were mercies, small ones. On Saturdays, the neighbor family—the retired Navy dad and the nurse mom— still waved him over for pancakes. Their kitchen smelled like coffee and warm syrup. No one asked questions with barbs on them. He ate seconds he pretended he didn't want and left with a ziplock bag of extras "for Evan, too." When he said thank you, the nurse mom put a hand on his cheek and said, "You're doing great, sweetheart," in a way that made him believe she wasn't talking about soccer.

Spring crept in. The team entered State Cup. Ethan played well enough to not be a problem and poorly enough to not be a solution. They bowed out in the quarters to a group of boys who celebrated like they'd won a war. Ethan watched them dogpile and felt nothing. Not anger. Not grief. Just the quiet space where feelings used to live.

He didn't quit the team. He didn't blow up at his mom. He didn't challenge the coach. What he did was smaller and, in some ways, braver: he decided to stop looking to other people to steady his ground. He wouldn't say it out loud—twelve-year-olds don't have manifestos—but the vow etched itself somewhere in him like a carving under a placemat: No more bargains with the ceiling. No more believing someone else can fix the house.

He still ran. He still passed. He still went to school and packed lunches and learned how to stretch a dollar farther than it wanted to go. But inside, he moved a step back from the places that used to define him. If the coach called his name, he answered. If Mom asked if he'd be home for dinner, he said yes. He learned to live in the pauses, to let silence be a language he understood.

One night—months after Anaheim, long after the whispers cooled into a new normal—Ethan lay in bed with Brandy's breath warm at his calves. Through the wall, the TV murmured a late rerun, laugh track steady as a metronome. He stared at the ceiling and watched the glow-in-the-dark stars find their faint light. He remembered the barefoot chase down the road after his father's car, the quicksand feeling in his legs as the taillights slid away. He realized the pool scene had felt the same: running without moving, reaching without touching, the important thing shrinking into a point of light you can't lasso back.

He rolled onto his side and pulled the blanket to his ear. Somewhere in the house, a pipe ticked. In the yard, a branch scraped the siding. He matched his breathing to Brandy's—inhale, exhale, inhale—and let his eyes close.

In the morning, there would be chalk lines and a whistle. In the afternoon, there would be homework and the soft slam of the mailbox lid. In between, there would be the quiet work of a boy deciding how to be in a world that had shown him too early that even the people who love you can crack the ground you stand on.

For now, there was sleep. For now, there was the dog. For now, there was the certainty, small but real, that he could learn to live with what couldn't be undone.

Chapter 3 — The Boots

By the time Ethan hit middle school, everything felt a half-size wrong. Even his shoes. They were Evan's old desert boots, cracked at the creases, laces that wouldn't stay tied. He could hear them a second before anyone else did—the soft slap, squeak, slap on the waxed hallway floors. Every step sounded like an apology for being late.

At home, nothing fit either. The house smelled like dog and old coffee. Brandy thumped her tail against the kitchen cabinets when Ethan came in, the whole back half of her wriggling with joy, as if she could wag the day off him. Mom would be between jobs, blazer still on, hair pinned back with whatever clip she'd found in the glove box. A stack of bills leaned against the microwave-less counter like a row of dominoes waiting for a breeze. The olive-green push-button phone on the wall had a fifteen-foot cord that snaked into the hallway; sometimes you could tell how Mom's day had gone by how tightly that cord had twisted while she talked.

"What's the homework situation?" she'd ask, toeing off her shoes.

"Manageable," Ethan would say, which could mean anything from "I did it at lunch" to "I'm going to make a volcano out of excuses."

Evan handled the stove: grilled-cheese roulette, canned soup with too much pepper, hot dogs split and fried till the edges curled like cartoon smiles. They ate at six when they could, a tradition hanging on by thread. The rule about finishing everything on your plate had softened to negotiations—"three more bites" was the going rate—but Ethan still hated the way peas felt like buckshot in his mouth. Brandy patrolled under the table, optimistic.

Dad was mostly a tailpipe now—headlights in the driveway for a weekend, then gone again, promises clattering behind him like loose lug nuts. When he did show up, he sat at the edge of the couch and watched Ethan like a coach who didn't remember what position his kid played.

School was the one place Ethan could control the narrative—sort of. He learned quickly that if they were laughing, they weren't looking too closely. The first time he made the back row convulse during a filmstrip—crossing his eyes so hard he saw two continents on the map—he felt something like relief. Laughter was a warm coat he could hide inside.

He got good at it. The pencil became a baton he twirled when Mrs. Harrell turned to write fractions on the board. He took attendance with the gym teacher's voice under his breath—"Reynolds present, Coach"—and the boys around him folded in half to keep from being seen laughing.

"Reynolds," barked Mr. Dempsey in math one afternoon, a man whose mustache was more famous than his equations, "if you put half as much effort into your homework as you do into your one-man circus, you'd be running this school."

The room cracked open. Ethan threw his arms wide, took a theatrical bow from his desk. The heat in his chest felt like pride, but lower down something turned over, heavy and private. Better the clown than the question mark, he told himself. He didn't want anyone tunneling past the jokes to the questions underneath: Why don't I ever see your dad at pickup? Why don't you ever come to the pool? Are those your brother's jeans?

His grades started to come back with red slashes and See me scrawled in the margins. He slid them into his backpack without looking and rehearsed a new bit on the way to the next class. Comedy as triage.

It happened on a Tuesday, the kind of gray day that made the school windows look like fish tanks. Ethan was late to math—again—hair mussed from a sprint down the science wing. He hit the doorway as the bell rang and spread his arms like an arriving celebrity.

"Nice of you to join us, Mr. Reynolds," Mr. Dempsey said, the sarcasm polished to a shine.

"You know me," Ethan said, backing into the room, "I like to make an entrance." The back row snickered.

He slid toward his desk, boots whispering on floor wax. The room had that chalk-dust glitter the light always found in late afternoon. So he didn't see the leg. A quiet little snare drum just under the desk line, slipped out at the last second.

His left boot caught and the rest of him kept going. He fell forward in a flail of elbows and binder rings, shoulder slamming the edge of Mr. Dempsey's desk. A stack of textbooks avalanched to the floor. The chalk tray jumped; a white cloud puffed up in slow motion and hung there like smoke from a small explosion.

For a beat there was silence. Then the room went feral.

A roar of laughter ricocheted off the cinderblock walls. Desks rattled. Someone wheezed like a broken accordion. In the back, a kid pantomimed the fall, clutching his chest. Ethan could feel it hit him the way cold water hits you when your shirt's still on—seeping, humiliating.

He pushed himself up, palms stinging, chalk dust smearing his shirt. The heat in his face wasn't stage heat; it was a burn that made his ears buzz. He looked automatically for someone to share the joke with—the eye contact that says We're in on it—but there was no one. He was the joke.

"Seat," said Mr. Dempsey, not unkindly, but not kindly either.

Ethan turned and saw the leg retract under a desk in the second row. Kenji. The quiet kid. He drew spaceships and room-sized dragons in the margins of his spiral notebook. He didn't travel in herds, didn't play the cafeteria trading game, didn't laugh loud. He wasn't smirking now, but Ethan's brain had already chosen the villain. His shame needed a face.

He slid into his seat, jaw throbbing from how hard he was clenching it, and stared at the side of Kenji's head. The numbers on the board swam; the only math in his body was subtraction—the way laughter had quickly cut away whatever armor he'd managed to build that morning.

When the bell rang the halls erupted into their usual clang and flow: lockers slamming like car doors, the wet-lipped squeak of sneakers on tile, a chorus of "Dude did you see—" trailing into stairwells. Ethan didn't go to his locker. He leaned against the wall outside the classroom, hands in his pockets to keep them from shaking, boots planted wide like he was riding out a wave.

He replayed the moment with the slow-motion cruelty of a replay screen—his boot catching, the edge of the desk, the laughter. He thought of Mom rubbing the bridge of her nose over a stack of bills, of Dad raising one of those proud, dangerous eyebrows and saying, That's my boy, as if that explained anything. He thought of Kenji's leg like a tripwire stretched across a hallway he'd already been stumbling through for years.

Kenji turned the corner with his books hugged to his chest, head tilted down as if he'd learned the trick of passing invisibly through crowds. He wasn't avoiding Ethan; he just wasn't looking for him.

Ethan stepped off the wall into his path, a quick, hard move that felt like catching a ball cleanly on the laces. "You think that was funny?" he said, voice low enough to sound like someone older.

Kenji blinked, surprised. "What?"

"You tripped me."

Kenji's eyes flicked back toward the door they'd both just come out of, then to Ethan's fists, then up to his face. "No," he said quickly. "I—"

Ethan didn't wait for the rest. The boots that never quite fit him took one decisive step, closing the space, and everything in him that had been vibrating all day found a single frequency. He pulled a fist out of his pocket and—

His fist found Kenji's nose with a sound like a knuckle rapping a watermelon. Kenji's head snapped back; a fine red mist dotted Ethan's wrist. For a second the hallway went pin-drop quiet, like everyone had sucked the same breath at once.

Then it broke open.

"Fight! FIGHT!"

Backpacks hit tile. A half-moon formed fast, kids shuffling for the best sightline, sneakers squeaking, lockers rattling as someone climbed for a better view. Ethan barely registered the faces—just the ring, tightening, a drumbeat in his ears that crowded out everything else.

Kenji staggered, dropped his books. The top one skidded under the drinking fountain; a pencil spun to a stop against the toe of Ethan's boot. Kenji's hands were up but untrained, palms out like he was warding off a dog.

"I didn't—" Kenji started, voice high and strangled.

Ethan hit him again.

The second punch landed on cheekbone, more dull thud than crack. Kenji twisted away, but Ethan was moving, boots heavy but relentless, the world narrowed to red and white. He heard himself breathing—harsh, animal—and somewhere far away, a girl yelped, "Get a teacher!"

Kenji tried to cover, forearms up, chin tucked the way older boys did when they boxed in the park. He wasn't fast enough. Ethan's fists kept finding him, anger steering them with a surety Ethan didn't know he had. He wasn't thinking about Kenji, not really. He was thinking about the laughter, and before that the green phone cord twisting, and before that the way a car's taillights can look like eyes as it turns the corner and doesn't come back.

"REYNOLDS!"

Mr. Dempsey shouldered through the ring, mustache first, face white. He grabbed Ethan around the chest from behind, a clumsy bear hug, and hauled him back. Ethan's feet kept going for a step, boots scraping grooves into the wax as if they could drag the rest of him forward by force.

"Enough!" Dempsey barked into Ethan's ear. His breath smelled like black coffee and chalk dust.

Kenji slid down the lockers to a sit, blood shining under the fluorescents, one eye already trying to close. A kid tossed him a fistful of tissues from a teacher's door; he pressed them to his nose and they went pink almost immediately. His shoulders trembled in little aftershocks, like someone who'd been running and had only just stopped.

"Everyone to class," Mr. Dempsey said, loud enough to reach the far end of the hall. "Now."

No one moved. He turned, found the assistant principal, Ms. Holloway, pounding down the hall in her sensible heels, jaw set. "Office. Both of you."

Ethan didn't resist when Dempsey steered him. His arms felt suddenly heavy. He looked at his knuckles—red, stinging, already rough with the start of swelling. He half expected to see someone else's hands attached to his wrists.

As they passed the drinking fountain, his boot clipped the edge of Kenji's notebook. It was open to a page of spaceships.

Not cartoonish ones—intricate, studded with rivets and antenna arrays, shadows worked in with the side of the pencil. A little universe you could tell he'd been building in the margins for months.

Ethan looked away. The heat in his cheeks rose again, a different kind.

The principal's office always smelled like burnt coffee and rubber bands. The plastic guest chairs could make you feel guilty even if you were there to drop off canned goods for the food drive. Ethan sank into one, heartbeat finally slowing enough to let the sounds of the school seep back in—the intercom's soft click, a copy machine grinding awake somewhere.

Kenji sat two seats down with a damp wad of tissues over his nose. Blood had run into the crease above his lip and collected at the corner, a dark comma. His mother stood behind him, small and composed in a navy cardigan, her hand on his shoulder. She was talking to him in a rapid whisper Ethan couldn't understand; the tone, though, was unmistakable— equal parts worry and steel.

Principal Carver folded his hands on the desk and looked from one boy to the other the way a referee looks between two boxers before the bell. He was a big man who wore his tie too tight; the flush at his neck climbed and receded like a tide.

"Boys," he said. "Middle school is not a boxing ring."

No one laughed. He flicked his gaze to a sheet of paper, then back up. "We've talked to witnesses. Kenji, you extended your leg. You tripped him."

Kenji started to speak; his mother's hand tightened on his shoulder and he looked down.

"Ethan," Carver continued, "you escalated it. A hallway fight? Repeated punches? That's not self-defense."

The room hummed quietly with the building's old HVAC. Outside, a flock of sixth graders thundered past like migrating elk.

"Accordingly," Carver said, voice flattening into the one adults use when decisions are already decisions, "you are both receiving one-week out-of-school suspensions. Starting tomorrow. You'll have packets of work to complete. You'll meet with your counselors upon return." He looked at Ethan and held the look. "And you will apologize. Both of you."

Kenji's mother exhaled, a sound more like a sigh than a word, and spoke to Carver in careful English. "My son…he is quiet. He does not fight. He is very sorry." Then, in a softer tone to Kenji, she added something in Japanese that made Kenji nod without looking up.

Ethan swallowed. The word sorry stuck like a dry pill. He glanced at Kenji; Kenji glanced back for the first time, and for a second all Ethan saw was not the leg or the laughter, but a kid who brought spaceships to school because it was better than talking.

"I—" Ethan started, but the door opened and the secretary leaned in. "Ms. Reynolds is here."

Mom arrived with her name tag still clipped to her blazer, hair escaping the barrette she'd jammed in at lunch. She stood in the doorway a fraction of a second longer than was polite— as if she were bracing herself against whatever version of reality lay on the other side—and then stepped in.

"Ethan," she said, half question, half warning, before she even sat.

Principal Carver did the script. Incident. Witnesses. Suspension. Packets of work. Apologies.

Mom's jaw worked the way it did when she was trying not to interrupt an insurance client who was wrong but important. "I understand," she said finally. "We'll take the packets."

In the parking lot she didn't start the car right away. The keys hung from the ignition, the little grocery store bonus tag clacking softly against the column. Brandy's hair clung to the passenger seat; Ethan brushed it into a little pile with the side of his hand.

"What were you thinking?" Mom asked, not looking at him yet. Her voice had an edge like a dull knife—no shine, all force. "Do you want to be like your father? Because this"—she flung a hand at his knuckles—"this is the start of that."

Ethan watched the reflection of clouds slide up the windshield. "He tripped me," he said. The words sounded small.

"And you hit him," she said. "Again and again. That's not strength, Ethan. That's losing control." She finally turned to him, and her eyes were tired in a way that had nothing to do with sleep. "I can't work two jobs and worry you're going to get expelled because you can't keep your fists to yourself."

He could have said a hundred things then. That he was tired of being the joke. That he had tried the laughing thing, and it had turned on him anyway. That sometimes it felt like he was walking around with a battery in his chest and no safe place to ground it. Instead he said, "Okay," because okay was safe. Okay ended arguments. Okay didn't make anyone cry.

At home, she set him at the kitchen table like he was five again. The Formica had a constellation of faint knife marks, some from years of dinners, one from a boy carving Pac-Man ghosts under a placemat long ago. She got the first-aid kit from the bathroom and dabbed his split knuckle with something that stung.

"Don't flinch," she said gently, and for a second the steel in her voice melted back into something softer.

"I'm not," he lied, and didn't.

She wrapped his hand with gauze. "Tomorrow you're home. You'll do the work they send. You'll help your brother with dinner. And when you go back, you'll apologize to that boy."

Ethan nodded. The bandage felt too clean for his hand.

"And Ethan?" she added, already halfway to the sink with the crumpled wrappers. "Whatever your father says about this—about 'standing your ground' or 'teaching someone a lesson'—you don't listen. You hear me?"

He nodded again. He heard. He did not promise.

That night the house had the small silence—sharp, cutting, the kind that made you notice the refrigerator's hiccuping cycle and the way the porch light hummed like an insect. Evan leaned in the doorway of Ethan's room later with two grilled cheeses balanced on a plate and held one out like a peace offering.

"So," Evan said around his first bite, "I heard you tried out for Golden Gloves in the B hallway."

Ethan let out a breath that wasn't quite a laugh. "Something like that."

"Mom's pissed."

"Yeah."

Evan chewed, frowned, then shrugged. "Well. Don't be dumb. But also—" He lifted the sandwich in a little salute. "— Kenji should keep his damn feet to himself."

Ethan smirked despite himself. "You're not helping."

"Never claimed to." Evan nudged his shoulder with the doorframe. "Eat. And ice your hand. Coach Evan's orders."

When the house finally went dark, Ethan lay awake and listened to the furnace kick on. His knuckles throbbed in time with it, a mechanical heartbeat. Somewhere down the hall, the long phone cord had been looped back neatly on its hook; in the morning it would be twisted again.

He closed his eyes and tried to picture the fall without the audience, to slow it down until it stopped mattering who watched. But every time he almost got there, the laughter rushed back in. He rolled onto his side and tucked his bandaged hand under his cheek like a kid, and for a while that was enough to make the day fade.

That night the blood on Ethan's knuckles wouldn't wash away. In the silence, he could hear two voices: his mother's— tight with disappointment—and his father's—loose with pride and old war talk that blurred people into enemies. He'd told himself Kenji deserved it, but under the sting he knew he hadn't thrown punches at a leg in a hallway; he'd swung at every laugh, every question, every look that made him feel small. The shame didn't fix anything, but it named the thing: he didn't want to be his father's kind of strong.

Tomorrow he'd start the work packets. He'd help with dinner. He'd stay quiet. He'd try.

And then, two days later, his father would show up with that easy swagger, the one that made rules look optional, and everything Mom had tried to build would tilt again.

Dad showed up two days into the suspension like a weather system—no forecast, just pressure. He knocked once and let himself in, the door catching on the throw rug the way it always did. He smelled like aftershave and gas station coffee and a kind of restlessness Ethan had learned to recognize before he could name it.

"Come on, champ," he said, clapping Ethan on the back as if they'd just won something. "Let's get out of here."

Mom was at work. Evan had taken the bus to a friend's house to study. Brandy circled Dad once, then chose Ethan's side, leaning hard into his shins. Dad grinned, unfazed. "Dog knows a winner," he said, and jingled the keys.

They drove past the Quarterdeck—closed for the afternoon—past the strip mall where the video store used to be, out to the diner off Route 1 with the neon coffee cup that always flickered. Dad slid into a cracked red booth like it was his office, nodded at the waitress like they were veterans of the same long campaign.

"Two burgers, two fries," he said, not looking at a menu. "Coke for him. Coffee for me."

When the waitress left, he drummed his fingers against the Formica, a rhythm that made Ethan think of the green phone cord at home: twist, release, twist. "Your mom called me," Dad said, voice casual. "Told me you got into it at school."

Ethan felt the bandage on his knuckles tighten just by thinking about it. "He tripped me," he said, staring at the napkin dispenser's warped reflection. "In front of everybody."

Dad's mouth tilted into a smile that was more show than joy. "And you showed him not to do it again."

Ethan didn't answer. Somewhere behind the counter, a radio hummed out an old song about leaving town.

"Some people will look you in the face and call you boy," Dad went on softly, almost like he was talking to himself. "Or they'll trip you and laugh. You can't let that stand, son. You hear me?" He picked up his coffee, took a long sip, set it down. His eyes sharpened. "Especially those people."

The words came out heavy, like rocks dropping into a well. Ethan looked up. Dad's jaw had that familiar notch in it, the one that showed up when he talked about the years Before: jungle heat, helicopters, night that sounded like bugs and fire.

"You don't know the half of it," Dad said, catching Ethan's look and mistaking it for a question. He leaned back, thumb worrying the edge of his cup. "We were kids, and they were everywhere. You couldn't tell who was who. One minute someone's handing you a canteen, the next—" He cut the air with his hand, sharp. "Your friend is gone."

He didn't use a slur this time, but he used a word Ethan had heard him use before, one Ethan had learned not to repeat at school or anywhere else. It landed between them like a dropped wrench. The diner clinked and hummed around it.

"Dad," Ethan said, unsure what he was asking.

"I'm not saying it's fair," Dad said, softer now, eyes glazing for a second like he was watching a screen on the far wall only he could see. "I'm saying that's how the world is. You need to be ready. You don't let 'em get one over on you. You stand your ground." He raised his coffee cup like a toast. "To that."

Ethan lifted his Coke because it was easier than not. The ice cracked against his lip. He felt the warm flare of being approved of and the cold sting of something else underneath, something that didn't fit right, like boots on the wrong feet. Kenji's quiet face flickered in his mind—the pencil-sketched spaceships, the way he'd held his hands up, palms out, not sure where to put them.

Their food arrived. Dad ate like he hadn't in days, big bites, fast swallows. When he finished, he wiped his hands on a paper napkin and grinned suddenly, conspiratorially. "Come on," he said. "Got one more stop."

They hit a sporting goods store with racks of camo in the back and fishing lures organized by color and threat. Dad didn't wander. He walked straight to the boots.

"Those?" He nodded at Ethan's feet with mock dismay. "Clown shoes. You need something that'll hold you up."

He made Ethan try on a pair of black leather work boots, heavy and sure. The laces bit in. When Ethan stood, the ground felt closer and farther away at the same time.

"Look at you," Dad said, laughing. "Like a man."

Ethan looked at himself in the sliver of mirror propped against a stack of shoeboxes. The boots changed the line of him. They made his calves look narrower, his knees more certain, his posture straighter. They also made his feet feel like they were encased in small, serious tanks. He took a few steps. The leather creaked. He didn't know whether to smile.

Dad paid in cash and slapped the box into Ethan's hands like a trophy. "Don't let your mother return them," he said lightly, but there was a dare inside the joke.

On the way home, he took the long route, windows cracked, his elbow hooked out like a wing. He told a story about a guy named Wheeler who could find a snake in the dark with his bare hands. He laughed at the part where Wheeler got bit and laughed harder at the part where Wheeler bit back. "You got to be the one who finishes the story," Dad said, turning the wheel with the heel of his hand. "That's what I'm saying."

Ethan nodded because it was simpler than not. The box was warm on his lap.

They pulled up to the house. Dad idled a second, engine rumbling. "I'm proud of you," he said, looking out at the yard like the words had to be aimed somewhere other than his son's face. "You didn't start it. But you finished it."

Ethan's hand tightened on the box. He wanted to say, I didn't finish anything. Or, He draws spaceships. Or, I think I made it worse. Instead he said, "Thanks," because thanks was a safe word that finished conversations.

Inside, Brandy danced circles until Ethan laughed for real. He took the boots to his room, put the box under the bed. The house had the big silence until Mom came home. Then it had the sharp one.

She stood in the doorway of his room, eyes going straight to the box like a metal finds a magnet. "What is that?"

"Boots," Ethan said, too quickly.

"I can see that." She crossed her arms, took a breath that seemed to hurt going in. "We talk about this when he calls."

"He's already called," Ethan said. "He's proud of me."

She went very still, like a deer that can't decide whether the sound is wind or hunter. "Of course he is," she said, voice level. "He would be." Then, softer, almost to herself: "He would be."

She didn't make him return them. She didn't tell him not to wear them. She just turned and left and the small silence took over, the kind that makes you hear your own breathing and wonder if you're doing it right.

Suspension days have their own weather. The sun feels like it's wasting itself on you. The mail doesn't come fast enough. The house is too small, the street too loud. Ethan did the work packets at the kitchen table, pencil scratching over photocopied lines. Evan quizzed him on vocab words while flipping grilled cheese without looking. Brandy snored by the door.

At night Ethan pulled the boots out and tried them on in the dark. He stood in them and listened to how they changed the sound of him, even when he wasn't moving. He pictured walking back into school with them—how the hallway would hear him coming and part like water.

He also pictured Kenji's eyebrow, already blooming purple at the edge, and the ships in his notebook, big enough to carry a person out of a moment like the Tuesday in math class and into some other kind of air.

On the last night of the week, Ethan dreamt he was running across the hot, pebbled street barefoot, chasing taillights that were getting smaller and smaller and never stopping, the way they had once before. When he woke, his feet hurt, the old way. He sat up and set the boots back into their box.

They made him apologize the first morning back. Ms. Holloway stood like a sentry outside the counselor's office, arms folded not like a threat but like a witness. The room smelled like dry erase markers and peppermint. A poster of a cat hanging from a branch said HANG IN THERE in bubbly letters.

Kenji was already there, perched on the edge of a chair. His eye had gone a sunset of colors; his nose was less swollen but still tender. He had his notebook on his lap, closed.

"Ethan?" Ms. Holloway said, one eyebrow doing the warning for her.

Ethan looked at the carpet, which had a pattern like TV static. "I'm sorry," he said. The words felt clumsy, too big for his mouth. "You tripped me. I thought—" He stopped. His brain was full of ands. "I shouldn't have hit you," he finished.

Kenji stared at his notebook like it might prompt him with a line. "I shouldn't have tripped you," he said finally, voice small but clear. "I thought it would be…funny." He winced once, not from pain. "It wasn't."

Silence widened for a second, and then Ms. Holloway nodded once, brisk. "Good," she said. "We own our part and we move forward."

They both nodded as if that were something a person could just do.

When Ms. Holloway stepped into the hall to take a call, Kenji flipped his notebook open like a nervous habit. The spaceship page flashed and Ethan couldn't help it. "That's really good," he said.

Kenji closed the book halfway, like he might have to defend it. "Thanks."

"You…draw a lot?"

Kenji nodded, wary and hopeful at the same time. "Yeah."

They didn't become friends right then. Movies get that wrong. But a new thing did wedge itself into place: when they passed in the hall, they'd nod, not just at each other but at the thing that had happened and the agreement, unspoken, not to let it happen again.

The world didn't change because two boys said sorry in a room that smelled like peppermint. But something in Ethan shifted a degree. Like a compass that had been stuck and then woke up.

At lunch, the kids still bartered fries for pizza squares and bragged about whose brother had what video game system. Someone asked Ethan where he'd been; he shrugged like he'd been bored at home instead of remade in small ways he didn't have language for. Humor came back less like a mask and more like something he could set down when his face got tired.

After school, he went to soccer. Coach blew the whistle and sent them on laps. Ethan ran like his legs were only legs and not something he had to prove. He beat the fast kid and didn't pump his fist about it. He passed early in scrimmage; he didn't try to score through three defenders. When practice ended, he stayed late and took shots on the empty goal until the light got gold and long.

"Boots, huh?" Evan said that night, seeing the box peeking from under the bed.

Ethan nudged it farther in with his heel. "Maybe later."

"Mom's proud of you for apologizing," Evan said, leaning in the doorway like always.

"Dad's proud I threw the first punch," Ethan said, not sure whether he was confessing or bragging.

"Both can be true," Evan said after a beat, surprising him. "Doesn't mean they're good together."

They fell asleep to the television's soft murmur and the click of the furnace. Brandy took turns checking both rooms, nails ticking the hall like a metronome.

The boots stayed under the bed for a while. Sometimes Ethan wore them to take out the trash, just to feel the ground different. Sometimes he laced them and stood still, letting their weight remind him he had choices about who he was going to be.

He learned where the hallway's floor buckled, the exact tile that rocked when too many kids stepped on it at once. He learned how to step around it, or to step square on it and ride the wobble without losing his balance. He learned that laugh lines can be a shield and a bridge, and that apologies can be a kind of map.

He learned that a boy can inherit more than eye color and last name. He can inherit stories told with coffee breath and a gaze that's somewhere ten thousand miles away. He can inherit the shape of a bootprint he's not sure he wants to fill. And he can also, slowly, learn to set the box aside and choose a different pair of shoes.

On a Friday a month later, Ethan caught Kenji drawing in the library—this time not ships, but a set of boots, detailed down to the stitching, a line of scuffs that told a story without words. Ethan paused, then slid a note onto the edge of the table before walking on: Those look heavy. But solid. When he glanced back, Kenji had added a second pair beside the first— lighter, thinner, more worn, but pointed in the same direction.

Ethan smiled, a small thing just for himself, and kept going. The hallway echoed, but for once the sound of his steps felt like his.

Chapter 4 — A New Divide

Spring didn't arrive so much as roll in—yellow pollen like dust on the hood of Mom's car, azaleas bursting in driveways, the air soft enough to make you think bad things might be far away. Ethan didn't trust it. By then he knew how quickly a blue sky could split.

Dad showed up on a Saturday with the usual thunder of confidence—front door open, boots in the hall, Brandy barking once and then wagging like a metronome. He didn't take his coat off. He clapped his hands, claimed the living room the way he did every space, and said, "Boys, take a seat. Got news. Big news."

Evan flopped into the recliner, one ankle crossed over a knee. Ethan took the edge of the couch, palms on his jeans to keep them still. The TV was on mute. A baseball game flickered in the corner with no sound, players mouthing words to a crowd you couldn't hear.

Dad smiled with his eyes and his teeth, showman-bright. "Cathy and I—" He paused like a preacher before the Amen. "We're getting married."

The word landed and kept landing, like a kid jumping from a low wall—one thump, then another. Evan's mouth opened and didn't close. Ethan's first thought was surprisingly small: So that's that. Like a door that had been cracked for years finally shuddered and latched.

"Congratulations," Evan said, voice neutral, trying it on the way you try on a shirt you're not sure is yours.

"Yeah," Ethan added, and even he could hear the hollowness in it. "That's…big."

Dad laughed, filled the silence with his own approval. "It is big. She's good people. You'll love her more once you know her like I do."

We know her, Ethan thought. He remembered Cathy's perfume—sweet like a bowl of fruit left on a counter too long—and the way she called them hon without looking up.

Dad's voice softened. "I want you both there. It's in North Carolina. Her hometown. Be good for the family to see my boys."

Her family. His boys. Ethan felt the words arrange themselves into teams.

They drove down two weeks later in Dad's pickup, through green that got taller and wilder as the miles stacked. Billboards promised peach stands, fireworks, and Jesus. The radio lost stations and found others—twangy guitars, preachers promising fresh starts. Dad pointed out the Blue Ridge as if he'd built it. "God's country," he said, one hand draped over the wheel. "Right there in front of your nose."

The church was small, whitewashed, and set on a ridge like a good idea. Inside smelled like lemon oil and old hymnals. Cathy's people filled the pews in careful clothes—women with hair sprayed into place, men with handshake grip that went a second too long. Ethan and Evan sat side by side, collars itchy, faces arranged.

Dad looked wrong and right all at once in a gray suit. He had a fresh haircut and a barber's line still faint at the back of his neck. When he took Cathy's hands, his smile turned real, the easy grin dropping into something quieter. The minister spoke of covenant and patience; the congregation responded the way a field does to wind—everyone bending the same direction.

Ethan watched his father say "I do" and felt the world tilt, not badly, just irrevocably. He thought of Mom's hands on a steering wheel, of the green phone on the kitchen wall, of the Tuesday he'd learned the floor could slide out from under you.

No more waiting for the reset, he told himself. No more pretending there's a switch somewhere.

The reception was at a cousin's place up the mountain, a house with a porch the length of a freight train and a view that looked like a paint-by-number landscape left unnumbered. Folding tables groaned under food—fried chicken, hushpuppies, deviled eggs with paprika freckles, a cherry cobbler that looked like it might still be breathing. Mason jars clinked. A record player scratched out a song people knew the steps to without thinking.

Cathy's uncle pressed a red cup into Evan's hand and another into Jesse's—the new stepbrother who was all elbows and fringe and the easy confidence of a kid on home turf. "A man gets married," the uncle said, "boys get to toast." Laughter and permission folded together.

Ethan sniffed his cup and set it down. He drifted to the edges, that place he'd perfected—close enough to be counted, far enough not to be consumed. He watched Dad make rounds, slapping backs, collecting congratulations like chips. He watched Cathy beam, watched her sister cry in that way that makes other women pat their own eyes, watched Jesse take a second cup and talk louder. He noted all of it the way you note exits in a theater.

By dusk, the porch swing held two sleeping boys—Evan and Jesse, heads tilted opposite ways, red cups canted into the dirt. Fireflies switched on in the yard like someone had found a very quiet light switch. Ethan stood by the railing and pretended the mountains could be counted like sheep.

Cathy found him there, the skirt of her dress held a little off the boards. "You doing okay, hon?" she asked, soft, almost careful.

He wanted to say, I don't know what to do with my face. He said, "Yes, ma'am," instead.

She followed his gaze to the two boys. "They'll feel that in the morning," she said with a small smile. Then, after a beat, "I know this is a lot."

He nodded, because it was both true and safe.

"I want it to be good," she said, looking out at the dark trees. "I want you to have a good place here." She didn't say home. She didn't try to make it that.

Ethan found that he could breathe a little easier around her honesty. "Thank you," he said, and meant the words—not necessarily the place, but the effort.

Dad appeared, flushed with happiness and beer, arm sliding around Cathy's waist like it lived there. "There you are," he boomed to no one and them all. "Family picture!"

They took one, then another, the flash bleaching faces into versions of themselves. In one Ethan smiled for real because Brandy—somehow included by virtue of being part of his definition of family—had wriggled between his knees and sneezed at exactly the wrong right time.

They stayed two more days, visiting people whose names ran together—Aunt-this, Cousin-that—and then Dad loaded the truck for the drive back to Richmond. He didn't mention the next piece of news until they'd cleared the mountains and the radio found the stations Ethan knew.

"We're moving," he said, as if he'd remembered to pick up milk on the way home. "Cathy and me. Kentucky. Got work out there, steady. Good folks."

Ethan kept his eyes on the white line that appeared and disappeared at the speed of the truck. "When?"

"Couple months." Dad checked his mirrors, his tone light. "Now look—this doesn't change anything. We'll work it out. Summers, holidays. I'll get you boys out there. You'll love it. Horse country. You can about taste the bluegrass."

Evan made a small sound that could have been agreement or indigestion. Ethan felt the words slide off him like rain off a porch roof. Doesn't change anything had been the prelude to every change that had ever knocked the wind out of him.

He pictured the map he'd studied in social studies, all states lined up like teeth. He imagined drawing a line from Richmond to somewhere in Kentucky and then trying to cross it every other week. He thought of Cathy's porch and the swing and the two sleeping boys; he thought of Mom's kitchen and the cold floors and the green phone. He knew without knowing how he knew that some distances don't measure in miles.

Dad glanced over, misreading the quiet. "I'll call you about baseball," he said, cheerful. "We'll get a game in next weekend. Maybe the Braves are in town." He thumped the steering wheel in time with a song Ethan didn't like. "Doesn't change a thing."

It changes everything, Ethan said in his head, and turned his face to the window so he could say it out loud to his own reflection.

Back in Richmond, the house seemed smaller, or maybe the air just fit tighter. Mom listened to the news on the couch without commentary, eyes doing that tired skim of a person who has run out of places to put any more information. Brandy paced the hall, unsettled by luggage smells and long drives. Evan took a long shower, then peeled out of the bathroom pink and damp and quiet.

In bed, Ethan lay on his side and counted the new cracks in the ceiling paint. Somewhere a car stereo thumped a bass line that tried to insist on optimism. He closed his eyes and saw the church—white against green—and Dad's mouth forming I do; he opened them and saw the outline of his own dresser and the box under the bed that still held the boots. He could feel the divide like a seam through the middle of him, stitched with the wrong thread.

A train sounded far off, long and then longer, and Ethan wondered who decided when a sound was a warning and when it was a lullaby. He decided it could be both. He decided he was tired of deciding. He rolled over and let the house settle around him, a ship he hadn't chosen to sail that was nevertheless carrying him somewhere he couldn't picture yet.

Spring kept pretending to be gentle. The dogwoods bloomed like folded handkerchiefs, and the days stretched long enough to feel like a promise. Inside the house, time felt tighter—measured in overtime shifts and the minutes Mom spent staring past the television with the volume low.

The first night back from North Carolina, the hot water didn't last through two showers. Evan came out pink and cussing under his breath, a towel slung around his neck. "Heater's on the fritz again," he said, rubbing steam off the mirror. "I'll hit it with the broom handle."

"Don't," Mom said from the hallway, not looking up. "It needs a new element. I'll call Mr. Dawson when I get paid Friday."

Friday became the Friday after.

Laundry migrated to the backyard line, underwear and jeans pegged like flags, stiff as armor when Ethan brought them back in. He tried not to flinch when the denim rasped his knees.

On the kitchen counter, a stack of bills grew like an extra piece of furniture. Some were folded neatly, a pen laid across them; some sat unopened like small white beehives. Mom arranged and rearranged them, mouth tight, a receipt always pinched between two fingers like a cigarette she didn't smoke.

"How much is it?" Ethan asked once, nodding at the pile.

"More than we have and less than the world demands," Mom said, then softened. "We'll make it. We always do."

He wanted to believe her because she spoke like a person who had wrestled a storm and knew where to plant her feet. But he also knew the thermostat game too well—how low can you go and still feel your fingers?—and the way Mom wrapped her hands around a coffee mug at night for warmth.

Soccer should have been the place where the air changed, where his lungs opened and the whistle meant what it said. It wasn't. Not fully. The coach still wore his "Italia" shirts, still barked for five more sprints, still praised Ethan's touch, but everything had a film over it. The boys passed him water bottles and talked good-natured trash the way brothers do, and none of that fixed the part of him that tensed when he saw the coach's car in their driveway. It was like finding a crack under fresh paint you couldn't unsee.

Some practices he flew anyway—touch clean, feet hot as if they were arguing with the ground. Other days, the ball felt like a stranger. When he laced his cleats, he told himself the same thing he had told the ceiling as a little boy: If I run hard enough, maybe the world holds.

Most afternoons he brought Brandy to the field and threw the ball for her until she panted with her whole body. She'd fling herself onto the grass and grin, tongue out, as if she had solved something big, and he would sit beside her and scratch the warm spot behind her ear and feel, for a few minutes, like he had a partner who didn't ask and didn't judge.

On his birthday, Mom came home with a grocery bag that didn't crinkle like groceries. She put it on the table and pushed it toward him with both hands. The corners were soft from being carried too hard.

"Go on," she said, and tried to arrange her face into casual. "It's not much."

Inside was an outfit—shiny parachute pants with zippers that went nowhere and a matching windbreaker that made that whisper sound when you moved. The kind of thing the coolest kids wore on Fridays. The kind of thing he'd stared at in a store window and calculated against the cost of oranges for halftime.

He touched the fabric like it might be a trick, then looked up at her. "Mom."

"Say you'll at least pretend to like it," she said, smiling without showing teeth. "They had red and black. I figured black won't show grass stains."

"It's perfect," he said, and watched relief bloom across her face like sunlight breaking clouds.

She made a cake from a box—slanted where it stuck to the pan—and frosted it with the patience of a person building a bridge. Evan sang off-key on purpose and smudged frosting on Ethan's cheek. Brandy put her chin on the table and stared at the candles like she might make a wish too.

The next morning, Ethan woke before his alarm. He stood in front of the mirror and put the outfit on slow, like a uniform that needed to be earned. He tied his laces in careful double knots. At school, the hallway did that humming thing it does when kids gather, and then people started noticing.

"Yo, Reynolds—look at Mr. Thriller," somebody called, and laughter bubbled up around him, but it was the good kind, the warm kind that doesn't burn. He let it wash over him. A hand slapped his shoulder. "Those zip?" another kid asked, and bent to flick one. "Sick."

He walked a little taller that day, not cocky—he wasn't built for that—just relieved. Even when someone said, two days later, "Didn't you wear that Monday?" he shrugged and said, "When you've got a Ferrari, you don't drive the Pinto." It got a laugh, and he filed the line away. He wore the outfit again Friday, washed by hand and air-dried on the line. The zippers caught the light under the fluorescent bulbs and he pretended the light belonged to him.

On the bus home, he pressed his forehead to the cool glass and watched their neighborhood roll by—porches with flags, porches with wind chimes, porches with nothing—and tried to memorize the feeling of walking down a hall and not being the poor kid or the kid whose mom was dating the coach or the kid whose father had moved to a different state and said it wouldn't change anything.

When he opened the door, Mom was at the sink rinsing coffee cups. She turned and her eyes did that soft thing again. "Good day?"

He nodded, still in the doorway, unwilling to cross into evening and risk breaking the spell. "Yeah," he said. "Good."

"Hang it up; don't throw it on the floor," she said, mock-stern. "We're not rich enough to iron parachute pants."

He laughed, and it felt like a small victory both of them could hold.

The calls from Dad came on weeknights after dinner, the green phone with the long cord snaking down the hall because Ethan had once swapped it out so he could talk from his room. You could tell by the first hello which Dad you'd get— booming and buoyant, or sharp around the edges.

This night was the bragging Dad. "Boys," he said, the word stretched, like he was clapping them on the back through the line. "Went to court today. Cleaned your mama's clock."

Ethan tucked the phone between his ear and shoulder and traced the pattern of the vinyl floor with his sock. Evan leaned against the doorframe, arms crossed, listening without trying to look like he was listening.

"Got me the best attorney in the county," Dad continued, pleased. "Man didn't break a sweat. Judge ate out of his hand. Child support? A hundred seventy-five a head. Three-fifty total." He laughed, a dry, satisfied sound. "Hell, I burn that in gas to get to work."

Ethan's jaw moved without words. He could see the backyard line in his head, clothes like flags. He could see the shut-off notice that had sat like a dare on the counter until Mom made a phone call that made her voice too sweet. He could see the hot water that ran out before it got to him.

"That's great," Evan said, flat.

"I'll have more for y'all when you're with me," Dad said quickly, an add-on tossed like a coin into a fountain. "Cathy's got connections. We'll get you boys a setup out here. Bikes, maybe a dirt track. Whole different life."

"Okay," Ethan said, because there was nothing else to say that didn't explode something.

Dad softened for a moment. "You been running?" he asked. "Keeping your head on straight?"

"Yeah."

"That's my boy." A pause, then the sound of ice against glass. "You know I'm doing what I can."

"Uh-huh." Ethan swallowed the rest—for who?—and let Dad talk about Kentucky highways like they were promises and not distances.

When he hung up, Mom was at the table sorting coupons, scissors flashing in the lamplight. She didn't ask what Dad had said. She didn't need to. She reached without looking and squeezed Ethan's wrist once, a silent translation: We keep going.

Mid-summer, the motorcycle arrived like a dare. Dad backed the trailer into the curb with a showman's flourish, slapped the tailgate, and rolled a gleaming machine down the ramp—chrome throwing back the sun, black paint so shiny you could have checked your hair in it. The neighbors' blinds did that subtle tilt thing. A kid from three doors down whistled, low.

"Oh, for the love of—" Mom started, then bit it off. She came out onto the porch and folded her arms. "What is that."

"Surprise," Dad grinned, as if he'd brought a golden retriever whose only trick was heal all wounds. "The boys need to feel the wind. Can't raise men without some noise in their ears."

Evan's eyes went wide as hubcaps. Ethan felt the old reflex—the part of him that loved machines and speed before he remembered cost. Brandy bounced around their legs, convinced the motorcycle might be a new, very fast kind of stick.

"Let's go," Dad said, tossing helmets like baseballs. "Around the block. We'll keep it clean."

Mom held Ethan's gaze in a long, level look that contained at least three entire conversations. He lifted a shoulder a millimeter. I'll be careful. She lifted hers back. Be careful won't fix everything.

The first time the engine barked, it ricocheted down the street. Dad straddled the bike and it made him look young. Evan hopped on and whooped as they rolled. They came back smelling like heat and gasoline and daring, Evan's hair mashed into helmet lines, eyes bright.

Ethan climbed on behind Dad and gripped the strap at the small of the seat. The engine throbbed under him, a living thing. They took the corner, and the world leaned with them, the houses tilting and righting. For a minute, he forgot everything except the feel of the wind pushing against his chest and the way the pavement blurred. For a minute, he remembered that there were kinds of joy that didn't ask permission.

They went up and down the street three times, the neighbors pretending not to watch while absolutely watching. When they idled back in front of the house, Mom was still on the porch, lips tight and white around words she'd swallowed for the sake of something larger than a fight none of them could win.

"Cool, right?" Dad said, killing the engine. The sudden quiet rang.

Ethan lifted off the helmet. He could feel the grin on his face like sunshine and then he could feel the guilt creep up behind it like a shadow. "Cool," he said, quieter, and caught Mom's eyes again.

After Dad left, Brandy curled at Ethan's feet and sighed in that dog way that says present accounted for. Mom stood at the sink longer than necessary, washing two plates and one glass like a ritual. The house held the echo of the engine the way a shell holds the sea.

That night the phone rang once and stopped. Ethan lay on his side and watched the long cord sway and settle. He thought about Dad's laugh when he'd said "three-fifty" and the way the wind had felt against his face on the turn and Mom's mouth pressed into a line. He thought about the church on the hill and the porch swing and Evan dead asleep with his mouth open, and about Kentucky and a line on a map you couldn't cross on gasoline alone.

The year stacked itself into contradictions. He could walk into school in parachute pants and feel like he'd tricked the universe into letting him belong, and he could come home to a shower that turned cold on his shoulders. He could fly down the block on a motorcycle and then sit at a table clipping coupons with Mom, measuring the week in cents. He could trap a ball with the softest touch he'd ever had and still feel his jaw lock when the coach waved from their driveway. He could hear Dad brag about winning and then see Mom count quarters and think this is what victory buys.

Some nights, before sleep found him, he made a list in his head of things that were solid:

Brandy's warm weight against his shins.
The smell of cut grass in August.
The clean click of a perfect pass.
The way Evan tossed him the last slice without looking like he was doing a kindness.
The whisper sound the windbreaker made when he moved.

He tucked those away like tools. He didn't know what he was building. He knew he'd need something sturdy.

On the first truly cool evening of fall, he took Brandy to the field after dinner. The lights were off, but there was enough moon to see the lines. He dribbled in and out of invisible cones until the rhythm came back, steady and even, like a heartbeat he could control.

"Again," he told himself, no whistle required. "Again."

He ran until his lungs burned the good way and his legs felt like they'd forgive him. He lay down at midfield with his hands behind his head and watched a plane blink across the sky, tiny as a gnat.

Somewhere west of him there was a new house with a porch swing and a woman who had tried to use the right words. Somewhere east of him there was a kitchen where a woman was washing a cup by hand so it wouldn't chip in a machine they couldn't afford.

He was here, in the middle, flat on his back on a field that didn't care who loved who or who had moved where. For the length of a long breath, he felt held by something that did not care and also, somehow, did not leave.

"Okay," he said into the night, to no one and to everyone. "Okay."

The fridge turned into a bulletin board for a life divided. Mom pinned the custody calendar next to coupons and Evan's practice schedule. Different colored highlighters carved the month into territories—Dad's weekends in blue, games in green, payday in pink. When Dad moved to Kentucky, the blue blocks migrated into long rectangles labeled SUMMER and CHRISTMAS (odd years) in Mom's careful print.

"Looks like a map," Ethan said.

"It is," Mom answered, tapping the paper. "Just happens to be of us."

The first trip west came in July. Dad arrived in a borrowed pickup with an ice chest in the back, honking like a parade float. Cathy waved from the passenger seat, her hair sprayed into an obedient helmet. Jesse sprawled in the extended cab, a baseball cap pulled low, pretending not to be curious.

"Load up, men," Dad called, as if the driveway were a staging area. "We'll make Knoxville by dark if we don't dilly-dally."

Evan tossed his duffel into the bed like he'd been born to migrate. Ethan folded his clothes twice, once in his room and once again at the door, then tucked them into the bag with the care of someone packing a part of himself. Brandy followed him back and forth, toenails ticking on the linoleum. When he knelt to hug her, she sighed into his neck like she understood maps and their meanness.

On the road, the landscape flattened then rose; the radio slid from oldies to country; billboards traded lawyers for fireworks and Jesus. Dad talked in wide loops—routes, gas prices, which counties had "real barbecue," which didn't.

Every so often he swatted the steering wheel like it had back-talked.

At a diner off I-40, the waitress called them "honey" and filled their cups with coffee and Coke without asking which belonged to which. Dad held court with his fork.

"Boys," he said, as if the word were a toast. "You're gonna like Kentucky. People mind their business and mind their manners. None of that city nonsense. We do things right."

Evan pressed ketchup into a spiral on his plate. "What's 'right'?" he asked, not quite looking up.

Dad grinned like he'd been waiting for the cue. "Right is work hard, say grace, look a man in the eye. Right is not letting people walk over you. Right is family."

Ethan thought, Which family? He sipped his soda and kept that thought on his side of his teeth.

They reached a subdivision of low, sturdy houses after dark, the kind with mismatched mailboxes and trucks in driveways. Dad's new place smelled like fresh paint and lemon cleaner, the air set a few degrees colder than necessary, as if to prove a point. The room that was "the boys' room" had twin beds with matching bedspreads and a poster of a basketball team Ethan didn't follow. Everything matched so perfectly it felt borrowed.

Cathy hovered kindly without being warm. "We've got a system," she said, showing them the chore chart on the fridge. "Trash Tuesday, mowing Saturday, dishes every night. You're part of this home when you're here."

Jesse rolled past in socks and said to no one, "Don't mess up my inning on Nintendo," which Ethan understood as welcome in a language that didn't want to admit it was being spoken.

Dinner was pork chops and green beans and a prayer. Dad's voice got big when he prayed, like he was standing in front of a congregation. Ethan bowed his head, but he memorized the table instead—the little nicks in the finish, the way Jesse's elbow spread like a wing, the spot where Cathy kept a salt shaker though she always said they didn't need it.

After, Dad turned the TV to the news and launched into a story about work—routes, drivers, the plant manager who didn't know a fifth wheel from a flatbed. "And then there's this fella from—well, you know—" he said, waving his hand in an ugly general direction of the globe. "Came over here and thinks he run the yard because he can count pallets. I told him a thing or two."

The word hovered between the living room and the kitchen, the kind that could collapse a room. Ethan felt it like a hand on his neck. He thought of Kenji. He thought of the quiet click of a pencil, the careful lines of a doodle. He looked down at his knuckles, long healed, and told them something without words: Not again.

Cathy cut a look at Dad that was half-warning, half-weariness. "We don't need to talk work at the table," she said, but her voice was small and the TV was loud.

Later, Dad took them around the block on the motorcycle, like he was giving them a tour of the night. The wind pressed Ethan's shirt to his back and smelled like cut grass and hot metal. For a few minutes, joy didn't apologize. For a few minutes, he thought maybe two truths could coexist: the one where the engine sounded like freedom, and the one where words still hung heavy in air-conditioning.

A church swallowed the next morning, the kind with a marquee out front that spoke in riddles: SEVEN DAYS WITHOUT PRAYER MAKES ONE WEAK. Inside, the air was butter-yellow. The ushers had matching jackets. A woman with white hair and a piano smile shook their hands like she was testing the ripeness of fruit.

"We'd like to welcome our new family," the pastor boomed, without asking if they wanted welcoming. "Brother Reynolds and Sister Cathy, and their fine boys."

Clapping unfurled like a flag. Ethan felt the heat rise to his ears. Evan stared at his shoes. Jesse winked at a girl two pews up.

After service, in the fellowship hall, somebody pressed a styrofoam cup of red punch into Ethan's hand and asked, "So you like basketball?" He nodded, because no would require a conversation. "We got a church league," the man continued. "Coach is strict, but it'll make a man of you."

I already had a coach, Ethan almost said. He sipped the punch and let the sugar spike then fade.

On the ride home, Dad was joyful in a way Ethan associated with winning. "See? Folks here are decent. The pastor's a stand-up man. Got me a breakfast meeting with him Thursday. They do father-son retreats. We could all go."

"Maybe," Evan said, which was family code for we'll see.

The last afternoon of the visit, Dad took them to the sporting goods store. The place smelled like vulcanized rubber and newness, the air charged like a dry thunderstorm. Dad prowled the cleat aisle with purpose.

"Pick 'em," he told Ethan. "The best ones."

"The best?" Ethan asked, fingers skimming the black, the white, the ones with studs like teeth. The price tags could have paid their electric bill. He knew that because he had seen the bill on the counter.

"The best," Dad said again, chin up like a challenge to an invisible judge. "You're not stepping on a field in garbage."

Ethan chose a pair that felt like future—light in his hands, balanced, a little mean around the edges. He laced them up and jogged a crooked line between aisles while Dad nodded like a foreman signing off on a load.

Cathy's mouth did a small thing when the cashier announced the total. Dad signed with a flourish. "Consider it an investment," he said. "My boy's got a rocket in his foot."

On the drive back to Virginia, Ethan kept the box on his lap. He imagined first touches like silk and a shot that curved late, impossible. He didn't let himself imagine the coach's face when he saw them, or the sidelong look from a teammate, or the way his mother would smooth the receipt with her palm and then tuck it into an envelope marked to be filed.

At home, he brought the cleats in like contraband and set them on his dresser, not taking them out of the box. He found Mom in the kitchen, counting tips and receipts, lips moving as she did math without paper.

"He bought you shoes," she said, not quite a question.

Ethan nodded. "They were on sale," he lied, because he wanted to soften something sharper than the studs in the box.

She looked at him a long time and then looked at the calendar. "First game's next Saturday," she said. "I'll be there. Might be late—second shift—but I'll be there."

He believed her. He also knew she would look at his feet first and then at his face and then at the grass, taking inventory of things she couldn't control.

The team gathered at dusk on a field that drank light and returned it in little breaths. When he laced the new cleats, the leather hugged his feet like they'd been waiting for each other. Coach blew the whistle and the drills started: passing ladders, one-touch rondos, the warm-up that was really a test.

"New boots, Reynolds?" Coach called, cupping his hands around his mouth.

"Gift," Ethan said, trying to keep the word plain.

"Use 'em like they cost something," Coach said, grinning, and then turned away to correct a spacing error, and Ethan resented him for being easy with his tone.

He played like the field was smaller than usual, like the ball had a secret route only he knew. When he struck a shot that kissed the bar and dipped in, his teammates howled and smacked the back of his head with approvals. He had to fight not to look for Mom at the fence line. Instead he glanced at the parking lot and saw a familiar silhouette leaning against a car: the coach again, off to the side, and next to him, Mom—arms folded, smile bottled, like joy had to be rationed.

Something thumped in his chest. For a second he wanted to punt the ball to the horizon. Instead, he picked it out of the net and jogged it back, telling himself, Play. Just play.

After practice, in the low light, the coach said, "Nice strike, E. Keep that footwork clean and the rest follows." It was a reasonable sentence from a reasonable man, and Ethan hated him for it.

In the car, Mom said, "That looked like fun," which was a sentence made of glass.

"It's a game," Ethan said, staring out at the faint reflection of his face in the window. "It's supposed to be."

She nodded once, like she'd been graded and the result had come back inconclusive.

The Kentucky visits settled into a rhythm over the next months: long drives, chore charts, church hellos, motorcycle loops, Dad telling stories that sagged under their own weight. Beneath everything ran the same quiet current: joys with a price tag, victories scored on the wrong field.

At Thanksgiving, Dad mailed a photo of him and Cathy on the porch swing, leaves red behind them, a caption on the back in his all-caps print: WISH YOU WERE HERE—WE'LL DO IT NEXT YEAR—LOVE DAD. Mom stuck it on the fridge with a magnet from the insurance office and wrote, in pencil, call: 7 p.m. so they wouldn't miss the time difference. The phone rang at 7:13.

On Christmas morning, Ethan opened a Walkman from Dad and a sweater from Mom. He thanked both with the same voice and then put the sweater on under his jacket and the headphones over his ears and took Brandy to the field, where music could be whatever he needed it to be.

He and Evan got good at translating two households into one boy. They learned which words could be said in which zip code, how long the silence could stretch on a call before it turned into a fight, how to say we're okay to a parent without promising too much. In the dark, when sleep was stubborn, Ethan would list small certainties again, like rosary beads he didn't have: the smell of Brandy's paws, the feel of the ball staying glued to his instep, the whisper of his windbreaker, the stubborn kindness of his mother's hands.

On the last night of the year, fireworks popped in the neighborhood like someone shaking tin foil. Ethan stood at the back door in sock feet, the air sharp in his nose, and watched red flare behind the trees.

Evan leaned his shoulder into Ethan's. "You think it gets simpler?" he asked.

Ethan thought about calendars, cleats, chrome, phone bills, and dinner prayers. He thought about the way the ball rolled perfect when he got his hips right. He thought about the line down a map and the way a person could choose to be the stitch across it.

"No," he said, and then surprised himself by not being sad. "But I think we get better at it."

Evan nodded like a coach had diagrammed something clean. "I'll take better."

They stood there until the last spark hissed out and the night went honest again. Then they went inside, closed the door against the cold, and set their boots by the heat vent—two pairs, drying, side by side.

Chapter 5 — The Challenge

High school didn't feel like a new beginning so much as a louder echo. Same desks, bigger rooms. Same questions, just with more eyes watching. Ethan told himself he'd rewrite the script this time—fewer jokes, more effort, maybe even a real backpack that wasn't fraying at the seams. But the second week in, a kid in a letterman jacket pointed at his shoes and said, "Vintage," and the row behind him snorted like geese. Ethan felt the old heat in his ears, the old rattle in his bones, the old reflex ramping up.

If they were laughing, they weren't looking too closely. If they were laughing, they weren't asking about divorces and court dates and long-distance fathers. He slipped the mask on and tightened the strap.

By October, teachers in three departments knew his name for the wrong reasons. In Algebra II he mouthed along with the announcements like a lip-synched opera. In Biology he ran a silent puppet show with a binder clip and two paperclips dressed as star-crossed mitochondria. In English he could drop a whisper-joke off the back row like a fisherman flicking a lure—never loud enough to draw a direct hit, always loud enough to ripple the water.

"Mr. Reynolds," his algebra teacher said one afternoon without turning from the board, "if your comedy timing was a fraction as good as your sense of when to do your homework, we'd be selling tickets."

The class laughed. Ethan gave a theater bow he didn't feel. The teacher chalked an integral and kept talking. The laugh rolled back into the room and settled somewhere in Ethan's stomach, heavy as a coin in a jar that would never quite fill.

Pep rallies on Friday were supposed to be combustible fun—school colors roaring, a drumline rattling ribs, the principal pretending to be a rock star in a blazer and striped tie. The gym was a bright box of noise and heat. Glitter signs rose from each class like amateur billboards: FRESH IS BEST, SOPHS RULE, JUNIORS = LEGENDS, SENIORS SZN.

Ethan stood wedged in the freshman section, shoulders pressed to shoulders, the cheap paint of a handmade sign flaking on his knuckles. The drumline hammered a cadence that vibrated through the bleachers. Across the gym, the sophomores went feral, a rolling wave of synchronized stomps and throat-tearing chants. They had the numbers, the height, the volume, the confidence of fifteen-year-olds convinced they were already kings.

The principal strutted out with the Spirit Baton—a ridiculous five-foot thing wrapped in blue and gold ribbons that everyone pretended to care about. He cupped a hand to his ear, performative, milking the moment. "I don't know…" he said into the mic, voice syrupy with suspense. "It's close this year…"

"Fresh-men! Fresh-men!" Ethan started, more to shake off his own nerves than to win anything. A few friends picked it up. The chant grew, gained a second row, a third. For a heartbeat Ethan felt the old soccer-field certainty—timing, space, wave-building.

"And this year's winner is—" the principal shouted, "—the Sophomore Class!"

The gym detonated. Blue and gold streamers flew. A sophomore waved his shirt and howled at the rafters. The baton dipped toward their section like a coronation.

Something in Ethan's chest tipped.

"Hell no," he muttered. He didn't think; his legs did. Down the bleacher steps, over a backpack, dodging a teacher's outstretched hand, sneakers squealing on the polished floor. Gasps rose like a flock of birds lifting.

The principal turned, startled deer in a tie. Ethan reached out and—yes—snatched the baton. The ribbons tickled his wrists. The mic squealed.

He pivoted toward the freshman section, adrenaline pitching time into slow motion. "Freshmen!" he shouted, and launched the baton in a high, arcing throw.

For one suspended second, it looked like a good idea.

Then the arc turned into a javelin headed at a knot of ninth-graders who panicked and parted. The baton clipped a kid's shoulder and pinwheeled under the bleachers.

Silence fell like a dropped curtain.

It lasted exactly half a heartbeat.

The sophomore section surged as one, a dam break of angry fifteen-year-olds pouring across the floor. Teachers dove at the front edge and got mowed under. A freshman screamed and then laughed because screaming sounded too serious. Someone yelled "GET HIM!" in a voice that belonged in a movie.

Ethan's first punch came from the left, a blunt thud to the shoulder that spun him. The second hit his ribs. He would say later that he saw it coming; truth was he barely saw anything— a wall of faces, a blizzard of hands, the slick floor skittering under his feet. He half-fell, half-scrambled, ready to curl, ready to spring, unsure which would save him.

"HEY!"

Evan arrived like a linebacker blitz, a senior with a chip that had never quite sanded down. He yanked Ethan up by the back of his shirt, set him behind his shoulder, and stepped into the wash of sophomores with a simple, violent logic. His first swing was clean and fast, a sharp left that dropped a kid who'd already started shouting his victory. The second pushed two more back, more herd movement than targeting.

"You touch my brother," Evan roared, voice tearing, "you deal with me!"

That lit the gym. Freshmen who had hesitated surged forward behind Evan's war cry. Juniors hopped the railings like they were dropping into a mosh pit. Seniors laughed and then jumped because there are only so many times you can see a fight and stay above it. Teachers screamed themselves hoarse. The drumline, bless them, kept playing for a full thirty seconds before collapsing into chaos.

Ethan ducked, covered, jabbed when he had to. He took a knee to the thigh that would bloom purple by Saturday and a glancing fist to the ear that left a buzz. He saw the principal's horrified face at the edge of the vortex and thought, I did this. He saw a girl he recognized from English hurl a pom-pom like a grenade. He saw a physics teacher try to pull two boys apart and get spun around. The whole gym had turned into a washing machine full of limbs and bad ideas.

A shriek cut through the din. Not a student—sirens, somewhere outside, growing louder, closer. The doors banged open and two uniformed officers waded into the mess shouting commands. The bullhorn feedback sliced the soundscape in strips. One of them grabbed Ethan by the elbow and pushed him back, then pushed back harder when the wave tried to close over them.

"Enough!" someone screeched into a mic. "ENOUGH! SIT DOWN!"

It took three full minutes and the authority of a badge for the room to remember it had rules. The chaos slowed, clogged, then finally broke into tired pockets. Kids sank onto the bleachers in panting knots. Pom-poms lay like exploded birds.

The Baton of Spirit was still missing under Section C, which somehow felt on-brand.

Ethan stood in the middle of the floor, hair stuck to his forehead, shirt stretched at the collar, chest heaving. Evan's hand landed on his shoulder like a steel clamp.

"What the hell, man?" Evan said between breaths. Not an accusation. A plea.

"I—" Ethan started, then stopped. The sentence I didn't think didn't feel like a defense. It felt like the diagnosis.

They sent twenty kids to the principal's office, five to the nurse, two to the ER for split eyebrows. Ethan, Evan, and three sophomores sat in plastic chairs outside the office in a row, wrists resting on their knees. The secretary typed as if the keys had wronged her. A poster on the wall said MAKE GOOD CHOICES in cheerful bubble letters.

Evan leaned in. "When we go in there, keep your mouth shut unless they ask you a question. Don't try to be funny. Don't try to justify it."

Ethan stared at a corner of the ceiling where a spider had made a perfect home out of neglect. "I wasn't going to—"

Evan snorted. "Brother. You were absolutely going to."

The door opened. "Reynolds. Both."

The principal's office smelled like old coffee and lemon cleaner, the school's two favorite scents. He took off his glasses and cleaned them with the edge of a tie already smudged from the gym.

"Do either of you wish to start?" he asked.

Evan shook his head. So did Ethan.

"Fine," the principal said, sliding a stack of incident reports into a square. "We'll start with what we know. You"—he pointed at Ethan with the hand that wasn't on his glasses—

"sprinted across a gym floor during a school-wide assembly, stole the Spirit Baton, and threw it into a crowd."

Ethan opened his mouth. Closed it.

"That action incited a brawl," the principal continued. "Your brother joined the fray and escalated it."

Evan lifted a shoulder. It was almost a shrug, almost a confession.

"Now," the principal said, leaning back. "Is there anything either of you would like to say that might persuade me to view this as a misunderstanding rather than an act of colossal stupidity?"

Ethan found his voice, smaller than usual. "Sir, I— I thought… it was a joke."

The principal stared. "A joke."

"I mean, to hype the freshmen. I didn't mean for—"

"For the riot?" the principal said mildly. "No one ever does." He put the glasses back on. "You will both receive out-of-school suspension. Three days for you"—he nodded at Ethan—"for instigating the disruption. Two for you"—to Evan—"for participating and striking other students."

Evan accepted it like taking a charge. Ethan felt it like a trap door opening under his feet.

"I want you to hear something," the principal said, voice softer. "This school is not the place you test the limits of your anger or your need to belong. Find a field. Find a stage. Find a teacher. Not a mob."

He let that hang. "You're dismissed."

Outside, Evan clapped a hand to Ethan's neck—firm, not unkind. "You're an idiot," he said. "But you're my idiot."

Ethan swallowed. "Thanks for coming."

"Always," Evan said, and meant it.

At home, Mom stood in the kitchen in her work blouse, a dish towel thrown over one shoulder like a flag of truce. She listened to the whole story with her hands on the table, palms down, chem-deep breathing in and out like she was keeping her own pulse steady.

"I can't afford to leave work early because the school calls," she said finally, voice rough with the day. "I can't afford to hear that you were the one who made the day worse for other people. You want to be funny? Be funny in a way that doesn't break things."

Ethan wanted to say he understood. He wanted to promise. Instead he nodded and took the dish towel and folded it because his hands needed a job.

Later, Dad called—news travels fast in the kind of network where exes still keep score. "Heard you stood your ground," he said, and Ethan could hear the grin. "Don't let people walk on you."

Ethan stared at the ceiling of his room, tracing the hairline crack that ran to the corner like a river on a map. "It wasn't standing my ground, Dad. It was just… dumb."

"Hmph," Dad said. "Sometimes dumb looks a lot like courage from the right angle."

When the call ended, Ethan lay in the dark and listened to the house settle—the ductwork pinging, the dog sighing in the hallway, the distant drone of a TV. He was suspended between two verdicts: Mom's weary do better and Dad's satisfied that's my boy. The verdict that mattered most had not yet arrived. It came in the form of a question he finally let himself ask: Who do I want to be when the crowd is gone?

He didn't have the answer yet. But for the first time, he wanted one.

The news came at the kitchen table, the same table where late bills were stacked under a salt shaker and homework got done in pencil because ink felt too permanent.

Mom set down her glass of water and kept her fingers on it like she needed the cool. "Boys," she said, eyes flicking from Evan to Ethan, "Coach and I… we're getting married."

The word hung there. Married. Ethan's fork hovered over the plate. Evan's jaw worked like he was testing a tooth.

Mom rushed into the silence. "It won't change who I am to you," she said, voice soft but steady. "It just— it gives us a chance to build something that isn't crumbling all the time."

Ethan looked at his mother's hands. The knuckles were nicked, a small cut he hadn't noticed before, probably from a box cutter at the store. He thought about the coach's blue Italia windbreaker, the whistle, the voice that could fill a field and make boys move. Two worlds he kept carefully apart were suddenly wearing the same ring.

"Okay," he said, because okay was easier than everything else he felt.

The ceremony was small, bare-bones—no aisle strewn with petals, no string quartet, no speeches that went on too long. The coach wore a navy suit that fit like he'd thought about it, Mom a simple dress the color of quiet dawn. In a room that smelled faintly of lemon oil and wilted carnations, a county clerk said the words and the papers made it real. Coach's kids—one older, one younger—stayed with their mother; they smiled in the photos and went home to a different address.

By July, a moving truck idled in front of a house Ethan kept calling the new place because home wouldn't stick in his mouth. The house was startlingly bright—fresh paint, fat baseboards, windows that let the sun pour in. It had an echo when you walked upstairs, a clatter of sound that made even footsteps sound confident. For the first time in his life, Ethan had a room with its own bathroom. He turned the faucet on just to hear what hot water sounded like when it arrived right away.

The two extra bedrooms—meant for a stepbrother and stepsister—sat perfect and unused, beds made with hospital corners, a pair of neat, hopeful lamps waiting to be turned on. Ethan stood in the doorways and felt… staged. Like a guest who hadn't decided whether to unpack.

Boxes bloomed in the living room like cardboard mushrooms—KITCHEN, LINENS, ETHAN—CLEATS / STUFF. Evan carried a box in, set it down, straightened. "Smells like new carpet and money," he muttered, not unkindly, just naming it.

That night, they ate pizza cross-legged on the floor because the table hadn't made it out of the truck yet. Mom laughed at nothing, at everything, the laugh she hadn't used much lately. The coach—stepdad, the word felt like a collar Ethan wasn't sure he'd grown into—opened a planner even before the plates were cleared.

"Okay," he said, the coach voice modulated down for inside. "Ground rules. We're not a team, but we are going to act like one."

Evan rolled his eyes and smirked at Ethan, but he listened.

"Curfew is ten on weeknights unless cleared in advance. Phones stay downstairs overnight—no exceptions. Dinner together when possible. And—" he looked at Ethan— "school matters. You've got a good mind. It's time to use it."

He pulled a legal pad from the stack and uncapped a pen. In four neat strokes, he drew a grid. "Incentive plan," he said, and wrote:

A = $100

B = $75

C = $50

D or F = $0

Ethan watched the numbers bloom in ink. A part of him bristled—bribery, whispered something inside. Another part did quick math without being asked. If he ran the table…

"Is this… real?" he asked, careful not to sound hungry.

"It's an investment," the coach said. "You meet me halfway; I meet you there."

Mom made a sound like relief and warning at the same time. "Don't do it for the money," she said. "Do it for yourself."

"I am," Ethan said. He surprised himself by meaning it.

The new school was its own country—brick buildings low and long, a campus peppered with trees and peeling spirit banners. In the morning the parking lot glittered, a dealership row of BMWs and Audis and the occasional throaty sports car that made the boys look up from their phones. Shirts had collars here, belts matched shoes, backpacks matched sneakers, and there were enough haircuts to staff a bank.

Ethan walked in wearing clean jeans and a t-shirt and felt like he'd shown up to prom in the wrong century. No one said anything cruel. They didn't need to. He'd learned to read the room years ago: you can be invisible and still feel seen.

What he hadn't expected was the quiet. Not silence—the school boomed at the seams with normal noise—but the quiet inside himself when he didn't have a crowd. His old clown routine required an audience who remembered the last bit. Here, nobody did. So he tried on something new.

He sat near the front. He took notes with a pen that didn't skip. He asked a question in Biology, voice steady, and the teacher's face lit like someone had just turned her microphone on. "That's exactly the right challenge, Mr. Reynolds," she said, and the click he felt was small but certain, like a gear finding its mate.

After dinner, instead of falling into the couch, he'd take his spiral notebook to the kitchen table and spread out. The house sounded different at night—dishwasher breathing, AC exhaling, the rote metronome of a clock on the wall keeping time no one asked it to keep. Coach would pass by and lay a hand on Ethan's shoulder, not heavy, not soft, a touch with a point to it. Mom would refill his water without a word.

The first quiz he aced was geometry. He flipped it over face-down on his desk so no one would see the 100 and didn't move until the bell. In English he wrote a passage about rivers and found the teacher had circled verbs like they mattered. In Chemistry he balanced an equation and felt, for three full seconds, invincible.

By midterms, the grid on the legal pad was filling with letters and dollar amounts like a scoreboard. A's lined up like little flags. When the report card came—A, A, A, A, A— Coach didn't blink. He just folded open his wallet and counted bills into Ethan's palm, slow, deliberate. "Well done," he said. Not a cheer; an acknowledgment.

Ethan took the money upstairs and put it in a cigar box under a stack of practice cones he no longer used. He didn't spend it. He loved the heaviness of it—the idea that he had made something appear by force of will.

Mom leaned in the doorway, arms crossed but eyes warm. "Proud of you," she said. "Proud of how you did it."

He smiled back and felt something he hadn't in a long time: control that didn't come from breaking a rule.

The Buick came that summer—the kind of car that smelled like vinyl and family reunions, a Buick Skylark the color of week-old rain. Dad rolled it into the driveway like a prize on a game show and slapped the hood with the flat of his hand. The engine ticked as it cooled, loyal as a dog.

"Take care of her," he said. "She'll take care of you."

The front seat had a bench that made you sit too close to anyone who rode with you. The radio was stubborn about tuning; you had to thumb the knob past static like you were trying to find a station with the right morals. The speedometer's needle trembled when you hit fifty-five, as if the car had its own opinion about limits. To Ethan, it was beautiful.

He drove loops of the neighborhood that afternoon, windows down, wind thudding his shirt against his chest. Freedom wasn't a highway. It was a cul-de-sac you could circle like a private track without anyone telling you to pull over.

On the first day of school in the fall, the parking lot looked like it had been detailed by a movie studio. Seniors slid out of German sedans in pressed polos. Girls in sundresses stepped into heels they would take off by third period. Ethan pulled the Skylark into a row of chrome and glass, killed the engine, and heard the rattle settle.

Two boys glanced over, not unkindly, just the way you glance at a relic someone else loves. One of them nodded. "Classic," he said, like he was being generous.

"Runs," Ethan said, pocketing the keys. "That's what matters."

He shouldered his backpack and joined the river flowing toward the doors. He didn't need to be the loudest person in it. He needed to get where he was going.

The house began to feel less like a model home and more like a place people lived. The extra rooms stayed ghost-quiet, but the downstairs broke into routines—Coach reading the paper at the counter, Mom humming without noticing she was doing it, Ethan dropping a ball of paper into the trash with the exact arc of a corner kick.

They ate together more nights than not. The conversation rotated predictable planets—work, school, the dog's new habit of sleeping sideways—but once in a while, it dipped into something deeper. Coach told a story about being the first in his family to graduate college. Mom told the one about chasing a customer into the parking lot because she realized she'd undercharged him five dollars and it wasn't right. Ethan listened and filed the details in the part of his brain he used for angles.

He started to see the grid the coach had drawn as something other than money. It was a scaffolding—a frame you built on until the shape could hold itself.

He still felt out of place sometimes. In English, a boy with perfect hair mentioned a trip to Nantucket and three people nodded like it was the grocery store. In Physics, someone said their dad could "talk to a guy" about getting the robotics team a new soldering station and twenty minutes later there was one. Ethan learned to work around the feeling the way you play with a blister—acknowledge it, adjust, keep moving.

When the first nine weeks ended, he pinned the new report card on the corkboard over his desk because it meant more there than in a wallet. Evan came in, glanced at it, nodded once. "Who knew?" he said, the smile crooked and proud.

Ethan did, a little. He closed the door and sat with the quiet for a minute. The house hummed, steady. The Buick clicked to itself in the driveway. The cigar box in the closet had weight.

He'd spent years perfecting the laugh that kept people at a safe distance. Now he was learning how to be the kind of person who didn't need it. The grid on the legal pad had turned into a map, and for once, the road ahead didn't look like a dare. It looked like a choice.

Top of Form

Bottom of Form

The first friends Ethan made at the new school didn't sit at the loud table. They occupied a corner of the library where the afternoon sun landed in a square and dust motes drifted like lazy snow. They liked proving each other wrong. They laughed at graphs. They argued over whether time felt different in a soccer stoppage than in a physics lab. They carried backpacks that creaked with textbooks instead of letterman patches.

"Reynolds," said a lanky kid named Jonah, "you're fast at more than just running." He tapped Ethan's geometry notes, where proofs lined up like careful dominoes. "You think in straight lines."

"Sometimes," Ethan said. "Sometimes I need the bend."

They traded homework tips and energy bars and terrible puns. At lunch, they huddled around a chess board that had lost a bishop and used a paperclip instead. No one demanded Ethan be funny. No one asked if his clothes felt new. When he did make a joke, it was a dry one-liner about parabolas that made them groan and clap anyway.

He picked up a job two nights a week at Whit's Market, a corner store three blocks from the new house where the soda cooler hummed all day and the Lotto machine sighed like a tired bus. Mr. DeLuca, the owner, wore a white apron that never looked clean even when it was.

"You're fast," DeLuca said on Ethan's first shift, watching him front the shelves so the labels lined perfectly. "Fast is good. Careful is better. Be both."

Ethan learned the rhythms: the after-school stampede for candy, the dinner lull, the nine-o'clock hush when the neighborhood walked its dogs and the same two women debated magazines at the counter like it mattered. He learned to count change without looking down, to bag eggs on top, to clock trouble before it walked through the door.

Some nights, DeLuca would lean on the counter and tell a story in a voice meant for radios. "When I was your age," he'd begin, which always made Ethan brace for a lecture and then thaw when the story ended somewhere sideways—on a fishing dock, or in an Italian bakery, or with a punchline about the first time he broke a bottle of Chianti and lied about the wind.

"What are you saving for?" DeLuca asked one night, after closing, when the store had settled into the metallic creak of cooling shelves.

"College. Gas. A little… buffer," Ethan said.

"Good. Money buys two things you need—options and time. Most folks waste both."

By senior year, "two nights" had become five when soccer didn't own the calendar. The cigarette case glinted like a temptation he never touched. The cigar box in his closet grew heavy in a way that made him feel tall.

On the field, fall brought back a kind of religion. Tryouts bit cold. Cleats chirped against frozen grass. Coaches watched with clipboards and the particular stillness of men who listen to feet. Ethan felt sharp again, alive. No mothers with coaches. No private politics. Just cones, whistles, breath.

He made the starting eleven as a sophomore, then fought to keep his name on the whiteboard. By junior year, the newspaper ran his photo, a blur of blue and white, ball tucked under his stride, headline shouting Cole Nets Two in District Win. Mom clipped it, smoothed the edges, and stuck it with a magnet to the freezer door. She didn't say anything. She didn't have to.

The bus rides to away games knitted boys into a kind of family—gum wrappers in the aisle, the hiss of a radio fighting static between towns, the ritual of shin guards and tape and muttered promises. They wore headphones and superstition. Ethan counted the lampposts that flashed by and pictured angles that would split a defense open like a zipper.

Senior preseason, his body revolted. Over one bizarre spring and summer he grew nearly seven inches. His feet shot forward like they were trying to leave him behind. He went from a size six to an eleven in months and tripped over his own certainty. New cleats blistered the backs of his heels. His tibias ached at night as if they were being carved longer by hand.

"You're running like a colt," Coach said after one session, a grin tucked in the corner of his mouth. "All legs. Your brain will catch up."

Ethan wanted to say his brain felt fine and it was the rest of him that couldn't keep time, but he just nodded and ran lines until the world melted to sweat and sky.

It took weeks. He learned the new math of his body— longer stride, different plant foot, the way a jump now took a second longer to land and could win a ball he'd never reached before. The angle of shots shifted; so did the swagger. By mid-season he was timing his runs again, slipping behind center backs who looked at him with the kind of annoyance that tasted like victory.

All-district came with a handshake and a certificate that felt like a thin golden shield. All-region followed, along with a second, smaller photo in the paper, where his face wasn't a blur anymore. DeLuca taped the clipping next to the register and pretended it made customers buy more Gatorade.

"Celebrity discount?" Ethan joked.

"You get paid in exact change," DeLuca said, deadpan. "Fame is your own problem."

Between shifts and drills, Ethan took the SAT in a gym that smelled like pencil shavings and nerves. He wrote an essay about rules and choice and the geometry of trust. He checked boxes for schools that his guidance counselor circled in blue—Virginia, William & Mary, Tech—places with brochures full of brick and lawns and kids in sweaters carrying coffee cups.

Then one evening, he spread the brochures across the dining room table like tarot cards. Coach walked in, tie loosened, jacket folded over his arm.

"Let's see it," he said, and did a slow lap around Ethan's future. He stopped at a glossy packet heavy with tradition—Southern Military Institute—a crest embossed like a dare.

"That one?" he asked, as if the page had volunteered to be a problem.

"I thought about it," Ethan said, which was true and not the whole truth. The idea had been hovering at the edge of things since a recruiter visited and spoke in sentences that had bones.

Coach tapped the cover with two fingers. "You? At SMI?"

The laugh was small. It still burned.

"What's that supposed to mean?" Ethan asked, and even he heard how fast it came out.

Coach chose his words with surgical care. "It means it's not like here. It's not even like soccer. The first year is designed to break you. Sleep deprivation. Constant pressure. People yelling on purpose to get in your head. You make bad jokes when you're exhausted. You get defiant when you're cornered."

"I get focused," Ethan said.

"You get loud," Coach said. "You'd never make it."

The sentence landed with a click like a lock turning. Ethan's jaw set. The room sharpened to edges—the legal pad grid framed on the fridge, the ghostly rooms upstairs, the Buick keys on the hook. He had spent a year building a life around the words You can. This was something else entirely.

"Watch me," he said.

That night he wrote the application essay in one sitting, longhand, then typed it so the letters wouldn't lean. He told them about chaos and choice, about the rules of the game that saved him and the rules of a house that didn't always make sense. He told them he wanted a place where the lines were painted and the whistle meant what it said.

He mailed it with a check he didn't let Mom see, paid from the cigar box and proud in a way that felt private.

The acceptance letter came on a Tuesday, as if Tuesdays had good news hidden behind their plain faces. The envelope had weight. The crest shone like a coin. He stood on the porch and held his breath until his vision fuzzed at the edges.

"Open it," Mom said, appearing at his shoulder, as if she'd been listening at the window the whole time.

He slid a finger under the flap and pulled the letter free. The words were brisk and official and kind all at once. We are pleased to inform you… He didn't realize he was smiling until his cheeks hurt.

He found Coach in the garage measuring a board for shelves he planned to build and never quite would. Ethan held the letter out without ceremony.

Coach read quickly, eyes skimming, then went back and read slower. When he looked up, the old coach grin was there, the one that started in the eyes and traveled.

"Well," he said, "looks like you'll last at least a month."

"At least," Ethan said.

They shook hands. It felt right—like a deal between men— even as Mom swept in and turned it into a hug that smelled like detergent and relief.

Evan smirked from the doorway. "Don't let 'em shave your brain," he said, but his eyes warmed. "I'll take the Buick if they do."

"Over my dead body," Ethan said, and the room laughed like a team who knew the play worked.

Dad called that weekend. "SMI?" he barked, as if the letters were an insult. "They'll shave your head and spit you out. Better learn to follow orders."

"I'm good at lines," Ethan said evenly. "And I run fast."

There was a pause, the line breathing. "Don't come crying to me."

"I won't," Ethan said, and didn't add I never did.

Spring of senior year, Ethan coasted academically for the first time in his life, but it wasn't lazy. It was the kind of coasting you do on a bike—legs still ready, eyes on the road. He worked Whit's three or four nights, stacked money, bought a belt for the uniform list he'd printed and folded into his wallet until the creases became part of the words.

Soccer ended with a playoff loss that didn't feel like failure. He knelt with his teammates under stadium lights that hummed like fluorescent bees and let the sound of the crowd fade into the sound of his own breath. He had outgrown the boy who needed to be loud to be seen. Now he knew how to speak without raising his voice.

On a warm evening in May, he parked the Skylark at the far edge of the school lot and sat for a minute, engine ticking in a rhythm he'd come to trust. He looked at the building that had made him prove things he hadn't known he needed to prove. He didn't feel small. He didn't feel big. He felt… ready the way a drawn bow feels ready, silent but charged.

The grid on the legal pad had become a map. The cigar box was lighter deposit made on a future he'd had the nerve to pick.

The house upstairs was still bright, still too quiet in places, but it was a quiet he could live in.

He closed his eyes and pictured the SMI parade ground, the lines perfect, the rules clear. He pictured the whistle and the moment right before it blew, the breath everyone took together.

He smiled into the windshield.

"Watch me," he whispered to no one and everyone, and stepped out into the evening.

Chapter 6 – The Road to Virginia Tech

The Ask

It started in the cafeteria, at the table where Ethan and the in-betweens ate—kids who weren't invisible but weren't orbiting the sun either. The starting goalkeeper cut through the noise and the smell of tater tots like he owned the room, broad-shouldered, swagger in his walk, eyes scanning until they landed on Ethan.

"Yo, Cole," he said, palming an apple like a baseball. "You wanna run down to Virginia Tech this weekend? Couple of my boys are there." He tossed the apple, caught it without looking. "Be a good time."

Ethan stared. "Me?"

"Yeah, you." The keeper's grin read easy charm. "Need a solid shotgun. You drive, right?"

"Sure," Ethan said, too fast. "Yeah. I drive fine."

"Cool. Roll out Friday after school. Blacksburg, baby." The keeper clapped his shoulder—friendly, heavy—and moved on, already telling a sophomore to save him a seat in study hall.

Ethan sat there with his tray cooling, heart kicking the back of his ribs. For a full minute he didn't eat, just watched the keeper's back recede, hearing the echo in his head: Me.

He wanted to feel purely chosen, but he'd grown up in a house where choice usually meant someone needed something. The thought arrived like a little gray cloud. Why me? Two beats later the answer did, too. Ride. Beer. Word gets around when your older brother can make those problem-solving phone calls.

It stung for half a second, then he shook it off. So what if it wasn't a fairy-tale invitation? It was an invitation. A weekend away from the same sidewalks and the same faces, a test drive of the life he said he wanted.

That night, over meatloaf and green beans, he tried to sound casual. "Mom, can I borrow your car Friday? The Civic?"

His mother looked up. He could tell exactly how her day had gone by the geometry of her hair and the set of her shoulders; tonight, everything sat a little off-center. "Your car works," she said, scooping beans.

"It does," Ethan said quickly, "but your Honda gets better mileage. And, uh, it's safer on the mountain roads." He did not mention that the Civic's brand-new stereo had a cassette deck clean enough to make even old tapes sound bright.

She lifted an eyebrow, a move that said I was seventeen once. "Where are you going?"

"Virginia Tech. Just for the weekend. A few guys. I'll be careful."

She chewed on that for a moment, then sighed. "Home by Sunday dinner."

"Done."

"And you fill the tank back up."

"Double done."

She held his gaze a second more, then slid the keys across the table. "You scratch it, you fix it."

"Understood," he said, trying to keep from grinning too wide.

Back in his room, he closed the door and leaned against it, grinning at the ceiling. Blacksburg. He grabbed a notepad and started a list: tapes—Buffett, James Taylor, Cat Stevens; toothbrush; hoodie; cash; cooler. His mind staged the whole movie—rolling into a campus lot with the windows down, stepping into a party without needing the punchline to enter, catching the kind of nod guys give other guys who already belong.

At ten, he knocked on Evan's door. His brother lay on top of the covers, headphones crooked off one ear, thumbing through a car magazine.

"You still friendly with that clerk?" Ethan asked. "The one who doesn't mind carding fuzzy?"

Evan slid the headphones down around his neck and studied him. "How much are we talking?"

"Eight cases," Ethan said, immediately regretting the number. He kept talking so he couldn't back out. "We'll take the Civic. I'll cover it."

Evan let a smile creep in. "Eight cases is a lot of 'we'll take the Civic.' What's the occasion?"

Ethan shrugged. "Trip. Tech."

"Who with?"

"Goalkeeper."

Evan made a face like of course. "You're not a mule, you know."

"I know," Ethan said, and he did. He also knew the feeling of not being invited and how heavy that silence could be. "It's a weekend. I'll pay you back for fronting it."

Evan sat up and swung his legs over the side of the bed. "Open your sock drawer," he said, nodding toward Ethan's room. "Bottom pair of white crews. There's thirty in there from when I sold the mower parts. Take it. Consider it a bad investment in your social life."

"You sure?"

Evan flicked a look that said yeah and be careful at the same time. "And if the wheels come off, you call me, not Dad."

"Deal."

For the rest of the week, time dragged like a bad signal. Ethan drifted through classes, only half-hearing teachers, the clock hands sticky and slow. He kept rehearsing how to exist by proximity—how to stand at a college party with an easy lean, how to nod like a guy who'd done this a hundred times and not like a tourist with a visitor's badge. He imagined the Virginia mountains rising and falling like a slow breath as the Civic hummed along, the dashboard lights soft, the cassette deck swallowing and spitting back a warmer world.

Thursday night he washed the Civic like it were a ritual—bucket, hose, sponge—running the cloth over every surface like he could polish the weekend into going right. He vacuumed the floor mats, Windexed the dash, adjusted the driver's seat until it felt like the car had been made for him. When he turned the key just to test the stereo, a song about beaches and bad decisions clicked into place, and he laughed alone in the driveway. He kept it to under ten seconds, respecting the house rule: no blasting after nine.

Friday after last bell, the keeper rolled up with a duffel and an energy that filled the doorway. "Let's roll," he said, already halfway back down the walk. At the curb, he eyed the Civic appreciatively. "This thing's clean."

"Just had it detailed," Ethan deadpanned, tossing the keys.

They loaded the trunk, which sagged obediently under the weight of the cases, and wedged a fisherman's cooler in the back seat, ice rattling like a promise. Ethan slid a tape into the deck and the opening guitar lilt unfurled. The keeper cocked an eyebrow.

"Buffett?"

"You'll live," Ethan said. "Trust me—road-trip medicine."

"As long as it's loud," the keeper said, cracking the first can as if the universe had granted him a permanent permission slip.

They hit the on-ramp for I-64 like a starting gate, Richmond shrinking in the rearview. The Civic purred; the sky was a clean-sheet blue. The mountains beyond Charlottesville rose in slow layers, purpled in the distance. The keeper drummed on his knees, talking about his buddies already at Tech and how the dorm floors had girls and the parties began before sunset and sometimes ended with someone jumping in a fountain, which was apparently a rite of passage.

At a gas stop near Gum Spring, Ethan topped off the tank because it felt like the responsible thing to do, then wiped a water ring off the hood because it felt like the right thing to do. An older guy at the next pump nodded at the car. "Good little machines," he said.

"Best in class," Ethan answered, which made the keeper snort-laugh and throw an arm around Ethan's shoulder. "Don't worry," he told the man. "We'll return it with more stories than miles."

Back on the highway, Ethan loosened into the seat, music pouring, the mountains opening. Every so often he glanced at the keeper—the way popularity fit him like a custom jacket— and wondered what it would feel like to wear confidence that easily. He thought about the math of invites and securities. He thought about being used and being included and how, at seventeen, sometimes those things braided into the same rope.

He turned the knob a little louder and let the guitar cover the thinking.

Just past the Charlottesville exits, the brake lights began, a red ribbon stretching to the horizon. It took a mile to realize they weren't pulsing; they were solid. Traffic slowed, then shuddered, then stopped like someone had cut the wire to the whole interstate.

"Uh oh," the keeper said, rolling the can in his palm.

Ethan dropped the car into park and looked up the slope of dotted lines and shimmering roofs. A door popped open in the lane beside them. Then another. The air above the asphalt trembled with heat.

"What do you figure?" Ethan asked.

"Something big," the keeper said, standing to scan over the roof. "Wreck? Hazmat?"

A guy in a trucker cap jogged down the shoulder, breathless dispatch. "Chemical tanker rolled a few miles up. Hazmat crew's out. They're sayin' hours."

"Hours," the keeper repeated, and then he grinned, the kind of grin that builds momentum. "We've got cold beer, a radio, and a captive audience."

Ethan looked at the heat wavering off the hood, the packed cooler in the back seat, the resigned faces of strangers unfolding like deck chairs. He thought about belonging and how sometimes all you had to do was open the door.

"Let's not be the only ones miserable," he said, and popped the locks.

They swung the doors open like wings. The tape clicked over to the flip side—sun, salt, promises—and the sound leapt into the stalled afternoon. Ethan tugged the cooler free and set it on the hood. Ice clinked. The keeper held a can up and scanned the immediate world. "First round's on the boys in the Civic," he said.

At first, people smiled without moving. Then a couple of college kids—VT hats, perfect timing—walked over, and everything began to tilt toward party.

Ethan watched it happen from a step off center, feeling the strange warmth that comes when a hundred tiny decisions gather themselves and say yes. He was not the awkward fringe kid for the moment. He was the guy by the cooler, the one you thank as you walk back to your friends, the one people nod to like you've been expected all along.

He caught himself smiling so hard his face hurt, and didn't stop.

For the first ten minutes, people just watched—smiles cracked, eyebrows lifted, shoulders un-hunched. Then the trickle began. Two college kids in Virginia Tech hats ambled over like they'd been summoned by a beacon only students could hear.

"Y'all serious?" one asked, already reaching for a can.

"As a heart attack," the goalkeeper said, popping his own with a crisp pssht. "Welcome to Exit Who-Knows-Where Fest."

Ethan laughed and played host, pressing cold aluminum into grateful hands. The cooler fogged in the heat, ice snapping under the cans as if trying to keep rhythm with the tape deck. The Civic's doors were flung wide like wings, Buffett's guitar lines drifting over the blacktop, buoyant and a little ridiculous, the exact medicine for a thousand stalled plans.

A man in a trucker cap walked up, curiosity on his face and a golden retriever at his heel. "You boys just saved I-64 from mutiny," he said, taking a beer and tipping it in salute. The dog sat, offered a paw to no one in particular, then wandered off to be adored by a group of girls sitting on someone's bumper.

By the time the tape thunked and clicked to the flip side, the shoulder of the highway had become a neighborhood. A guy in a tie loosened it and used it for a headband. A woman in nursing scrubs kicked her clogs off and double-dutched with two college girls using a bungee cord for a jump rope. Somebody produced a frisbee from a hatchback and a perfect little arc sailed over lanes that had forgotten they were supposed to be going anywhere.

Ethan became the de facto DJ of Exit Who-Knows-Where. He ejected one tape, spun a pencil in the little wheel to rewind another, fed it back into the deck. Buffett gave way to Tom Petty, which gave way to Springsteen, the music rotating through the decades like a lazy fan. Every time a new track landed just right, people whooped as if they'd requested it hours ago and had finally been heard.

"Hey—hey, host with the most," a girl with sunburned shoulders called, hopping lightly across the painted lines. "You got anything not beer?"

"I've got… half a warm cola rolling around under the passenger seat," Ethan said, grimacing.

"Sold," she laughed. "My head is going to be a crime scene if I keep this up."

He dug around, surfaced with the sticky can like a prize fish, and offered it with a little bow. She clinked it against his empty can. "Thanks, Civic guy."

"Ethan," he said.

"Jess," she answered, then wove back to her group, the name looping in his head a couple of extra times because it was said with friendliness and not out of necessity.

The goalkeeper, born for this, worked the perimeter like a politician on a fairground—knuckling guys he'd never met, promising to visit dorms he didn't know existed, flirting shamelessly with anyone who wandered within six feet. He was natural at it, and Ethan felt that old, familiar twinge—envy and admiration standing shoulder to shoulder. But for once, the feeling didn't sting. Here, now, he wasn't the satellite. He was the center of gravity, the guy with the cooler and the chords and the nerve to open the doors.

"Underage, underage," a voice hissed as a couple of freshmen-looking kids edged closer, eyes hungry for free handouts. Ethan stepped in front of the cooler and tilted his head toward the shimmering shoulder.

"Water's in that camper three cars up," he said, as gently as he could. "Go make friends with the guy in the Hawaiian shirt. He looks hydrated."

They rolled their eyes in the universal language of seventeen-year-olds denied, but they moved on. Ethan exhaled, surprised at himself—this little flicker of responsibility amid the red Solo cups and the laughter.

A highway patrol cruiser rolled up the opposite shoulder, lights off, window down. The trooper slowed, looked across the barrier at the pop-up block party—music, frisbees, a guy stretched flat on his hood staring skyward like he'd found religion—and shook his head. He lifted two fingers off the steering wheel in a kind of half-salute, half-warning, and rolled on. The crowd booed half-heartedly and then cheered at their own audacity.

By hour two, the asphalt radiated back every bit of daytime heat it had swallowed. The air smelled like hot rubber and spilled beer and the faint sweetness of someone's bag of oranges that had been opened and shared down the line. The sun slid a notch lower and shadows lengthened, the light going syrupy.

A trucker with a silver mustache wandered up, his handle embroidered on a patch over his pocket: SHORTSTACK. He held a Styrofoam cup like a chalice. "Y'all on the box?" he asked, jerking a thumb toward his rig. "CB says it's a mess up there. Hazmat boys laid out like ants on a Popsicle."

"Hours?" Ethan asked.

"Hours and change," Shortstack said. He squinted at Ethan. "You look like a good kid. Keep it under the porch light when we get moving."

"Yes, sir," Ethan said automatically, and Shortstack's mouth tugged into something like approval before he wandered back into the human tide.

As the afternoon softened, the edge came off everything. Even the impatient had been soothed into patience by necessity. People told stories because there was nothing else to do: a couple from Ohio on their way to a wedding with a cake in the backseat ("God help us if it melts"), a grad student with maps who talked about the quick way to Boone as if he were reading weather patterns, a mom with two kids who had turned the whole thing into a scavenger hunt ("Something red! Someone named Mike! A dog with a bandana!"). The retriever obliged them by returning in a Stars-and-Stripes kerchief, posing for a picture he would never see.

The keeper slid back to Ethan's fender and nodded at the cooler—low enough now that ice and cans were indistinguishable. "We're gonna be folk heroes," he said, eyes bright.

"Or cautionary tales," Ethan said, grinning. He tipped his own can and felt the hollow lightness when it was very nearly empty. "We should pace. When this opens, we're not in shape to be decent citizens."

"We'll pull off," the keeper said, already reading the ending as clearly as the beginning. "Crash at a gas station. Rally later or head back. Either way, story's better than the plan."

A guy with a guitar appeared as if conjured by the glow of the gathering and started picking, badly at first, then better with encouragement. He didn't know all the words to anything, but neither did anyone else, and that seemed to be the point—people sang the parts they knew, hummed the rest, and clapped at the end like it had been perfect. The dog barked at the applause and was applauded for barking, and for a while everything felt like it fed everything else.

Ethan looked out across the lanes—bumper stickers, laundry baskets visible through rear windows, strangers sitting cross-legged on the shoulder sharing grocery-store cookies. He thought about how many kinds of lives were presently braided into the same inconvenience, tricked into community by the failure of forward motion. He thought about his own life, how often it felt like this—stuck, then suddenly, inexplicably, almost joyful because he'd decided to roll the windows down and open the doors.

"Hey," Jess said, reappearing, cheeks a little less red, holding the now-empty warm cola like a trophy. "Your DJ set? Epic."

"Years of training," Ethan said. "I once did a full cassette flip with a Bic pen in under ten seconds."

"Teach me your ways, master," she said, mock-serious, then bumped his shoulder. "I'm Jess, by the way."

"You told me," he said, then immediately wanted to crawl under a car. "Sorry. Ethan. I'm Ethan."

"Hi, Ethan-I'm-Ethan," she said, deadpan, and he laughed because he deserved it.

When the traffic finally began to twitch—not a rumor this time, but a real, collective shiver—there was a murmur like someone had announced extra innings for free. People tossed last sips into the brush, crushed cans under heels, folded lawn chairs as if they had all rehearsed together. The guitar guy strummed a little fanfare. Couples did quick math with their eyes about who should be driving. The nurse slipped her clogs back on with the air of a woman about to return to a calling.

Ethan closed the doors, the Civic suddenly looking smaller now that it had been a stage. He stowed the limp, sloshy cooler on the floor behind the passenger seat, wiped condensation rings off the hood with the edge of his shirt, and turned the key. The engine caught without complaint, the dashboard lights winking awake. Beside him, the keeper buckled in and immediately reclined the seat, tipping his head back like a man boarding a red-eye.

"Exit, left," he murmured. "Soon as we can. I'm seeing double."

"Noted," Ethan said, throat dry. He took a breath and felt a flicker of pride that had nothing to do with popularity—just a simple we didn't do something stupid.

They rolled as a unit, lanes sloughing forward like a glacier suddenly remembering it's a river. Past the jackknifed tanker they went—men in hazmat suits moving with careful choreography under bright floodlights, a world apart from the party a few miles down. Ethan drove like Shortstack had asked—under the porch light—hands at ten and two, eyes soft but awake.

At the first exit with a gas station, he eased off and pulled into a lot washed in fluorescent hum. The keeper peeled his seat upright with a groan. "Bathroom, water, potato chips the size of a hubcap," he declared, then added, "Nice work, host."

"Thanks," Ethan said, and watched him stumble inside.

He stayed in the driver's seat for a second longer, the car ticking as it cooled, the bourbon-colored afterglow of the day hanging on. He could still hear the echoes of that pop-up community—laughter, guitar strings, the retriever's bark. He rubbed the heel of his hand over the line the seat belt had pressed into his T-shirt and smiled. He had been invited because someone needed a ride and a favor. He was leaving with something else.

When the keeper returned with armfuls—water bottles, chips, two Snickers bars like mercy—Ethan cracked one of the waters and drained half of it, feeling clarity return cell by cell. They ate in the quiet way you do after a long day—greasy, grateful, present.

"You good to steer us home?" the keeper asked.

"Home," Ethan repeated, and it felt right in his mouth.

They slid back onto the road, the world finally doing what it was built to do. The mountains were darker now, a single black shoulder against a deepening sky. Ethan kept the stereo low, a song he could hum to without words, something that let him think. He thought about how the day had zigged from his plan, then zagged into a story—how sometimes belonging was as simple as opening the doors and turning the volume up.

By the time the highway flattened into the familiar slide toward Richmond, the keeper was snoring lightly and the ice in the cooler had surrendered to water. Ethan's fingers relaxed on the wheel. He felt older than he had that morning, in a way that had nothing to do with age.

At a red light near home, he glanced at himself in the rearview mirror. He looked like a kid who had been outside all day—flushed, a little wind-burned, happy. He smiled at himself, small and private, and rolled through the intersection when it turned green.

He pulled into the driveway just before midnight, the Civic's engine purring like a cat that had seen things. Porch light on. Kitchen light off. The kind of quiet that meant someone was awake and listening.

Ethan killed the ignition and sat there a second, palms pressed to the wheel. He could still feel the highway under his feet, the phantom sway of a day that had been all motion and no miles. The cooler sloshed when he reached back to grab it— mostly water now, with a few orphaned cans that felt like relics from a museum exhibit on Poor Choices.

He wiped the last condensation ring off the hood and carried everything inside. The door squeaked the way it always did—the house's tell. Mom was at the table in her robe, elbows on Formica, doing a crossword in pencil. Coach leaned against the counter, arms folded, the posture that read respect me or at least pretend to.

"You're late," Mom said, voice soft but heavy.

"Yeah," Ethan said, setting the cooler down on the vinyl with a dull thunk. "Traffic."

Coach sniffed the air. "Traffic smells a lot like beer."

Ethan winced. He'd cracked the windows the last twenty minutes, but the Civic still wore the day like a cheap cologne. "We… got stuck on 64," he said. "Chemical spill. Four hours. Everyone was outside their cars. We—" He hesitated, then decided: if he was asking to be treated like an adult, he could start by acting like one. "We threw a highway party. Music, frisbee. I passed out beers. We didn't drive drunk. We pulled off and sobered up. But, yeah. We were drinking."

Mom's eyes narrowed—fear, then anger, then something older that had nothing to do with him and everything to do with nights she'd sat up waiting for another man to come home. "You drove my car."

"I know."

"With beer in it."

"I know."

"And you drank."

He nodded. "Then I didn't drive. We slept at a gas station for a couple hours." He lifted a shoulder, tried for a small truth. "It was… kind of amazing. People were nice to each other."

Coach pushed off the counter and stepped closer, not looming, exactly—just making sure he filled Ethan's frame of view. "Keys are contracts," he said. "You take them, you sign your name to a set of decisions. Some of yours were good. Some weren't."

"I know," Ethan said again, and this time he meant I was scared too.

Mom sighed, long and old. "The car's fine?"

"Yeah. I cleaned the… uh… the rings on the hood."

"Of course you did," she said, and one corner of her mouth twitched, the ghost of a smile that wanted to live but didn't quite trust the light. She reached out and took his wrist for a second, thumb pressing onto the lines like she was memorizing a map. "Thank you for telling the truth."

Coach nodded once, like they'd completed step one of a drill. "Consequences," he said, and Ethan waited for the hammer. "You're not grounded. But for the next two weekends, the Civic stays here. You want to go somewhere, you ask, and you take your clunker. And if you drink, you hand over the keys before the first sip. Every time. No cowboy stuff."

"That's fair," Ethan said, relief mixing with a prickle of shame. "It won't happen again like that."

"Good," Coach said. "Because next time I'll sell the stereo for parts." He let it hang just long enough to see Ethan blanch, then cracked a smile. "Kidding. Mostly."

They let him leave it there. Mom kissed his cheek on the way past—the quick press that said I'm mad and I love you, in that order. He showered, the water lukewarm but honest, and crawled into bed smelling like borrowed soap and sunburn. When he shut his eyes, the highway unfurled again—music rolling over heat shimmer, strangers waving as if they'd known him all his life.

On Monday the story walked into school half an hour before he did.

By first bell, he'd heard three versions of it that bore no resemblance to reality—one with a marching band, one with a state trooper dancing on a cruiser, one where the goalkeeper heroically resuscitated a fainting grandma with a funnel and a keg. By lunch, people were calling it Buffettstock, which he had to admit was pretty good.

The goalkeeper stood on a cafeteria chair, thumbs hooked in his backpack straps, doing a play-by-play that featured him heavily as visionary and Ethan as "my guy with the aux."

Ethan laughed along; it cost nothing to give the keeper his spotlight. When someone turned and said, "Yo, Reynolds, you really DJed the interstate?" he shrugged.

"Civic's got a tape deck and a dream," he said, and the table cracked up.

He slid his tray down near the middle of the room where the friend groups bled into each other—athletes leaning back on two chair legs, theater kids doing stage-faint dramatics for an audience of five, a cluster of AP students constructing a Jenga tower out of milk cartons with concentration usually reserved for surgery. He was nimble between them now, bilingual in goof and grind. For once, he didn't feel like he had to choose.

"Man of the hour," said Raymond from Algebra, slapping Ethan's shoulder as he sat. "I heard you got a trooper to do the worm."

"Fake news," Ethan said. "He did the sprinkler. Very different energy."

They ate. People drifted over, tossed in lines, grabbed lines he tossed back. The story belonged to everyone now. He had helped make a moment, and then he had let it go. It felt… adult, somehow.

On his way to History, he found Evan at his locker, spinning the dial like a safecracker. Evan took one look at him and shook his head. "I heard, I heard," he said. "You turned a hazmat scene into spring break."

"It wasn't like that," Ethan said, and explained—the dog with the bandana, the nurse with the jump rope clogs, Shortstack's porch-light advice. Evan listened all the way through, which was his gift. At the end, he clapped Ethan on the neck.

"That's a good story," he said. "Make sure the next one doesn't need the same disclaimer."

"Working on it," Ethan said.

Evan smirked. "Also—Mom doesn't know about the eight cases."

"She knows enough," Ethan said. "Trust me."

"Uh-huh," Evan said, shouldering his bag. "Just remember Dad taught us what not to be proud of."

The bell rang. They split in opposite directions. Ethan felt the weight of it—not heavy, exactly. Just present.

In History, the teacher started in on reconstruction and the bright idea of binding a country back together with a thread and a threat. Ethan took notes he'd actually read later. When his pen paused, he found himself doodling a rectangle with four open doors and little music notes floating out. He shaded it in: Civic as clubhouse.

After school, he drove the Skylark to the car wash, because the Civic had earned a day off and the Skylark had earned forgiveness. He fed quarters into the machine and watched gray water spit off the fenders. The old Buick shuddered under the spray like a dog shaking off river water.

As he scrubbed, he replayed the weekend again—this time without the noise. He thought about how quickly he'd stepped into hosting, how natural it had felt to set a tone, to look around and see who needed water, who needed music, who needed a small nudge toward better. He wasn't the fastest or the loudest there; he'd just… decided. We're going to be okay, together, for a minute.

On the way home, he swung by the convenience store and picked up a bouquet of grocery flowers for Mom—carnations dyed colors not found in nature, baby's breath like little clouds. He set them in a vase and scribbled a note: Thanks for the keys and the trust. —E.

She didn't say anything that night when she found them, just set the vase square in the center of the table like a boundary and a blessing.

Before bed, he popped a cassette into his own battered boombox—one that warbled if you turned it too loud—and lay on the carpet, hands tucked under his head. The music was low enough that he could hear the house breathe, the dryer thumping once every revolution because it had a bad leg and refused to admit it.

He thought about the keeper and how their friendship was real where it was real and transactional where it was transactional. He thought about Jess and the warm cola and the way strangers can be kind for no reason other than the world is easier that way. He thought about Coach's line—Keys are contracts—and how maybe that applied to more than cars.

He fell asleep there, on the carpet, the tape clicking to a stop and then hissing in that steady, forgiving way that sounds like the ocean if you want it to.

In the morning, the Civic keys were back on the hook where they lived. He stood and looked at them a beat longer than usual. Not as a prize this time, but as a promise: be the version of yourself who deserves to hold these.

When he walked out to the Skylark, the sky was that sharp blue that only happens after a storm you didn't realize you'd weathered. He slid behind the wheel, turned the ignition, and let the old engine cough itself awake. The car smelled like soap and a little like hope.

He pulled into traffic under the porch light.

Chapter 7 – Across the Parade Deck

The barracks rose like a fortress around the grassy parade deck, a rectangle of trimmed sod that drank the moonlight. From a distance, it looked like a castle. From inside, it felt like a cage.

Every cadet knew the pecking order by heart. First floor belonged to the seniors—kings with keys and long memories. Juniors held the second, sophomores ruled the third. Rats got the attic: the fourth stoop, where the wind cut hardest in winter and the sun baked mercilessly in August.

Ethan and Jack weren't Rats. Not yet.

They were Pre-Strains, a kind of limbo species—summer-school cadets living inside the walls, tasting the rhythms of the place without the full brutality of the Ratline. No gray blouses. No braced chins and pinned elbows. No upperclassmen nose-to-nose screaming their names out of existence. Not yet. For a few thin weeks, they were freer than they'd ever be again.

They leaned on the fourth-stoop railing, looking down at the deck. The air smelled like hot stone and cut grass; somewhere, a lawn sprinkler clicked in a steady metronome. Ethan hooked his fingers through the cool iron balusters and grinned.

"Feels like we're kings up here," he said. "Kings of the chimney."

Jack snorted. "Kings of nothing. Clock's ticking."

From the third stoop, two sophomores lounged against their own railing, watching with lazy, proprietary amusement. One of them drew his chin down until it vanished into his collar and marched in place, elbows pinned, eyes bulging—his perfect Rat impersonation.

"This'll be you in a month!" he called up. "No names, no smiles. Just Rats."

Their laughter drifted upward like smoke. Jack's fists bunched at his sides, the tendons standing in his forearms.

Ethan bumped him with an elbow. "Relax. They're just getting their reps in."

Jack watched the sophomores a beat longer, then looked back at the night. "I'm not built to be quiet," he said.

"Nah," Ethan said, half-smile returning. "You're built to be a problem."

The barracks folded into a restless hush. Box fans rattled in windows. Pipes ticked. Somewhere down the stoop, a cough answered the creak of a mattress frame. Ethan lay on his back with his hands laced behind his head, counting the seconds between sprinkler clicks.

"You awake?" Jack whispered.

"Unfortunately."

"Town?"

Ethan's grin lifted in the dark. "Thought you'd never ask."

Five minutes later they were slipping their feet into sneakers, easing the door closed behind them. Their room still smelled like laundry soap and shoe polish—summer's attempt at order—but beyond the stoop railing the night was a wide, open mouth.

The field lay before them—dark, dew-wet, stretching to the back gate. Crossing it was forbidden after hours, but it was the shortest line to the back gate. The long way around hugged the barracks interior, past doors and guard posts, a tour of opportunities to get caught.

"Shortcut," Ethan said.

Jack didn't answer. He was already moving.

They hopped the rail, dropped to the deck, and jogged. Their sneakers softly thudded through the damp grass as they cut across the deck. One hundred yards in, the back gate looked almost touchable.

That's when the shout cracked the night.

"HEY! Stop right there!"

A flashlight beam tore the dark. A guard cadet charged from the far side, bootfalls drumming along the interior stoop before he vaulted down the stairs. The light found their faces, climbed their chests, pinned them like insects.

Ethan threw his hands out from his sides, trying to conjure a story—latrine run, heat exhaustion, anything. The guard closed fast, breath loud, eyes bright above the glare.

Before Ethan could speak, Jack stepped into the light.

"Don't," the guard barked, voice breaking on the word.

Jack's fist flashed. The punch landed with a wet, cracking pop that seemed to vibrate through the air. The guard's head snapped sideways; his legs forgot their job. He folded. Jack hit him again on the way down, then drove a kick into his ribs that made a sound Ethan felt in his own.

"Jesus, Jack," Ethan hissed, shock detonating in his chest. The beam skittered across blacktop and died, the flashlight rolling away.

Jack's eyes were flat and bright. "Run."

They ran.

Across the deck, across their own fear, through the shadow of the back wall and out the gate into town, where the streetlights were warm and the windows glowed and nobody cared whether you were a Rat or a king.

They found a greasy diner just off Main—a horseshoe counter, red vinyl booths, a waitress who called everyone honey. They slid into the corner and became civilians by force of will.

"Burgers?" the waitress asked, pen already hovering.

"Two," Jack said. "And fries. And whatever pie is a religion in this place."

"Coconut cream," she said, proud. "It'll change your life."

"Then two of those too," Ethan said, because it felt like the kind of night where you said yes.

They ate like animals. Burgers bleeding onto wax paper, fries salted to resurrection, Coke so cold it cut. Jack kept glancing at the door, the windows, the sheriff's cruiser rolling past outside with bored blue eyes.

"You dropped him," Ethan said finally, quiet.

Jack chewed. Swallowed. "He shouldn't have chased us."

"That's literally his job."

Jack shrugged. "So's mine."

Ethan watched the neon OPEN sign buzz and flicker. "What's your job exactly?"

Jack smiled with one corner of his mouth. "Not getting eaten."

A booth over, locals told lies about fish. A TV over the register murmured about weather and minor catastrophes. For a few stolen minutes, the Institute felt far away—just some stone walls on a hill.

"Hey," Jack said, voice softer. "You okay?"

Ethan thought about the flashlight, the sound a rib makes under a boot, the part of him that had jumped at the violence and the bigger part that wanted to pretend it hadn't.

"Ask me tomorrow," he said.

They slipped through the back gate just before two, stooped silhouettes against the barracks wall. The deck lay quiet again, a black lake under a thin moon. No lights moved. No voices rose.

In their room, Ethan peeled off his shoes and sat on the edge of the bunk. His hands wouldn't stop pulsing. He could feel his heart in his wrists.

"What if he reports it?" he whispered.

Jack rolled onto his pillow, voice muffled. "He won't. Nobody volunteers to tell the Corps they just got dropped by a Pre-Strain."

"You broke him."

Jack's breath evened. "Then he'll keep his distance."

The fan in the window rattled; a moth fretted against the screen. Ethan lay down but didn't close his eyes. He'd thought the walls were the worst part—the rules, the eyes, the ranks. He'd thought the fear would come from above, from the upper floors and the sophomores' smirks and whatever waited inside the Ratline.

He stared into the dark and revised the math.

Sometimes the danger came at you with a flashlight and a pair of boots. Sometimes it slept ten feet away, already dreaming.

He watched the ceiling until it turned from black to charcoal to blue. When reveille finally ripped through the morning, he was already awake.

Reveille shredded the dawn.

Ethan rolled out before his feet knew what they were doing. Somewhere beyond the limestone walls, a bugle sawed the sky open; inside, bunks rattled, curses hopped from mattress to mattress, and a hundred box fans tried to pretend it was still night.

"Up," Jack muttered, already on his feet. His knuckles were faintly swollen, a purplish seam blooming along one joint.

They fell into the summer rhythm—muster on the stoop, a shuffle of sleepy bodies in t-shirts and shorts, then a jog to the mess hall that stitched the companies together into one uneven thread. The coffee tasted like it had been filtered through a boot heel. The eggs had the resilience of racquetballs. No one complained. You didn't complain around here; you ate with your head down and pretended you were somewhere else.

At the end of the table, a pair of guard cadets sat close enough for Ethan to see the edge of a bruise beneath one boy's eye. The kid wore his pride like a splint; the bruise only made it tighter.

Jack didn't look. Ethan did. For a second, the guard's gaze lifted and clipped his. Recognition rippled—then the kid dropped his eyes and lifted his cup. The moment slid away like a slick card in a deck.

"See?" Jack said around a mouthful of toast. "Ghost story."

"Ghosts have a way of coming back," Ethan said.

Jack grinned and tapped his knuckles against the table. "Then let 'em."

Days stacked up: PT at gray-thirty—pushups on hot asphalt, cadence building from a mumble to something that felt like purpose—then summer classes in bare rooms that smelled like chalk and old sweat, then work details that taught you how many ways there were to move a broom.

They learned the geography by foot: the echo under the archways; the section of deck that held heat like a stove; the "long way" along the inner walk where shadows clung; which staircases complained, which kept secrets. They learned the faces of the cadre who would be their world in a few weeks— the corporal with the railroad-tie jaw, the sergeant who grinned when he yelled, the lieutenant who seemed bored by everything, even his own authority.

Sophomores treated Pre-Strains like appetizers.

On the third stoop, one boy would clap his hands together when Ethan passed. "Eyes front, Pre," he'd snap, chin welded to his throat. Ethan would oblige, not because he had to, but because he wanted to practice. Sometimes the sophomores would chuckle and melt back to their railing, satisfied; other times they'd pepper him with trivia about the Institute's founding or the name of a statue in the courtyard—questions with answers he'd learn soon enough or else.

Jack never played along. He'd stop, look them full in the face, and let the silence thicken until the sophomores looked away, wondering if their curiosity had just discovered a bigger animal.

"Pick your battles," Ethan would mutter when they moved on.

"I'm shopping," Jack would say.

Even in limbo, the Institute taught its codes.

You didn't cut across the parade deck unless you were in formation or invited by a cruel necessity. You didn't walk on the brass in the archways. You kept your room squared away because even if no one inspected it today, someone might remember what it looked like tomorrow. And you didn't leave a brother to eat alone.

One evening, Ethan came back from extra PT to find Jack sick—head over the trash can, face gray. The infirmary was closed; the upperclassman on duty was uninterested. Ethan cleaned the room anyway, set a fan just so, smuggled crackers from the mess hall, and sat on the floor until the clock coughed past midnight. Jack dozed, woke, squinted at him.

"You don't have to babysit me," he mumbled.

Ethan shrugged. "We share air."

Jack snorted, half laugh, half cough. "Hate this place."

"You chose it."

"Maybe it chose me."

Ethan didn't answer. He watched the fan blades blur.

They learned town by daylight too. On Saturdays after details, they'd walk down the hill in clean shirts and pass the places they'd only seen by neon—the pawn shop with a trumpet in the window, the barber who could shave a head with three flicks, the diner that redeemed a week's worth of eggs with one plate of chicken-fried steak.

They sat at the counter and listened to old men who treated the Institute like a weather pattern—sometimes welcome, always there.

"Y'all Pre-Strains?" a man with newspaper-ink fingers asked one morning.

"Unfortunately," Ethan said.

The man winked. "That place'll break your back and give you a backbone. Most folks don't understand how both can be true."

Jack chewed and stared through the glass at the hill where the walls sat like a squared-off cloud.

Ethan asked for another coffee.

On the walk back, they cut through a used-book store whose ceiling fan had three blades and one mission. Ethan found a dog-eared paperback on infantry leadership; Jack bought a pocket Bible he said he'd never read. "Insurance," he said. "Maybe they go easy on believers."

"You plan to hold it between you and a sergeant like a talisman?"

"If it works."

"Then buy two."

They were halfway up the hill when a guard truck rolled past them, slow. The passenger was the bruised cadet. He didn't look their way.

Jack watched the truck go. "Told you. Ghost."

Ethan watched too, seeing the slight tightness in the boy's shoulders, the way his driver said something without looking at him and the ghost shook his head.

"Ghosts have friends," Ethan said.

Jack smiled without humor. "So do we."

One late afternoon, the cadre held a "voluntary" drill for the Pre-Strains. Voluntary meant no one had to show up. Everyone showed up.

They formed on the deck in uneven ranks. A corporal stepped out front, voice both bored and delighted.

"Some of you think the deck is where you walk to town. You're wrong. The deck is where you learn to be a unit. It's where you stop being You and start being Us. It's where you're taught that your left foot belongs to the guy next to you."

He made them mark time in the heat until their shirts were Rorschach blots and their calves sang. He had them dress right, dress left, dress forward until they finally understood what straight meant in this place.

Ethan found the rhythm early, how to breathe and move with the man beside him, how to swallow the urge to glance at the sophomores on the railing. Jack found it too, though when the corporal barked eyes front, Jack's eyes stayed just north of defiant.

At a break, the corporal wander-patrolled down the line and stopped in front of Ethan.

"You," he said. "You got a name for a month?"

"Sir," Ethan said. "Not yet, sir."

"You got a reason for being here?"

Ethan felt the answer first as heat at the base of his skull. He could say a dozen things—scholarship, challenge, a dare he couldn't resist. What came out surprised even him.

"Want to be better than I am, sir."

The corporal's mouth twitched. He looked past Ethan to Jack.

"And you?"

Jack's jaw flexed. "I like a fair fight, sir."

"Nothing fair about what's coming," the corporal said, almost kindly, and moved on.

Back in the room that night, Ethan wiped down the sink and lined up the toothpaste and razor like he'd seen in a room down the stoop that looked like a museum exhibit.

"You believe him?" Jack asked from the bunk. "About nothing fair?"

Ethan folded a towel into a neat square. "Fairness has never been a thing I could spend."

Jack stared at the ceiling, hands pillowed behind his head. "We could have left, you know. The moment we saw the rules. Or the guard."

Ethan thought of the guard's eye, of the diner, of the voluntary drill that wasn't. "We still could."

"Not my style," Jack said.

Ethan slid the towel into the drawer. "Not mine either."

Somewhere two stoops below, a group of sophomores laughed too loud, then cut it off like they'd remembered themselves. The building inhaled and exhaled and held its breath for the coming season.

By mid-week the story broke the way stories always break inside stone: as an echo.

A guard had gotten "rocked by some townie" near the back gate. A cadet had "tripped like a clown" and kissed the deck. A Pre-Strain had "cold-cocked" a guard for fun. Depending on the teller, the guard had been in the wrong place, the wrong mood, or the wrong body.

Ethan said nothing. Jack said less.

On the third stoop, one of the earlier hecklers looked Ethan over with new measurement and jerked his chin toward Jack. "Your buddy a problem?"

"Depends on who's asking," Ethan said.

The sophomore smiled a genuine smile for the first time. "Good answer."

He didn't bother them the rest of the week.

The day they'd all been pretending not to see finally found its way onto a whiteboard by the guard room: MATRICULATION – 10 DAYS. Someone underlined it twice. Someone else drew a tiny rat's face in the corner with Xs for eyes until a corporal wiped it off with the heel of his hand.

New cadets' parents started arriving on scouting trips—nervous dads counting steps between stoops, moms peering at rooms as if their gaze could improve ventilation. The barracks took on the scent of brand-new, as if the stone itself had been polished for the next crop. Boxes appeared in rooms. Haircuts got shorter.

Jack stood on the railing and looked at the deck that had felt like an ocean and now felt like an altar.

"Last few days of being nobody," he said.

Ethan nodded. "After that, we'll be nobody together."

He felt a shiver of something he didn't have a word for: fear braided to excitement, doubt woven with a curl of pride. He'd come here because someone told him he couldn't. He was staying because the place was daring him to become someone he didn't yet know how to be.

"Tonight?" Jack asked, as the sun dropped behind the mountains and turned the deck into a burnished sheet.

"Diner," Ethan said. "Pie like religion."

"And after?" Jack's grin sharpened.

Ethan looked across the black rectangle to the back gate and shook his head. "No shortcuts."

Jack laughed, a sound that made the stone blink. "Look at us," he said. "Already learning."

The ten-day countdown dissolved one square at a time until there was only the word MATRICULATION and the date under it. The night before, the barracks went preternaturally quiet, as if the building itself were drawing a breath and holding it.

Ethan lay awake listening to the fan tick-tick-tick. Jack tossed once and then stilled.

"You call home?" Ethan whispered.

Jack: "Left a message. You?"

"Mom picked up. Said she was proud. Said to eat breakfast."

Jack snorted softly. "Tell her the coffee here counts as a food group."

They didn't talk about the other voice Ethan sometimes heard when things were hard—the one that said he wouldn't last a month. He didn't say it out loud because if he did it might turn solid and sit on his chest.

Matriculation morning smelled like starch and cut grass. Families flowed through the arches in a nervous river, arms full of garment bags and shoe boxes, cardboard crates with names scrawled in black marker. A brass band was warming scales somewhere, each note like a drop of paint on the stone.

Ethan and Jack stood at the edge of the courtyard in issued PT shorts and t-shirts, a paper packet under each arm. Their names were typed at the top of everything, like the place wanted to make sure it knew who it was about to swallow.

Ethan's mother appeared at the arch, small in a blue dress, hair pinned back the way she did when she needed to look composed. She saw him, smiled so hard her eyes shone, and then the smile trembled. She hugged him, then stepped back as if afraid she'd wrinkle the day.

"You okay?" she asked.

"Yeah," he lied. "You?"

"Of course," she lied back.

Jack's folks had the practiced briskness of people who'd spent years at ballfields and sidelines. His dad shook Ethan's hand, clapped his shoulder once, hard, then turned to Jack with instructions about oil changes and saving pay stubs. Jack's mom straightened his collar even though there wasn't a collar to straighten.

Uniform issue was a hot, humming line through a low building that smelled like wool, cardboard, and someone else's sweat. They received two sets of khakis, two gray shirts, one dress blouse, socks folded into hockey pucks, and boots that could stop a lawnmower blade. The quartermaster spoke in declarative sentences: Sign here. Try that one. Next. A sergeant laced Ethan's first boot up to the eyelets, yanked it tight, and tied a knot that looked like it would require a crowbar.

"You'll break before these do," the sergeant said, not unkindly. "That's the point."

Haircuts were next. The barbers moved like men trying to beat a clock the rest of the world couldn't see. Clumps fell onto capes, skittered down necks, collected in soft drifts below the chairs. A kid two seats down had to remove his earrings; they rattled like coins in his palm. When Ethan's turn came, the clipper teeth buzzed a line up the back of his head and he felt the day take another bite.

He stepped outside and rubbed his scalp. The air felt different against his skin, as if part of him had been listening in there all along and could finally hear.

Afternoon heat puddled on the parade deck. The brass band had found its stride; the notes bounced off the inside walls and came back larger. Families clustered along the inner walks, clutching programs like passports.

Cadre formed two facing lines under the archway that led from the deck into the open center of barracks. Their bodies made a tunnel, their sleeves sharp with creases. Between the lines, a narrow canyon of shade and shouting waited.

"New cadets," a captain called from a small platform. "On my command, you will cross the parade deck and enter the barracks. Once you pass between those ranks, you are in our house. You will move with purpose. You will say nothing unless spoken to. You will listen."

Ethan found his place in the formation. Jack slid in next to him, jaw set.

"Ready?" Ethan asked.

"No," Jack said. "Let's go."

"Forward—MARCH!"

They stepped.

The deck radiated heat straight through the soles of their new boots. Sun hammered the back of Ethan's neck. Halfway across, the world narrowed to sound—the slap of three hundred pairs of boots, the band, a stranger's voice whispering I'm proud of you that had to be someone's mother, maybe his.

As they neared the arch, the shouting got teeth. Cadre voices ricocheted off stone and into bone.

"Button that pocket!"

"Eyes front!"

"Fix your gig line!"

"Pick up your FEET!"

They entered the tunnel.

Faces on either side, inches away, eyes bright. Names were read from index cards and flung back as corrections, as commands.

"You will strain! Chin in! Chin in means CHIN IN!"

Ethan felt a hand at his sleeve, a tug, a microscopic correction that somehow made him feel more balanced and yet disassembled. Spit dotted his cheek—not deliberate, just physics, words fired this fast. He strained, locked his eyes on the brick six inches ahead, and felt time slow to river speed.

Halfway down the tunnel a sergeant stepped into his path. Bruise-yellow bloomed under one eye, faint now, like a shadow of a shadow.

Ethan knew that face. The guard from the deck.

The sergeant's eyes registered, then went flat.

"New cadet," he barked, "your belt line is a disgrace. Drop. Push."

Ethan hit the ground, palms skidding against grit. He knocked out push-ups as the tunnel thundered around him. The sergeant counted his last three in a calm voice a teacher might use.

"One. Two. Three. Up." A beat. "Fix yourself. Move."

Ethan sprang back into the stream. Jack's eyes flicked once toward the sergeant, a spark there and gone.

No one said ghost.

They burst into the quadrangle—a square of sun, flags shivering on faint wind, the band cutting off mid-bar as if someone pinched the air. New cadets scattered to assigned companies, herded by corporals with clipboards and voices refined into scalpels.

"Name!" a corporal barked at Ethan's company area, though everyone knew the answer by the card pinned to his chest. It was about volume and obedience.

"New Cadet Ethan, sir!" He almost said his last name; swallowed it.

"Wrong." The corporal's smile was surgical. "You don't have a name. You have a title. Try again."

"Sir, this Rat reports as ordered, sir!"

"Better. You will speak of yourself in the third person. You will strain every second you are in this barracks. You will move fast. You will never cut across the deck. You will never, under any circumstances, think you are special. Do you understand?"

"Yes, sir!"

"I did not ask for your opinion. Do you UNDERSTAND?"

"Sir! Yes, sir!"

"Good. You're going to hate me and I'm going to sleep like a baby. Room assignment—down the walk, last door on the left."

Ethan moved like someone had wound him with a key. Jack was shunted into the neighboring company; the last time Ethan saw him that afternoon, Jack was nose-to-brick, a sergeant explaining the metaphysics of dust.

Inside the new room, a stranger was already there—tall, farm-strong, eyes wide and sincere.

"Hey," the kid whispered, then flinched at his own voice. "I mean—this Rat—uh—"

Ethan dropped his gear and offered a hand without looking directly at him. "This Rat will help you square your locker after we square this Rat's."

"Thanks," the kid breathed. "This Rat's from Amelia County. You?"

"Richmond."

They built a friendship out of folded t-shirts: three fingers from the seam; edges like paper; socks rolled exactly twice; boots tagged; belts coiled like obedient snakes. Every five minutes, the door exploded inward and a cadre member stood there like a thunderclap and asked a question about founders' names or the year a cannon was cast. Wrong answers equal push-ups. Right answers equal push-ups, too. The lesson: outcomes are not your business; effort is.

At dinner formation they stood in a block on the deck that was somehow both smaller and larger than it had been an hour earlier. The band played. Parents lined the inner walk and pretended not to cry. A chaplain spoke; the words slid like cool water over hot rock.

Ethan stared at the flag and felt his body trying to memorize this posture, this breathing, this way of fitting himself into a machine without losing his shape.

I want to be better than I am, he'd told a corporal days ago. He repeated it now, silently, like a cadence no one else could hear.

By Taps, voices were hoarse, boots new-blistered, beds made and unmade twice. Lights went out and the barracks breathed again, the exhale long and relieved.

From the dark came a whisper through the wall vent.

"Hey, Rat," Jack said, voice a low grin. "Still want to take the shortcut?"

Ethan's laugh was a cough he turned into a pillow. "No shortcuts."

A beat. "You okay?"

Ethan thought of his mother's hands on his shoulders, the sergeant's calm count, the feel of stone so close to his nose he could smell heat baked into it. He thought of the words he'd been dared by, the ones he'd been carried by.

"This Rat is okay," he said.

In the next room, Jack tapped the wall once, twice, three times—an invented code that meant I'm here.

Ethan tapped back: Me, too.

Outside, the parade deck held the day's prints under its skin, then let them go, ready to take new ones in the morning.

They woke to a sound that belonged to the place as much as stone and flag: reveille bursting like a fistful of nails in a coffee can. Ethan rolled out of the rack before his brain arrived, feet hunting for boots, chin tucked, eyes on the wall. A corporal slid the door open with two knuckles, didn't step inside, just said, "PT formation. One minute," and vanished like a stagehand.

Outside, dawn had only just scraped a line of light across the mountains. The air smelled like wet grass and metal. Rats formed up in shorts and gray shirts, breath ghosting, everyone pretending they weren't shivering.

"Company—atten-tion!" a cadet lieutenant called. "Welcome to morning PT. It is not complicated. It is not negotiable. It is every day."

They ran.

Out the arch, down past the river and back, shoes drumming in ragged time, cadence calls thrown over shoulders and answered on the exhale.

"I don't know but I've been told—"

"—SMI Rats are mighty cold—"

The hill back to the arch looked reasonable from a distance and like a wall up close. Ethan's lungs lit with a clean kind of fire. He liked that about running: pain that told the truth. Beside him, a kid from Amelia County started to fold; Ethan nudged his elbow without looking. "On me," he said between breaths. "Just match feet."

They made it. Push-ups on hot asphalt, sit-ups until the world narrowed to sky and counting, flutter kicks that set hips on fire. When it was over, they jogged back into barracks, sweat pooling in the smalls of backs, the stone echoing their footfalls like approval.

"Two minutes to shower. Move," a corporal said, checking a watch as if time were his personal property.

By noon the barracks had found a rhythm: square-away checks, knowledge questions, brief moments alone that were never actually alone, then a knock, a voice, another correction.

"Mail call!" someone barked down the stoop, and for a heartbeat everyone was twelve again.

A cadet sergeant—different face, same haircut—stood by a laundry cart of envelopes. "When your name is called, sprint. You are excited to hear from the outside world." He started in alphabetical order and weaponized the pauses. "Benson. Davis.

Glover. Hernandez. Jones. No letter? Must be lonely. Kramer. Lee. Mason…"

When "Reynolds" came, Jack snatched a thick envelope, the corner already soft with whoever had carried it to the mailbox. He didn't open it until later, shoulders square to a wall, eyes moving fast. He folded two pages into his pocket like a talisman, said nothing.

"Gre—" The sergeant squinted. "Ethan." He lifted a thin white envelope between two fingers. "From Mommy." A few chuckles, the cheap kind; easy to ignore when you had something to hold.

Inside was a single page, neat block letters. A photo fluttered out—Brandy, tongue out, eyes bright, brown fur gone gray around the muzzle. Eat when you can, sleep when they let you, and remember who you are, his mother had written. At the bottom she'd drawn a ridiculous little boot with wings.

Ethan slid the picture behind his ID in his wallet and felt braver by half.

That afternoon they were marched to Jackson Hall, a room that smelled like old paper and wax. The Honor Court stood at the front, cadet officers with faces scrubbed free of jokes.

"A cadet will not lie, cheat, steal, nor tolerate those who do," the president said. No flourish, just a sentence that sat like a weight in the middle of the room. "This is not a suggestion. This is not a slogan. This is how we protect the value of the thing you're breaking yourselves to be part of."

Ethan thought of all the ways he'd learned to survive— masking, smoothing, telling partial truths to keep the peace— and felt a complicated twist in his chest. He raised his right hand with the rest of them and said the words anyway. He wanted to be worthy of something that didn't shift underfoot.

On the way out, a corporal leaned in. "You don't get extra points for being clever," he said softly, not unkind. "You get to sleep at night. That's enough."

The bruised sergeant found them again before evening mess.

He stopped Ethan outside the company door, boots planted, hands behind his back. Up close, the yellow had faded to sallow green.

"Rat," he said, even. "Do you learn fast?"

"Yes, sergeant."

"Good. Because you don't get to be the story again." He held Ethan's gaze one beat longer than the handbook would prefer. "Pass it along."

"Yes, sergeant."

Ethan strained through dinner, eyes on the cup at the precise angle, fork and knife at the approved width. Later, with the door shut and the checks complete, he told Jack what had been said.

Jack's mouth tightened. "He want to make something of it?"

"No," Ethan said. "He wants us to disappear into the standard."

Jack lay back on his rack, hands laced behind his head. "That's not really our brand."

Ethan smiled into the dark. "Maybe it is for a while."

Saturday night they were given one hour that wasn't quite theirs. Some Rats wrote letters with pencils chewed flat. Some washed socks anyway. Ethan and his roommate pulled every stitch of clothing from the footlocker and re-folded it just to keep their hands busy. Down the stoop, someone's harmonica found three notes and made a whole song out of them.

Sunday morning they learned the liturgy of the parade. There was a way to lace leggings that made calves look carved.

There was a way to hold a rifle that would make your shoulder bruise and your cadre nod. There was a way to stand so still the world had to circle you.

On the deck, the Corps formed into a geometry that felt ancient. Drums rolled like distant thunder. The command snapped down the line and snapped back. Forward—MARCH. The whole machine moved.

Ethan kept his eyes where they told him to keep them and used the edge of his vision for air. Families dotted the inner walk in their Sunday best; a little boy on a father's shoulders saluted with the wrong hand and no one corrected him. The flag popped once on the breeze and then stretched, full and certain.

As they wheeled past the reviewing stand, Ethan felt the weirdest thing—pride unhooked from ego. Not look at me. More like look at this. The line held. Shoes hit in time. The music and the motion braided into something that hummed in his ribs.

When it was done, they flowed back under the arch and into the cool shadow, the noise collapsing behind them like a tent.

That night, the room smelled like polish and damp wool. Blisters had learned to be quiet. The Amelia County kid was already asleep, mouth open a little, the day still leaking out of him.

Through the vent came three slow taps.

"You still there?" Jack's voice, sanded down by 48 hours of shouting.

"Here," Ethan whispered back. "This Rat is still here."

"What'd you think of the parade?"

Ethan thought of the way the deck had held them, of the letter in his pocket, of how the honor code felt both impossible and like a map. He thought of the sergeant's even voice, of his mother's drawn boot with wings.

"This Rat thinks he might belong," he said.

Silence. Then Jack again, softer: "Yeah. Me too."

Outside, the fortress dimmed one bulb at a time until only the moon carried the watch. Inside, two Rats slept like boys who'd run a long way to get to the starting line.

And in the morning, they'd get up and do it again.

Chapter 8 – Skunk

The fourth-floor barracks room smelled like every bad decision made in July—sweat and wet leather, ramen broth, a sour hint of old socks. A box fan in the window rattled like loose coins in a coffee can, pushing the same hot air from one corner to the other. Thirty bodies wedged into a space made for three, voices stacked on voices until the cinderblock walls hummed.

Ethan Cole sat cross-legged on a bottom bunk with a warm Coke sweating in his palm, trying to take up just the right amount of space—not so much that anyone noticed, not so little that he disappeared. The room wasn't his, but Darnell Jackson lived here, and Darnell was gravitational. Six-four, two-fifty, the kind of linebacker frame that made doors look narrow, he laughed in a way that made everyone else laugh along, as if they were afraid not to.

"Hey—move your big head," Darnell barked at a kid blocking the fan. Then he grinned, clapped the kid on the shoulder hard enough to sway him, and went back to his story about a summer-league game where he'd "accidentally" forearmed a defender into the track. Groans, cheers, a "no way" from someone who wanted to be impressed.

On the desk—really a scarred board on two file cabinets—a radio hissed between stations, catching a snatch of guitar before drowning it in static. Pizza boxes leaned by the trash like collapsed monuments. Cleats dangled from the bedframe, little knives of black rubber dried to curved claws.

Jack Reynolds posted by the door with his arms folded, a bouncer in a T-shirt. He didn't say much, didn't need to. When he shifted his weight, the room adjusted around him.

Ethan laughed in the right places, nodded when that seemed smart. He liked being near the heat without having to tend the fire. In rooms like this—rooms where a pecking order set itself like concrete—he'd learned to move careful and quiet.

The topic ricocheted from football to intramural basketball to whether the mess hall meatloaf qualified as a crime. Somebody on the far bunk—scar over one eyebrow, name stitched crooked on his T-shirt—leaned forward and lobbed a question into the noise.

"Yo. Skunkweed—y'all know what that is?"

A few hands lifted in vague I-heard-of-it shapes. Somebody said, "Some kind of chemical?" Another guy made a face. "Nah, that's ditch weed. Garbage." Laughter. A third shrugged. "Bad pot."

Ethan's mouth opened before he told it to. "Wrong."

The word was soft, but the room hinged toward it. Ethan felt his ears go hot. Well, hell—too late now.

He leaned his Coke on his knee, found the tone he used when he knew a thing and didn't want to sound like he knew it too much. "Skunkweed's the opposite of bad. It's strong. You smell it before you see it—hits the room like you left a tomato skunk under the bed. People call it skunk 'cause it stinks like one. First time you light it, everybody three floors down knows."

A perfect beat of dead quiet. Then the room burst like someone had spiked the Coke with fireworks.

"Yo!" Darnell howled, head thrown back. He smacked Ethan between the shoulder blades and sent a sticky splash down his jeans. "This kid knows his skunkweed!"

"I'm serious," Ethan said, half laughing now because it was safer to laugh. "Like—open the bag and you've already smoked it."

"Say less," a lanky cadet in glasses crowed. "From now on, you ain't Ethan—you Skunkweed."

The chant caught quick because everything catches quick in a room of sweaty boys desperate for a story: "Skunk-WEED, Skunk-WEED, Skunk-WEED!"

Ethan shook his head, palms up, faux modest, but the grin gave him away. The name felt like a coin dropped into a slot and hitting the right tumblers. He'd spent years letting other people name him—poor kid, clown, quiet. This one he'd earned with a sentence and a stupid smile.

"Skunk!" Darnell boomed over the chorus, cutting off the "—weed" like he was doing Ethan a favor. "Short. Mean. Stinks up a room. That's you."

"Wow. Thanks?" Ethan said, playing the beat.

Darnell chopped the air with one hand. "All in favor?" A forest of arms shot up. "All opposed?" One tepid hand bobbed and vanished under glares. Darnell turned back, solemn as a judge. "Motion carries."

"Yeah, yeah," Ethan said, still laughing. "What do I get— certificate? Sash?"

Darnell flowed up from the chair like a tide lifting a pier, grabbed a black marker off the desk, and caught Ethan's wrist. He turned Ethan's palm up and scrawled SKUNK in block letters across the skin.

"There," he said, capping the marker with his teeth. "Stamped."

"Like a hazard label," someone cracked.

"Like a warning," Jack added from the doorway, a smile that didn't quite make it to his eyes. He shouldered through bodies and bumped Ethan's fist. "Fits."

The chant subsided into a low hum of jokes. Questions started coming at Ethan like tennis balls on a practice machine.

"You smoke a lot, Skunk?"

"Nope," Ethan said. "I read a lot."

"Uh-huh," Darnell said, grin wide. "Where you read that—High Times?"

"My neighbor's older brother's garage," Ethan deadpanned. "Primary sources."

Laughter again—good-natured, the kind that folded you in instead of cutting you out. Someone slid a slice of pizza his way. Another guy shoved a cold Coke into his free hand like a peace treaty. Across the room a kid with a crew cut started humming "Low Rider" on a loop and couldn't stop.

Through it all, Ethan felt the strange, giddy click of belonging. He had not asked for the room to see him. He'd just corrected a fact. But now the room had a hook to hang him on, and hooks mattered here. Hooks kept your name in people's mouths in a way that didn't taste like pity.

The door banged open. A sophomore cadre stuck his head in, eyes sweeping the sea of illicit camaraderie.

"What in the actual—" He stopped, recalculated. Too many bodies to write up, too much paperwork on a Saturday. "Jackson, kill the circus before I come back and start making examples."

"Roger," Darnell said smoothly, already turning the volume dial on the radio down from static to whisper.

The cadre's gaze snagged on Ethan's palm. SKUNK in thick black. One eyebrow hitched. "Cute." He shut the door with a knuckle.

"See?" Darnell said, pointing at the door like he'd won a debate. "Branding works. He'll never forget you."

"Not sure that's what I want," Ethan said.

"That's exactly what you want," Darnell said, grinning. "Invisible gets eaten."

The party drained toward the hall in little shoals, boys peeling off in twos and threes with excuses about laundry and guard duty and "my roommate's gonna knife me if I don't give him the bed back." Ethan helped stack boxes, righted a toppled cleat, scooped two wet ramen noodles off the floor with a wince.

Darnell bumped his shoulder. "Good hangs, Skunk."

"Appreciate the knighting," Ethan said, flexing his palm to crack the drying marker. He glanced toward the door where Jack had re-taken his sentry spot. "You know he's going to call me that until I'm eighty."

"That's the point," Darnell said. "Better a name you can say out loud than the one you never hear."

They stepped into the corridor, the heat somehow thicker out there, the air tasting like mop water and old dust. Down the stoop, a knot of cadets saw him and tried it out like a new pair of boots:

"Yo, Skunk!"

"Skunk—hit the canteen later?"

"Hey, Skunk, you really smell like one or what?"

Ethan lifted his palm like a badge and kept moving, smile tucked into the corner of his mouth where it couldn't get him in trouble. Jack fell into step beside him.

"You good with it?" Jack asked.

Ethan shrugged, letting his head tilt, letting the answer be whatever it needed to be. "Could be worse."

"Could be Rat," Jack said dryly.

Ethan's laugh bounced off concrete. "Give it a week."

They cut across the stoop, the fan-noise fading behind them, Darnell's last laugh still a low echo. Somewhere a door slammed. Somewhere a whistle blew. The barracks felt both smaller and bigger with a name echoing down its spine.

And as they neared their own room, a thought slid through Ethan's mind with surprising warmth: in a place determined to strip him down to parts, he'd just been handed a piece of himself he could keep.

Jack's room felt colder than the hallway, the way some rooms do even in July—like the cinderblock had decided to keep a secret from the sun. Two of his roommates were already knocked out, one on his side with his mouth open, one starfished and snoring into a government-issue pillow. The third—Caleb Rourke—sat on the edge of his mattress with a spiral notebook on his knees and a cheap mechanical pencil whispering across paper.

Jack peeled off his shirt, tossed it into the open drawer, and watched the pencil move. Slow, deliberate strokes. Pause. Scratch. Pause. Scratch-scratch. It was the rhythm that did it— too patient for a kid their age, like someone copying a map instead of writing thoughts.

"What is it this time?" Jack asked finally, voice low so as not to wake the others. "Poetry?"

Caleb didn't look up. "Observations."

"About what?"

"People," Caleb said, same as before. Then, after a beat, like he was offering a mercy, "Us."

Jack let the silence stretch until it hummed. "You taking notes on me?"

Caleb's mouth twitched. "On everyone."

There was nothing outright hostile in his tone. That almost made it worse. Jack crossed the narrow slice of floor, sat on his own bunk, and unlaced his boots—one, two, tug, thump. His fingers itched to snatch the notebook and throw it out the window, but that would be a whole… thing. Jack didn't like "things." He liked problems he could solve with his hands.

The pencil kept moving. Row after row of tiny block letters. Jack's eyes drifted to the page despite himself. The handwriting looked like it belonged to a meticulous ten-year-old—or a bomb tech. He caught fragments:

Jackson: laughs from the belly, left knee stiff after runs, always leaves door cracked

Cole: deflects with humor, checks exits, right-handed, adjusts watch before chow

Reynolds: watches exits, favors right shoulder; will swing first if cornered

Sgt. Hatcher: checks lights 2310; smokes by stairwell facing parade deck; keys jingle 15 paces out

Jack's chest tightened. He recognized names. He recognized details he hadn't thought of as details—little tells a stranger shouldn't have.

"The hell you writing the guard schedule for?" Jack asked, voice kept flat through effort.

Caleb's pencil paused. He tilted his head, eyes still on the paper. "I like patterns."

"Patterns like… keys jingling?" Jack's laugh came out wrong. "What are you, writing a manual?"

Caleb touched the eraser to the page, made a small correction, then finally looked up. His eyes were dark and tired, like someone who'd been up for days listening to the building breathe.

"Patterns keep you alive," he said simply.

Jack didn't have a good answer for that. He lay back, hands behind his head, staring at the hairline crack that ran from the light fixture to the top of the window. He told himself not to let it get to him. Plenty of weird birds came through SMI. Half of them left after October with medical withdrawals and thousand-yard stares. The other half kept their heads down and let the place sand them smooth.

The pencil started again. Jack shut his eyes and tried to hear past it: a truck downshifting on the road beyond the wall, the throat-clearing roar of a distant generator, footsteps up on the third stoop, measured and military. When he finally drifted, he dreamed he was back on the parade deck in a fog so thick he could only see his own boots. Somewhere a pencil scratched, steady as a metronome.

Morning split the room open with a trumpet blast from somebody's bedside clock-radio. Jack was on his feet before he knew he'd moved. Caleb sat already upright, notebook tucked away, blanket folded to a razor's edge.

"Sleep?" Jack asked, dragging a brush through his hair.

Caleb blinked once. "Enough."

They filed into the corridor and joined the small river of summer cadets moving toward the stairwell. On the fourth stoop, Ethan—Skunk now, whether he liked it or not—leaned against the railing with Darnell and a handful of hangers-on. The nickname had traveled faster than gossip. It seemed to find him from both ends of the hall at once.

"Skunk!" a kid from the next room called, already turning to walk backward so he could keep talking. "We running laps after chow?"

"Yeah," Ethan said, drawing the word into an easy grin. "If I don't melt first."

Another cadet slipped past and tapped the letters still faint on Ethan's palm. "Better redraw that before cadre decide it's graffiti."

"Please," Darnell said from behind a yawn. "Cadre love branding. Saves them the trouble."

They poured down the stairs, heat rising to meet them. On the second stoop, two juniors paused their conversation and watched the flow of fourth-floor bodies with proprietary smirks.

"Morning, Pre-Strains," one said. "Heard some of y'all think you're celebrities now."

Darnell didn't even break stride. "Only the ones with fan clubs."

The junior let them pass, shaking his head in mock sorrow. "Names won't save you in August."

"Neither will yours," Jack muttered under his breath, loud enough for Ethan to hear and grin at, quiet enough that it became their private joke.

The mess hall smelled like burnt toast and bleach. A fan over the dish return turned in a slow, heroic circle. Ethan queued for eggs that had been scrambled into a single yellow topography and grabbed two slices of white toast that would become shrapnel when bitten. He slid onto a bench beside Jack and Darnell.

A sophomore cadre with a square jaw and a fresh haircut paused at their table. He scanned faces, landed on Ethan, and let the corner of his mouth lift.

"Skunk," he said, trialing the name like a coin on his tongue. "You must like attention."

Ethan swallowed a mouthful of dry toast. "Sir, attention likes me."

Darnell choked on a laugh and turned it into a cough. The cadre's jaw flexed. After a beat, he moved on.

"Careful," Jack said without looking up. "That kind remembers."

The day stretched long in that summer-camp-with-sharper-edges way—PT that baked sweat into the seams of their shirts, classroom sessions where visiting instructors tried to make land navigation sound romantic, barracks inspections that found dust in places dust had no right to be. Ethan wore the new name like a jacket he wasn't sure fit yet. Every time someone called it down a hallway or across the deck, he felt his shoulders lift, then settle.

At mail call a kid from D Company shouted, "Skunk—letter!" and waved an envelope with ETHAN COLE typed plain as day. Ethan jogged over, took it with a nod, and slipped it into his pocket unopened. It felt better to be called than to read. Reading meant quiet. Quiet meant thinking. Thinking meant… well. He'd spent enough years thinking.

Jack spent the afternoon in the weight room where the air smelled like iron and iodine. He put plates on a bar and moved them until the world narrowed to breath and burn. When his head was clear and his shoulders shook, he racked the weight and sat on the bench, forearms braced on his knees. Across the room, Caleb did pull-ups with a slow, perfect cadence, chin above the bar, down in a measured count, up again like he'd been built for gravity and wasn't impressed by it.

Back in the room at lights-out, Jack found the spiral half-tucked under Caleb's mattress while he bent to clear a candy wrapper from under the bed. He didn't mean to look. He didn't mean to read. That's what he told himself as his thumb found the corner and his eyes slid across the page.

Laundry room: lock sticks; kick low left; 0140–0210 usually empty

Back gate: motion light #3 flickers 1/4; blind spot under camera housing; guard rotation 0000/0200

Reynolds: will step between; avoids confrontation if witness count > 3; runs toward sound, not away

He let the paper fall back and straightened slowly. Caleb watched him from the bunk, his face as blank as the wall.

"You planning a prison break?" Jack asked, soft, almost amused.

Caleb tipped his head. "Planning is how you don't become the plan."

Jack held the stare for a heartbeat longer than comfortable, then blew out a breath, a laugh without humor. "You do you, Roomie."

Caleb slid the notebook fully under the mattress without breaking eye contact. "I always do."

Jack flicked off the lamp. Darker than it should have been, somehow. He lay awake longer than he wanted to admit, hearing Ethan two doors down tell a story in a voice made round by laughter, hearing Darnell's booming bass punch through like a drum, hearing, beneath it all, the faintest scratch of pencil on paper.

The nickname spread faster than a rumor with a drumline. By the weekend, "Skunk" was painted on a paper cup above Ethan's sink in black Sharpie; someone taped a crude skunk tail under his nameplate on the door; a Rat from another company leaned into their jamb, sniffed theatrically, and said, "Smells like trouble."

"It's efficient," Darnell declared. "One syllable. Yells well. Looks good on a T-shirt."

"It's not going on a T-shirt," Ethan said, but he couldn't help the grin that kept showing up uninvited.

In the heat-limp afternoon, he jogged the parade deck alone, counting laps by the rhythm of his breath. The walls threw his footsteps back at him. On the third circuit, two sophomores drifted down the stairs and matched his pace along the rail.

"Skunk," one called conversationally. "Word is you know your strains."

"That so?" the other said. "Smart thing for a man at a military college."

Ethan didn't break stride. "Word's half right," he said. "I know what not to do here."

They laughed like they'd been practicing. "We'll see," one of them said, and peeled off toward the sally port.

Back upstairs, the room felt unusually orderly. The fan had been shut off. His locker door—always left a hand's width ajar—sat latched. A faint citrus cleaner smell cut through the usual stew of sweat and ramen. It took half a heartbeat too long for his brain to clock the difference.

"Jack?" he called into the hall. No answer—Jack was probably in the weight room again, turning steel into quiet.

Ethan spun the dial, heard the familiar thunk of the lock and swung the door wide. At eye level, perched like a dare on his folded PT shirts, sat a squat metal tin with a yellow label. A cartoon skunk grinned up at him, thumb out.

SKUNK BRAND STINK BAIT—DO NOT OPEN INDOORS

He stared, breath held. A novelty gag? Or something worse smuggled inside a gag? Either way, it had been planted with care and timing. If cadre popped in now, the optics would be simple: nickname, tin, story.

He listened. Voices down the hall, the slam of a door, Darnell's bass ricochet, distant laughter. He could take the tin straight to the sink and wash it down the drain. He could chuck it out the window and pray it didn't detonate midair and gas the stoop. He could leave it and risk inspection.

A soft knock on the open jamb.

Caleb leaned past the curtain. "You might want to step back," he said.

Ethan blinked. "You put this here?"

"No." Caleb slipped inside, closed the locker with two fingers, carried the tin by the rim as if it were a live coal. "But I saw who did."

"Who?"

"Third stoop soph with a long stride and too much free time," Caleb said, flat. He crossed to their tiny sink, set the tin inside, and turned on the water to a thin thread. "They thought it would be funny if you set it off yourself. Loud stories write themselves."

Ethan stood there, arms hanging stupid, as Caleb worked. He pried at the curl of label with a short nail, found the seam, and eased the lid. A stink so sour it almost tasted jumped for the air and got caught under the faucet, beaten flat and driven into the drain.

"Stink bait," Caleb said, like announcing a lab result. "Harmless to everything but your social life."

Ethan let out the breath he'd been holding and leaned back against the cinderblock, heart drumming. "Why are you helping me?"

Caleb rinsed the tin, shook it twice, wrapped it in a brown paper towel and tucked it into his cargo pocket like evidence. "Patterns," he said.

"That again?"

"They were watching the rail," Caleb said. "Waiting for noise. You didn't give them any." He wiped the sink with the heel of his hand. "Now they'll try something else."

Ethan studied him. The kid's face didn't hold triumph or mischief—just an eerie, methodical calm. "You always like this?"

Caleb thought about that, which was the oddest part. "I always take notes," he said.

Darnell shouldered in, shoulders sun-slick and grinning. "What's this, a book club?" He took in the closed locker, the running faucet, Ethan's expression. "I miss something?"

"Just Skunk being popular," Caleb said, and ghosted back out, leaving Darnell to fill the room up with oxygen again.

"Man," Darnell said, chuckling. "You got them working overtime. Sophs don't like a story they didn't write."

Ethan poured water over his wrists to cool them. "I didn't write this one either."

"Trust me," Darnell said, "you're writing it now."

Night laid a velvet hand over SMI. From the second stoop, a cadre's whistle shrieked short and sharp; from somewhere near the sally port a burst of laughter flared and died. Jack and Ethan took their usual place on the fourth-floor rail, elbows propped, watching heat wobble above the deck.

"I'm beginning to hate how pretty this place is," Ethan said.

Jack snorted. "It's gorgeous from a distance. That's the trick."

The third-stoop soph with the long stride wandered into view below, chin up, hands tucked just so behind his back. He glanced up, met their gaze, and gave Ethan a little salute that wasn't a salute at all.

Ethan smiled with all his teeth.

"Careful," Jack said softly. "You poke a hive, you better run fast."

"That's what I'm built for," Ethan said, and meant it, and didn't.

A door banged open down the run. Sergeant Hatcher stepped out like a punishing idea made flesh—square shoulders, sleeve creases sharp enough to slice. He had a cigarette between two fingers and a key ring that sang faintly with each step.

"Evening, gentlemen," he said, voice mild. "Enjoying your summer?"

"Yes, Sergeant," they chorused.

"Good," Hatcher said. He flicked ash into the air; it fell like bright snow. "Enjoy the names, too. Always a joy to hear new favorites echoing off the stone." He let his eyes rest on Ethan.

"You understand names you don't earn get proved one way or another in August."

Ethan swallowed. "Yes, Sergeant."

Hatcher's gaze slid to Jack, weighed him. "And some of you have names behind your eyes, whether you want them or not."

He tucked the cigarette into his mouth, turned, and walked the length of the stoop with a metronome's patience. Keys chimed. Boot soles clocked. Caleb's notebook had been right.

"Friendly, that one," Ethan murmured.

Jack exhaled through his nose. "He's a weather report. You either listen or you get soaked."

They stood there without speaking while the last thin light drained off the parade deck. Somewhere a radio played a Motown song on a half-static station; somewhere a kid cried and then didn't; somewhere a phone rang twice and went quiet. The Institute held all of it without comment.

A whisper rippled from the far end of the fourth stoop, a game the summer cadets played when cadre weren't close enough to kill it. One kid cupped his hands and called softly, "Skunk?"

A beat, then the answer came back from the other side: "Skunk!"

Down on second, a junior snapped, "Knock it off," and the sound died in throats.

Ethan rubbed the heel of his hand over his forearm where gooseflesh had risen against the heat. "Feels like the building knows my name now."

"It knows all our names," Jack said. "It'll decide which ones stick."

"Think yours will?"

Jack watched the dark square where the fallen guard had hit the deck weeks back, a stain only he could still see. "Doesn't matter what they call me." He glanced sideways. "What matters is what I do when the lights are on."

Ethan nodded, quieted by that. Below them, the deck lay still as a held breath. Somewhere, out of sight, a pencil began its minute-long scratch and pause, scratch and pause. Caleb, mapping routes none of them could see yet.

"August is coming," Ethan said.

"It always was," Jack said.

They stayed until the insect hum grew loud enough to feel in their teeth and the stone gave back the day's heat in tired waves. When they turned in, Darnell was already snoring like a foghorn. Ethan lay on his back and listened to the building breathe. Across the hall, Jack lay on his side and stared at the hairline crack in the ceiling, the one that ran toward the window like a route on a map.

"Skunk," someone whispered from a bed two doors down, like a boy trying on a word in the dark.

Ethan didn't answer. He tried his real name out in his head—Ethan Cole—and then let the new one wash over it like paint. Tomorrow, the count would tighten, the runs would lengthen, the cadre would find new ways to make the walls feel closer. Names would either harden or flake away.

For now, the fan rattled, the notebook turned a page, and the parade deck waited in the black like an ocean they'd soon be ordered to cross.

Chapter 9 — The Boots

After taps, SMI breathed differently.

During the day the barracks felt like a factory—boots clacking, doors banging, voices ricocheting off stone. But when the bugle faded and lights snapped dark, the place settled into a low electrical hum: fans churning warm air through open windows, the flag halyard pinging the pole, the soft coughs of men pretending not to be awake. Shadows pooled under the stoops and the parade deck turned the color of ink.

Ethan sat on the fourth-floor rail with a sweating Coke bottle hooked in his fingers. His calves dangled over a hundred feet of black emptiness. The stone under his shirt had absorbed a day's worth of sun and still radiated heat, gluing his shoulder blades to the wall. Around him, a handful of Pre-Strains drifted in ones and twos, summer-cadets who belonged and didn't belong all at once. Jack leaned against the jamb, arms folded, a solid outline in the dim.

A flare of orange down the stoop pulled every eye. A third-classman—thin as a fence post, jaw like a hatchet—cupped a cigarette from the light night breeze and drew slow. He had the unbothered posture of someone who had already been fed through the woodchipper and come out the other side still grinning.

"Y'all new ones know the Honor Code?" he asked, like a man asking the time.

"Don't lie, don't cheat, don't steal," a Pre-Strain piped up too quickly, as if speed could make it true.

The upperclassman nodded, smoke curling from his lips. "And the part you conveniently forget?"

Blank looks. A cough. A nervous laugh swallowed halfway.

"Or tolerate those who do," he said. "Which means if your roommate lies and you know it, and you keep your mouth shut? Same rope, boys."

Someone tried bravado. "So, what—get yelled at? PT at dawn?"

The cadet's mouth twitched. "You get drummed out."

The words landed like a dropped barbell. The stoop quieted, even the fan blades seeming to turn softer.

He tipped ash with a practiced little snap. "They form the Corps on the deck. Drums start low, like thunder too far away to get wet. They walk you out with your cap under your arm. Read your name. Your rifle number. What you did. Every set of eyes watches you cross the bricks and step through the gate. When that latch clacks behind you, you don't come back. Not for reunion, not for a football game, not for a picture on someone's mantle. You're gone."

A boy near Ethan swallowed. Another muttered, too lightly, "All for one dumb lie?"

"All for any lie," the cadet said. No heat in it. Just the fact.

He took another drag, gaze drifting across the black square of the parade deck. "Some don't take it like gentlemen."

"How do you mean?" Ethan asked before he could stop himself.

The upperclassman looked at him, then past him again, as if watching a film on the courtyard. "Shame's heavy. Heavier than a ruck. We had one a few classes back step off the third stoop headfirst. Another put a pistol in his mouth in his trunk room. They say you can still hear boots some nights, after taps. Marching when no one's on the bricks. Straining—chins tucked, shoulders locked—like the Ratline never let 'em rest."

A couple of Pre-Strains snorted too loud. "Yeah, okay— ghost cadets."

"Sure," the cadet said. "Ghosts." He flicked ash again. "Or maybe it's just the wind banging the flag line. Maybe it's your heartbeat getting ambitious. Whatever it is, you won't catch me crossing that deck after midnight."

"Is that a rule?" someone asked.

"Worse," he said. "A habit." He ground the cigarette against the rail, ember flaring, then straightened. "You boys think it's all pushups and demerits. It's not. It's who you are when no one's watching." He tucked the butt into his breast pocket—no trash on the stoop, not on his watch—then gave them the smallest of nods and faded into the dark of the stairwell.

The fan kept humming. The halyard ticked the pole once, twice, though not a leaf moved in the sycamores beyond the wall. A radio down the hall clicked off.

"Man loves his stories," a Pre-Strain whispered, trying to inject some swagger back into the air.

"Stories make rules stick," Jack said from the doorway.

Ethan turned his Coke bottle by the neck, condensation slick in his grip. "You believe that stuff?" he asked, aiming for easy and missing.

Jack didn't answer right away. He was staring at the deck like he could see footprints baked into the tar. "Doesn't matter if I do," he said at last. "He does. So will the ones who can make our lives hell."

The little knot of summer-cadets broke apart, pretending they needed water, pretending they'd always meant to go. Someone made a joke about ghosts haunting the latrine. No one laughed. The stoop carried the sound to the corners and dropped it.

Ethan stayed put. Heat bled through his shorts from the stone. Somewhere below, a night bird chirred and then fell abruptly silent. The Coke fizzed in his mouth, metallic and sweet.

Okay, he told himself. Don't lie, don't cheat, don't steal. Sounds simple written on a brochure. But the older cadet's voice wouldn't leave his head—or tolerate those who do. He pictured a drumline starting up like thunder, pictured walking between ranks of stares, pictured the gate's latch catching, the sound you'd hear in your bones.

He tried on a grin, found it didn't fit, and slid off the rail. Jack pushed off the jamb and fell into step beside him. Neither of them said anything as they crossed the threshold into the dim corridor. The heavy door swung on its hinges and shut with a hollow clank that echoed down the stoop like a distant cadence.

In his bunk a few minutes later, Ethan lay on his back and watched the fan limp its circles. A roommate snored, the building breathed, the night pressed its palm to the screen. He told himself he was listening to nothing. He told himself stories were just stories.

Still—beneath the fan's whir and the throat-clearing somewhere down the hall—he heard it, or thought he did: a slow, measured clomp… clomp… clomp across the black square below, the footfalls of men who had gotten the rules wrong, marching because they didn't know how to stop. He closed his eyes and tried to count his breaths. The counting helped until it didn't.

Honor, he thought. Heavy as a rifle. He pictured the third-classman's flat tone. He pictured the gate.

He didn't sleep easy.

The ghost talk didn't die with the cigarette. By noon the story had grown a ribcage—dates, names, a cousin's friend who swore he'd seen a cap roll across the deck on a windless night. By dinner it had a spine.

"Midnight," Darnell said, thumping his tray down beside Ethan. "We go put a Coke on the base of the flag. Come back in one piece, it's all bull."

"You're out of your mind," someone said.

Darnell grinned. "Probably. Skunk, you in?"

Ethan glanced at Jack out of reflex. Jack raised an eyebrow that said: really? Ethan felt heat crawl up his neck. He didn't want to be the one who blinked. "I'm in."

"Reynolds?" Darnell asked.

Jack chewed, swallowed, wiped his mouth like the decision needed a napkin. "I'll keep you idiots from dying."

They agreed on a time—twenty-three thirty, fifteen after taps. Long enough for the building to exhale. Short enough to outrun their second thoughts.

—

In the room, lights out, the fan spun its lazy ellipses. Caleb Rourke sat on his bunk with his back to the wall, the little lamp clipped to the frame casting a cone of yellow over his notebook.

"You're going to cross," he said without looking up.

Jack paused with his bootlaces in his hands. "Who told you that?"

Caleb turned a page. The pencil made its dry little hiss. "You did. At dinner."

Ethan sat, suddenly aware of how loud his heartbeat sounded in his ears. "You want to come?"

Caleb's mouth twitched—something like an almost-smile, or maybe a muscle spasm. "No."

"Why not?"

He wrote a word. Then another. "Because I will hear them either way."

Jack snorted. "Creepiest roommate in America."

Caleb's pencil paused mid-stroke. "Don't let the Coke bottle rattle," he said. "It carries."

—

The stoop after taps felt like the inside of a closed hand. The sycamores beyond the wall leaned over the parade deck as if to listen. Somewhere down on first stoop, a door clicked softly and then the sound fell through the building like a coin in a well.

"Ready?" Darnell breathed.

"No," Ethan said, and stepped off the rail anyway.

They moved in a crouched jog, the three of them—Darnell in front, Ethan a step behind, Jack ghosting their right flank. The deck underfoot was still warm, springing sound back at them in empty gymnasium echoes. At fifteen yards Ethan could feel the space open around him like an ocean at night, nothing to break the feeling of being seen by everything.

At the flag base they dropped to a knee. Darnell unscrewed the Coke, poured a darker circle on the black, and set the bottle on the concrete ring like an offering.

"That's that," he whispered.

"Let's go," Jack said.

They were five paces into their return when they heard it— faint and far at first, like hearing your name from another room. A measured clomp… clomp… clomp. Not the sharp heel-toe of dress shoes. Not the slap of sneakers. Boots. Heavy. Unhurried. Coming from the far side of the deck where shadow swallowed shadow.

Ethan's feet glued themselves to the tar. Darnell went statue-still. Jack slid a half-step in front of them without thinking, shoulders squared to nothing.

The sound continued. Clomp… clomp… Then stopped.

No wind. No flag line ticking the pole. The building held its breath.

"Guard?" Darnell mouthed.

"Too slow," Jack whispered back. "Guards run."

Ethan felt his mouth go dry. He thought of the third-classman's flat tone—Some don't take it like gentlemen. He told himself he was listening to his own pulse. His pulse didn't sound like leather.

From their left: two quick, lighter steps—the skitter of a rat—or a shoe catching the edge of a brick. Ethan's scalp prickled. He didn't realize his hand had found the back of Jack's shirt until he felt the cotton under his fingers.

"On me," Jack breathed, and they moved—not a run, not a walk, something in between designed to make as little noise as possible while covering ground. The deck stretched itself longer. The shadows invented corners.

Behind them, closer now: clomp… clomp… clomp. Three beats, four. Then silence again, like a held breath that wouldn't let go.

They hit the shadow of fourth stoop and collapsed against the wall, lungs burning, ears straining. Nothing. No shout. No flashlight. No guard boots hammering toward them. Just the fan's small heartbeat, the building's slow exhale.

Darnell let out a sound that started as a laugh and ended as something else. "Told you," he said too loud. "Told you it's—" He cut himself off. No one believed him, not even Darnell.

Jack's eyes were black coins in the half-light. "Inside," he said.

—

In the room, Ethan closed the door with exaggerated care. He didn't turn on a lamp. Didn't want the room to look at him. Caleb's lamp was still on. His pencil was still moving.

"Well?" Caleb asked without inflection.

Ethan swallowed. "We heard… something."

Caleb nodded, like a man marking inventory. "Time?"

"Twenty-three forty-five," Jack said.

Caleb wrote the digits. "You took the deck." It wasn't a question.

Darnell flopped onto his bunk and threw his forearm over his eyes. "Y'all can take your ghosts and—"

A sound cut him off: the halyard pinged the pole—ting—a lonely, accidental note.

No wind.

No one spoke for a long breath. Then Caleb turned a page. "Sometimes it's the wind," he said, like a mercy. "Sometimes it isn't."

Jack toed his boots under the frame and sat, elbows on knees, head down. "Whatever it was," he murmured, "it wasn't walking to help us."

Ethan lay back and stared at the ceiling. His skin still buzzed with the feeling of open space on every side. He had expected to come back with a better joke, something to make the stoop laugh again. What he had instead was the taste of pennies at the back of his tongue and the understanding that the story wasn't just a story anymore, not to him.

He closed his eyes and saw a Coke bottle glint at the base of a flag in the middle of a black sea, and he heard—clear as if it were in the room—the slow, patient rhythm of boots that didn't belong to anyone alive.

Top of Form

Bottom of Form

Morning made liars of a lot of things. The courtyard looked small again, like a basketball court instead of a sea; the barracks returned to being stone and steel instead of a throat. Sun pooled on the blacktop and turned last night's terrors into heat shimmer.

Ethan, Jack, and Darnell drifted to the fourth stoop rail with the others after chow, leaning out like boys at a pool edge. The flag snapped lazily in a real breeze. Ants worried a dark ring at the base.

"The Coke," Darnell said, squinting. The bottle was gone, but a sticky halo remained, dust clinging to it like fur. A single heel print cut through the tack, deeper than a sneaker would make, the chevron tread crisp in the sugar.

"Guard," someone said.

"Maybe," Jack answered. He didn't sound convinced or unconvinced. He sounded like a man setting down a fact and choosing not to pick it back up.

Ethan watched two sophomores cross the deck in daylight with a rugby ball, cut diagonally, laugh, cut back. The echo came back wrong—thin, harmless. He told himself the night had played tricks. He told himself a lot of things.

Down on first stoop, a folding table had appeared at the guard desk. On it sat a miscellany of contraband and lost-and-found: a deck of cards, a pair of sunglasses, a cheap watch, and—on the corner—a dented Coke bottle with its label half-peeled.

Darnell elbowed him. "Souvenir?"

"Pass," Ethan said, though some part of him wanted to tuck it into his trunk like proof that the whole thing had happened.

The third-classman from the night before came out of the sally port with his cover cocked back on his head, a clipboard under his arm. He glanced up at the fourth stoop, caught Ethan's eye, and held it a fraction too long to be an accident. No smile. No wink. Just that look like a man who knew where you'd been at midnight without having to be told. He kept walking.

"Gotta love a place where the walls take attendance," Darnell muttered.

—

They made it to noon labs before the memo hit. A cadet corporal stuck his head into physics and read from a sheet with the stiff satisfaction of a man delivering bad medicine.

"Attention on deck. Effective immediately: no cadet—Pre-Strain or otherwise—will cross the parade ground after taps without authorization. Violators will be written and referred. That is all."

Chairs scraped. A kid in the back whispered, "Somebody got cute." The instructor cleared his throat and started talking about vectors, but the room was already calculating the angle at which an order intersects a story.

Ethan felt the note settle on him like an extra layer under his shirt. He kept seeing that heel print in the syrup, precise as a signature.

After class, in the shade of the arch, Jack said, "We don't go back out there at night." He said it like a rule he wished someone had handed him when he was younger.

Darnell opened his mouth, then closed it. "Fine," he said too loud, and then, softer, "Fine."

—

At mail call, Ethan got nothing and didn't expect to. Caleb got a thin envelope from nowhere and slid it into his notebook without breaking stride. Back in the room, Caleb opened it with the care of a man disarming a trap and read it with his face arranged into nothing.

"You ever going to tell us who writes you?" Darnell asked from his bunk.

"No," Caleb said, and went back to the pencil.

"Course not," Darnell muttered. "This place is like living with a haunted filing cabinet."

Caleb kept writing. Then, without looking up: "The trick isn't to stop hearing them." The pencil ticked. "It's to decide which ones you march with."

Jack made a noise in his throat that might have been agreement. Or indigestion. It was hard to tell with Jack.

Ethan lay back and watched the ceiling fan carve the air into slices. He didn't know yet which boots he'd choose, only that he could hear more than one pair now—the measured cadence of something old that lived in the stone, and the sharper rhythm of the real men who would own the deck in August, and maybe, if he listened past both, the jittery rush of his own feet trying to keep up.

—

That evening, a company of rising seniors took the deck for silent drill. No commands, just motion: rifles flashing, arms cutting, heels striking in a precision that made the air straighten its spine. From the stoop the sound came up clean—clack at four-to-the-bar, a metronome with muscle.

Ethan felt the hair lift on his arms. Same surface, same echo, different meaning. Those were not the boots that had walked behind them last night. These belonged to men who were still making their shame and pride in real time.

"See the difference?" Jack asked quietly.

"Yeah," Ethan said. He did. The night had felt like being measured by something you couldn't argue with. This felt like an invitation and a warning at the same time: line up right, or get cut out of the song.

When the drill ended, the seniors filed off without a word. The deck took back its silence in a way that felt less hostile now and more like a room between verses.

They stood there longer than they needed to, the three of them, not talking. The sun slid behind Afton Mountain and painted the barracks a color you didn't call anything in front of other men.

Finally Darnell huffed. "I'm starving," he announced to no one, which in Darnell meant everyone. "Let's go find something that used to be chicken."

They turned to go. At the stairwell, Ethan looked back at the flag base. A fly worried the sugar ring, its tiny feet skittering in the varnish. He felt a ridiculous impulse to go wipe it clean, to leave no trace, to keep the deck from remembering the shape of them in the dark.

He didn't. He followed Jack into the stairwell where their footsteps became that hollow stairwell thud you could recognize in your sleep after a week.

—

That night he slept. Not deeply, not cleanly—there were still moments where he came up from the surface a little too fast, convinced he'd heard something pacing the length of the stoop—but he slept. When reveille split the gray with its brass knife, he sat up at once, boots already within reach, laces already in his hands.

On the way out he passed Caleb's bunk. The notebook lay open face-down, a pencil run under the coil to hold the place. On the margin, visible for an instant as the page lifted, was a line he couldn't help reading: You are what you do in the dark.

Out on the fourth stoop, the Corps was already moving— platoons forming, lines straightening, the prelude to a day. Ethan fell in with the others and the building made that sound he was beginning to know, the sound of a thousand heels agreeing on a beat.

He listened to it and felt the old night-rhythm shiver under the new one like a bass note. He didn't know yet which one would own him. He only knew he was stepping into both.

The deck took their weight. The day began. And somewhere, past the places you could point to, a pair of boots kept time.

Chapter 10 – Moonshine

By week four, the days at SMI clicked like a metronome: classes in the morning, drills in the afternoon, soccer in the haze between sunset and dark. Ethan and Jack moved inside the schedule the way fish move inside current—resistance felt pointless, so you learned the eddies and saved your legs.

Meals were the only place the Institute didn't have them by the throat. The mess hall was a money trap, and their pockets were mostly lint and laundry tickets, so dinner lived in a wobbling pyramid of Chef Boyardee cans stacked in the corner like a fort you built when you were six. Ravioli. Beefaroni. Spaghetti. Each lid cranked open with the squeal of a P-38 can opener, each meal eaten cold with a spoon that had been bent and re-bent into the permanent angle of resignation.

"Gourmet dining—SMI-style," Ethan would say, lifting a can as if he were toasting a white-tablecloth crowd.

Jack snorted. "You're going to rot your guts out, Skunk."

"Rot's cheaper than roast," Ethan said, and dug back in. If he kept the jokes flowing, he didn't have to hear the hollow in his own stomach.

The one class that didn't feel like a tax was Advanced Mathematics. Numbers behaved for Ethan. Where other cadets threw up their hands, he found the rhythm tucked inside the mess and made it sing. Dr. Maddox, tall and spare with ink-stained fingers and a nervous little pulse jumping at one temple, would light up when Ethan raised his hand.

"Exactly, Mr. Cole," he'd say, tapping the board with the nub of chalk. "Linearity here is your friend—don't treat it like the enemy."

By mid-July Ethan held a perfect hundred. After class one morning, Maddox stopped him in the corridor, his voice still carrying a lecturer's carry.

"You have a gift, Mr. Cole. Don't squander it."

Ethan gave him the easy grin he wore like a mouthguard. "Yes, sir."

But the words stayed with him the way a song does, humming under everything else.

That night the fourth-floor air stuck to skin. The fan rattled in the window and only pushed the heat from one corner to another. Across the stoop, Jack sat at his desk hunched over a sheet of lined paper, handwriting slow and careful like a man stepping around tripwires.

"You write more letters than the postman," Ethan said, shuffling a deck of cards until the edges went soft.

Jack grinned without looking up. "Caroline. Three years now." He sealed the envelope with a firm swipe and held it, thumb pressed to her name like it was a talisman. "She's the one. I'm going to marry that girl."

"She looks perfect," Ethan said, and meant it. The photo on Jack's shelf made her look like sunlight.

"She is." Jack leaned back, studied Ethan. "What about you? Anyone back home?"

Ethan shrugged and made the cards bridge. "A few dates. Nothing serious."

"Because you hide behind jokes," Jack said, not unkindly. "Girls see it."

"Guess I'm doomed, then."

Before Jack could fire back, the door swung wide and Billy Ray Carter slid in sideways like a salesman ducking a closing door. Wire-thin, quick eyes, grin that could talk a wallet into walking—Billy had a mason jar tucked under his arm, the clear liquid inside catching the light like it was alive.

"Evenin', gentlemen," he drawled, flourishing the jar. "Skunk, you ever had the real stuff?"

"What's the real stuff?" Ethan asked, though the jar had already answered.

"White lightning. Mountain dew. Straight from my uncle's still in Tennessee. Burns like a brushfire, and if you listen close enough you can hear it hum." Billy set the jar on the desk with a glassy thunk. "Put hair on your chest and sin in your smile."

Jack didn't even stand. "You're going to get us tossed, Carter."

"No one's checking tonight," Billy said, confidence rolling off him like heat. He looked at Ethan, eyes twinkling. "C'mon, Skunk. Just a taste."

Ethan hesitated. He was a beer guy when he was anything—cheap, predictable, the kind of buzz that widened a grin without bending your knees. The jar was a dare, gleaming. Maybe he was tired of being the shy one, the jokester, the kid who was always the buoy in other people's water. Maybe he wanted to feel like he could set something on fire and make it behave.

"What the heck," he said.

They poured into mismatched plastic cups—one from the PX with a faded logo, one that had once held instant noodles. The smell came up like paint thinner turned mean.

"To the hills," Billy said.

"To terrible choices," Ethan added, and they clinked.

The first swallow was fire. The second was gasoline. The third threaded the fire and the gas with a wire of sugar that hit the back of Ethan's throat and yanked tears into his eyes. He coughed so hard his ribs twinged, then laughed at himself because everyone else was laughing and laughter was a raft.

"Lord, he's a natural," Billy crowed, topping him off.

Jack capped his pen, leaned back, and watched with the patient disgust of a man who had already decided who he wanted to be. "I'll pass," he said. "Caroline'd kill me if the Institute didn't get there first."

"Suit yourself," Billy said, uninsulted. "More for Skunk."

The jar did its slow disappearing act. The heat in the room turned into a second sun. The radio on the shelf—some forgotten country station with the treble cranked—blurred into a friendly buzz. Ethan felt that floaty, dangerous sense that his body had become a thing he could lean on without checking the bolts.

"Another," he said, surprising himself with the eagerness in his own voice.

Billy obliged. The room titled a few degrees left. Ethan set the empty on the desk and missed. It bounced once and spun to a stop. Everybody laughed. He laughed too, because that was the rule he'd made for himself a long time ago: if they were laughing, you were winning.

"Skunk," Jack said gently, "enough."

"Skunk's fine," Ethan said, and then, because the word had a way of tattooing itself on his tongue, repeated it: "Fine."

He meant to stop. He did. But Billy was telling a story about outrunning a county sheriff in a dented pickup, and someone to Ethan's left slapped the table at the funny part, and the jar came back around with the inevitability of a planet. Ethan took it like a handshake.

Time got strange. The hands on Ethan's cheap plastic watch seemed to lurch forward in big jumps and then freeze. He was laughing one minute and standing another and then sitting again, and at some point his spoon-angled can from dinner had toppled, red sauce drying in the curve like a Rorschach.

"Skunk," Jack said again, closer now, the kind of voice you use to call a dog off a road.

"Mm?" Ethan answered, and the room answered back with a soft fold in the edges.

Billy's grin blurred into two. Somebody said something about the back gate, and somebody else said something about being invisible, and the fan chopped the air into eight slow pieces.

The last clear thing Ethan remembered was the jar on its side, a clear ribbon of liquid running toward the edge of the desk and dripping to the floor with a sound like a clock.

He reached to right it and missed.

Then the night went to black.

Ethan woke to a knife behind his eyes and a mouth like a dustpan. Sunlight hacked through the blinds, carving his bunk into stripes. For a long, floating second he couldn't place the weight in his gut or the sour sting in his nose. Then the mason jar hit him like a shove.

He rolled and the room spun. The fan chopped the air into slow, vindictive pieces. Somewhere in the barracks a bugle practice scale went wrong, and the wrongness drilled into his skull.

The clock on his desk said 07:50.

Advanced Mathematics final at 08:00.

"Sh—" He didn't finish. He was already on his feet, jamming legs into trousers that felt like they belonged to a taller, meaner cadet. His shirt went on inside out; he knew it and couldn't fix it. Buttons missed holes. He yanked his belt tight, slipped on boots without laces, and staggered for the door.

"Skunk." Jack's voice from his desk, level as a plumb line. "Stop. Look at me."

Ethan blinked at him, eyes watering. "Can't. Final."

"You smell like a parts cleaner." Jack stood, crossed the room in two strides, and straightened one side of Ethan's collar with quick, practiced hands. "You do this again, I'm done dragging you out of fires you start."

"I'm fine." Ethan's tongue was leather. "I got it."

Jack held his stare for a beat. Something like disappointment fixed there, the kind that doesn't shout because it doesn't need to. Then he stepped aside.

Ethan took the stoops in a sloppy half run, half tumble, palms grazing the rail at each turn. Heat rose off the quadrangle already, the parade deck gleaming like a griddle. He cut across the shadows, lungs burning cold around a hot center, and shouldered through the academic door with three minutes to spare and none to spend.

Dr. Maddox stood at the front like a kept promise—hair combed flat, tie slightly crooked, chalk dusting his cuffs. He handed out stapled packets with a little nod for each cadet. When Ethan reached him, Maddox's expression softened.

"Mr. Cole," he said quietly, as if saving the words for just the two of them. "Finish how you've begun."

Ethan tried to return something like a smile, but it broke on his face.

He sat. The paper swam.

Problem One should have been muscle memory: diagonalize a $3{\times}3$, prove the eigenbasis, compute the power of A without multiplying yourself to death. He could do it in the time it took the chalk to squeak. Instead the matrix crawled like ants. The numbers wouldn't hold still long enough to be counted.

He closed his eyes, pinched the bridge of his nose until little sparks popped, and opened them again. Still ants.

He wrote anyway. His pen skittered across the page, dragging half-formed symbols after it—the mathematical equivalent of slurred speech. He lined out a wrong path and dove into a worse one, scribbled a proof that refuted itself halfway through, boxed an answer he didn't believe. Sweat pulled at his shirt where it clung to his back. The room tilted a degree to port and stayed there.

A cough somewhere behind him. A chair leg scraped. The second hand on the wall clock clicked, loud as boot heels on the deck.

Problem Three: nonhomogeneous differential equation, method of undetermined coefficients. He stared at the forcing term as if it were written in Cyrillic. His brain offered him song lyrics, a half-remembered joke, and the taste of gasoline. None of it helped.

He set the pen down, knuckles white, and breathed in through his nose the way Coach taught before a penalty kick. In through the nose, out through the— The room lurched. He swallowed hard and pushed through Problem Four like a cadet punching a heavy bag after taps: swing, miss, swing again.

Time ran, and then time was gone. Papers shuffled. Chairs scooted. Dr. Maddox's shadow crossed the aisle and stood beside his desk. Ethan handed the booklet up without meeting his eyes.

"Thank you," Maddox said.

Ethan nodded and fled.

The hallway hit him like bright water. He leaned against cool brick and counted ten of something that might have been breaths. His hands shook. Shame found the soft place under his ribs and sat there, heavy.

Back in the room, Jack had his duffel half-packed, one boot on and laced, the other by his knee. He took one look at Ethan and didn't bother to ask.

"How bad?"

Ethan tried to make a joke out of it and couldn't find the edges. "Numbers were… interpretive."

Jack's jaw worked. "You did this to yourself."

"Yep."

"And to Maddox. He stuck his neck out for you every class."

Ethan felt the flinch and let it land. "I know."

Jack pushed the unlaced boot aside and stood, hands on hips, the way upperclassmen did when they meant to break you down and build something better in the wreckage. "I don't care if you drink a beer after practice. I don't care if you tell jokes until taps. But when you let Carter's jar run your life? When you step on the one thing you're better at than anybody in the room? That's not funny, Skunk. That's wasting."

Ethan stared at the floor. "I got it."

"Do you?" Jack's voice softened without losing any steel. "Because I love you like a brother, and I'm telling you—no jar is worth being small. You hear me?"

The word brother went through Ethan like a hot wire. He nodded, throat thick.

Jack picked up his second boot and sat. "Caroline wouldn't let me get away with it," he said, almost to himself.

"Lucky you," Ethan said, and managed half a smile.

"Lucky me," Jack agreed.

They packed for leave in a quiet that felt different from other silences—this one like a promise Ethan didn't know how to make yet. Down the stoops, the summer session moved on like nothing had happened: a squad marched past in cadence, a whistle trilled, some poor Pre-Strain trotted with a laundry bag for a backpack. The Institute didn't care about one cadet's headache or one botched exam.

That afternoon, Jack slung his duffel and clapped Ethan on the shoulder. "Call me when you're home."

"Yeah."

"And Skunk?"

Ethan looked up.

"Leave the jar alone."

Ethan wanted to say easy. He wanted to say done. Instead he said the only true thing he could manage. "I'll try."

Jack nodded once—the kind of nod men use when they know a battle won't be decided today—and headed for the stairwell. Ethan watched him go until the landing swallowed him.

The room was suddenly too neat, too bright. Ethan sat on the edge of his bunk and laced his boots slowly, threading shame and resolve through each eyelet, one after the other, like he could tie something inside himself that had come undone.

Home was supposed to rinse SMI out of you for a few days. Instead, it made everything louder.

On the third morning of leave, Ethan was sitting at the kitchen table with a bowl of cereal going to mush, the house heavy with the smell of coffee and lemon cleaner, when the phone rang. He almost didn't pick up. Then he did.

"Ethan Cole," he said, out of habit more than pride.

"Mr. Cole," came the crisp reply. Dr. Maddox. No preamble, no throat-clearing, just that careful, precise voice that made equations feel like machinery. "I've finished grading the finals."

The spoon in Ethan's hand suddenly weighed a pound. "Yes, sir."

"You earned a ten." Maddox let the number land—softly, but unavoidably. "Out of a hundred."

Ethan closed his eyes. The kitchen faucet dripped once. He could hear his own breathing in the line. "Yes, sir."

"I don't know what happened," Maddox continued, his tone softer now, threaded with disappointment and something worse—care. "All session you've demonstrated perfect command of the material. I don't say that lightly."

"I… had a bad morning," Ethan managed, the shame sour in his mouth. He couldn't bring himself to say jar.

"I suspected as much." Paper rustled on the other end. "Given your work, I have discretion. I'm entering a C as your final grade. You passed."

Ethan gripped the phone harder, like he might fall without it. "Sir, I—thank you."

There was a pause. "You have a gift," Maddox said, a repetition of the compliment that had buoyed Ethan all summer, only now it felt heavier. "Gifts can be neglected. Don't neglect this one."

"Yes, sir."

"Enjoy your leave," Maddox said, which was as close to mercy as a mathematician could offer. The line clicked dead.

Ethan stood there a moment with the receiver pressed to his ear, listening to the flat hum. The kitchen clock ticked. Outside, a dog barked twice and went quiet.

He set the handset down gently, like it might break, and stared at the cereal until the flakes sank.

When the dial tone died, Ethan sat very still, tasting metal. Maddox had handed him mercy he hadn't earned, and it felt heavier than a failing grade. He taped the EpiPen-bright promise to himself in the only language he trusted—numbers. One screw-up had turned a 100 into a 10; one choice could turn a semester. He tucked the lesson away like a blade: don't waste the gift.

His mother came in, heels in one hand, tote bag in the other, halfway between jobs again. "You okay, honey?" she asked, reading his face with that tired, laser-accurate gaze.

"Yeah," he said. "Just tired." It came out too quickly.

She kissed his temple anyway. "Get some rest today, okay?" And then she was gone in a flurry of keys and apology—a door closing, an engine catching, the familiar retreat of someone carrying more than one life at a time.

He rinsed the bowl, watched the milk whirl down the drain, and saw his reflection warp in the steel basin—eyes bloodshot, jaw tight. The kitchen smelled like mornings when he was ten and trying to be brave; it made the shame feel older than it was.

He laced his running shoes and went outside. The air had that Virginia thickness, like trying to breathe through a damp towel. He ran anyway—past the line of hedges he'd trimmed a hundred times, past the mailbox with its crooked red flag, past the houses where dads washed cars on Saturday and kids chalked hopscotch on the sidewalk. He ran until the stitch in his side pulled like wire, until sweat soaked through his shirt and stung his eyes, until thought burned down to a small, stubborn coal.

When he got home, he dug a spiral notebook from his duffel—the one with problem sets and scratch work and a half-doodled soccer formation in the margins. On the inside cover, beneath his name, he wrote two lines with a force that tore the paper a little:

Don't waste what you're good at.
No more jars.

He tore the page free and folded it into his wallet, behind an old movie stub and a wrinkled photo of him and Evan in muddy cleats. Then he copied the same two lines on an index card and slid it under his barracks cap in the footlocker. He wanted the reminder where it could ambush him—at the vending machine, at his desk, pulling on uniform.

The phone rang again that evening. Jack.

"You live?" Jack said by way of hello.

"Barely."

"Caroline says hey." The smile was in his voice, easy and earned. "You breathing smarter yet?"

Ethan stared at the note on the table, the ink still wet enough to shine. "Working on it."

"Good," Jack said. "You get one free swing at stupid. You already took it."

"Copy," Ethan said, and meant it more than he knew how to say.

They talked about nothing for a while—soccer conditioning, some guy from their hall who shaved his head crooked, Caroline's dad teaching Jack to grill like it was a rite of passage. Normal things. The call steadied Ethan in the places his promise hadn't reached yet.

That night, when the house finally went quiet and the fan in his window did its futile best, he lay awake and replayed the exam. The snakes of numbers. Maddox's voice. The word gift arriving like both a blessing and a warning.

He almost told his mother before bed. He almost dialed Jack again just to say ten out of a hundred. He didn't. The shame felt like a thing he had to carry by himself for a while, like a ruck you shoulder because it's yours.

In the morning he packed for the return: shirts folded tight, socks rolled, boots buffed until they reflected a slightly better man. On impulse he took the mason jar—only an inch remained, the clear liquid catching light like a trap—and walked it out to the trash can at the curb. He twisted the lid, poured the rest into the grass, watched the blades darken and twitch as if even they didn't want it. The smell rose, harsh and medicinal, and then the breeze took it.

Back at SMI, the walls looked the same and different at once. The parade deck threw heat like a furnace. The stoops hummed with rumor. Somewhere a cadre voice barked a name and a Rat snapped to attention, chin tucked, eyes pinned on nothing.

Ethan set his duffel on the bunk and slid the index card under his cap again, like stowing a compass. Jack dropped his own bag, thumped him once on the shoulder, and nodded at the empty corner of the desk where Billy Ray's jar used to sit like a dare.

"Good," Jack said simply.

That night, taps fell like a curtain and the barracks settled. Ethan lay in the dark, listening to fans and footsteps, to murmurs thinning to silence, to the deep, slow exhale of a place that had trained itself not to sleep.

Under the hum, he thought he heard it again—the old story's echo, faint and steady: clomp… clomp… clomp—boots on the deck, marching toward a line you cross once and never back.

For the first time all summer, he didn't feel like he was already a Rat. He felt like a cadet who had been given a second chance and a smaller, sharper burden to carry: not honor in the abstract, but a promise he'd written in his own hand.

He closed his eyes with that note folded in his wallet and under his cap, the words pressed against him in two places, and let sleep find him at last.

Chapter 11 — Hell Week

The Corps was back.

Sun bounced off four stories of stone like heat off a forge. Brass flashed from a hundred chests on the stoops, eyes hard as rifle barrels peered down, and the parade deck turned into a skillet where sweat beaded fast and stung faster. The Rats stood in ranks that weren't quite straight, trying to become statues. Ethan Cole could feel a trickle working under the collar of his scratchy gray T-shirt and disappear between his shoulder blades. His chin tucked, shoulders locked back: the "strain." It already hurt.

Silence first—the kind that feels like somebody's hand on your throat.

Then the sound came.

Boots. A moving earthquake, soles hammering the deck in perfect rhythm—left, left, left-right-left—until the air itself vibrated. The cadre wheeled with parade-ground precision and stopped in a single sharp crack of heels. For a half-breath they were marble. Then they erupted.

"YOU ARE THE WORST CLASS I'VE EVER SEEN!"

"HEAD UP, RAT! EYES FRONT! ARE YOU LISTENING TO ME?"

"YOU THINK YOUR MOMMY CAN HELP YOU HERE?"

Spit stippled Ethan's cheek. He didn't flinch. Jack Reynolds was beside him, jaw clenched, eyes boring dead ahead as if he were willing a tunnel through the chaos. Ethan could feel Jack's heat, his coiled energy—not the cocky grin, not today. Today even Jack knew the rules: you don't talk back to a storm.

A sergeant with a voice like gravel shoved his face so close Ethan could count whiskers. "Name, Rat!"

"This Rat is—"

"WRONG. You have no name. You do not exist. You are what I say you are. You are FAILURE wrapped in SKIN. Start over."

"This… Rat, sir."

"What?"

"This Rat, sir!"

"Better. Barely."

The sergeant moved on. Another cadre materialized and the volume went up again. Strain, breathe, don't lock your knees, don't pass out. Ethan focused on one thing—the glint of a brass buckle two cadets down—until the buckle blurred and the world narrowed to a tunnel made of noise.

"MOVE!"

They moved.

Shorn

The barbershop was a conveyor belt of humiliation. Laughing boys went in; pale-headed strangers came out. On the floor, dark drifts of hair looked like winter road slush. The barber didn't bother with small talk; he set the clippers to Ethan's scalp and pushed, the vibration buzzing through bone. Tufts skittered down the cape and onto Ethan's lap. He watched his fifth-grade self appear in the mirror—ears he'd forgotten were that big, eyebrows suddenly too much face.

"Next," the barber said to the room, not to him.

Outside, Jack rubbed his own skull and winced. "Damn. Windburn."

"Brandy used to lick my head like this," Ethan said before he could stop himself.

"Your dog?"

"Yeah." He shrugged it away. "Keep moving."

Issued and Owned

The issue room smelled like wool and starch and impatience. They were measured in barks and handed the rest in heaps: trousers that bit at the hipbones, tunics with collars engineered to chafe, low quarters with soles like anvils, caps that never sat right no matter how you tipped them.

"Rat! That tunic's not your size till I say it is."

"Yes, sir!"

Heft after heft until Ethan's forearms burned. They were cattle shunted through pens—belts, brass, hangers, laundry bags, shoe brushes, canteens. Each item came with a rule; each rule came with a consequence. He mouthed the instructions as they marched, terrified of dropping a number he'd need later.

On the mess-hall steps a corporal slapped a small, heavy booklet into his hand. "Do not lose it."

"What is it, sir?"

The corporal's smile was all teeth. "Your life, Rat."

The cover read Southern Military Institute — Cadet Handbook. Inside: dates, founders, battles, mottos; the Alma Mater; the sequence of every flag raising since the nineteenth century; names of buildings and men and wars, a catechism of pride and penalty. Some pages were already slick with generations of nervous thumbprints.

Jack flipped his open and muttered, "Phone book from hell."

"WHAT WAS THAT?" a voice cracked across them.

"NOTHING, SIR!" Jack barked, eyes snapping forward.

Ethan slid his own handbook into his breast pocket where the fabric scratched and the weight sat like a dare. He could memorize plays and proofs. Could he memorize a place?

The Strain Lesson

On the fourth stoop a lieutenant demonstrated the strain like a museum piece. "Chin in, chin in, MORE—good.

Shoulders back, elbows pinned, hands at the seams. You are a fence post—no, you are WORSE than a fence post, because a fence post is useful."

He stalked down the line, sculpting Rats with a crooked forefinger. When he reached Ethan, he pressed until Ethan's traps trembled. "You will hold this until I get bored. I never get bored."

Time slowed to syrup. Ethan tried to breathe without moving anything that could be seen to move. His face ticked. His scalp itched. A fly landed near his eye and did not care that he was becoming a statue. He thought of soccer wind sprints, of Maddox's clean chalk arcs across a board. He thought of nothing.

"Recover," the lieutenant said at last, and the entire line exhaled like punctured tires.

"Do not confuse mercy with habit," the lieutenant added. "I do nothing from mercy."

First Formation, First March

By afternoon, the deck was a griddle. They formed again, now in uneven gray, brass unshined, belts crooked. An upperclassman with a voice made for PA systems took them around the rectangle. "LEFT—LEFT—LEFT RIGHT LEFT." Arms swung too high, too low, out of rhythm. A pair of Rats clipped heels and dominoed. The cadre pounced, and for two hot minutes the world was pushups.

"Count, Rat!"

"One, sir!"

"I can't hear you."

"ONE, SIR!"

When they popped back up, Ethan's palms burned and left dusty handprints on the deck when he wiped them on his trousers. Jack grinned sidelong—we're alive—and the grin got knocked off his face by a barked "EYES FRONT!"

The Braced Meal

Dinner was not dinner. Dinner was a ceremony where everything you did was wrong.

They filed into the mess hall in ranks, shoes suddenly too loud for tile. The room shone—long tables, plates aligned like latitude lines, silver that could see itself. Heat, meat, steam. Ethan's stomach tightened and didn't know whether it was hunger or dread.

"BRACE!" The command hit and every Rat snapped to the angle—chin buried, shoulders back, elbows locked to ribs. Eyes on your plate. There were rules about the menu—one Rat per table recited it; rules about who poured; rules about who asked; rules about the question itself.

"Sir," the first-table Rat quavered, "the menu this evening is roast chicken, rice, peas, salad, rolls, and tea."

"Speak like you've met a noun before," an upperclassman said mildly.

They ate at forty-five degrees of misery. Fork and knife at attention; hands never higher than chest; bites small; chewing silent; questions answered in third person, because first person wasn't for Rats. When a fork clinked too loud, a voice cut: "The instruments on this table are not percussion, Rat." When a napkin slipped, someone sighed—audible, disappointed.

Across from Ethan, Jack's jaw worked steadily. His eyes stayed in his "boat"—an imaginary rectangle the cadre had drawn two inches above his plate. Jack wanted to smirk at the absurdity; he did not smirk. Ethan watched the way Jack's knuckles whitened around his fork and copied the grip. When he risked a glance up, an upperclassman's eyes were already on him. Ethan snapped his gaze back to peas that tasted like salt and rules.

"Sir, may this Rat be excused?" The table voice again.

"You may," came the verdict, which felt like a pardon.

They stood as one, chairs sliding in as if on rails, and filed out into air that felt almost cool only because the hall felt like a furnace.

Evening Study

Back on the stoop the light went honey-gold, then bruised purple. Orders were posted. Shoe shines were inspected. Belts were measured with thumbs and found wanting. Somewhere a trumpet ran scales and turned into taps in the imagination before it actually did.

On his bunk, Ethan opened the handbook and started with what he thought he could keep: founders, dates, the creed printed in block letters on the inside cover. I will not lie. I will not cheat. I will not steal. Nor will I tolerate those who do. His lips moved without sound. He underlined with a pencil he wasn't supposed to have. On the top margin he wrote Don't screw this up and erased it until the paper fuzzed.

Jack slid onto the foot of his bunk, rubbing his scalp. "You good?"

"Define good."

Jack snorted. "Can you feel your traps?"

"No."

"Then you're good."

A shadow crossed the doorway. "Lights out in five. Secure your trash, Rats."

"Sir, yes, sir."

Ethan slid the book under his pillow like a talisman. He lay flat, collar biting, ears ringing with orders that would echo even if the building fell down. Through the screen, the parade deck was a dark sea, and if he listened—really listened—he could hear the cadence trapped in the stones.

Hell Week had not broken him. It had barely introduced itself.

The Court

They marched the Rats into a room that smelled like oiled wood and old verdicts. Portraits of dead men lined the walls—generals, founders, faces that had never smiled for a camera. At the front sat cadets in dark sashes, motionless as furniture. The Honor Court.

No yelling here. Just the scrape of chairs and the hush that follows church.

A senior with bars on his collar stood. "SMIs honor system is simple," he said, voice carrying without effort. "I will not lie. I will not cheat. I will not steal. Nor will I tolerate those who do."

He let the last clause hang.

"If you cross that line, you will come back to this room. Your name will be read to your peers. Your offense will be read to your peers. You will walk out—alone—and you will not return."

He didn't raise his voice. He didn't have to. Ethan felt the words like weight plates laid across his chest. He thought of Dr. Maddox giving him a mercy C when he'd earned a disaster. Mercy didn't live here. Here, you earned, or you left.

A sophomore near the back coughed. The sound sounded like blasphemy.

"Memorize the creed," the senior finished. "Live it. Or this institution will reject you like a bad graft."

They were marched out as quietly as they'd come in. The sunlight on the stoop felt harsher than before.

Meeting the Dykes

"Your Dyke owns you," a cadre announced that evening on the first stoop. "He will keep you from drowning. You will keep his brass bright, his boots shined, his room squared away. You will show up when he snaps his fingers and disappear when he blinks."

Names were called, Rats peeled off and followed upperclassmen down echoing corridors. Jack got lucky fast.

"Reynolds!" A tall first-classman shouldered through the crowd—clean-lined uniform, easy authority. Captain Harris. Soccer captain, campus royalty. He stuck out a hand like he was choosing a starter. "You're with me."

"Yes, sir," Jack said, and for the first time all day his voice had color in it.

Harris led him into a first-floor room that looked like a recruiting poster—bed tight as a drum, boots aligned like coordinates, brass that caught the light and threw it back sharper. Cleats hung from a nail. A ball rested on a folded gray blanket.

"You hustle for me, we'll keep you alive," Harris said, checking Jack's belt with a glance and fixing it with one tug. "Practice starts the minute Hell Week ends. Until then, two jobs: don't get written up, and keep this place shining." His grin broke quick and bright. "Welcome to the team—sort of."

Across the quadrangle, Ethan's path ended in a room that sounded like a language lab. Laughter in quick Vietnamese, the smell of Tiger Balm and shoe polish. Tran Nguyen didn't look up right away. When he did, his face was even, unreadable.

"Cole," Tran said. Not Rat. Not Skunk. Just the name on the roster. He tossed a pair of low quarters across the room. They hit Ethan in the chest. "Shine. Mirror. Ten minutes."

"Yes, sir."

Ethan found a spot on the floor between a trunk and the wall and opened the battered tin: black paste, the sweet chemical bite of solvent. He wrapped the rag around two fingers like he'd been shown in orientation videos, breathed, and started small circles at the toe cap. The world shrank to leather and light.

The other cadets kept talking, joking, switching to English when they needed to pull a word they liked. None of it included him. Tran checked his watch, then crouched, tilted the boot. Ethan saw his own face in the blur, distorted and dull.

Tran handed it back. "Again."

"Yes, sir."

By the time Tran nodded once, Ethan's fingers were black to the cuticles and the room had thinned out. Tran slid a list across the floor—brass to polish, laundry pickup times, inspection windows, a schedule of when Ethan would exist to him and when he would not.

"Questions?"

"No, sir."

"Good. Don't be late. Late is loud."

Errands and Lessons

They ran the Dyke circuit until the deck went purple. Ethan learned the geography of service: where to queue for Brasso, which stairwell was fastest, which sergeant hated dust strings and which hunted belt mis-measurements like trophies. Jack learned Harris's rhythm—practice plans pinned to a corkboard, a toothbrush reserved for cleaning cleat studs, a towel that better be folded in thirds, never halves.

On the fourth stoop, Rats compared quick notes in eyes, not words. A cadre drifted by and their chins vanished into their chests.

"Sk—Ethan," Jack corrected, catching himself, "you good?"

"Tran likes mirrors," Ethan said. "I like not breathing."

Jack huffed. "Harris wants me at 0600 to run before formation."

"Show-off," Ethan said.

"You jealous."

"Envious," Ethan said. "Jealousy's about loss. Envy's about want."

Jack smirked. "Shut up and shine."

The First Night

Taps poured through the quadrangle like cool water. Lights snapped out, then back to a disciplined dim. The day's noise unspooled into a soft chorus of fans, muffled orders, somebody's low cough two doors down. Beyond the screen, the parade deck was a dark pane of glass.

On his bunk, Ethan slid the Rat Bible back under his pillow and felt the ridge of it press into his ear. He mouthed the creed again. I will not lie. I will not cheat. I will not steal. Nor will I tolerate those who do. He didn't know yet how heavy tolerate was going to be.

Jack turned in the top rack, the springs giving a small metallic sigh. "Hey," he whispered into the dark, "we'll eat 'em alive once we can breathe."

"Deal," Ethan said.

"Reynolds!" a voice snapped from the hallway, too sharp for the hour.

Jack's feet hit the floor instantly. "Sir!"

Harris leaned in the doorway, a shadow cut out of darker shadow. "You up at oh-five-fifteen to run. Don't make me come get you."

"Yes, sir."

Harris's tone softened half a click. "You'll be fine, Cole." Then he was gone—boots whispering on concrete, not quite a sound, more a suggestion.

Ethan stared at the ceiling and listened. Somewhere out on the deck, a flag clip ticked the pole in a breeze he couldn't feel. Farther off, a heel struck stone—one, two, three beats and then nothing. He thought of the third-classman's ghost story and decided, firmly, that he didn't believe in ghosts.

He believed in rules.

He believed in tomorrow coming whether you were ready or not.

He closed his eyes.

Sleep came in pieces—ten minutes here, twenty there—interrupted by dreams of collars that tightened when he breathed and boots that wouldn't shine no matter how hard he rubbed. When the knock came at 0510—two quick taps on the doorframe—Ethan was already awake, hands black-stained in memory, the creed drumming time with his heartbeat.

Hell Week had a second day. It would not be kinder.

Sweat Party

Day Two didn't start so much as pounce. The doors blew open to a wall of voices.

"RATS TO THE DECK!"

They poured out in gray shirts and fear. The cadre formed a horseshoe around them and began the music of misery.

"Front leaning rest—MOVE!"

Palms hit hot asphalt. Pushups bled into mountain climbers, into flutter kicks, into eight-count body builders that made the world narrow to counting and the taste of pennies. Sun burned their scalps. Sweat pooled in their ears. If someone lagged, everyone paid. If someone sounded off weak, everyone paid.

Ethan found a rhythm—breathe on the down, grit on the up. To his right, a kid from Norfolk started to fold, elbows trembling, eyes glassy.

"Finish," Ethan hissed through his teeth. The kid heard something in his voice and did three more. It cost Ethan a couple sloppy reps. A sergeant spotted it.

"You two are a matched set now—down!"

They went down together. It was almost a relief to be singled out; at least it meant someone knew you existed.

When the whistle finally blew, the Rats rolled to their knees and the deck spun. The cadre's faces didn't change. They never changed.

"On your feet. Chow."

Square Your Meals

The mess hall wasn't food; it was a system. Rats entered single file, eyes locked on a spot on the wall known as the boat, hands pinned, elbows clamped. They called the menu—too fast and you were wrong, too slow and you were wrong—for meals you hadn't yet seen.

"Rats will square their meals!" a corporal barked, and every fork in the room began its stilted ballet: lift, ninety degrees, left—mouth—down, ninety degrees, right—plate. Eyes stayed in the boat; conversation didn't exist. If you needed salt, you didn't. If you needed water, you didn't.

Ethan could feel the cadre drifting the aisles like sharks. One stopped behind him and whispered—soft, almost kind.

"Lift your chin, Rat. We eat like soldiers, not strays."

Ethan lifted his chin. His fork kept making little squares. He swallowed without tasting. Across the table, Jack squared his milk like it was a grenade and somehow found a way to smirk without moving his face.

Knowledge Checks

Afternoons were for knowledge. The Rat Bible had more land mines than the deck. Dates, names, founders, mottos, order of battle, which general had coughed where in which war. They were pulled at random from formations and ambushed on the stoops.

"Rat Cole!"

Ethan snapped to brace—chest out, chin tucked, eyes frozen on the horizon.

"Recite the Creed."

"I will not lie. I will not cheat. I will not steal. Nor will I tolerate those who do."

"Who was SMI's first superintendent?"

"Colonel Addison Farr, sir."

"What year did the Stone Barracks burn?"

"Eighteen seventy-eight, sir."

"Wrong. Eighteen seventy-nine. Push."

His palms hit stone. He didn't argue; arguing was air you didn't have. As he pumped, he heard another exchange behind him:

"Rat Reynolds! Regimental motto!"

"Per ardua fortis, sir."

"Translation?"

"Through adversity, strength, sir."

"Show me."

"Sir?"

"Fifty."

Jack dropped without a sound. When he stood again his shirt had turned a darker gray. Harris watched from the end of the stoop, not intervening, not saving—just clocking his Rat's recovery time with an old coach's eye.

Dyke Time

Evenings belonged to the Dykes. Harris handed Jack a schedule that looked like a season: runs at dawn, lifts at dusk, touch-a-ball every chance between.

"You'll be our motor," Harris said, cleats in hand. "But the Ratline comes first. Do the work, keep your mouth shut, and I'll keep the wolves off you."

Across the quadrangle, Tran handed Ethan a different kind of season: shoe dates, brass polish, inspection windows, a laundry plan that could have supplied a platoon. Tran never raised his voice. He didn't need to. He checked seams with a thumbnail and found dust in places Ethan hadn't known existed. When Ethan got something right—a mirror that actually looked like one, a belt that sat perfect—Tran gave him a single nod that felt like a trophy.

"Don't be late," Tran said once, eyes flicking to a second hand. "Late is loud."

Ethan wasn't late again.

The Test Inside the Test

The fourth night, a corporal swept into Ethan's room and ran a finger under the bed. He held it up: a gray arc of lint like a crime.

"Disgusting. Whose room is this?"

"Rat Cole's, sir."

"Cole, did you clean this room?"

Ethan's mouth went dry. He had. He had missed the dust, but he had cleaned. The easiest lie in the world rose up like a handrail—No, sir, it wasn't my duty block—and for a heartbeat he wanted it. The Honor Court's portraits stared at him from the back of his skull.

"Yes, sir. I cleaned it. I missed that."

The corporal's eyes didn't change. "Finally. An honest Rat. Fix it." He dropped the dust on Ethan's shoulder like a snowflake. "And while you're at it—push for the room you left behind."

Ethan hit the deck. He pushed until the world narrowed again. When he stood, his shirt clung, his hands were grit-streaked, and something inside was strangely lighter.

That night, on the stoop, Jack bumped his shoulder. "You could've skated."

"Would've been worse," Ethan said.

Jack nodded once. He understood.

Rat Mass

By Day Five they weren't twenty dozen strangers; they were Rat Mass. They moved like a single organism: stumbles synced, breath synced, yes-sirs fused into one hoarse hymn. The cadre noticed and made it harder. That was their job.

During an evening "sweat," the Norfolk kid folded again, knees knocking. Before the sergeant could pounce, a half-circle tightened around him, Rats counting louder to cover his ragged breaths. Ethan stepped a half pace closer and matched the kid's cadence, low and steady.

"Finish," he said again, and this time the kid did.

The sergeant prowled their line, hearing what had happened and pretending he hadn't.

"Better," he said, too quietly to be a compliment. "Do it again."

They did.

The Night Before

The last night of Hell Week was a machine of drills. Inspections bled into knowledge which bled into runs that had no destination. Somewhere around midnight the cadre relented long enough to let them square one more meal, slap water on their faces, and stare at the dark deck that had become a mirror for everything they weren't sure about.

On the fourth stoop, Ethan and Jack stood shoulder to shoulder, elbows barely touching. Below, the flag hung limp on the pole.

"You hear 'em?" Jack asked without looking at him.

"The boots?" Ethan said. "Sometimes. Might be my heart."

Jack huffed. "Same rhythm."

They didn't say more. There wasn't more to say.

The Line

Dawn pulled a thin line of light across the quadrangle. The cadre assembled with the precision of a knife being laid back in its slot. The Rats formed up opposite—raw, shaved, squared, smaller somehow and larger at once.

A first-classman stepped forward, sash dark against his tunic. He looked like he hadn't slept, which meant he had and was disciplined enough to hide it.

"Rats," he said, and the word didn't sound like an insult anymore, "you have survived Hell Week."

No one cheered. No one moved. He let the quiet ring.

"You are not cadets. Not yet. You are in the Ratline. You will earn what others wear. You will earn what you will one day demand of those who come after you. Look left. Look right. Those are the only people who will make that possible."

He raised his hand. The Corps snapped to salute. The flag climbed the pole inch by deliberate inch, the halyard clips ticking a clean metronome against the metal. When the colors broke, the sun found them.

"Sound off," a sergeant barked.

"SOUTHERN MILITARY INSTITUTE!" the Corps roared.

"RAT MASS!"

The Rats answered, late by a hair, ragged by a hair, but together. Ethan felt the shout tear his throat on the way out and didn't mind. Jack's voice braided with his on the last syllable.

They were dismissed not with a smile but with the absence of an order. The absence felt like a gift.

On the stoop, Jack's grin finally split his face. "We're in it."

"In it," Ethan said. He looked down at his hands—polish still in the cuticles, one knuckle scabbed, the lifeline on his palm etched black with Brasso and deck dirt. He flexed them once.

The system hadn't forgiven him anything. It hadn't forgotten anything. But it had given him a clean, brutal line to push against.

He found his place in formation for the next evolution, Rat Bible back under his arm. The cadence started up—left, right, left—and somewhere under the echo on the stone he thought he heard the other boots, the ones that never stopped marching. He didn't know if they were ghosts or history or just the sound of his own resolve.

Either way, he kept step.

Chapter 12 — Stripped

"STRIP!"

The word ricocheted off the stone like a shot, and shirts, belts, and brass buckles went to the floor in a panicked clatter. The fourth-floor corridor filled with shaved heads, pale shoulders, and the iron smell of boot polish leaking from still-warm leather. Cadre flowed through the confusion with the cool impatience of men moving furniture—tugging, yanking, snatching uniforms into a growing heap like they were clearing brush.

Ethan had his tunic folded tight against his ribs when a sergeant hooked two fingers into it and ripped it free.

"Think this is yours, Rat? smi owns your skin. Move."

They were driven through the steam-heavy doorway into the shower bay: a long, tiled trench with a spine of pipe overhead and no partitions anywhere. Valves spun. Water exploded cold and punishing, the kind that steals breath before it reaches the lungs.

"LINE UP! NUTS TO BUTT!"

Bodies closed until the column became a single trembling shape. Shoulder blades pressed into chests. Elbows pinned. The spray came in from every angle, stinging scalp and spine, needling the soft hollows where heat had pooled all day.

"EYES FRONT!"

Ethan locked on the far wall—a veil of white steam and the faint, wavering ghost of his own outline. The cold was a knife, then a burn, then something worse: a command.

"SAY YOU LOVE THIS WATER!"

A shaky chorus: "I love this water, sir!"

"LOUDER!"

"I LOVE this water, sir!"

His teeth were chattering by the time the sergeant nodded, satisfied that conviction could be learned like a marching song. Someone behind Ethan yelped as the spray swung harder. The yelp disappeared under the roar of pipes and the drum of the cadre's boots.

It wasn't a shower. It was a lesson. They could take anything from you, and you would call it love.

They were marched dripping into the corridor—bare feet slapping tile, water ticking from elbows and ears—then turned again, this time into the latrine. The smell hit first: bleach, damp concrete, the faint metallic tang of old fixtures. Along one wall, a row of toilets stared at them, proud and unashamed. No stalls. No doors. No mercy.

"DROP TROU AND SIT! MOVE, RATS!"

Ethan's feet stuck where he stood. Some part of him reached for a handle that wasn't there, for a curtain to pull, for anything that would make this a private act instead of a spectacle. The order came again, flatter, closer to bored than angry. He obeyed. Around him, porcelain thumped in a staggered beat as a dozen boys sat in unison, the cadence of a dignity being redefined.

On his left, Jack dropped, forearms resting across his knees, mouth bent toward a grin he wasn't dumb enough to show the cadre.

"Guess we're family now," he murmured, just loud enough for Ethan to hear over the hiss of a mop head somewhere behind them.

Ethan kept his eyes on a cracked tile the color of old bone. He tried not to hear the cough two seats down, the nervous laugh that died instantly, the slow, predatory circuit of a sergeant's boots behind the line. He told himself to breathe. He told himself that if he survived this moment, the rest might come easier. He didn't believe it.

The mop found his ankles. A private first class with a fresh chevron and an older man's eyes sluiced water past his feet like he was clearing a gutter.

"Don't get soft on me, Rat," the PFC said without looking up. "Soft breaks."

Ethan swallowed. "Yes, sir."

"Did I ask you to speak?"

"No, sir."

"Then don't."

The line finished in silence.

They were herded back into the corridor where their uniforms—SMI's uniforms—had been flung in a wet, gray tangle. The sergeant who'd torn Ethan's tunic from his arms earlier pointed at the heap.

"Dress. You've got thirty seconds. If it doesn't fit, that's on you."

Buttons fumbled. Belts reversed. Someone swore under his breath and swallowed the word whole when a corporal's shadow slid across him. Ethan's trousers went on backwards and then right; his belt bit a notch tighter than before; the damp collar found the raw stripe at the base of his skull where the clippers had carved a new border.

"Time!"

They froze—half-buckled, sleeves misaligned, water still pooling at their heels. A corporal walked the line, face unreadable, fingertips tracing seams and stopping on sins like a dowsing rod.

"You are not individuals," he said finally, quiet enough that they had to lean with their ears to hear. "You are rats. We will strip you to bone. When there's nothing left that belongs to you, we'll see what's worth building."

He flicked lint from Ethan's shoulder with the delicate disgust of a jeweler rejecting a flawed stone. "This is filth. Fix it."

Ethan wiped the speck with his cuff, felt it smear, felt his throat go dry again.

Jack's voice drifted from two down, the grin back in it now that the cadre's eyes had moved on. "You're learning, Skunk. Keep your chin, keep your yes-sir, keep your hands moving."

Ethan didn't answer. The floor was cold through his socks. His collar itched. Somewhere deeper in the barracks a whistle blew, thin and mean.

"Formation in five!" someone shouted.

Five minutes to be dry, squared, aligned, silent. Five minutes to be owned.

They moved.

Outside, the parade deck was already swallowing the late light. The fans in the windows hummed their useless hum. As Ethan fell into file, he felt the day's lessons settle over him like a second uniform—heavier than wool, tighter than the belt:

You will be seen. You will not be known.
You will be touched. You will not be comforted.
You will be broken. You might be built.

He kept his eyes front and waited for the next order.

By the second morning, even walking had rules.

Rats strained everywhere—chins tucked, shoulders back, fists welded to seams, eyes locked on a point that was never a person and never a view. Corners were taken like parade turns, ninety degrees on a dime. In the arches, they braced—heels together, spine ironed flat, breath boxed and stacked—until a cadre's shadow passed like a storm cloud and moved on.

"Rat Cole requests permission to speak, sir!"

Ethan learned to make the sentence a single blade of sound, no ragged edges, no personality. The wrong word—I—could trigger an hour of being smoked in the stairwell. Rats did not have first person. Rats did not have persons at all.

Square your meals

The mess hall looked almost kind under morning light—long tables, the clatter of trays, steam lifting from pans. Then the rules unfolded and the room shrank.

"Eyes in the boat, Rats! Your plate is the ocean. That plate is your whole universe."

They ate in silence, shoulders square to the table, elbows pinned. Bread at the upper left corner. Glass aligned with the knife tip. Forks stacked like railroad ties. Every bite traveled along invisible right angles—up, over, down—no diagonals, no looping wander. Napkin folded twice on the thigh, crease parallel to the table edge.

Ethan's stomach roared; the food tasted like cardboard and salvation. He almost looked up when sunlight flashed on brass across the hall—instinct, just a flick—but a hand slammed the table near his tray.

"WHAT'S OUTSIDE YOUR BOAT, RAT?"

"Nothing, sir!"

"Correct. Keep it that way."

He ate rectangles of eggs and squares of toast and drank water in measured sips, counting them like penance.

At the end of the meal, everything reset: silverware stacked just so; cup at forty-five degrees to the plate; crumbs gathered and buried as if evidence of appetite were a crime. Stand. Push chair in with exactly one hand. Pivot. Strain.

Order could be taught. Hunger could be ignored. Both lessons stuck.

Knowledge ambushes

The Rat Bible rode everywhere with them—small, thick, and smug in Ethan's pocket. The paper smelled like ink and talc. Dates, founders, mottos, battlefields, colors, songs—pages of a language he did not yet speak.

"Rats! Knowledge!" a corporal barked in the arch.

Ethan and Jack locked into a line. The corporal didn't look at the book; he didn't need to.

"Page twelve, paragraph three. Mission of the Institute. Cole."

Ethan felt the words before he heard them. His mouth was dry. He had underlined that paragraph at 0400, whispering to the fan.

"The mission of Southern Military Institute is—" His voice snagged on Southern. "—to produce citizen-soldiers of… character, discipline, and—" He reached, came up empty. "—and… service to—"

"Drop." The corporal's tone was almost bored. "Front-leaning rest. Cadence on me."

Ethan hit the tile. Palms slid in a film of old wax. His arms pumped while the cadence counted and the floor rose and fell. Somewhere past push-up twenty the words snapped back into place, whole and unhelpful.

"Up."

The corporal's eyes went to Jack. "Reynolds. Page thirty-four. Mottoes. All of them."

Jack rattled them off, voice flat, pace perfect. The corporal's eyes didn't blink.

"Correct," he said, unsatisfied. "Reynolds, teach your Rat. If he fails, you both sweat."

Later, in the stairwell, Jack pressed a thumb into Ethan's Rat Bible hard enough to dent the page.

"You're close," he said, not unkindly. "Stack the first letter of each sentence. Make an acronym. When your brain fogs, the letters won't."

"I had it," Ethan muttered.

"Then have it faster."

Dyke economics

Ethan's Dyke, Tran Nguyen, lived on first stoop where the air felt two degrees cooler and the floor polish gleamed. His room smelled like starch and eucalyptus, like a tailor shop packed into a footlocker. Tran spoke softly in English and rapidly in Vietnamese, the latter blooming into laughter that didn't include Ethan.

Tran set expectations in ten words: "Shine boots. Press blues. Brass bright. Room inspection perfect."

He handed Ethan a boot whose toe reflected the world like black ice. "This is yours," Tran said calmly. He placed its dull twin in Ethan's palm. "Make that look like this. Thirty minutes."

Ethan worked the cotton in tight circles, water and polish and breath and heat until his fingers cramped and the leather finally caught the light. Tran didn't nod. He just turned the boot three degrees, found a faint swirl, and passed it back.

"Again."

There were errands—laundry runs at a dead sprint, belt brass redeyed to mirror, ribbons measured with a ruler to the sixteenth, a dust line on a windowsill that became a sermon. Once, when Ethan paused with the iron in hand to flex his aching wrist, Tran's voice drifted without looking up from his own paperwork.

"You want mercy, Rat?"

Ethan blinked. "Sir?"

Tran's mouth twitched. Not a smile. Not unkind. "Then be excellent."

Across the quad, Jack's Dyke—Captain Harris—operated like a coach who ran the whole field. He met Jack at evening formation with two boots and a grin that wasn't friendly.

"You'll lead your Rat Mass tomorrow on the morning run," Harris said, voice low enough to sound like a favor. "If anyone falls out, you pay in brass. Bring the pace up after second hill."

Jack nodded, eyes brightening like he'd been told to invade a small country.

"And Reynolds," Harris added, sliding a folded index card into Jack's palm, "the first stanza of the Institute Hymn. If you can't sing it, don't make me hear you."

Jack flicked a glance at Ethan that said both this is a gift and don't fail me. Gifts at SMI were just debts with better packaging.

By midweek, the ritual at meals tightened a notch. A sergeant walked the aisle like a metronome.

"You will not stab. You will cut. You will not chase peas. You will corner them."

Someone's fork scraped. The sound was a offense.

"Front-leaning rest under the table," the sergeant said softly, and a boy slid to the floor like a puppet with its strings cut. The rest of the Rats cut quieter.

Ethan felt the heat building in his neck—the rage, the comedy, the old instinct to raise a line that would make the table snort and the sergeant blink. He ate his peas in a neat formation and swallowed the line whole. The joke would keep. His place here wouldn't if it slipped out.

"Rats to the pit!"

The basement was cooler and meaner. Concrete. A stripe of rubber matting. The smell of humanity steamed into it. They moved—push-ups, mountain climbers, flutter kicks at a cadence that didn't care about lungs. Ethan caught Jack's eye at twenty-five, both of them in the same plank of pain, and for a second the whole place felt like a team instead of a test.

A minute later, Jack was on his feet, counting the last ten for the Mass as if he'd been born on that cadence. Harris watched from the doorway, face blank, hands behind his back. When it ended, he nodded once—barely—and vanished.

On the way back up, Ethan paused under first stoop to catch a breath he hadn't been given permission to take. Tran's roommate, Bao, appeared in the corridor with a paper napkin packeted around something warm. He held it out without a word.

Ethan blinked. "Sir?"

Bao's eyes flicked toward the arches. "Eat," he said, the single syllable neutral. "Don't tell."

Ethan slipped the steamed bun into his palm and kept walking, heart hot in his throat for reasons that had nothing to do with food.

A way through

That night, Ethan made flashcards out of an old legal pad, slicing them into squares, writing Founding, Colors, Mottoes, Hymn, Founders in block letters and underlining the first letter of each line. He practiced at the sink, in the arch, in queue, whispered the phrases into the hum of the fan until the words stuck to the rhythm of his breathing.

When the next ambush came—"Page seven, Colors and their meanings, Cole"—the answer fell into place like drill:

"Gray for sacrifice; white for honor; blue for the Commonwealth; gold for the standard we are sworn to uphold, sir."

The corporal stared at him a heartbeat too long, looking for the join, the place where the line might split. Then he moved on.

Jack bumped Ethan's shoulder as they strained down the hall, a contact quick as static.

"See?" he murmured. "Stack the letters. Win the game they're playing."

Ethan didn't trust himself to answer. He let the posture hold him upright and the rules carry him across the tile and told himself the truth he could stand:

He was still being stripped. But he'd found a seam he could grip.

Sunday didn't arrive so much as pause the noise.

The Corps formed on the bricks in dress grays, the air still and glassy, the sun bleaching the parade deck to a sheet of light. "Chapel detail!" and the Mass moved as one—no talking, no wobble, chins pinned. Inside the small stone chapel, the cool hit first, then the hush. The chaplain spoke about duty like it was a door everyone had to walk through. Ethan didn't catch the verses; he felt the silence sit down beside him and refuse to move.

When they filed out, the tap of heels on slate sounded almost gentle. For ten whole minutes, no one yelled.

It didn't last.

Mail call was a riot held together with rules. A sergeant stood on a milk crate with a canvas sack and a voice like gravel. "Reynolds!" A padded envelope flew. Jack caught it one-handed. Caroline's looping script flashed in the corner. He tucked it inside his blouse like a talisman and never broke strain.

"Cole!" A thin white envelope, Mom's careful print. Ethan slid it into his cover and felt, for a second, the shape of her kitchen in his chest—the hum of the old fridge, the smell of coffee even at night. He didn't dare read it on the stoop. You learned quickly what privacy wasn't.

He waited until lights were out, the fan a soft saw above them, then angled the envelope toward the window's thin moon and read. Just a paragraph: she was proud of him; money was tight; she'd fixed the dryer herself with a coat hanger twist; "eat when you can, sleep when you can, be kind when you can." He folded the page into the smallest square he could make and tucked it into his Rat Bible. That made it feel safer than the wall locker.

Inspections turned kindness into contraband. White gloves slid along shelves and stopped. "Dust." A single fleck could cost a platoon ten minutes of mountain climbers. Gig lines had to be so straight they looked drawn. Brass had to throw a face back at you. Shoe heels had to be black as a lie.

"Locker, Cole." The sergeant's fingers walked along the top shelf, paused over t-shirts rolled like shells, then stopped over the Bible. He flipped it open. A paper square fluttered to the floor. Ethan's heart fell with it.

The sergeant's eyes didn't soften. He toed the square toward Ethan. "Keep your sentiment squared away like your socks, Rat. This stays closed unless you're studying." A beat. "And study."

"Yes, sergeant."

Ethan retrieved the tiny square like it might evaporate, slid it deeper between pages—the mission on one side, mom on the other.

The Road arrived on a Tuesday, late, when the heat had already worked all day. "Rats to the Road!" and they were off the bricks and onto the gravel path that circled the parade deck and disappeared toward the ridge. It was a loop made of bad decisions and good intentions—sun-baked, sharp underfoot, with a hill that took the name out of your lungs.

Harris appeared on the flank without announcing himself. "Reynolds has the pace." Jack moved to the front without breaking stride; his count slid under the sound of feet and turned the mess into a cadence.

Ethan fell in with the mass, every breath a match struck in his chest. The hill took the talking away from all of them. Sweat ran behind his ears and down the notch of his spine. Somewhere to his left, a Rat began to drift—gait going crooked, eyes glassing. Ethan didn't think; he slid an elbow into the kid's ribs and a hand into the small of his back and pushed him back into the lane.

"Don't fall, man," Ethan hissed. "Not here."

The kid's eyes focused just enough to nod.

They finished as a rag with holes. Harris didn't smile. He lifted two fingers—almost nothing—and Jack gave him the smallest nod back. It was the first time Ethan believed the day might not beat him bloody.

Nguyen's room that night ran like a watch. Bao's needle snapped through a trouser hem, Tran's pen moved over a form in tight, precise lines. Tran didn't waste syllables.

"Your brass is good," he said, glancing at the buttons Ethan had laid out in a row. "Your laces are not. S-turn the ends. It holds better. Do it now."

Ethan pulled the lace, made the snake, tucked, crossed, cinched. Tran watched exactly long enough to be sure he'd learned it and then looked back at the form.

"Sir—" Ethan heard his own voice before he decided to use it. Tran looked up. "Thank you."

A faint tilt of the head. "Be excellent," he said again, as if it were an address you were either moving toward or away from with every tiny thing you did.

On first stoop, as Ethan strained back to his room, he passed three older cadets speaking Vietnamese, laughing softly. He remembered his father's voice in some long-ago diner—those people—and felt how small that sentence sounded inside these walls. Nguyen's cover sat on the shelf a perfect sixteenth from the edge. Excellence didn't care about anyone's war.

The rooms on fourth stoop smelled like Brasso and damp cotton and boys trying not to be boys. Jack tore open Caroline's padded envelope with his fingernail and drew out a Polaroid of her in a sundress, hair blown to one side by the kind of wind that only exists in towns without regulations. He looked at it the way some men look at orders.

"Don't let them get in here," he said, tapping two knuckles against his sternum and then setting the photo inside his wall locker like an icon.

"Who?" Ethan asked.

"Anybody." He grinned without amusement. "Even me."

Ethan didn't have a picture. He had a square of paper tucked into a book. It felt like the same thing.

Knowledge checks got meaner after the Road. "Rat Mass— Hymn. Stanza three." Voices staggered, caught, recovered, became one. "Founders. Full names." Not just last names— full, mouth-filling names with middle initials and birthplaces. Ethan learned to stack them like blocks in his mouth: name, year, bullet of a fact. He didn't know if he believed in any of them. He believed in not failing in public.

At chow, a corporal set a silver dollar on the tip of Ethan's boot. "If it slides, you slide." It didn't. Not today. The coin caught a straight line of light. Ethan felt something not quite like pride, but adjacent.

On the way out, a Rat two spots down dragged a heel and sent the coin skittering. Ten push-ups. Twenty for the smirk he didn't hide fast enough. The Mass paid in sweat for the single mistake. Ethan filed that fact under Laws That Always Enforce Themselves.

That night, storm light rattled the windows and made the shadows flicker in the corners like nervous men. The fans chopped the air into square breaths. Ethan lay flat, damp dog-eared pages of the Bible fanned on his chest, and let the day play backward.

The showers had stripped him. The toilets had humiliated him. The strain had sanded off the parts that wanted to look around. The Road had forced him to choose between the easy alone and the hard together. The inspections had taught him that excellence could be measured with a ruler and a white glove. Nguyen had put a phrase in his pocket: be excellent. Harris had put a promise on Jack's back: don't make me chase you. Mom had put a sentence in his bones: eat, sleep, be kind.

He found, under all of that, a thin seam that hadn't snapped—the piece of him that could learn a rule in the morning and use it by night, that could turn a lace into a lock, a boot into a mirror, a panic into a pace.

Ethan exhaled. "Be excellent," he said into the dark, just loud enough to make the words real.

Outside, the flag halyard tapped the pole in a rhythm no ghost could own. Somewhere down the stoop, a cadre's boots passed, then faded. Jack's breathing settled into its metronome across the room. Ethan slid the little square of his mother's letter deeper into the Rat Bible and closed his eyes.

They were still stripping him. They would keep stripping him.

He would keep what they couldn't take.

Chapter 13 — Sweat Parties

Part 1: The Midnight Ambush

Sleep at Southern Military Institute was a rumor you chased and never caught.

Near midnight, the barracks finally went still—fans rattling thinly in the windows, the parade deck outside a black sheet of silence. Ethan felt the wool blanket scratch his knees and, for a breath, believed he might actually drift.

The door blew open like a shell burst.

"UP, RATS!"

Flashlights carved the dark into hard white slices. Boots hit floorboards. Hands ripped sheets. Bunks slammed back against cinderblock. By the time Ethan's eyes found focus, his heart had already outrun him into the hallway. He stumbled barefoot into formation with the others—shaved heads shining, breath already ragged from panic alone.

"DOWN!"

Palms slapped concrete. Heat soaked up off the stoop like a griddle.

"Front leaning rest—MOVE! Push-ups!"

Arms bent. Bodies dropped. The night became a saw-toothed rhythm: down-up, down-up, knuckles slipping in sweat, chests smacking stone when triceps quit too soon. Voices overlapped—no single order to obey, just density, volume, heat. Ethan's elbows wobbled. Rep twenty tasted like blood.

Jack set beside him like a metronome—wide frame steady, breath a deep engine.

"Don't quit, Skunk," he said through his teeth. "Not here."

Ethan's arms failed anyway. His chest kissed the deck.

A cadre was on him, nose-to-nose, flashlight haloing sweat into a crown.

"You QUIT, Rat? Already? You don't belong at SMI."

"No, sir—" Ethan forced air, pushed, arms shaking like wire. The lockout barely happened before he slid again.

"Flutter kicks! Six inches—LOCK IT!"

Backs hit concrete. Heels lifted. The bright knot in Ethan's lower abs lit and kept burning.

"Left… right… ready—MOVE!"

Toes scissored. Calves screamed. A Rat two spots down gagged quietly and swallowed it back. Cadre boots paced. Someone laughed—not the good kind.

"Mountain climbers! FASTER!"

Hands thumped. Knees pumped. Gravel dust turned to paste under palms. Time fell apart: fifteen minutes, thirty, forever—none of it mattered. There was only the next rep and the next breath and the watery tunnel forming at the edge of his sight.

"Burpees! Drop—push—JUMP!"

Ethan's legs felt borrowed. He hit the deck, pushed, staggered up into a squat-jump that never quite left the ground. Jack banged out full reps like he was fueled by anger alone.

"They want us broken," Jack growled low. "We don't break."

Ethan wasn't sure. The night made a good argument.

The heat, the spit, the luminous rage of the cadre's faces— somewhere in it the point disappeared. This wasn't instruction. It was a kind of liturgy: a ritual performed so often it no longer needed meaning to work.

"Recover!"

Just like that, it stopped. Boots receded down the stoop. The flashlights went with them, leaving moon and fan-light to reassemble the corridor.

No one spoke. Rats sprawled where they'd collapsed, chests heaving, sweat finding new paths through old salt. After a long minute that might have been ten, bodies peeled themselves off the floor and drifted back to rooms, silence a pact none of them had to sign.

Ethan crawled onto his bunk and felt the mattress give in all the right ways. His shirt clung cold. His lungs still clawed at the air like they didn't trust it.

Across the room, Jack lay flat on his back, forearm over his eyes, breathing heavy but even.

"You ever… think we made a mistake?" Ethan whispered.

Jack's jaw moved as if he were chewing on the words first. "Mistake?" He let it sit. "Maybe." A beat. "But we're here. And if we're here, we survive."

Ethan watched the bunk slats above him blur and sharpen. He wanted to borrow Jack's certainty, to hang it on a nail next to his cover and pick it up in the morning. Instead he found only the echo of the ritual in his bones—down-up, left-right, drop-push-jump—and the small, dangerous knowledge that SMI's night had a way of getting inside your head.

Somewhere down the stoop, a door banged and a boot heel clicked twice, a sound like punctuation. Ethan closed his eyes and tried to catch the rumor of sleep before the next ambush found them.

Morning didn't so much arrive as pry the barracks open with a crowbar. Reveille crashed through metal vents and rattled the window frames. Ethan rolled to his feet on legs that didn't feel signed out to him anymore. Every muscle had a complaint; most filed it loudly.

The hallway smelled like bleach, wool, and old adrenaline. Rats moved in a quiet caravan—hobbling, taped, already sweating through gray before the sun cleared the walls. No one mentioned the midnight party. SMI etiquette: if it broke you, you didn't advertise; if it didn't, you didn't brag.

Small Rules for Staying Alive

By noon, a code had formed—passed in whispers between chow line and formation, a survival gospel written in sweat:

Never be last. Last gets noticed. Noticed gets punished.

Eat fast. Fork, swallow, fork. Thirty chews was for people with rights.

Water when they're not looking. Not gulps—sips. Cadre could smell thirst like fear.

Shine buys time. If your brass blinds, they look at the next Rat.

Know something. A date, a motto, the second stanza— recite clean, earn a breath.

Jack added his own: "If you can't be strong, be steady."

Ethan added his: "If you can't be steady, be invisible."

The Work of Being Presentable

Afternoons became a scrap-yard of minutes welded into use. Ethan learned to love the sink's rough porcelain. The boot brush bit his palm; the wax warmed like tar under his thumb. He built a shine in circles the size of dimes until the leather held a sky of its own. It wasn't just polish. It was penance and prayer.

Tran Nguyen—quiet, unreadable—watched from his bunk while Ethan worked the Dyke's boots. At first Tran gave only tasks. Then, one evening, a sentence:

"Brass is your first language here."

Ethan looked up.

"Speak it fluent," Tran said. "They yell at accents."

He didn't smile when he said it, but he left an extra tin of polish on the desk and a square of real cotton—soft as permission.

Laundry became logistics. Rats traded hanger wire and stolen seconds in front of the steam press. Someone learned that a dab of shampoo cut salt rings out of collars. Another swore by cornstarch for razor burn. Foot powder was currency; moleskin, gold.

The barracks echoed with small domestic sounds: spoons tapping dented cans, laces slapped flat against soles, toothbrushes scrubbing at the seam where leather met welt. Busy hands gave the mind less room to panic.

Turning Noise Into Math

Ethan found a trick to get through formations: make math of it. Ten counts to each breath; five breaths to the minute; four minutes to the inspection. Convert the cadre's orbit into vectors. Plot his path, predict the glare. When fear tried to sprint, numbers made it walk.

At night, he built mnemonics for the Rat Bible—dates knotted to images, mottos set to the rhythm of a chant. He whispered them to the kid from C-3 who stuttered when cornered and to the lineman whose hands shook during recitation. By the end of the week, those two could fire the founding year and Latin crest like rifle drill.

"Teacher Skunk," Jack teased, dropping onto Ethan's bunk. "Careful. They'll draft you to chapel to tutor the Almighty."

"Almighty already knows the second stanza," Ethan said, deadpan. "You don't."

Jack smirked and tossed him the booklet. "Then teach me."

So they traded: Ethan's mnemonics for Jack's breathing. In the stoop's heat, Jack showed him how to box oxygen—four in, four hold, four out, four hold—until the edges of the world stopped fizzing. When cadre lit them up again, Ethan lasted six more push-ups and didn't see the tunnel.

Humor With the Edges Filed Off

Humor survived—filed down, pocketable. On day three, a slow leak formed where last night's sweat puddled. Someone christened it Lake SMI. Another cut a paper fish from the back of a chow pass and floated it there until a cadre boot crushed the joke. They didn't laugh loudly; they laughed inward, the kind you could deny if asked.

When a Rat from Alpha Company puked mid–mountain climber, a cadre planted a boot an inch from the mess and whispered, "Leave it. You can have it back at breakfast." The line quaked, and then—God help them—someone snorted. Even fear had limits.

The Second Party

It came two nights later, no preamble: lights, boots, the hard bark of "DOWN!" The body remembered faster than the mind this time—hands found placement, cores fired, breath boxed itself. Ethan rode the wave—not strong, not smooth, but steadier. When his triceps failed, he rolled clean to flutter kicks without a cadre's nose on his face. Small win, stamped in sweat.

Halfway through, a thin Rat from Echo sagged and stayed down. Cadre crouched, lips at his ear, voice surprisingly soft: "Breathe, son." A canteen cap clicked open. Water touched his tongue. The next command hit like thunder again, and the softness vanished, but Ethan kept that single second like a pebble in his pocket. SMI had edges. Somewhere, a curve.

Afterward, back in the room, Jack tore open two packets of saltines and split them, then slid Ethan the bigger half.

"Fuel," he said.

"Vintage," Ethan answered.

They ate in synchrony, crumbs falling like ash onto gray blankets.

The days took pieces. Nerves frayed along private seams— one Rat snapped at another over a scuffed cover; two nearly came to blows over whose turn it was at the sink. But then the pendulum swung back: a hand to steady a tray; a word prompted during recitation; a shoulder presented for leaning against during a surprise wall-sit that went long enough to warp time.

Tran's room stayed a cipher. Sometimes he'd say nothing at all, take the boots, nod once. Other nights he'd ask Ethan a single history question out of nowhere—obscure, unfair—and listen to the answer without moving. Twice, he corrected Ethan's posture with two fingers and a breath, and both times the cadre drifted past him like he'd turned slightly less visible.

"Why me?" Ethan asked once, before he could swallow it.

Tran's gaze was unreadable. "Because you ask."

It was not affection. It was investment. In SMI terms, that might be more durable.

Quiet Accrual

By week's end, the Rats didn't look tougher so much as more exact—creases truer, brass brighter, faces arranged in the careful blank of men who had learned where to put their eyes. The midnight parties still hurt. The days still bit. But something else had begun—an accrual so slow it only showed when you voiced it aloud:

He lasted six more push-ups.
He didn't stutter the crest.
He timed the breath.
He kept the shine.

Ethan fell asleep that night with the Rat Bible under his hand and Jack's box-breath pattern ticking like a metronome in his ribs. When the door banged again—because of course it did—he was already turning, the floor cool under his feet, the fear there but smaller, contained inside the count.

Out on the stoop, boots gathered like weather. Somewhere in the dark below, SMI watched and weighed. And for the first time since the doors first blew open, Ethan felt something quieter than terror settle in beside it.

Not confidence.

Just the faintest outline of cope.

By the end of the first week, the midnight ambushes almost felt predictable—like thunderstorms that formed over hot pavement, cracked the sky, and rolled off toward the mountains before dawn. What didn't feel predictable was the silence between them. That was when you felt watched.

Word of the Honor Court moved like static through the barracks. No one ever saw them organize—just rumors that they took their coffee black, their notebooks neat, their faces set in a kind of disappointed patience. You didn't have to see them to know they were there. You just had to feel yourself making smaller choices with larger hands.

The Bill

It was a Sunday morning, quiet as Southern Military Institute ever allowed. Sunlight slid along the fourth stoop, turning dust into a slow flock of gold. Ethan stepped out with two missions: twenty minutes at the sink to press a crease that had drooped, and sixty seconds to breathe a box of air before formation snapped him back into angles.

He almost missed it—a rectangle against the concrete, tan as the stoop. Twenty dollars. Crisp, face up, Andrew Jackson staring like he'd been waiting.

His first thought—automatic, human—was that someone was running back for it right now. The second was SMI's: this is a test.

Boots scuffed behind him. Jack.

"Don't," Jack said, low.

"I wasn't," Ethan lied. His leg had already bent.

They stood over the bill the way two hikers stand over a copperhead, admiring and refusing it at the same time. The stoop was empty except for them. Somewhere, a radio clicked off.

"What's the move?" Jack asked.

Ethan heard Dr. Maddox in his head—You have a gift, don't squander it—and Trans's sentence—Brass is your first language here. He straightened his spine until it felt like a ruler. When he spoke, his voice came out steady enough to surprise him.

"Witness," Ethan said. "We ask for a witness."

Jack nodded once, then louder: "Cadre presence requested!" The sound carried down the railings, bounced from stone to stone, pulled a figure out of the shadows like a conjuring trick.

A second-classman stepped into the light, cover squared, eyes unreadable. "Issue, Rat?"

Ethan kept his hands at his seams. "Found currency on the stoop, sir. Request permission to turn it in to the Guard Room with a witness."

A pause long enough to taste.

"Proceed," the cadet said. He didn't bend either. He let Ethan describe the bill without touching it, then gestured to a third Rat to fetch a scrap of paper and an envelope. Ethan dictated the time, place, and amount while the third wrote in shaky block letters. The cadet watched the whole dance with no expression, then took the sealed envelope and the witness with him toward the Guard Room.

Jack let out a breath he'd been folding into his ribs. "They'll still say we wanted it."

"Then we'll still say we didn't," Ethan said. His mouth was dry and his palms were sweating and he felt—strangely— upright.

The Cap

The next evening brought the mirror image. A cover lay on the far end of the parade deck—alone, too alone, white disc like a dropped moon. A few Rats glanced, then snapped their eyes front so hard you could hear necks resist.

It was the last place a Rat wanted to be seen: open ground, no shadows to hide in, no excuse to offer that didn't smell like a story. Ethan felt his shoulder twitch toward it. Jack, by his side, didn't blink.

"Not ours. Not our lane," Jack whispered.

"Not our test," Ethan answered, and they marched past it like a lighthouse—note it, steer around it, let it be what it was for whoever it was for.

Someone behind them peeled off. The sound of footsteps changed—hesitation has a rhythm—and then sped up again. Ethan didn't turn. He didn't have to. SMI would tell him later whether that was a choice or a mistake.

Later came the drumbeat no one had to invent.

They formed at dusk, heat still rising from the deck, the air already thinking of night. An officer read names for drill, for duty, for a hundred small rotations that made up the Institute's clock. Then the tone shifted.

"All present will stand fast for an announcement."

Silence collected in the corners. Two cadets from the Honor Court stepped forward, dark sashes breaking the monotony of gray. One unfolded a paper with care. The sound of the crease opened the whole Corps.

"Private William McKay, Echo Company," the cadet read, voice unhurried. "Violation of the Honor Code: theft. You will remove yourself from formation."

A hole opened where a boy had been. He stepped forward, alone in a way that made Ethan's throat constrict. No one hissed. No one jeered. That was the most unnerving part: the respect remained, even as the place revoked his right to stand in it.

McKay set his cover under his arm, squared his shoulders, and walked. Across the deck, beneath windows holding a thousand eyes, into a history that would not footnote him. When he reached the archway the echo of his boots shortened and died.

"By order of the Honor Court," the sash continued, "you will leave the Institute at once."

The formation did not breathe for a long, measurable second. Then the clock restarted—commands resumed, heels struck in unison, the body of the Corps moving on, because that was what bodies did when they lost a piece.

Ethan's palms went slick. He wasn't thinking about the twenty dollars anymore. He was thinking about every small decision with a shadow attached. He scanned the windows without moving his head. If ghosts existed, this was where they would stand.

The Pact

That night they sat on the stoop with their backs against the rail, boots unlaced just enough to let ankles swell. The parade deck glowed the color of old nickel. Crickets sang in the grass beyond the wall like the earth had no idea what humans did to each other inside it.

Jack spoke first. "No shortcuts."

Ethan nodded. "No stories."

"No favors we didn't earn," Jack added.

"No lies we tell ourselves," Ethan said, and that one landed heavier than it sounded.

They didn't shake. SMI made you shake hands with enough devils as it was. They just breathed together, matched counts like drill, and let the pact set like concrete in the heat.

When the door blew open again—because of course it did—they were already standing. The party that night lasted twenty-one minutes by Jack's watch. Ethan counted breaths and not the burn. When a cadre demanded the second stanza of the school hymn, Ethan's voice didn't crack on the line that always felt like a lie.

Afterward, sprawled on the floorboards, salt crusting where shirts met skin, Jack tapped the Rat Bible with one finger.

"They mean for this to be a leash," he said.

Ethan turned the booklet in his hands, felt the cheap staple pinch his thumb. "Or a map."

Jack considered. "Same thing, if you let it be."

Ethan set the booklet on his chest and stared at the ceiling where centuries of sweat and ambition had left a patina the color of old bone. "Then we won't."

He wasn't sure whether he believed himself. He only knew that the twenty dollars had stayed on the concrete, the cap had stayed in the open, and he had stayed inside his own skin a little better than he had the day before.

The Small Victory

Tran waited when Ethan brought the boots that night. He held them to the light, turned one, then the other, and set them down.

"Less streak," he said.

"Yes, sir."

Tran's eyes flicked to Ethan's face and away again. "Good choice on the stoop."

Ethan worked to keep his chin where it belonged. "Which choice, sir?"

Tran's mouth nearly made a curve. "Exactly."

Back on the fourth floor, Jack had already pulled blankets straight and cracked two warm Cokes like a sacrament. They drank in silence, the carbonation burning a clean line down throats rubbed raw by yelling.

Across the deck, the flag halyard knocked against the pole—lonely, metallic, patient. Somewhere below, boots crossed stone. Maybe they were living. Maybe they were memory. Either way, Ethan listened and didn't flinch.

The Institute had taught him a handful of things in seven days. Some of them hurt. One of them didn't:

When the floor tilts, pick a thing that doesn't move and make yourself face it.

For now, that was Jack at his left, the code in his hand, and the narrow corridor of choices between them.

Chapter 14 — Jimmy Buffett

At Southern Military Institute, the outside world wasn't just far away—it was banned. No radios, no TVs, no Walkmans. If you didn't give yourself over, the place would take you anyway.

Ethan had a loophole the size of a cassette.

The Sony Walkman lived under a towel at the bottom of his locker, battery door taped to keep it from rattling. Most nights, after study hour dulled into that slow scrape of pages and pencils, he'd slide the foam pads over his ears and press play. The first strum of Jimmy Buffett felt like oxygen entering a sealed room. Steel drums. Lazy guitar. A voice that made worry sound like a bad habit you could shrug off. In those minutes he wasn't Rat Cole or Skunk or a number written in grease pencil on a whiteboard. He was just Ethan, someplace warm that smelled like salt and sunscreen.

He always put it back carefully, towel smoothed, lock clicked. And for weeks, he got away with it.

Until he didn't.

The door blew open at reveille like a battering ram. "ROOM INSPECTION!" Six cadre poured in—hands under mattresses, fingers in desk seams, boots kicking open trunks. Sheets left in ropes on the floor. Notebooks flung like birds. The air went bright and hot with barked orders and the rip of tape.

Ethan locked his chin, eyes drilled to a knot in the cinderblock, every muscle pretending it didn't know how to tremble.

"Got something!" a voice crowed.

A cadet rose holding the Walkman by its cord, headphones dangling like a noose. Laughter rolled through the room.

"Well, well," another sneered, turning the player so the light ran along its black shell. "Rat Cole's a tourist. Enjoy your beach, Rat?"

By noon a slip found his hand: Report to the Rat Disciplinary Committee—Chapel, 2000.

The Chapel was colder than the barracks ever managed. Stained glass threw bruised colors across the stone floor; saints stared down like they knew everyone's worst thought. A long table waited at the front. Upperclassmen behind it sat too still.

Center seat: Marcus Steele.

Six-four and built like a doorframe, Steele had the posture of someone who slept at attention. Word said he'd done mini-BUD/S already and smiled while other men learned to hate sand. To the Corps, he was less a cadet than a consequence.

"Rat Cole," Steele said, voice like gravel poured slow. "Possession of unauthorized electronics. Violation of the Ratline." The words climbed the rafters and came back harder.

Ethan swallowed. "Yes, sir."

"You think you're special?" Steele asked, leaning forward. "Think you get a private pipeline to paradise while your class sweats?"

"No, sir."

A thin smile. "Punishment is as follows. Every day at lunch you will report to Cadet Daniels of this Committee. You will conduct physical training while listening to Jimmy Buffett—" a few snickers sparked and died, "—on your Walkman. You will continue until the batteries die. You will pray they die quickly."

Heat rushed into Ethan's face. He kept his eyes front. "Yes, sir."

"Dismissed."

Outside, night air pressed hot and damp against his shaved scalp. The chapel door thudded shut behind him like a verdict.

At noon the next day, while Rats swarmed the mess hall, Ethan turned down the empty corridor to Daniels's room. His stomach growled at the smell of gravy drifting up the stairwell.

Daniels didn't bother with preamble. He dropped the Walkman into Ethan's hands. "Put it on."

Click. The world narrowed to foam pads and a lazy riff. Changes in Latitudes slid into his skull.

"Down, Rat."

Push-ups. Then sit-ups. Then flutter kicks. Then burpees. Sweat ran into his ears; Buffett's breezy chuckle washed through it like a joke with teeth.

"Faster," Daniels said, watching the second hand crawl. "Paradise should hurt."

The first day hurt. The second day hollowed him out.

By the third day, Ethan's noons had a cadence: knock at Daniels's door; Walkman slapped into his palm; foam pads over ears; click; a lazy riff curling into the skull; "Down, Rat."

Push-ups until his triceps quivered. Sit-ups until the world narrowed to ceiling, knees, ceiling, knees. Flutter kicks while Margaritaville mocked him with salt and lime. On Fins he did burpees; on Volcano he mountain-climbed; when Come Monday drifted in like a kind wind, Daniels only smiled and whispered, "Faster."

No lunch. No tray line chatter. No ten minutes to inhale calories and pretend to be part of the herd. Just Buffett and concrete and a stopwatch that ticked like it hated him.

By formation he shook through his sleeves. In afternoon drill his rifle felt heavier than steel had a right to be. On the practice field, Captain Harris eyed him once, then twice.

"You lose a step, Cole?" Harris asked, neutral as a judge.

"No, sir," Ethan said, and willed his legs to remember how to be his.

He looped a fresh notch into his white belt that week. Then another the next. Boots that had fit like a squeeze now felt like borrowed shoes. His cheeks hollowed, jaw sharpening. The other Rats tried to make it into a joke.

"Skunk doesn't eat," someone said in the mess line, stage-whisper loud. "Runs on Buffett and spite."

"Wastin' away again," another sang, off-key, and the table snickered until a cadre's shadow fell and the noise died.

Ethan grinned when they looked at him—automatic, easy—but the smile never reached his eyes.

At night the songs wouldn't let go. He'd lie on his bunk, shaved scalp buzzing against thin pillow, and the choruses kept circling his head, bright and relentless as noon sun on brass. He tried to hate them. It didn't take much.

Jack started slipping him contraband calories. Half a roll wrapped in a napkin. A smear of peanut butter on an index card like a joke. A protein bar cut into three pieces so it looked less like a thing that could get them both burned.

"Eat," Jack muttered, eyes on his book at study hour. "Quiet."

Ethan palmed the food without looking, chewed fast and careful, throat tight. Gratitude sat in his chest like a hot coal. So did shame.

Tran Nguyen, his Dyke, didn't say a word for two weeks. Then he tossed a can of peaches onto Ethan's bunk without slowing.

"Eat. Shine boots when you're done," Tran said, voice flat, face unreadable. It was as close to mercy as the Institute knew how to speak.

Day after day, Daniels ran his private show. Ethan learned the length of batteries by muscle burn more than minutes. The "A" side of his cassette was worth two hundred push-ups and a hundred sit-ups if Daniels didn't switch tracks to speed him up.

The "B" side stretched thinner and meaner; on Cheeseburger in Paradise Daniels always, always called for burpees.

He lived for the skip, the stutter, the telltale sag in treble that meant power was fading. Each noon he listened for it like a drowning boy watches for a rope.

It never came.

Mid-September brought a damp, early chill to the stoops and a rumor about extra inspections. Ethan came out of Daniels's room wrung-out and light-headed, the Walkman damp with his sweat. As he turned down the corridor, voices stopped him—Daniels and another cadet talking low in the half-open doorway.

"…plug it in after study hour," the other voice said. "He'll never know."

"Already do," Daniels answered, and the smirk in his tone was a thing you could hear. "He thinks he's waiting out the batteries." A small electric click. A red LED blinked to life on a wall outlet charger Ethan hadn't noticed before. Two AA cells slept there, fat with promise.

The hallway tilted under Ethan's boots. For a second he thought he might put a fist through the door. Instead he tightened his jaw until it hurt and walked.

On the fourth-floor stoop he sat hard on the rail and stared into the parade deck's square of evening. The air smelled like cut grass and old stone. A few Rats ghosted past, heads down, strain tight. Jack slid in beside him and didn't speak for a while. The quiet felt like a blessing.

"They're charging them," Ethan said finally, voice low and flat. "Every night. It's not supposed to end."

Jack's mouth went tight. He nodded once, like a man confirming the obvious cruelty of gravity. "Yeah."

Ethan's laugh came out wrong. "Steele told me to pray the batteries died." He shook his head. "Guess God's on a charger too."

Jack didn't smile. He watched the dark gather in the courtyard and said, "So make it yours."

"What?"

"The music," Jack said. "They think they took it from you. Take it back. Count to it. Breathe to it. Own it until it's just a metronome and you're the one setting tempo."

Ethan stared at the deck. A squad crossed below, boots in unison. He thought about how the Walkman had felt the first week—a doorway. He thought about Steele's smirk and Daniels's blinking charger and how small he'd felt holding plastic and wire like a leash.

He nodded, once.

The next day at noon he still went hungry. He still shook. Pencil Thin Mustache still sounded like a grin with teeth. But he matched his breath to the chorus, locked his reps to the kick drum, let the steel drums become a clock. When Daniels snapped, "Faster," Ethan shifted the count, not the beat. In his head, he wasn't chasing the song anymore. The song chased him.

Small victories were all the Institute left you. He took them.

Word about "Buffett PT" spread faster than anything official ever did. Rats he didn't know clapped him on the shoulder in the stairwell and said, "Hang in there, Skunk." Upperclassmen smirked when he passed and hummed bars under their breath. Somebody chalked a tiny palm tree near his locker—two lines and three leaves, a joke that made him want to laugh and move the drawing where no one could see it at the same time.

He stopped losing weight so fast. He stopped waiting for the skip in the tape like salvation. He stopped thinking about batteries.

One night, after study hour, Jack slid him half a grilled-cheese he'd bartered off a kitchen Rat for two brass polishes and a promise.

"You good?" Jack asked.

"No," Ethan said honestly, then took a bite. Butter and salt and heat hit like news from home. "But I'm here."

They sat on the stoop until Taps sent its last, lonely note up into the dark. Somewhere a fan rattled. Somewhere a cadre's laugh clipped off short. In Ethan's head a steel drum ticked, and for once, it didn't sound like a taunt.

The punishment hadn't ended. It probably wouldn't.

But the music—at least for now—was his again.

Noon came on a gray Tuesday that smelled like wet stone and brass polish. Ethan's stomach had learned to be quiet by then, to fold in on itself and wait. He knocked. Daniels opened without speaking, shoved the foam pads into Ethan's hands, and pointed at the floor.

Click.

A lazy guitar rolled in like warm surf. Changes in Latitudes again—Daniels' favorite opener. Ethan dropped to plank, matched his breath to the first verse, and let his body slide into the tempo like a train catching its track.

Push-ups. Sit-ups. Flutter kicks. Burpees on the chorus. The same cruel choreography. Sweat pooled and disappeared into concrete. His arms shook, then steadied. When Daniels snapped "Faster," Ethan didn't race the song; he moved the count.

Halfway through Fins, the sound hiccuped.

A tiny, almost polite stutter. Then silence.

Daniels blinked. Ethan did not. He kept the rhythm anyway—four-count down, one-count hold, drive up—breathing like a metronome. One-two-three-four—up. One-two-three-four—up. In his head, the steel drums kept time because he told them to, because Jack had been right: if you made the music yours, no one could weaponize it against you.

Daniels frowned, popped the battery case with his thumb, shook the dead AAs into his palm. He reached toward his desk drawer for a fresh pair.

"Up," Ethan said—to himself, not to Daniels—and finished the set as if the chorus still swayed through the room. He rolled to sit-ups, laced his fingers, and worked the count through closed teeth. Thirty… forty… fifty. Silence became the cleanest song he'd heard in weeks.

Daniels watched for a beat too long. The new batteries clicked in. He raised a brow, then pressed play.

The music came back bright and grinning. Ethan didn't flinch.

By formation that afternoon, the rumor had already grown legs: Skunk kept moving when the tape died. Nobody could say who told it first. By evening study hour, a fourth-classman hummed Margaritaville under his breath as Ethan passed on the stoop, but this time there wasn't a smirk in it. Just the shared fact of a thing endured.

Tran Nguyen said nothing for another week, which was exactly on brand. Then, after taps on a night when the stoops still sweated from an early rain, he paused in Ethan's doorway. He didn't look in. He didn't soften.

"Walk," Tran said.

Ethan fell in a step behind. They moved past the silent trophy case and the Honor Court doors that seemed to breathe on their own. Tran stopped under a pool of light at the first-floor turn, where the stone stayed cool even in August.

"You are still here," Tran said into the air.

"Yes, Dyke," Ethan answered.

Tran held out a small, dented tin. Sardines. The smell hit before the lid fully peeled—a tidal wave of salt and oil. Ethan swallowed the reflex in his throat, took the tin, and tipped the fish into his palm. Tran started walking again before Ethan finished chewing.

"Shine boots," Tran said over his shoulder.

"Yes, Dyke."

It was the closest thing to praise the Southern Military Institute taught.

Soccer kept its own calendar. On a Thursday scrimmage Captain Harris pinned a bib to Ethan's tunic without comment. The turf steamed under the late sun. Balls pinged. Cleats hissed. Ethan's legs felt carved and light, every touch landing on the beat he'd been counting for weeks. He stepped inside a tackle, heard a phantom steel drum, and split two defenders with a pass that kissed the grass like a secret.

"Well done, Cole," Harris said evenly—the kind of compliment that meant more for being rationed. After cooldown a training Rat palmed him an orange like contraband; Ethan peeled it at the far fence, juice running down his wrists, sugar hitting his head like a bell.

At lunch the next day, Daniels upped the cruelty.

"Sing it," he said with a soft smile when Cheeseburger in Paradise landed. "Loud enough for the hall to hear."

Ethan tasted bile and battery acid in equal parts. He sang anyway, voice rough, breath coming in sawed lengths between reps. A verse in, the absurdity tipped from humiliation to something else. He couldn't quite name it. Daniels paced with his hands behind his back, measuring. At the chorus, Ethan was almost laughing. Not at Daniels. Not at himself. At the strange, stupid fact of a life where you could be starving, sweating, and belting out a beach song to please a man who wanted you small—and somehow not be small.

Afterward, he leaned on the cool hallway wall until the dots cleared from his vision. Jack found him there, slid a folded napkin into his palm. Two bites of bread lived inside, pressed flat and perfect as contraband.

"You look like hammered death," Jack said mildly.

"You smell like sardines," Ethan shot back.

Jack snorted. "That your Dyke?"

Ethan nodded. "I think it was a kindness."

"At SMI, a kindness just means it won't kill you," Jack said, then tipped his chin toward Daniels's door. "You good?"

"No," Ethan said again—truth as discipline. He tucked the bread under his tongue like communion and pushed off the wall. "But I'm here."

Steele watched him once, weeks later. It was a nothing moment, built of quiet—a slow Friday noon with half the Corps at drill and the mess hall clatter drifting thin through the windows. Daniels had him on a plank with one foot lifted, Volcano muttering about pressure and time, when the corridor air shifted. Ethan didn't lift his head; Rats didn't. But boots spoke a dialect you learned fast. These boots landed soft and certain.

"Carry on," Steele said from the doorway, voice like a weight set down gently. Daniels stiffened. The music played on. Ethan held the count until his forearms burned clean, then longer.

When it was over and he stood to strain at attention, eyes front, chin pinned, he felt Steele's gaze slide across him and keep going—as if taking inventory, as if noting a tool that had refused to break.

The batteries never died again. Daniels stopped bothering with the theater of letting them run out. He clicked fresh ones in without hiding it, and Ethan stopped praying for silence. He didn't need an ending to win. Little by little, the punishment became a room he could walk into and out of without leaving pieces behind.

On a cool night in October, a wind found its way over the parade deck and plucked at the flags until they snapped clean. The stoops smelled less like summer and more like metal. Ethan sat with Jack where they always sat, on the fourth-floor rail with his boots hooked under the bar so a cadre couldn't claim they were dangling.

"They can pick the music," Jack said, eyes on the dark square of the deck. "They can set the time, the place, the rules."

Ethan listened to the flag halyards clack, the fan in four-two rattle, the quiet that came when the Corps finally slept.

"But they don't get to write the song," he said.

Jack's mouth twitched. "There you go."

Lights-out rolled over the barracks like a tide. Somewhere, a lone voice down on first called cadence to an empty hallway, the sound bouncing and thinning until it turned into nothing. Ethan felt the beat of it in his ribs and didn't flinch.

He would still go hungry tomorrow. He would still sing stupid lyrics for a man who enjoyed it for reasons Ethan didn't care to understand. He would still polish Tran's boots until his fingers went black with paste and shine.

But the Walkman had turned back into what it had been the first time he pressed play: a door. He couldn't step through it, not yet. Not here. So he did the next best thing.

He kept the key.

Chapter 15 — Specials

At Southern Military Institute, nothing was small.

Not mistakes. Not consequences.

A crooked gig line, a loose thread, a thirty-second slip at formation—each one got the same treatment: Specials. The system was simple and merciless. You didn't wait to be caught. Waiting meant whispers. Whispers led to the Honor Court. So you marched yourself to the guard desk, took a thin slip of paper called a bone sheet, and confessed in your own careful handwriting.

Everyone learned the verb fast: boning.
Boning was SMI's sacrament—public guilt in triplicate.

The slips came back stamped and official. At the bottom, three boxes sat like a bad joke the Corps never tired of:

Correct.

Incorrect.

Correct, but wish to explain.

The cadre loved that last one. "Might as well read: Please, sir, don't kill me," Jack muttered one night, flicking his bone sheet with a thumbnail. Laughter skittered around the room, the nervous kind that died fast.

Ethan didn't laugh. Because when his first Special hit, nothing about it felt funny.

Ethan's first bone
Inspection Saturday. The kind that started with boots in the hallway and ended with someone dry-heaving into a trash can. Ethan had spent an hour on his rifle, oil worked into the walnut, metal bright enough to catch his own shaved reflection.

Sergeant Leary stopped at the rack, eyes like calipers. His gaze flicked once, then fixed.

"Your sling is twisted, Rat."

Ethan blinked. "Sir, I—"

"QUIET." The word slammed the air. "Bone yourself. Now."

The order landed like a sentence. That night, under the jaundiced glow of the guard station, Ethan filled the sheet with hands that wouldn't stop sweating.

Offense: Rifle sling out of alignment.
Response: Correct, but wish to explain.

He stared at the words, knowing they were a mistake even as he wrote them. But pride is loud, and he wasn't ready to let go of the tiny voice saying I checked it. I did.

The summons came at morning formation.

The Superintendent

Superintendent Hartley's office was colder than the rest of the barracks, as if the portraits on the walls demanded lower temperatures to keep from cracking. The frames held SMI— men in sepia uniforms, jaws set forever. Ethan stood at strain, the Special shaking just enough to make the paper rasp.

Hartley read without looking up. "Rat Ethan Cole. Rifle sling out of alignment. Correct, but wish to explain."

His eyes lifted, quick and sharp. "Explain."

Ethan's throat tightened. "Sir, I checked it twice before inspection. The leather must have shifted when—"

Hartley raised a single finger. The room went silent. "Excuses."

A couple upperclassmen along the wall exhaled their amusement through their noses. Ethan felt heat flood his ears.

"You chose 'wish to explain,'" Hartley continued, voice like a gavel. "And your explanation is worthless. Do you know what that makes you?"

Ethan swallowed. "No, sir."

"A Rat who cannot follow orders. And worse, a Rat who talks back on paper."

The phrase hit harder than a shove. Talking back on paper. He hadn't meant it that way. But the effect was the same.

"Ten penalty tours," Hartley said. The pen scratched. "You will march every evening this week—rifle on the shoulder—until the lesson takes."

Ethan's mouth went dry. "Yes, sir."

"Louder."

"YES, SIR."

"Dismissed."

Ethan saluted, pivoted, and walked out on legs that felt like borrowed wood. Outside, the hall air was warmer, noisier—the living world resuming—yet he carried the cold with him like a second uniform.

Paper weight

Back on fourth stoop, the bone sheet felt heavier than its ounces. Jack was waiting, leaning against the rail like trouble couldn't stick to him.

"Well?" he asked.

"Ten tours," Ethan said.

Jack whistled low. "Over a sling. They're tight this week."

Ethan nodded, jaw locked. He could still hear Hartley's phrasing, the way the room had enjoyed it—talks back on paper—like they'd been waiting to use that line on someone.

That evening, the bell for tours sounded and the courtyard filled with slow, miserable circles. Ethan fell into the line, rifle nestled into the notch of his shoulder, barrel sliding against his ear with each turn. The stock rubbed a raw crescent he knew would open by lap six. Upperclassmen lounged on the stoops with Cokes, commentary drifting down like cigarette smoke.

"Look at Buffett's boy," one called. "Marching to Margaritaville."

Laughter spattered the stone.

Ethan kept his eyes forward, chin pinned, steps clean. The cadence was slow enough to hurt—a pace designed to make time claw.

By the fifth lap, sweat stung his eyes. By the tenth, his thighs shuddered. By the fifteenth, he knew if he stopped and put a hand to his knee, the bell would reset and he'd live the hour again. So he didn't stop. He counted bricks on the inner wall, let the numbers stand between him and the ache.

When the release finally came, his blouse clung to him, salt whitening the seams. Back in the room, Jack clapped a palm on his shoulder, then hissed when he felt the heat through the cloth.

"Could've been five," Jack said, eyes sympathetic. "You picked the wrong box."

"Yeah," Ethan said. He set the rifle down gently, as if it might bruise. "I picked the wrong box."

He lay awake later, the ceiling a shade lighter than dark, replaying the moment he'd checked Correct, but wish to explain. Pride had wanted a say. SMI had answered.

He promised himself he wouldn't make the same mistake again.

The ledger at the guard desk became a second attendance sheet for Rats who'd stumbled. A chalkboard hung above it with names and tallies like a scoreboard no one wanted to lead. Every evening at 1800, the bell sounded; every evening at 1801, a slow file of gray uniforms and pale scalps formed in the courtyard, rifles slung, eyes locked front.

The pace was deliberate cruelty—thirty-inch steps, heels rolled, corners taken at a crawl. If you scratched an itch, if your sling slipped, if your eyes flicked, the watch cadet reset your count with a voice that carried to the fourth stoop. The rifle stock carved a half-moon into Ethan's shoulder each night, a raw crescent that never healed because it never got the chance.

"Tours ain't punishment," Jack said, rolling his shoulder as they formed up. "They're time. You can use time."

The bell clanged. They stepped.

Around the deck, upperclassmen lounged with Cokes and commentary.

"Smile, Skunk! Think sunny beaches!"
"Margaritaville, two o'clock!"

Ethan kept his chin pinned and counted bricks—five to a section, twelve sections a side. Numbers were safer than faces.

On Jack's fifth lap of his own first Special, he slid past Ethan on the opposite arc and grinned like he'd found a hack no one else could see.

"Correct," he murmured, so low only Ethan could hear.

He'd circled the box without flinching, stood before the Superintendent like a statue, taken five tours for a collar unbuttoned after taps, and walked out smiling. That night, he marched them like wind sprints, exaggerating the heel-roll, clipping corners so sharp the sling sang against brass.

"Hell," Jack breathed as they crossed again, "this is conditioning."

Ethan wanted to believe that. Wanted to inhabit Jack's trick of turning shame into fuel. But every time he passed the guard desk, every time his name glared from the chalk, a weight tugged at his ribs. To him, Specials weren't time; they were proof.

So he adapted a different way.

He learned the bone-sheet rhythm—ink straight, letters square, no flourish, no plea. He stopped choosing Correct, but wish to explain; he stopped wanting to. He boned himself before anyone could tell him to, handed the slip in with a steady hand, and walked out without looking at the board.

"Own it and go," he told himself. "Don't feed it."

The Corps noticed. Not with kindness—SMI didn't do kindness—but with a different sort of silence. No one mocked a Rat who boned fast and marched clean. They saved their laughter for the wafflers, the explainers, the ones who argued the angle of a gig line to a man whose ruler had already decided.

By the third week, Ethan and Jack's evenings were a choreography. Lunch hour: Ethan disappeared for Buffett-PT, stomach empty, sweat slicking his blouse. Afternoon: drill, classes, barracks inspections that turned pockets into grenade craters. Evening: the tours bell, the long slow circles.

On cool nights, breath fogged the air and boots clicked like metronomes. On hot ones, the stone radiated anger and the rifle felt heavier by the lap. Somewhere on fourth stoop, a radio (illegal, always) leaked a whisper of static until a door slammed and the sound died.

"Use it," Jack would say on the pass.
"Count it," Ethan would answer.

Different strategies for the same sentence.

One Friday, the bell released them early—two tours canceled for weather or mercy or a clerical error no one dared question. The courtyard emptied. Ethan sat on the inner wall and unlaced his boot, flexing his raw shoulder. Jack tipped his canteen and drank until his throat clicked.

"You see the trick yet?" Jack asked, not looking up.
"Which one?"

Jack screwed the cap back on. "They make you carry it like shame. But it's just work. If you let it be work, it can't own you."

Ethan nodded. "And if it still owns you?"

Jack glanced over, the grin gone. "Then we shoulder some of it together."

They sat in the dim a minute longer, the barracks humming with far-off voices and the clink of brass. When they finally stood, Ethan felt the weight shift—not gone, not even lighter, exactly—but redistributed, like a pack settled properly for a long march.

The next Special that hit his hand, he checked Correct without a tremor, signed, and turned away before the ink dried. That night, as he traced his slow circle in the heat, the chalkboard above the guard desk felt less like a verdict and more like a clock.

Time to be paid. Time to be used.

Saturday brought the kind of inspection that made Rats feel like insects under glass. The cadre moved down the hallway in pairs—one with a ruler, one with a notebook—peeling back bedsheets, sighting down gig lines, running a white glove along the lip of lockers like a judge passing sentence.

Ethan had been careful. He'd ironed until the room smelled like burned starch, shaved in cold water to keep the skin tight, polished his brass with cotton torn from an old T-shirt. He'd even rehearsed the order of his answers—"Yes, sir. No, sir. Correct, sir."—so his mouth couldn't betray his hands.

The glove came away from his locker with a faint gray crescent.

"Dust," the notebook said.

A ruler touched the hem of his curtain. "Quarter inch low."

A finger pressed his belt. "Buckle off center."

Stacked—three slips in five minutes. The notebook tore them loose and handed them over like receipts.

Jack caught Ethan's eye across the room and did a small, almost imperceptible shrug: Use it.

Ethan nodded once. He took the bone sheets to the guard desk, filled each one with the same quiet handwriting.

Offense: Locker dust.

Response: Correct.

Offense: Curtain hem low.

Response: Correct.

Offense: Belt buckle off center.

Response: Correct.

No plea. No explain. No oxygen for the fire.

That night, the bell sent him out with both shoulders already tender and a rifle that felt an ounce heavier per mistake. By the fourth lap, sweat stung his eyes. By the seventh, his legs moved on rails. By the tenth, he'd stopped hearing the jeers from the stoops.

He recited instead.

Dates, mottos, the Rat Bible's first pages by gritted-teeth rhythm. Founder's name on the turn. Battle streamers at the corner. Creed on the long side. When the rifle bit down into the raw crescent on his shoulder, he doubled the cadence in his head and pushed the pain into the facts.

On the twelfth lap, a voice drifted down from second stoop.

"Rat's memorizing, sir."

Another, drier voice: "Good. Let him learn something while he pays."

No laughter followed. Not a compliment—SMI didn't do those—but not a whip, either. It felt like stepping into a pocket of still air.

Ethan finished his laps and slid the rifle back into the rack with a care that bordered on prayer. He didn't feel proud. He felt… aligned. The way a buckle feels when it finds the center by touch alone.

The Corps supplied its own cautionary tales. Two rooms down, a Rat named Holbrook tried to thread a needle through Correct, but wish to explain on a Special for a loose button. He stood before the Superintendent and delivered a dissertation on cheap thread, on how the button had been pulling since issue day, on how he'd planned to fix it after study hour.

Hartley let him finish, then folded the paper neatly and set it aside like an exhibit.

"Ten tours for the button," he said evenly. "Five for the explanation."

Holbrook walked out pale and blurring at the edges. That evening, when their circuits crossed, he looked gutted. Ethan kept his eyes front. Sympathy was a luxury here—if you loaned it out, you never got it back.

"Pick your fights," Jack murmured later, toeing off his boots. "And if it's not a fight you can win, don't swing."

"I'm not swinging," Ethan said. "I'm sanding corners."

Jack laughed softly. "Good. They can't cut what's already smooth."

Small rituals grew in the gaps where sleep should have been. Ethan laid his blouse flat and sighted down the gig line like it was a rifle barrel. He tied his tie by feel with the window dark and his jaw sore. He cut a square of old T-shirt and tucked it in the flap of his cap, a secret talisman for brass that dulled the moment you looked away. Every night before taps, he set his rifle on his knees and ran a fingertip under the sling, hunting for the twist before Sergeant Leary's glove could.

Jack's rituals were louder. He did sets of push-ups until the cot creaked, a private war with gravity. He timed himself on making a rack so tight a coin would pop, then did it again because it wasn't tight enough.

Different liturgies, same church.

Grant Hall — Correct But Wish to Explain

By mid-October, the chalkboard over the guard desk still knew their names, but not as often. Jack's tally spiked on weeks he baited the line—"conditioning," he called it, grinning around the rifle stock as if he'd gamed the place. Ethan's numbers thinned to single digits. Some afternoons he stood under the board and felt nothing tug in his ribs at all.

On a cold evening when breath smoked and the stone gave back the day's heat like a banked stove, Ethan rounded the outer corner and almost collided with Captain Harris. Jack's Dyke leaned against the rail, arms folded, watching the slow file of Rats in orbit.

Harris's eyes flicked to Ethan's sling, then to his belt, then to his boots. He didn't speak. He nodded—once, barely—and set his gaze downrange again.

Ethan didn't smile. He didn't break stride. But something settled behind his sternum that held through the rest of the laps and well into the night.

Specials didn't stop. SMI never ran out of small edges to cut skin. A thread would snag. A head would turn. A sleeve would crease wrong in the rain. The bell would clang and the slow sorrowful parade would form up again.

But something had shifted. The bone sheet no longer felt like a confession; it felt like a ledger entry. The tours didn't feel like a public flogging; they felt like a currency he could spend with intention. The chalkboard was still a scoreboard—but it had also become a clock.

Time to pay. Time to use.

Near lights-out one night, Jack rolled onto an elbow and squinted across the dark.

"Still counting bricks?"

"Sometimes," Ethan said. "Mostly I count the things I don't want them to take."

Jack grunted. "Hold onto those."

Ethan set his blouse for morning and smoothed the gig line with the back of his knuckles. Outside, boots clacked on the stoop, a late pair making their own slow circle. Inside, the barracks breathed—cots settling, a cough in the next room, the tiny hiss of a Zippo closing somewhere far down the hall.

At SMI, small things drew blood: a dusty lip of steel, a crooked buckle, a bad word in the wrong box. But small things could save you, too—the square of cloth, the extra glance at a sling, the choice to write Correct and walk away.

The system hadn't softened. Ethan hadn't outsmarted it. He'd learned where his edges were and sanded them until they didn't catch.

And when the bell called him to march, he lifted the rifle, found the raw crescent on his shoulder by feel, and stepped into the long, slow arc as if he'd chosen it.

Chapter 16 — Drumout

It happens when the barracks is so quiet you can hear the blades of the fans fight the heat. When the last joke has flattened into sleep and every Rat is wound into a thin blanket, praying for one more hour before reveille.

The doors blow open.

"ON THE STOOP! NOW!"

Boots, fists, voices—stone turns into a drumhead. Ethan jerks upright, heart ramming his ribs, fingers fumbling at the fly of his trousers. He gets one leg half in, the belt backward, and stumbles into the corridor with everyone else, shaved heads and white eyes, a herd trapped between sleep and terror.

Then the sound.

Not cadence. Not a march.

A single, slow, merciless crack of snare.

Rat—

…a…

—tat.

The note goes up the walls of Southern Military Institute like a flare and falls back as an order. Rats choke the stoops, straining into formation, bare feet slapping stone, half-buttoned blouses hanging crooked. Down on the parade deck, floodlights burn the courtyard into a pale stage.

The Honor Court enters as if it has been carved from the granite under SMI itself. Full dress coats catch the light, gold buttons lined like coins, white gloves without a tremor. They move at half-time to the drum, each step a verdict, each turn a sentence. The Court President carries a folded paper. No one looks up. No one looks anywhere.

Rat—

…a…

—tat.

The Court circles the deck once. Boots strike. The drum cracks. The air feels brittle. Ethan's mouth dries until his tongue sticks to his teeth. He has heard about Drumouts like you hear about a car wreck at an intersection you've never driven through. Seeing the twisted metal is different.

They wheel as one. The Court President steps forward and opens the paper with a softness that makes the floodlights seem loud. His voice carries like a bell through the four stories of stone.

"The Honor Court has met."

No rustle. No cough. SMI holds its breath.

"Cadet Thomas Kelly has been found guilty of three counts of cheating."

The name hangs in the heat. A tray flashed in Ethan's mind—yesterday—in the mess hall. A laugh over something stupid. Kelly's chin tucked in study hour, lips moving as he memorized.

"His name shall never again be spoken within these walls."

The drum answers.

CRACK.

CRACK.

Silence.

The Court turns and leaves the way it came, the snare fading until it's only a shape your ears remember. For a long moment, no one moves. The floodlights buzz. Somewhere, metal ticks as it cools. Ethan hears his own pulse where the drum was, a ghost beat in his neck.

On fourth stoop a Rat crosses himself quick and small, like he's hiding even from God. Another's lips move in a prayer learned before rank, before rifles, before this place had a claim on his breath.

Kelly's room will be empty before reveille. Sheets stripped, name scraped from the roster slate, footlocker hauled away. The men on his hall will talk around a vacant door the way you walk around a hole in the sidewalk. By noon, you'll be told you imagined the shape of him.

"Back inside!" a cadre barks, voice lower than usual. The formations dissolve into a silent trickle. No one jostles. The stone drinks up their footsteps.

Ethan lies on his bunk and stares at the black bands the window frame cuts across the ceiling. The drumline keeps time in his chest. He tries to reverse-breathe it away—inhale on the downbeat, exhale on the space—but the rhythm won't obey.

He pictures Kelly in a motel—there's always a motel—two lamps the color of tea, the air humming in the window unit. A suitcase zipped. A payphone in the lobby where he will make the longest call of his life. I failed. I cheated. They read my name. They played a drum. Ethan imagines the pause after, the weight of a parent's silence.

Across the room, Jack turns once and goes still. He doesn't say anything. There's nothing you say after a drum.

Ethan flips his pillow to the cool side and doesn't sleep. Every small sound—the click of a Zippo somewhere down the stoop, a mattress spring settling, a cough that's held too long—comes wrapped in that phantom cadence.

Rat—

…a…

—tat.

At SMI, honor is iron. The drum is the hammer that proves it. And tonight, every Rat has learned the shape of the anvil they live on.

Reveille split the morning like a pane of glass. The bugle sounded too bright, too clean, as if the night hadn't happened, as if the drum hadn't rolled through every chest on post.

Ethan dressed on muscle memory—shirt, belt, lace, lace again—then stepped onto fourth stoop and stopped. Halfway down the run of doors, there was a vacancy your eyes tried not to see. Kelly's nameplate had been scrubbed with solvent until it was just a faint rectangle where brass had been. The room itself stood open and airless, mattress pulled, footlocker gone, a square of dust on the floor where a chair had been. Someone had mopped, leaving a pale crescent the shape of a drying moon.

Nobody paused, not obviously. But the pace changed for a heartbeat as each Rat slid past. Heads didn't turn. That was part of it—the erasure depended on your cooperation.

"Eyes front, Rats," a cadre said, not even loud. He didn't have to be.

Formations ran tighter that morning. Chins tucked deeper, thumbs tighter to seams. In ranks, Ethan could feel the correction running down the line like a wire under current— shoelaces double-checked, covers squared, rifle slings retensioned twice. Beside him Jack stood perfect and motionless, jaw locked, everything about him saying no openings.

At breakfast the mess hall sounded wrong. Utensils were quieter. The open-mouthed laughter from the firsties' table had a forced edge. Rats ate like prisoners—tray down, stare at chow, ten minutes gone. Someone somewhere dropped a cup; the clatter cracked and then died as if the sound itself had broken a rule.

Halfway through, an upperclassman in sash and saber appeared at the head of the hall with two Honor Court men flanking him. He didn't need a mic.

"Listen once," he said. "You won't hear this twice." Conversations stopped. "At SMI, honor is not a word. It's the stone under your boots. Step off it and you will fall. Last night was proof. Eat your chow."

That was all. They left to a silence you could fold and put in your pocket.

Back in the barracks, superstition bloomed like mold in damp corners. Rats tied and retied laces at their doors. One kid from C Company ringed his nameplate with shoe polish as if to keep bad luck from smearing it. A Catholic Rat touched the tiny medal under his blouse before he stepped into the hall. Another wouldn't cross the threshold near Kelly's room; he took the long way to the latrine and pretended the detour was for speed.

Cadre leveraged it the way a blacksmith uses heat.

"Cheaters don't sleep on my stoop," a sergeant said at noon formation. "They vanish. Let that save me breath."

Ethan lasted through morning classes without hearing a word the instructors said. In Advanced Military History the maps looked like puzzles designed to be unsolved. In Calculus the numbers marched by in ranks he couldn't join. Twice he realized he'd been staring at the margin and tracing a rhythm with his thumbnail: rat—…a—tat.

He found Jack behind the gym where the wall baked in late sun and the dumpsters baked in their own way. No cadre back there, just air that smelled like rubber, grass, and hot brick. They leaned against the wall, elbows touching mortar.

"It's still in my ears," Ethan said, softly. "I keep thinking about him in a motel. What do you even say to your dad? 'Hey, we're not allowed to say my name anymore.'"

Jack rolled his shoulders as if the set of them bothered him. "You don't say anything. You move. You work. You don't give them a reason to read yours."

"It feels… medieval," Ethan said. "Like they like the spectacle."

Jack's mouth made a shape that wasn't quite a smirk. "Yeah. And that's why it works. They don't whisper consequences here, they parade them. Scares the hell out of the rest of us." He looked over, eyes flinty. "So don't give them an opening, Skunk. Not one."

They stood like that a while, letting the heat pull the moisture from their shirts. A freshman team jogged past at the corners of the field, knees high, arms chopping, a corporal barking cadence that had nothing to do with drums and still made Ethan flinch.

By afternoon drill the Corps moved like a single machine. You could feel the fear sharpened into precision—heels hitting crisp, rifles flipping tight, commands caught in the air and executed like the air itself had order arms. The cadre didn't shout as much. They didn't need to. Every Rat had seen the syllabus.

On fourth stoop at study hour, Ethan pretended to read the Rat Bible again. The words swam. We will not lie, cheat, or steal… His eyes slid to the blank patch where Kelly's name had been. Somebody had run a fingernail along the stone and left a thin white crescent, a mark the mop had missed or ignored. He couldn't stop seeing it.

A sophomore stuck his head into the room. "Cole. Reynolds. Tours will form at 2000 for those with Specials. Square yourselves away and don't be late." He looked at the empty corner of the stoop and amended, "Don't be stupid."

Jack lifted his chin. "We'll be there."

When the bell rang for penalty tours, Ethan shouldered a rifle and joined the slow orbit of the courtyard. The loop felt longer than last week's laps, and the rifle stock dug into a spot already sore. Jack passed him on the opposite arc and gave the tiniest nod, a move you'd miss if you weren't looking for it.

"Keep stepping," Jack murmured on the cross. "No holes."

Above them, upperclassmen leaned on railings and watched the parade of the flawed with the detachment of men watching rain. One of them, a firstie Ethan only knew as "Red" for the color of his hair, called down in a voice that carried just far enough, "Hear that, Rats? That quiet? That's the sound of a name being swallowed."

Some of the marching Rats looked up. Ethan didn't. He kept his eyes on the line of his world—the seam of the courtyard, the barrel shadow sliding ahead of his boot, the next step and the next and the next. The drum wasn't there. His body kept supplying it anyway.

Back in the room, after taps, Jack spoke into the dark.

"We're not them," Jack said. "We don't lie, we don't cheat, we don't steal, and we don't tolerate. Say it."

Ethan stared at the underside of the bunk above him. The pledge felt like a rock he could hold in his hand. He breathed once, and then again.

"We don't," he said.

"Louder."

"We don't," Ethan repeated, and a piece of the drumbeat loosened its teeth.

On the stoop, someone coughed. A fan clicked as it turned. Somewhere far off, a train's horn dragged a long line over the hills. Ethan listened hard, expecting the phantom cadence to come striding back out of the dark.

It didn't. Not yet.

But he understood now that SMI didn't need to strike the drum every night. Once you'd heard it, you did the rest yourself.

Sunday brought chapel formation, white gloves and hard shoes, the Corps aligned by company and height until the whole yard looked gridded by a draftsman's hand. A breeze lifted the flags, took the edge off the heat, and pushed the faint smell of brass polish from the ranks. Ethan stood in that clean geometry and felt the absence more than the order—the way a perfect line can still hold a missing point.

They marched past first-floor stoop where Kelly's door was shut now, not open and airless. A new nameplate waited in masking tape, blank—space reserved for whatever freshman would inherit the room and the silence that went with it. The Corps kept moving. That was the lesson too.

After service, the barracks ran on weekend rules—lighter, which at SMI meant merely less brutal. Cadre were fewer and further between. Sun laid squares of light on the stoop. A ratty paperback did a slow migration down the hall—The Old Man and the Sea, its cover soft as cloth from too many hands. Someone left a tin of Kiwi open on a windowsill, a black flower in a metal cup.

Ethan decided to clean. Not because a cadre had said so— because he needed to do something that had a beginning and an end. He took apart his rifle on a towel, lined the pieces like bones, oiled and reassembled until the bolt slid like thought. He pulled his blouses one by one and shaved loose threads from seams with a razor. He ironed covers until the piping lay straight enough to please a plumb line. The work steadied him the way numbers did.

Jack came back from the gym with a sheen of sweat and a look that said he'd been outrunning something on the track. He watched Ethan crease a sleeve with the heel of his hand.

"You'd make a tailor nervous," Jack said.

Ethan kept his eye on the crease. "It's the only thing today I can control."

Jack leaned in the doorway, arms folded. "Then control it. All of it." He tapped Ethan's temple. "Start here."

Later, on an errand to the guard desk for fresh Brasso, Ethan hit the test he and Jack had promised each other they'd never fail. It lay on the third step like a cold coin of sun: a twenty-dollar bill, crisp enough to cut. Two sophomores lounged on second stoop, talking too casually. Across the courtyard, a firstie with binoculars pretended to be very interested in the pigeons on the armory roof.

Ethan didn't think. He lifted the bill between forefinger and thumb like evidence and called out without turning his head, voice clear enough to bounce.

"Twenty on deck!"

The sophomores flinched a fraction. The firstie's binoculars stopped pretending.

"Guard desk," Ethan said to the air. He kept walking. At the counter he put the bill down and said, "Found on third stoop." The corporal behind the blotter looked bored and disappointed at the same time.

"Logged," the corporal said, scratching in the ledger. He slid a tin of Brasso across. "Don't smear it."

Back on fourth stoop, Jack raised an eyebrow.

"Trap," Ethan said.

"Sprung," Jack replied, the word clipped and satisfied. He didn't say good. He didn't need to.

That evening brought tours again for the unlucky and the careless. Ethan wasn't on the list, but he laced his boots and walked down anyway. Jack glanced over, surprised.

"You don't have to," he said.

"I know." Ethan settled his cover. "I'm going to walk a lap with you."

They stepped onto the slow orbit. The rifle on Jack's shoulder rode easy; he carried weight like a man born for it.

Ethan walked empty-handed, matching cadence. He could feel eyes on them from the upper rails—why is Cole there if he's not on the sheet?—but the questions stayed in throats. You don't heckle a Rat for marching more than he owes.

Two laps. Three. The courtyard took on the strange, meditative quality it only got at dusk, when the light stopped arguing and everything admitted the day was ending. Somewhere a radio in a firstie room put out a thin thread of country music—authorized by class, loud enough to be heard by accident. The melody snagged on stone and drifted away.

"Drum's quieter today," Jack said at last.

"It's still there," Ethan answered. "Just… further back."

"Keep it there," Jack said. "Make it useful."

After taps, the barracks breathed like a sleeping animal. Ethan lay on his back, hands flat on the blanket, and tested the silence for that phantom cadence. What came instead was the hollow clack of a night guard's baton meeting his boot heel at the corner—two taps, routine, not ritual. He let his shoulders sink.

He thought of Kelly again, but the image shifted—not a motel this time, just the blank of a life that had to be rewritten. He wondered if the boy would be a mechanic, or a lineman, or a man who never told anyone about a night with a drum. He wondered if he'd ever stop hearing it.

Across the room, Jack spoke into the dark. "Hey, Skunk."

"Yeah."

"We're not going to be names they say," Jack said. It wasn't bravado. It sounded like a plan. "We're going to be names nobody has to say because we did it right."

Ethan turned that over and felt something click into place, the way a bolt finds home. The Honor System's edges were still sharp enough to cut, but the shape of it made sense now:

not just a threat, a boundary. A line you could choose to step inside and stay.

"Then we do it right," he said.

"Then we do it right," Jack repeated, like a cadence only two people could hear.

On the wall, the ratty paperback slept under a paperweight. On the sill, the open Kiwi had dried to a dull skin. Somewhere down on first stoop, a door eased open and closed; a Dyke checking that his Rat's shoes would pass muster at reveille. The place worked on itself even in the dark.

When sleep finally took him, Ethan dreamed of marching—but it wasn't the drum this time. It was the steady, ordinary rhythm of boots moving in step because the men wearing them chose to. He woke once, late, and realized the beat in his chest had slowed to the pace of his breathing.

SMI hadn't let go of him. It wouldn't. But he had found a way to stand inside it without letting it hollow him out: one crease ironed straight, one twenty turned in, one lap walked he didn't owe, one word kept with a friend.

What stays after the drum fades isn't fear, he thought. It's what you decide to hold.

Chapter 17 — The Forced March

When Ethan filled out his Southern Military Institute application, the question felt like a trap disguised as courtesy.

Do you have any allergies?

He'd grown up as the punchline—spring pollen turning his face blotchy, mystery picnic foods making his throat itch, EpiPen lectures from the school nurse. But at SMI, weakness wasn't a medical note; it was a target. He stared at the little box until the paper blurred. Then he checked No, sealed the envelope, and mailed it like he was mailing a version of himself he wished were true.

By October, that lie began to hunt him.

Saturday rose cold and thin, a blade of a Virginia morning. Rats rolled out to the sinks, faces numb under water that never quite got warm, razors skipping over the new geography of red, sandpaper chins. Uniforms went on hard and exact: gray blouses, creases like rules, boots that spoke in hard syllables on stone. Dykes inspected, corrected, dismissed. The flag climbed. The courtyard filled with the hollow thunder of formation.

In the mess hall, Ethan moved with the line, tray in both hands, eyes on the stainless counter the way Rats were taught to—see nothing, want nothing, be nothing but efficient. Most mornings he could navigate the danger without looking afraid: bread over gravy, fruit over unknowns, coffee poured black and safe. Today the corporal on the serving line—five-foot-five, all blade—snatched the tray from his fingers and slapped down a scoop of eggs, a biscuit, two links of sausage.

"Eat, Rat," he said without looking. "You'll need it."

The smell reached Ethan before the doubt could. Not pork. Sharper. Wrong. Chicken sausage: the cheap kind, spiced to taste like something else. His throat tightened at the thought, a phantom itch blooming behind his tongue. He should speak. He should say I can't.

But the Honor System had no mercy for past-tense honesty. Admitting an allergy now was admitting he'd lied then. Lying meant the Court. The Court meant a drum in the night and a life folded up like a uniform you no longer had the right to wear.

He lifted a fork, forced it through the casing, chewed and swallowed like swallowing a dare. The table clattered around him. Jack, three seats down, had his head bent over his tray, inhaling calories like a man loading a kiln. He didn't see Ethan hesitate.

They formed up in the chill outside, rucks on, rifles balanced, breath smoking from shaved scalps. The cadre laid out the terms without poetry: Eighteen miles. Mountain road. Keep up or get left. Then the column bent itself to the gravel and began to move.

Jack took to it like he'd been waiting all week to be allowed to hurt. The fifty-pound pack sat on him like it belonged there. He cracked a line to the Rat behind him, got a strangled laugh, started humming something off-key and defiant—"Country Roads," just to irritate the Virginians. Cadre barked pace. Boots answered. The ridge line unspooled ahead in a brown-and-gold ribbon.

Two miles in, Ethan's chest began to cinch. It didn't feel like the usual climb-strain, the muscular squeeze of effort; it felt chemical, a tightening from the inside that ignored willpower. By mile three, his ears throbbed, his tongue felt thick, and the world narrowed at the edges like someone was slowly pinching the frame of his vision. He fixed on Jack's shoulders a few files over, broad and steady, and made a simple private vow: one more step.

One more step. One more. The gravel seemed to blur under his boots, the sound of the column—boots, breath, bark—sliding away like it was happening behind glass. He swallowed and found his throat sandpaper-dry. He tried to lift his hand. It didn't feel like his.

The road tilted. Or he did.

He went down without drama. No stumble, no act of theater. One moment he was part of the machine; the next there was just a Rat-shaped absence in the moving line and a body on the shoulder of the road.

"RAT DOWN!" someone found the air to shout.

Everything stuttered. The cadence blew apart. Cadre converged—shadow, brass, boot leather—voices hard and layered.

"Pack off—"

"Check airway—"

"What did he eat—"

"Eyes open, Cole! Stay with me!"

Ethan tried. The sky above the ridge looked bleached. Faces leaned in, edges too bright. The five-foot-five corporal who'd barked Eat an hour ago appeared at his shoulder, dropped his own ruck like it was nothing, and in one hard, practiced motion hauled Ethan across his back in a fireman's carry.

"Don't you die on me, Cole," he grunted, and started to run.

Three miles. Gravel spitting, boots slamming, the column stuttering around the absence, cadre sprinting ahead to flag the medic truck, Jack turning his head mid-march and going stone-still for a heartbeat as he took it in—the small man under the weight, the big one atop it, Ethan's limp hand bobbing with each stride.

Jack's fists opened and closed against his rifle sling, knuckles white. There was nothing to hit. Nothing to fix with force. So he did the only thing the road allowed: he kept moving. He made room for the medic truck when it shouldered past. He stared front and swallowed the taste of copper.

At the ambulance, the corporal lowered Ethan like he was setting down something he didn't trust the ground with. Doors flew. Hands took over. A mask covered Ethan's face. Someone shouted numbers. The rig swallowed him. For a moment, Jack saw his friend's eyes—wide and far away—then the doors clanged and the siren lifted like a blade into the cold morning.

The column re-formed. The road waited. A cadre's voice found the cadence again.

"Step it out. Move."

The ride in the ambulance existed in shards. Oxygen hiss. Gloves snapping. Someone calling out numbers like they were trying to count him back into his body.

"Pressure tanking—"

"Pulse… single digits—"

"Epinephrine now."

Fire in his thigh, heat flooding his chest, a ceiling light smearing into a comet. The next thing he knew, the world came back all at once—too bright, too loud, a machine beeping with bossy certainty. A masked nurse leaned over him, calm eyes in a storm. Someone lifted his wrist, squeezed, nodded.

"Back with us, Mr. Cole."

Ethan tried to answer and found his tongue felt enormous, his throat sandpaper-dry. Sound came out as a croak.

"Easy," the nurse said. "You had a severe anaphylactic reaction. You're safe now."

Safe. The word felt like a blanket he didn't deserve.

A doctor appeared, sleeves pushed up, chart in hand. "You've got a poultry allergy," he said, no drama, just the cleanness of fact. "That sausage did it. We've started steroids and antihistamines to calm the system. You'll go home with an auto-injector. Use it if your throat tightens or hives spread. Then 911. No bravado."

Ethan blinked. "My file—" he rasped. "SMI… the form…"

The doctor's eyes flicked up, quick and knowing. "Your medical file says 'anaphylaxis—poultry confirmed.' That's what needs to be there to keep you breathing. Who you were last month is less important than you being alive next month." He tucked the chart under his arm. "We'll keep you a few hours for observation."

When the curtain whispered shut, the shame arrived, clean and cold. He hadn't lied to get out of trouble. He had lied to get in. And almost didn't get out again.

He dozed in the rubbery half-sleep hospitals hand out. When he woke for real, Jack was in the chair by the bed, elbows on his knees, big frame folded small.

"You scared the hell outta me, Skunk," Jack said without preamble.

"Guess… I'm not as invincible as you," Ethan managed.

"You were never invincible." Jack tried to grin and couldn't find it. "You were blue, man. Like a fish that jumped on the dock. Don't do that again."

"Working on it," Ethan said, and the joke was thin but it held.

Jack leaned back, eyes on the heart monitor like he was bargaining with it. "They said you'll carry a pen now."

"Yeah."

"Good." He sat up. "You tell your Dyke?"

"Not yet." The shame flared again, hot. "I'll have to. Medical… they're logging it."

"Then you tell him before someone else does," Jack said. "On your feet, not your knees."

An hour later the curtain moved and the corporal stepped in—five-foot-five of purpose, cap under his arm, eyes that did not look away. Ethan pushed himself upright.

"Sir," he started. "Thank you."

The corporal waved it off with something almost like irritation. "You keep your lungs working next time," he said. Then his gaze softened by a degree. "You owe me a pair of boots. I ran the heels off mine."

"I'll shine them till they blind you," Ethan said, voice ragged.

"You'll march them off again," the corporal replied, but there was a faint crease at the corner of his mouth as he left. The curtain fell back into place, the visit already turning into a story.

The monitor beeped steady as a metronome. Ethan stared at the ceiling tiles and replayed the checkbox he'd lied on—No allergies—and the moment a five-foot-five corporal threw him over a shoulder and ran. SMI could shred you, but it would also carry you when you fell. He palmed the plastic of the EpiPen the nurse had left and decided he'd never lie on a form again, not about something that could end a life.

By evening, the IV was out, a packet of instructions and a bright yellow EpiPen were in his bag, and he was cleared to return to barracks with two days of light duty. Jack walked him to the truck in silence, hands shoved into his campaign sleeves like he didn't trust them.

Back at SMI, news traveled fast but sideways. Rats didn't ask; they glanced and cataloged. A few clapped Ethan's shoulder as he passed. One kid muttered, "Hardcore," like almost dying was a flex. Another, pale and sincere, whispered, "Glad you're back," and fled before Ethan could answer.

Tran, his Dyke, listened in his usual unreadable stillness while Ethan delivered the facts in clipped sentences:

"Anaphylaxis. Chicken. EpiPen here." Tran tapped the injector once, nodded, and handed it back.

"You tell the mess line you pass poultry," Tran said. "If anyone gives you grief, they can come see me."

Ethan blinked. He'd expected a lecture about weakness, a scalpel of contempt. Instead he got logistics.

"Yes, sir."

Tran's gaze held him a moment longer. "Next time you think lying makes you harder, remember today."

"Yes, sir," Ethan said again, and the words sat different in his mouth.

That night, the barracks smelled the same—sweat baked into stone, polish, starch. The parade deck outside glowed a dull silver under the moon. Sounds fell into their familiar places: boots, doors, a laugh ill-timed and punished immediately. Ethan lay on his bunk, the EpiPen on the shelf where his hand could find it in the dark, the humiliation and gratitude braided together in a knot he couldn't pull apart.

Jack appeared in the doorway, hands full: a pilfered orange from somewhere, a plastic cup of ice, contraband kindness.

"You're on light duty," Jack said. "So I'll complain on your behalf. My feet hate you for making me finish that march."

"Your feet hate everyone," Ethan said, and this time the grin found both of them. Jack tipped the cup of ice into Ethan's hand.

The next morning he reported to the mess line early, shoulders square. He met the same corporal's eyes across the steam table.

"Poultry allergy," Ethan said. The words no longer stuck.

The corporal nodded once, clipped and practical, then ladled eggs onto a tray with a gap like a small respect.

"Don't pass out in my line again," he said.

"No, sergeant."

By Wednesday, the rhythm folded him back in—a shorter version, modified and watchful. He ran stairs without a pack, then with an empty one, then with ten pounds. Cadre yelled as they always had. Jack barked at him to hydrate like he'd invented water. Tran stopped him at the top of the stoop one afternoon, placed a hand flat on his chest for one slow count, then took it away as if confirming the engine still turned.

What changed was inside. He ate carefully and without apology. He showed the pen to the Rat in his room and to the one who bunked across the hall, said, "If I go quiet and my face goes red, you stab me right here," tapping his thigh, then added, "and call the medic." He didn't try to turn it into a joke. He didn't need to.

Jack went the other direction. The forced march had carved something into him—clean lines, hard edges. He seemed taller, though he wasn't. He looked like he'd tasted the road and wanted more. When he laughed now, it had a new sound, low and satisfied, like a man who'd discovered the lever that moved him and planned to pull it often.

One night on the stoop, the air brittle and honest, Jack bumped Ethan's shoulder with his own.

"You didn't quit," he said.

"I fell over," Ethan answered.

"You didn't quit," Jack repeated, and made it a verdict. "Different thing."

Ethan watched his breath lift away and disappear. The drum from a past midnight lived somewhere in his bones. The road that had almost killed him stretched ahead in a hundred other forms: inspections, courts, sweat parties, the quiet traps of small decisions. He could see the shape of the place more clearly now—how it broke and bound, punished and protected.

SMI didn't make sense if you looked at it in one direction. But if you turned it in your hands, the contradictions clicked like parts of a rifle. The same man who stripped you for a crooked sling would carry you three miles when your throat began to close. The same system that humiliated you for a Walkman would log your allergy so exact the mess line turned their ladles.

He wasn't forgiven. He wasn't fearless. But he was still here.

He closed his eyes for a moment, let the cold burn his lungs, and opened them again on the lit rectangles of barracks windows—the hive he belonged to, whether he wanted to or not. The EpiPen weighed almost nothing on the shelf. The truth of it weighed more. He could carry both.

Light duty lasted forty-eight hours, which at Southern Military Institute felt like a rumor. On the third morning, Ethan buttoned his blouse with deliberate fingers, slid the EpiPen into the sewn-on pocket Tran had ordered him to add to his trouser seam, and reported for formation.

"Canteen?" Tran asked.

"Full, sir."

"Pen?"

Ethan tapped the pocket. "Here."

Tran's chin dipped once. Approval, SMI-style.

Word of the collapse had filtered through the Corps and then thinned into the background hum. Nobody said "allergy" to his face. They said "you good?" with a glance at his throat, or they said nothing and made space a half-step to his left in ranks, just enough that if he fell again he wouldn't take anyone with him. It was more kindness than anyone would admit to.

That evening, while most of Bravo Company attacked equations under fluorescent light, Ethan sat cross-legged on the floor of the corporal's room, buffing a pair of boots he had, technically, not scuffed.

"You said shine 'til they blind you," Ethan muttered, working the toe in tight circles. "I'm aiming for solar eclipse."

Across the room, the corporal grunted—noncommittal, but he didn't take the boots back. When Ethan set them on the desk, the leather caught the lamp and threw it back in a hard, clean line. The corporal looked at the reflection, then at Ethan.

"You keep that pen close," he said, softer than a shout, which for him counted as something like gratitude. "And you speak up in the line. Nobody wants a repeat."

"Yes, sergeant."

"Good. Now get out. You're ugly and you're blocking the light."

It was almost a joke. It landed like mercy.

Two Saturdays later, the company roster posted a six-mile conditioning march. Not eighteen. Six. Rucks at twenty pounds, rifles slung. The route cut along the same spine of road that had eaten him.

At first formation, Jack slid into place beside him, massive and loose, like he was already chewing the miles.

"You don't have to do this," Jack said under his breath.

"I do," Ethan said. And found that he meant it.

They stepped off at dawn, boots ticking the asphalt, breath white in the brittle air. The pack bit but did not crush. Ethan had eaten carefully—toast, fruit, black coffee—and checked the labels on the powdered eggs himself. Tran had signed his chow card like a countersign. He counted his inhale for four steps, his exhale for five, settling into a rhythm that felt like learning a song by ear.

Mile three was where he had gone down last time. The shoulder of the road there was rougher, scattered with gravel the color of old teeth. He felt his pulse jump as the curve rose to meet them, an involuntary memory—the way the sky had tilted, the sudden weight of the ruck like a hand on the back of his neck.

"Left, left, left-right-left," Jack called lazily from the next file over. It wasn't an official cadence. It was a rope.

Ethan tightened the shoulder straps one notch, slid a hand over the EpiPen to feel its shape, and kept moving. He didn't push the fear away. He packed it, neatly, beside the water and the pen.

"Hydrate," Jack said without looking.

Ethan drank.

At mile five, the road flattened and broke into a broad view of the valley. The sun had shaken itself awake and was laying copper over the fields. Cadre rotated down the line with their usual mix of threat and encouragement.

"How's the throat, Cole?" one barked.

"Open, sir," Ethan said.

"Keep it that way."

"Yes, sir."

They turned the last corner and the barracks came into sight—stone shouldering into sky, parade deck a dark rectangle. Ethan's calves twitched, a warning. He shortened his stride by a hair, refused to sprint. He crossed through the arch not with a finish-line lunge but with enough left in his legs to stand at attention without swaying.

"Time," someone called.

"Within," someone else answered, and that was the real grade.

Jack bumped him with an elbow as they stepped off their rucks. "Look at that," he said. "Mile nine comes for you, and you walk it at five."

Ethan snorted. "Math checks out."

Jack grinned. "Nerd."

"Meathead."

They laughed, and the laugh didn't crack.

The next week handed Ethan a different test in a smaller box: an inspection Special for a loose gear strap. He could feel the fork in the road—the old instinct to explain it away, to write a paragraph that was really a plea. He remembered the Superintendent's eyes on his last "wish to explain." He remembered the drum.

He wrote in neat block letters:

Offense: Loose strap on ruck.

Response: Correct.

Five tours. He marched them without chewing the inside of his cheek to shreds, without narrating a defense to himself. Rifle across his shoulder, he watched the light turn honey along the top edges of stone and decided this, too, was conditioning.

On the fourth lap, he looked up to see his corporal on the stoop, posture accidentally casual, boots he had shined catching a seam of light. The corporal didn't nod. He didn't need to.

Jack's reward for the march came more public. The company commander pulled him after PT and handed him a strip of cloth and a weight.

"Guidon bearer," the lieutenant said. "Try not to hit anyone with it."

Jack tried to look unmoved and failed. The next morning, he stood at the front of Bravo with the guidon pole braced, pennant snapping in the brittle breeze while the Rats formed behind him. He didn't look back, but when Ethan fell in, he felt taller for it. Pride borrowed is still pride.

Tran appeared at Ethan's shoulder without sound. "You did not fall," he said.

"No, sir."

"Good." A pause, brief as a blink. "Protect your yes. Do not say it to things that kill you."

"Yes, sir," Ethan said, and filed the sentence where he kept the EpiPen.

That night they sat on the fourth stoop with paper cups of contraband powdered lemonade that tasted like cold chalk, the parade deck set in shadow like a stage waiting on actors. Somewhere below, someone laughed too loud and was corrected immediately. Fans hummed in windows. The world felt held.

"You know what I was thinking," Jack said, "when we crossed that bend where you ate gravel?"

"Enlighten me."

"How I wanted to carry you then." He looked annoyed at his own honesty. "Hated that I couldn't."

"You did," Ethan said. "Just… later."

Jack considered that, then let it stand. "You gonna tell your mom about the allergy?"

"Yeah," Ethan said, surprising himself. "And what it means. And that I'm not dead."

"Add that last part," Jack said. "She'll like it."

They watched the barracks windows glow and go dark and glow again as rooms cycled through their evening drills. Ethan thought about the lie in a box on some admissions shelf and the truth written everywhere else now—in the mess line, on his gear, in his squad's heads. He thought about the man who had called cadence at the edge of his collapse and about the one who had carried him three miles. He thought about the battery of small choices that would make up the rest of his year.

"Hey," Jack said, as if remembering something, then let it go. "Never mind. Save it for tomorrow."

"For what?"

"Whatever they throw," Jack said, and for once it didn't sound like a dare. It sounded like a plan.

Ethan tugged his collar straight, felt the pen's light weight against his leg, the heavier weight of what he knew now. He wasn't invincible, and he wasn't broken. He was exactly what the place made you if you let it and fought it at the same time: alert, stubborn, honest when it counted.

The night settled deeper. Somewhere distant, a drum from memory tapped once and faded. He breathed in for four, out for five, and the math worked. Tomorrow would ask again. He'd answer.

Chapter 18 — Breakout

Southern Military Institute never promised redemption. It promised a system. Break you down, then build you back the way the stone walls preferred. Recognition—Breakout—didn't live on a calendar. It lived in the moment the Corps decided you'd earned a name.

That winter, the fuse was blood.

The Fight at the Frat House

A Rat slipped the wire one Friday—crossed into the civilian campus with his haircut and his hunger showing. The bar he found was dark and sticky, pitchers sweating on scarred wood, cheap beer trying hard to taste like freedom. He called to a girl as if he were already part of their world.

She wasn't.

Her boyfriend and his friends introduced him to the alley— brick, snow, and fists. By the time they lost interest, the Rat's face had been remapped. Teeth on the ground, a halo of red where his cheek met ice.

News runs fast in a place built on cadence. It sprinted the length of the stoops in under an hour.

"They jumped one of ours," a Rat said, flat as a verdict.

Jack didn't bother with words. His fists closed as if they'd rehearsed it.

That night, Bravo and Alpha didn't need orders. Nearly four hundred Rats pulled on BDUs and moved as one tide across the frozen quad, boots laying down a drumline the civilians had never heard. The fraternity house looked smaller with their formation filling the street. Someone rang the bell. Someone else didn't wait. The door gave. Windows turned to sugar. Voices became noise and then became the kind of quiet that happens after a storm has done its arithmetic.

They didn't stay. They didn't need to. They came home in step, steam rising from their shoulders, knuckles split, eyes bright in a way the barracks hadn't seen since August.

Waiting at the arch, the RDC president stood with his hands behind his back, face cut from stone. "All Rats are confined," he said, voice carrying. Then the corner of his mouth moved—so small you could argue you imagined it. "And I could not be prouder. That is how we take care of our brothers."

Ethan felt it land. Not fear. Not performance. Something older. His ribs ached with it.

The Week Before Breakout

The Institute doesn't let a fire burn without feeding it. February tightened like a tourniquet. Sleep went thin. The hour hand meant nothing.

"RATS, UP!"

Flashlights combed bunks, sheets snapped from bodies, boots pounded tile. Into parade dress at 0100, out on the deck at 0104, running the perimeter with the brass biting your collarbones. Back inside at 0217, stripped to shirtsleeves and dumped into a classroom that smelled of chalk and damp wool, handed a surprise quiz on SMI founders while sweat marked the paper. Pencils down before you finished writing the date. Back to the hill. Back to the deck. Back to the corridor for wall-sits until your quads shook like bare wiring.

Behind the barracks, the fire department hosed the slope every afternoon until the ground went from frozen to treacherous to something between the two. A black-brown glisten laid over clay and grass until it looked like an animal crouched and breathing in the cold.

"Breakout," someone whispered on the stoop, as if the word itself could trigger it.

Ethan learned how to nap standing up—chin tucked, eyes locked forward, brain slipping for ninety seconds at a time and returning at the first scrape of a boot. He learned the shape of his EpiPen through fabric without looking. He learned there were versions of hunger you could name and deeper ones you couldn't. Jack didn't grow quieter. He grew sharper, like steel drawn to a colder edge. He ate the miles in PT and spat out the last rep with a grin that made cadre bark louder.

On the third night without a real sleep, Ethan and Jack sat hip-to-hip on the fourth stoop, cups of contraband lemon powder pretending to be a drink.

"You feel it?" Jack asked, voice low.

"What."

"They're not asking anything new. Just more of it, all at once."

Ethan watched the hill shine under the floodlights. "You think that makes us ready?"

Jack's mouth twitched. "It makes me hungry."

Ethan didn't trust that hunger. But he trusted Jack.

By Thursday, boys were moving like ghosts—hollowed eyes, lips cracked, uniforms polish-sharp over bodies that looked like they'd been boiled down to tendon and will. Cadre took attendance not with names but with stares that counted souls. Tran Nguyen stopped Ethan in a hallway and checked the pen with two fingers, a small nod serving as both order and permission.

On Friday before dawn the bugle cut the dark in a clean line. The stoops filled in seconds. A cold wind came off the valley and moved through shaved heads, through gray wool, through the place where nerves end and resolve begins.

"Formation!" someone shouted, but they were already in it.

They marched past the arch, past the chapel, past the place Ethan still heard drums when it was quiet. The Corps—nine hundred strong—was already there when they rounded the corner to the back slope. Upperclassmen ringed the hill in four tight ranks, boots planted, shoulders squared. From a distance the formation looked like a single body—a wall with a heartbeat.

The floodlights made the mud glow. It was not a hill anymore. It was an idea.

Alpha Company was called to the line.

Jack rolled his shoulders once, like a boxer. He didn't look at Ethan but his voice found him anyway, casual as a tossed coin. "See you at the top."

Ethan swallowed air that tasted like iron and turned his eyes to the crest. He searched for Tran and didn't find him.

The whistle came down like a blade.

The whistle sliced the cold. Alpha Company hit the mud like a thrown net.

Upperclassmen poured down the slope in a living avalanche—hands, knees, forearms, boots—turning the hill into a churn of bodies. Rats tried to climb; the Corps taught them gravity. Faces went in first. Mud found mouths and ears. Shoulders were wrenched back by collars. Every foot of gain came with a fist in the ribs or a boot grinding a hand from its hold.

Jack took the first hit like it was a greeting and the second like it was advice. He rolled to his knee, slid, found a root, planted. Someone hooked his ankle and yanked; he rode the slip, came up laughing through gritted teeth, eyes fixed high.

"Down, Reynolds!" a voice barked, and three cadets converged. Jack dropped his shoulder and drove, not through them but into the space they didn't own yet. For every shove, he gave two inches of compliance and stole three inches of hill on the recoil. He didn't look for help; he looked for a seam.

At the crest, Captain Harris stood like a standard—cap perfect, brass clean even in the misted light. He didn't move at first. He didn't have to. He let the Corps teach Jack the lesson, let the slope write its argument across Jack's uniform. Then, when the scrum tightened, when five bodies made a gate that opened and closed with elbows, Harris stepped down two strides, reached in, and found Jack's sleeve.

"Move, Reynolds," he said, voice low, as if they were alone. "Earn it."

Fingers like a winch. Jack clawed. Harris pulled. Hands slapped at their grip and missed. Mud gave and took and gave. Jack's knee slid, hit a rock, lit a flare up his thigh; he swore once and kept going. A cadet got both hands on his webbing and yanked; Harris bared his teeth and hauled harder. For a moment they were a single engine—effort knotted to expectation.

Jack's palm hit the crest. The world changed angle. He rolled over the lip, came flat on his back in the runoff, chest heaving, grin wide and ugly with mud.

"On your feet," Harris said, not unkindly.

Jack got up. He turned, looked down, and found Ethan in the sea below—just a quick flash of shaved head, then bodies over him again. The grin drained from Jack's face. He didn't call out. You weren't allowed to from the top.

"Bravo Company!" The call cracked across the formation.

Ethan stepped into the pit.

The cold licked through his uniform with small, precise teeth. He took two quick breaths—shallow, measured— touched the EpiPen shape against his thigh without looking, and raised his eyes to the rim one last time. He searched for Tran Nguyen's narrow shoulders, the straight line of his cap.

Nothing.

The whistle blew.

Hands found him. A forearm across the mouth. Someone palmed the back of his head and pressed him into the slope like a stamp. Mud slid up his face and over his scalp. He tried to turn his cheek to breathe; a knee found his ribs and convinced him otherwise. Sound went muffled and big—roars traveling through earth and bone.

Up. He had to get up.

Ethan tucked his chin, turned his palms into paddles, and swam through clay. He found a root and pulled. Someone pried his fingers loose one by one. He kicked, boot heel skidding, came to his knees, took one hand's worth of hill—and a body rolled across his shoulders and dragged him back into the cold.

"Keep him down!" a voice laughed close to his ear.

He learned the hill's grammar by pain. If he fought straight, it punished him with weight. If he yielded a second, the press eased and he could steal a breath. He began to hunt for that beat between offense and pile-on, the half-syllable where bodies took air and hands shifted. In that thinnest of spaces, he planted a palm, a knee, a hope.

Time didn't pass so much as repeat. His lungs burned first, then his forearms, then the small muscles along his spine that he didn't know had names. His eyes stung; mud scratched glass. Somewhere a cadet's boot slipped and scraped skin from Ethan's knuckles; the sting was neat and bright, then lost to the general ache.

He reached the middle slope and saw sky. That was a mistake. Hands filled the sky. He went under again, face first, the world narrowing to pressure and the drum of his own heartbeat in the mud. A flash of panic—loud and stupid—rose in his chest. He buried it. Panic made thrashing; thrashing made piles; piles made stillness. He forced himself small, waited for that half-syllable, and surfaced with a cough that tasted like pennies.

"Where's your Dyke, Rat?" someone jeered.

Ethan didn't answer. Saving air was the only rule that mattered.

He clawed for another inch. And another. At some point his jaw caught a knee. Stars pulsed behind his eyes. He blinked them into smaller stars and kept going. A cadre crouched to his left, face inches from Ethan's. "Quit," he said conversationally, as if discussing weather. "You can sit it out and try again next year."

Ethan closed his mouth around a noise that wasn't a word and pushed.

At the crest, Dykes pulled their Rats over the lip, slapping backs, barking pride into faces they'd been barking at since August. Almost all of Bravo was up now—bent over, hands on thighs, steam rising from uniforms in ghost-threads that the floodlights loved. Down below, one form kept moving. Not cleanly. Not heroically. Just…moving.

Ethan didn't know he was last. He only knew there was still hill.

Minutes burned into him and left no ash. The world beyond the slope narrowed to pulses of sound—the Corps' chant, the whistle of breath in his own nose, a single barked "Enough!" from some nameless upperclassman when three cadets pressed him too long under. A hand he didn't recognize brushed his shoulder once—brief, almost a mistake—and was gone.

He reached a lip that wasn't the crest and mistook it for mercy. Bodies corrected him. He slid three feet, gouged his fingers into clay, saved two of those feet, lost them again, took one back. He was arithmetic done on a shaking table.

At some point—later, much later—a shadow came down from the ring and cut through the pack like it had rank. Two hands—gloved, strong, indifferent to ceremony—closed on Ethan's webbing and hauled.

"Up," the voice said with no flourish.

Ethan found his feet, lost them, found knees, lost those, found a scrap of purchase under his boot that held because the hand at his back made it hold. There was silence at the crest for a heartbeat—not the Corps, never that, but a small held breath—as the last Rat came over.

He rolled onto his side and didn't get up. The sky above the floodlights was the color of a new bruise. His chest heaved like a bellows with a hole in it. Mud had dried in a shell along his cheekbone. He tried to blink and felt grit scrape the whites of his eyes. The world went soft at the edges.

Voices blurred. Names were shouted—real names—Rats no longer Rats. Laughter cracked open along the ring, bright and too loud after so much night. Somewhere below, a mess-hall door boomed open and the smell of meat drifted up the hill—brown, rich, impossible.

Ethan turned his head toward it and saw nothing but gray.

"Medic!" someone called.

He didn't see the stretcher. He felt hands that weren't trying to teach a lesson lift him simple and clean. He let his body be carried, for once, and didn't argue with the dark coming in from the edges.

Jack stood at the crest with Harris, mud drying in a map across his face, and watched the stretcher move through the gap the Corps made without talking about why. He didn't move. He didn't shout Ethan's name. He put his palm flat to his own chest, once, as if to settle something searching there, and followed the flow down the hill toward the mess hall he'd spent months dreaming about. He paused at the door and looked back at the slick, gouged slope.

"Earned," Harris said, as if answering a question Jack hadn't asked.

Jack nodded, but the word didn't sit right. Not yet.

Ethan came back to consciousness in pieces: the sting in his eyes first, a high white burn each time he blinked; then the ache along his ribs, deep and specific, like fingers pressed under the bone; then the hum of the fluorescent light above him, an insect caught in glass. The sheets were too clean. The air smelled like alcohol and lemon. Hospital.

A nurse's face drifted into view, round and kind. "Welcome back, sweetheart." She checked the line taped to his arm, then the pulse at his wrist. "You gave the boys on the hill a scare."

He tried to speak and found gravel. "Did…we…?"

"You made it," she said, understanding the question he could manage. "All the way." She hesitated, then added, softer, "Happy birthday, by the way." She tapped the plastic bracelet on his wrist. "Nineteen today."

The word hit him like a misplaced laugh. Birthday. He let his eyes close a second and saw the hill again, the slope moving under him as if it were alive, the moment a hand—no one's he knew—had closed on his webbing and made up the difference. He didn't feel proud. He felt…empty, the sort of emptiness that follows a storm that somehow hasn't finished.

When he opened his eyes again, Jack sat in the chair by the bed, elbows on knees, hands knotted. Mud had dried in a map along Jack's jaw, cracking when he smiled.

"Hey, old man," Jack said. "Caught a nap?"

Ethan tried for a grin. It came out crooked. "How's the steak?"

Jack huffed. "Overrated." A beat. "They said you were last Rat up the hill." He didn't make it a question. "They said you wouldn't quit."

Ethan looked past him to the square of window, where the dawn was ironing color into the mountains. "Didn't have the option," he said.

Jack clicked his tongue. "That's the point." He glanced at the doorway, dropped his voice. "They recognized us last night. We're not Rats anymore." He let the words sit between them, strange and bright. "We're cadets."

The word should have warmed Ethan. Instead, it felt like he was hearing it from across a river. He found Jack's eyes. "Tran show?"

Jack's jaw tightened. "Didn't see him."

Ethan nodded once, as if agreeing to terms he hadn't read. "Figures."

"Doesn't matter," Jack said, too quickly. "You made it. That's what they'll remember."

A doctor came, then another, and then a volunteer with a tray that had nothing in common with steak. Jack stood, squeezed Ethan's shoulder once, hard. "I'm coming back tonight."

"You don't have to," Ethan said, and meant it two ways.

Jack gave the half-smile that always looked like a dare. "Yeah I do."

He was discharged the next afternoon with a bottle of eye drops, a ribbon of tape over his ribs, and a paper bag that held an EpiPen and a folded sheet of instructions he'd already memorized. The air outside bit his teeth; the sky was the blue you only got after a storm. The Institute's walls looked less like a cage and more like an old, blunt promise.

When he stepped back through the arch, the barracks breathed different. Conversations didn't stop when he walked past. Heads turned and didn't snap away. Names traveled openly—first names, last names, nicknames used without a sneer. The invisible line that had separated his class from everyone else had been pulled up like tape after a race.

"Cole," someone called from a second-floor stoop. Not Rat. "Good to see you upright."

He looked up. A third-classman with mud still under his nails raised a Coke in salute. Ethan lifted the paper bag in return and kept moving.

The room had been attacked by joy and left to heal on its own. Wet uniforms draped from bedposts. Someone's brass shone in small suns along a desk. Jack's boots sat on a towel, cleaned to the point they looked new. On Ethan's bunk: a mess-hall napkin crumpled around something heavy.

He unfolded the napkin. It was a steak bone, stripped clean, tied with a shoelace like a prize. On the napkin, in Jack's block letters: For the one who earned it twice. —J

Ethan snorted once—the sound halfway to a laugh, halfway to something else—and set the bone on his shelf like a joke he'd keep.

Evening brought the formal part. The Corps assembled on the parade deck under a sky being smudged into dusk. The class formed in a block—no longer in the desperate hush of Rats, but in the uneasy quiet of something still becoming itself. Company by company, Dykes stepped forward and called their men by name. There were handshakes that snapped like salutes, brief embraces disguised as corrections to collars, words too brief to be overheard.

Captain Harris found Jack, and the way he said "Mister Reynolds" turned the air. Harris pinned nothing—there was nothing to pin—but the gesture had weight anyway. Jack's chin lifted a fraction, then settled. He'd been taller since the hill.

When it was Bravo's turn, Ethan stood still, hands flat to his seams, and waited for a name that didn't come. Tran was a gap where a man should be. Ethan felt the eyes of others, not unkind, resting on his shoulders for a beat and then moving on.

An upperclassman from another company stepped into the space Tran had left.

"Cole," the cadet said simply, offering his hand. No flourish. No speech. Just a steady grasp and a nod that didn't pretend to be anything more. It was enough. It was not enough. Both truths fit.

"Thank you," Ethan said, and made sure his voice was level.

Afterward, the class flowed back to the stoops, loud in that stunned way that follows pain: laughter half a pitch too high, stories that already didn't match what had happened. Someone produced a boom box—the legal kind now—and let a guitar tumble into the lights. Not Buffett. Not a punishment. Just music.

Ethan stood with Jack at the railing and watched the parade deck take on its gentle night color. The oily sheen of the mud hill had been fenced off and already looked smaller from this angle, as if distance and ceremony could level it.

"You were alone a long time," Jack said, not looking at him.

"I wasn't, then." Ethan thumbed the EpiPen in his pocket, then let it go. "Somebody pulled. Not the one who should have. But somebody."

Jack's mouth worked, a thought traveling to speech and deciding against it. "We're done being Rats," he said instead.

Ethan listened to the word done and found how elastic it was. The Ratline was over. The work wasn't. The Court still waited for names. Tours would still be walked. Specials would still find pockets. The hill had given him a birthday he'd never forget and a mirror he didn't love—one that showed a boy who would drag himself forward an inch at a time even when no hand reached.

"Yeah," he said quietly. "We're done."

From somewhere below, a voice bellowed a first name with a joy that would have been punished last week. It bounced off the stone and came back as a chorus of answers. The barracks felt—if not kind—at least less cruel.

When the lights finally blinked for taps, Ethan and Jack didn't move right away. They stood until the deck emptied and the flag's halyards clicked softly against the pole in the small wind. At last Jack pushed off the rail.

"Tomorrow," he said, a promise disguised as a schedule.

"Tomorrow," Ethan agreed.

He killed the light in their room and lay back, ribs complaining. In the new quiet, he heard the familiar phantom: boots across stone, the echo that had once sounded like ghosts. Tonight it sounded different. Not the condemned. Not the condemned at all.

Marching. Forward.

Chapter 19 — Natty Bo

Part 1: Smuggling Freedom

Life after Breakout wasn't freedom. At Southern Military Institute, nothing that easy existed. But the leash loosened. The nights were quieter. No one ripped sheets off their bunks at 0200 just to count push-ups. No one held them under mud. The word "Rat" stopped slashing across the air like a whip, replaced—warily—with "fourth-classman."

For Jack, the change was visible. He walked the stoops like a man who finally fit the uniform that had tried to contain him. No five-five tyrant snapping in his face, no thin shoulders with big voices picking at him because they could. If anyone wanted to test him now, they thought better of it.

For Ethan, the change tasted better than it looked. He could sit in the mess hall at noon and eat. Not shovel in three bites and sprint. Not lunge and strain in a side room while "Margaritaville" mocked him from a Walkman he no longer owned. He put a fork in real food and didn't apologize for it. That felt like a small miracle.

The barracks breathed different, too. Voices carried without fear of being noticed; laughter rose and wasn't punished for trying. The parade deck still owned their feet, the Honor Court still owned their names, but the day-to-day pressure had eased just enough that you could lift your head and look around.

That's when Captain Harris slipped in a taste of the outside world.

He came at dusk, the stone of first stoop already giving back the day's heat. Harris wore it casual—gray undershirt, sleeves rolled, posture that said he was in charge without having to announce it. He tapped Jack's door with two knuckles and slid inside like the corridor belonged to him, which in a way it did.

Under his jacket: a case of brown bottles.

Jack's eyebrows went up. Ethan blinked once. Harris grinned.

"Don't make a mess," he said, setting the case on the floor. "And don't be stupid." Then he was gone, leaving the door clicking gently in the frame and thirty-six ounces of trouble sitting between them.

Ethan crouched, peeled back the soft cardboard. The label smiled up at him with that one-eyed sailor and a name that felt like a joke if you'd never had it: National Bohemian.

"Natty Bo," Jack said, like a secret handshake.

"How much?" Ethan asked, already knowing money would make the story better.

"Four bucks a case." Jack hooked a thumb toward the window as if the bargain itself were parked out on Washington Street. "You return the bottles, you get a dollar-fifty back."

Ethan snorted. "So we're drinking for two-fifty."

"Best deal in Virginia."

They cracked the first two. Caps skittered under Jack's bunk; foam climbed, slow and lazy, and spilled down Ethan's knuckles. The smell hit first—warm, skunky, metallic at the edges. He wrinkled his nose.

"Smells like the inside of a radiator," he said.

Jack raised his bottle anyway. "To surviving."

They clinked glass. The first swallow was worse than the smell—flat bread and rust with a little sun-baked cardboard thrown in. Ethan grimaced and laughed around it.

"Terrible," he said.

"Perfect," Jack countered.

Heat pressed into the room like a second ceiling. The barracks in summer didn't believe in mercy. No air conditioning, one fan somewhere down the stoop doing more rattling than moving air, windows open to a night that hummed with cicadas and didn't cool a thing. Sweat darkened their gray shirts and ran past their collarbones; the bottles grew slick in their hands.

They sat cross-legged on the floor, backs to opposite bunks, voices low enough not to carry. The talk started easy: Harris hinting at a starting spot next fall, the way the team's shape would change if Jack owned the middle; Dr. Maddox's note, a neat paragraph of praise that Ethan kept folded twice in his desk like a ration he didn't want to spend too fast. They worked through two more bottles and let silence have the room for a minute.

"Remember when a Friday night meant getting jumped into the mud?" Ethan said.

"Remember when a Friday night meant doing burpees to Jimmy Buffett non-stop?" Jack shot back.

Ethan raised his bottle in half salute. "Too soon."

They laughed. Not the nervous kind they'd learned to throw like chaff. The actual kind, the one that loosened something in your ribs. For the first time in months, nobody flinched at a bootstep outside the door.

He'd learned at SMI that moments of calm were always rented. But you could still enjoy what you'd paid for.

Jack tipped his bottle, studying the one-eyed sailor like he expected it to wink. "Tell me again how this costs four bucks."

"Less if you do the return," Ethan said. "We should be sending thank-you notes to Baltimore."

"Dear Natty Bo," Jack intoned, putting on the solemn voice he used when he wanted to make a joke sound like a prayer. "Thank you for your service."

Ethan choked on a laugh and wiped foam with the back of his hand. "Amen."

They made a plan—half kidding, half serious—to sneak the empties out past the guard to the grocer off Main, clink their way through a dollar-fifty, and pretend that accounting was a sport. They talked about Christmas leave—who might fly home, who had to drive, whether ribs healed faster if you pretended they didn't hurt. Jack was certain of the future the way some men are certain of sunrise.

"Next year," he said, and his eyes got that fixed, faraway look he wore on the last mile of anything, "we won't be scraping. We'll be handing out pain, not receiving it."

Ethan nodded, not because he believed in the math but because he believed in Jack believing. He set his empty on the floor between his heels and watched the glass settle.

"You realize we made it," he said quietly.

Jack lifted his chin. "Made it where?"

"Through the worst." Ethan didn't say Ratline; the word still tasted like metal. "We're still here."

Jack turned the bottle in his palm, label to, label away. "Damn right," he said, and for once he didn't try to decorate it. "They tried to break us."

He didn't finish the sentence. He didn't have to.

Another cap popped somewhere down the hall. Someone coughed, then laughed too loud and shushed himself. On the stoop, an upperclassman's voice chased a story and caught it; the punch line ran up the rail like a wave and fell silent at their door.

They finished the case slower than they started it, time stretching the way it does when you stop measuring by formation and start measuring by conversation. When the last bottle clinked down, Ethan leaned back against the cinderblock and closed his eyes. The heat had softened his muscles. The beer's small courage made the room feel bigger than its measurements.

"You know what I miss?" he said without opening his eyes. "Eating without looking over my shoulder."

"You're eating now," Jack said.

"Yeah," Ethan said. "That's why I noticed."

They sat in the comfortable quiet you only get with someone who's earned it beside you. Out in the dark, cicadas droned on. Somewhere, a flag halyard ticked against its pole with the little wind that managed to cross the parade deck after sunset.

When Ethan finally stretched out on his bunk, sweat cooling on his back, he felt the old weight of the walls settle— less crushing than before, but still there. SMI never forgot to remind you who owned your hours.

He set one empty bottle on the sill, the sailor facing inward like a lookout who understood his duties. Then he turned out the light.

The beer was gone. The tests wouldn't be. But for one night, in a room that still smelled like rust and cheap yeast, freedom had come in brown glass and a four-dollar grin.

They hid the empties under Jack's bunk and slept like men who'd earned a little quiet. Morning came with the usual bugle, the usual scrape of boots on stone, but the edges felt softer. Even formation looked different when your head wasn't welded to the mud.

By afternoon, the two of them had a mission.

"Returns," Jack said, kicking the case. Glass clinked like wind chimes in a storm. "Dollar-fifty buys the next mistake."

They loaded the bottles into a laundry sack—towels on top, contraband below—and timed the walk for a shift change at the guard desk. The corridor smelled like floor wax and hot metal. Ethan kept his eyes front, the sack over his shoulder, the way you carry something heavy you're pretending is light.

On first stoop, the guard cadet glanced up, bored. "Laundry?"

"Laundry," Jack said, not breaking stride.

They crossed the parade deck with that casual-not-casual pace every fourth-classman learns: fast enough to look official, slow enough not to look guilty. At the gate, the sentry squinted, then thumbed them through. One more right turn and the town opened like a different country—brick storefronts, chalkboard menus, a sun that felt less owned.

The grocer's bell gave a tired ding. Mr. Kellam—wire glasses, radio murmuring baseball—looked up, saw the sack, and didn't bother hiding his smirk.

"Back again already?" he said.

"Recycling," Ethan answered, setting the bag gently so the glass didn't rat them out. "We're environmentalists."

"Patriots," Jack added.

Kellam counted bottles like a banker and slid three quarters into Ethan's palm, then three more into Jack's. The coins felt heavier than they should have. Money earned on a loophole made a sweeter sound.

On the way back, they didn't talk much. The case was lighter; the air wasn't. The stone walls of SMI rose at the end of Main like a reminder you could see from anywhere in town. Ethan rolled the quarters in his fist, listening to the dry rattle.

"Feels stupid," he said.

"What does?" Jack asked.

"To feel proud about a dollar-fifty."

Jack shrugged. "You take freedom where it fits."

Back inside, the afternoon settled into a rhythm they hadn't had time to notice before. Jack laced up for off-season drills; Harris ran the squad in tight, punishing patterns on the lower field, whistle carving the hour into clean slices. Ethan watched from the bleachers with a notebook open on his knee, pencil tapping out derivatives and limits while the ball zipped across the grass. He wasn't on the field, but the repetition, the numbers, the way everything resolved—somewhere in it his breathing evened.

When practice ended, Harris jogged by and clapped Ethan's shoulder. "He'll be starting," the captain said, motioning after Jack. "He keeps his head right."

Ethan nodded. "He will."

He believed it.

Dinner in the mess felt almost normal. Trays slid, forks chimed on plates, the constant hum of a hundred small lives running side by side. Ethan ate slow out of stubbornness— chewed every bite, swallowed without glancing at the door. He'd promised himself he would notice simple things and then notice that he noticed them.

From somewhere down the table: "Skunk! You look less like a ghost."

Ethan raised his cup. "I switched to a liquid diet," he deadpanned, and the guys groaned, grateful for the bad joke because it made the good food taste better.

After evening study, they sat on fourth stoop with their backs against the rail, watching dusk drag purple across the mountains. The parade deck went from hard gray to soft black, the flag halyard ticking a patient metronome. A pair of upperclassmen crossed below, laughter rising, then dissolving.

"You think it gets easier from here?" Ethan asked.

Jack rubbed the heel of his hand along a scab at his hairline that never quite healed. "No," he said. "But it gets clearer."

"Clearer?"

"Who you are. Who you're not. Who you can't be and still make it." He turned the words like a stone. "They can't take that part."

Ethan let the silence sit. He thought of the jar of moonshine, the exam he'd butchered, the professor who'd called anyway. He thought of the drum at 0300 and the way the courtyard swallowed names. He thought of a two-dollar-and-fifty-cent beer night that felt like a jailbreak.

When they finally stood, lights had winked on in half the windows. Somewhere within the maze of stone, a trumpet found the first notes of taps and tasted them, then stopped—too early. They walked the corridor back to their room, quarters in their pockets, sweat drying on their shirts, the day clicking into its bracket.

At lights out, Ethan lay with his forearm over his eyes, the barracks humming its low, familiar song—pipes, fans, somebody's radio two stoops over too quiet to locate. The sailor on the empty bottle watched from the sill like a tiny witness.

The leash had slack, the walls still close, the next test already writing itself in a room he couldn't see. But for now, two things were true: he'd eaten lunch, and the quarters in his desk drawer meant there would be another night they could afford to call their own.

Word of their "investment strategy" leaked the way everything did at SMI—sideways. A corporal's roommate's buddy asked, too casually, if the grocer in town still paid cash for returns. Jack only grinned and said soda bottles worked the same. Ethan added, "Be a shame to litter," and they let the subject drift.

They set rules because rules kept you alive. Two bottles each, never three. Open by the window, caps in the pocket, glass rinsed and dried, labels scraped, everything wrapped in a towel and buried at the bottom of the laundry sack before lights out. No smell on the stoop. No loose tongues in the hall. If a knock came, the towel became a pillow and the sack became a seat. Innocence lived in choreography.

By the second Friday, the heat had broken, leaving the room only stifling instead of molten. They called it Two-Fifty Friday because names made hard things easier.

"Inventory?" Ethan asked.

Jack held up four fingers—two for them, two for ghosts. "And a nickel profit if we find a bottle in the trash," he said, winking.

They toasted lightly—no clink, just a shared lift—and sat cross-legged on the floor. Through the window, the parade deck looked almost gentle under moonlight. You could forget what it had done to you for a minute.

"What're you doing after taps tomorrow?" Jack asked.

"Calculus review. Maddox sent a practice set." Ethan shrugged. "If I don't treat my brain like a muscle, it turns on me."

Jack snorted. "My brain lifts lighter." He tipped his bottle. "But I'll run steps at dawn if you'll quiz me on stats after."

"Deal."

They were halfway through their second when footsteps hammered the corridor. Jack had the towel over the bottles in a single motion. Ethan slid the window shut on instinct, then cursed—the room immediately smelled like the inside of a drum.

The door flew open. A third-classman stood framed in the light, eyes scanning, nose twitching. Daniels. The same upperclassman who'd smiled while Buffett punished Ethan at noon all fall.

He stepped in. The pause was surgical. "Smells… festive," he said softly.

Ethan felt his stomach drop. Jack's face didn't move.

Daniels' gaze slid to the desk, over the beds, down to the towel. For a heartbeat Ethan saw the chapel again—stained glass and steel voices—and braced for the barked order that would end this small freedom, maybe more.

Instead, Daniels stepped back into the hall. "Ventilate, rats," he said, bored. "Smells like a wet locker in here."

The door clicked shut.

They didn't breathe for a count of five. Then Jack leaned his head back and laughed without sound, chest heaving.

"Why—" Ethan started, voice thin.

"Because he remembers," Jack said. "Buffett at lunch. Maybe he figured you'd earned a night."

"Or he's waiting to see if we're stupid," Ethan said.

"That too." Jack lifted the towel, slid the empties into the sack, and tied it in a neat knot. "We won't be."

After taps, the barracks hummed. Ethan lay awake, the earlier scare still pulsing in his ribs. He thought about how easily everything could vanish—how quickly a knock turned into a drum. SMI had taught them that every gift was rented.

Saturday dawn came cool and blue. They paid back the beer with miles—down the hill, around the track, up the stadium steps until their legs shook, words coming only in fragments.

"Stats. After chow," Ethan panted.

"After I nap," Jack shot back, then added, "And you're eating. No Buffett penance, no 'I'm not hungry.'"

Ethan saluted with two fingers and managed a grin.

The weeks found a shape. Harris kept feeding Jack minutes in scrimmages, pushing him, praising him, barking at him harder than ever. Ethan's name showed up on a bulletin board he hadn't looked at before—Dean's List, fall preliminary. At night he tutored two classmates on derivatives, and they taught him how to tape a sprained ankle without bubbles. They found favors that didn't cost too much to owe.

Some afternoons, when the light hit the mountains just right, they took their books to the top row of the bleachers. From there, SMI looked less like a trap and more like a geometry problem—angles, arcs, a proof you could work if you were patient. Jack sprawled in the sun, eyes closed, reciting definitions for a quiz while Ethan corrected without opening his own.

"See?" Jack murmured. "I'm educable."

"Barely."

"That's still an -able."

On the third Two-Fifty Friday, a thin envelope arrived with Ethan's name, the paper soft from being re-folded too many times. He opened it slowly. Dr. Maddox's spidery handwriting spilled out—three lines and a postscript.

Proud of the work since summer. Keep your head. Talent is a knife; learn where to cut. P.S. – Numbers forgive, but only if you ask them before midnight.

Ethan read it twice and tucked it into the back of his notebook like a talisman. When Jack asked, he only said, "He thinks I'm not hopeless."

"Smartest man on campus," Jack said.

They returned the bottles in town at last light, the grocer's radio calling balls and strikes while quarters slid across the counter. On the walk back, a pair of civilians in hoodies drifted past, not seeing them at all. The invisibility felt almost luxurious.

"Funny," Ethan said. "We fight to be seen here. Out there, being nobody feels… good."

"Out there," Jack said, "we're just two guys with laundry."

They stopped at the gate and looked up. The flag snapped once in a stray gust, then sagged, limp against the line. Somewhere in the maze of windows, a trumpet found taps for real, the first note clean and mournful as a blade.

Back in the room, Ethan set two quarters in the top drawer—the ritual now—and slid the sack under the bed.

"What's next, you think?" he asked, switching off the lamp.

"Next is always heavier," Jack said in the dark. "But we're stronger than last time."

Ethan let the quiet spread. He thought of the hill, the hands, the drum, the jars, the beer that tasted like rust and victory. He thought of how they'd learned to measure freedom in ounces and inches and coins, to take it seriously so they could keep it.

The barracks settled, stone exhaling, as if satisfied for one night. Tomorrow would tighten everything again—formations, sprints, the look in an upperclassman's eye that meant a new line to toe. That was the deal.

For now, the window was cracked to the September air, the sailor on the bottle label half-smiling from the sill, and two quarters waited like a promise for a Friday that had already earned its name.

Chapter 20 — Sophomore Year: Broken Hands & Broken Hearts

Part 1: Whispers, Clippings, and the Letter

Southern Military Institute didn't welcome you back with banners and brass; it greeted you with inventory and silence. Sophomore year opened like that—no speeches, no soccer drills, just a sense that something in the barracks' bones had shifted while everyone was gone.

It started as a small absence. Caleb Rourke's rack stayed made, his footlocker unclaimed, his name strip still stuck flaking on the doorframe like a label on a crate that never shipped. Guys shrugged. People washed out, people quit, people vanished in the long summer and sent a postcard from civilian life. SMI was built to swallow names.

But this wasn't that.

Two weeks into the term a thin manila envelope made the rounds, passed from hand to hand on the fourth stoop like contraband scripture. Inside was a newspaper clipping, local rag print, the kind of gray photo that made everyone look haunted. The headline said enough without the rest: LOCAL MAN ARRESTED IN GIRLFRIEND'S MURDER.

Someone read the body in a low voice, watching the words for confirmation none of them wanted: the timing, the town, the age. It was Caleb. He'd been arrested weeks before reporting to pre-strain summer. The article was clinical, cold— charges, timeline, a sentence about "dismemberment" that made even the hard cases swallow.

Jack took the page last. He read it through once, slow, then again, faster, like speed might change the ending. The paper trembled in his hands just enough for Ethan to notice.

"That stare," Jack murmured, voice flat. "He looked like he'd already fallen in a hole."

No one laughed. The stoop, that eternal amphitheater of jabs and jeers, held its tongue. For a few beats, the barracks felt smaller, as if the stone had cinched one notch tighter around the Corps. They had slept ten feet from a kid carrying something like that. They had lived with him, loaned him toothpaste, complained about the same chow line. The walls didn't only hold drills and sweat and songs; they held men, and men brought ghosts.

The clipping made its way down the steps and disappeared. Life at SMI did what it always did: continued at attention. But a seam had opened, a hairline crack in certainty. If a face across your room could hide a headline like that, what else could the Institute be housing? The whisper traveled—watch everything—and even the loudest learned to listen harder.

Ethan filed it away in that mental cabinet where SMI stored all its contradictions. You could be made and unmade here. You could come to survive or come already ruined and keep it secret until the day a manila envelope arrived.

But Caleb Rourke wasn't what broke Jack Reynolds.

That arrived in a white envelope with a name he loved on the front.

Caroline's handwriting had always looked like Sunday: clean loops, steady lines, a kind of grace on paper. Seeing it snapped something warm and familiar into Jack's eyes. He tore the flap with a thumb, sat on the rail of the fourth stoop with the parade deck falling away behind him, and read.

Ethan leaned a shoulder to the iron post and pretended not to watch.

Jack's mouth moved at first, silent, pacing the lines as if he could walk them back where they started. Then his lips stilled. The color ran out of his face. When he looked up, it wasn't toward anyone—just toward a blank mid-distance where sentences go when they're trying not to be true.

"She's gone," he said. Like reporting a casualty. No story, no defense. Just the fact.

Ethan didn't try for wisdom. SMI had trained advice out of him. He kept his body still beside Jack, an anchor that didn't pretend to be a rope.

That night Jack didn't show for dinner. The next night he didn't, either. By morning formation he was a rumor: "Reynolds missed PT?" "Not like him." "You hear about the letter?" The cadre noticed on day two and barked; by day three they were threatening tours; by day four they started using his name like a tool—REYNOLDS, STAND UP STRAIGHT IN ABSENTIA—as if volume alone could drag him out of bed.

It couldn't. Heartbreak closed around him like a boot pressing down. He stopped shaving. Stubble shadowed the jaw that had once cut clean in profile. Sheets soured. The room took on the ruined-fruit heat of a space not aired. He missed class, then lab, then formation. Ethan brought him bottled water and a sandwich and left both untouched on the desk. The Corps could make a man love a cadence or hate a hill; it couldn't lift a letter's weight.

"Come on," Ethan said on day five, voice careful, like the floor might creak. "You gotta move. Mess hall. Ten minutes. You don't have to talk."

"For what?" Jack's voice came back from the pillow like it had to travel miles.

Ethan didn't have an answer that would matter. He set the sandwich on the locker and sat. They breathed in the same air for a stretch. Outside, someone laughed too loud on the stoop; it sounded obscene in the doorway.

What had always made Jack powerful at SMI wasn't just his body—it was his direction. Even in pain he had pointed at something: a drill to crush, a test to ace, a teammate to outrun. Now the compass spun. SMI had taught them both what to do with rage. It had never taught them what to do with grief.

Around them, life proceeded in the square-edges way of the Institute. The bell; the rifles; the crunch of boots on gravel as Fourths double-timed across the deck to a formation Jack should have led. Coach Harris asked Ethan if he'd seen him. "He'll be back," Ethan said, because the only other sentence felt like treason.

On the sixth morning, Ethan woke to a sound he couldn't place at first—a jittering, a clatter like screws in a coffee can. He rolled over and saw Jack, barefoot, shirtless, throwing his room apart and putting it back together. Boots to the corner. Sheets stripped, then stretched tight enough to bounce a coin. Books squared like bricks. Brass laid out, dull metal awaiting hands.

He moved like a man trying to repair a flood with a broom.

Ethan fought his way up from sleep, guard duty from the night before still weighing his bones. The one mercy of midnight pacing was simple: you could leave your rack down after sunrise. He kept his blanket where it was and rubbed his eyes.

"Leave it," he muttered.

Jack didn't turn. "Get your bed up."

"I'm on guard," Ethan said, edge sharpening without his consent. "I can leave it."

Jack stopped moving. When he looked over, the eyes were the same ones that stared through the mud at Breakout—feral, unlit, hunting a handhold anywhere. "I said get it up."

Ethan felt something in him flick hard, a circuit popping. "Shut the hell up."

Later, Ethan would replay the next part a hundred times and still not quite understand which part was decision and which was gravity. He remembered the space between them shrinking. He remembered Jack's breath—heavy, hot—and the angle of his shoulders. He remembered thinking don't and hearing do.

Jack swung first. It came fast and flat, a glove-less cross without aim beyond impact. Ethan ducked. His own fist came up by reflex, a left jab thrown wrong from the start, and Jack caught it with the same terrible calm that had carried him up the hill in February. He didn't wrench or twist. He just folded Ethan's hand back one finger at a time until the pain sharpened into a white edge that cut through breath.

The scream tore out of Ethan before he could swallow it. The sound yanked a door down the hall, then another, and boots thudded, and a classmate shouldered the frame and shouted, "Knock it off, idiots!"—and the spell broke.

Jack backed away, chest heaving, eyes wild and empty at once. Ethan cradled his hand to his chest, knuckles already blooming purple. The air smelled like sweat and metal and something scorched—shock, maybe.

They glared. Words came out like reflex, like men reaching for knives that weren't there.

"You're a bastard," Ethan hissed.

"You're soft," Jack threw back, but it landed like a stone dropping in wet sand—no bounce, no ring.

Outside, the bell for section rang. Inside, a silence so loud it made the light buzz.

Jack was the first to speak again, voice too casual, like a truce offered on a table no one had set. "You want to get breakfast before the hospital?"

Ethan blinked at the absurdity, at how SMI could turn even a fight into an appointment. Pain throbbed in his palm to his elbow, but he found himself nodding. "Yeah," he said, and surprised himself with the steadiness. "Why not."

They rolled their racks, buttoned their shirts, tucked in their anger with their tails, and walked out side by side into a morning as crisp and indifferent as any other.

They ate in a corner of the mess hall like two men sharing a ceasefire. Ethan fumbled eggs with his left hand, wincing every time the fork clinked the tray. Jack stared at his food until the steam died and the sheen went dull.

At the infirmary, the medic didn't ask for stories. SMI medicine moved like a pit crew: assess, set, secure, shove you back onto the track. A captain with readers on a lanyard prodded Ethan's swollen hand, hummed, and sent him for films. The X-ray looked like a treeline in winter—five stark branches, two of them angling wrong.

"Fractures," the medic said, kind but brisk. "Index and middle metacarpals. You'll keep this on three to four weeks. No contact drills. You can run." He wrapped a fiberglass cast that hardened into a white club and signed the corner with a quick —Dr. M.

Jack leaned against the cinderblock wall the whole time, arms crossed, jaw working. When the cast set, he reached for Ethan's sling, tied the knot with a neat square sailor's hitch he'd learned from Harris, and stepped back like a workman inspecting a repair.

"You good?" he said.

Ethan flexed what fingers he could. "Define good."

The corner of Jack's mouth moved. Not a smile. An acknowledgment. They walked back across the deck in the flat glare of ten hundred, rifles and cadence echoing from formations they weren't in. Neither of them spoke about the reason why.

SMI noticed. It always did.

The Company TAC pulled Jack aside that afternoon. The door stayed mostly closed, but voices carried through wood like heat—low at first, then sharp, then the TAC's measured baritone cutting through: "You're circling the drain, Mr. Reynolds." Silence. "Fix it or I'll fix it for you."

Word got to Harris inside of an hour. He didn't come to commiserate. He came to collect. He found Jack on the third stoop, took in the stubble, the stare, the posture that had lost all its angles, and didn't raise his voice.

"Field. Fifteen minutes," he said, and walked away like the only possible answer was roger.

Jack showed. Harris didn't ease him in—he strapped him to a ladder of sprints, shuttles, and box-to-box repeats until Jack's breath rasped like a saw. "Again," Harris said. "Again." When Jack bent double, palms on knees, Harris toed his boot. "Up. I can't start you if you can't stand up." It wasn't cruelty. It was permission to rejoin gravity.

Ethan watched from the sideline, his cast thumping against his thigh with each jogged warmup lap. He couldn't touch a ball, so he ran. Laps in the cinders. Stairs until the burn hit a clean, wordless place. The trainer looped elastic around his waist and made him lean into resistance. When he slept that night, the ache in his legs had its own slow pulse. It felt almost like peace.

Jack returned late, salt crust drying on his collar. He paused in the doorway like a man checking a threshold for tripwires. Ethan looked up from a calc text and a page of scratch-work numbers and lifted his cast an inch in a half-wave.

Jack nodded once. He said nothing. He didn't have to. He gathered Ethan's muddy boots from beneath the rack, set them on a towel, and shined them until the leather turned mirror-black and the toe caps showed a boy with a white club for a hand looking back.

The next morning Ethan found two protein bars on his desk, still in the PX plastic, and a note ripped from a green memo pad: 3rd period I'll run your tours if they hit you for missed drill — J. The pen had dug a little too hard on the downstrokes.

That was the apology. Not words. Deeds.

He took it.

Consequences still landed. The Company Clerk slid a Special across Ethan's blotter for "UNIFORM DISCREPANCY: IMPROPER GLOVE/SLING CONFIGURATION," the paperwork equivalent of a shrug and a smirk. Ethan checked Correct. The Superintendent gave him three tours—marching circles with his rifle balanced in the crook of his good arm, the cast itching beneath the sling. Jack showed up beside him on the second lap, unassigned, a rifle across his shoulder and a grin that looked almost like defiance. "Conditioning," he muttered, same as before. They circled the courtyard in tandem until the bell released them into evening.

At night, Ethan practiced math with his left hand, cramped and slow. The numbers came anyway, obedient as ever. Dr. Maddox had slipped him a line in the hall—"Don't let circumstance be your excuse, Mr. Cole." Ethan had nodded like a recruit receiving ammo. Circumstance wasn't an excuse; it was a weight vest.

Jack, stripped back to the frame, rebuilt himself by increments. Harris hounded him but also floated a lifeline: "Travel squad's not a charity. Earn it." Jack did—eight miles at dawn, weights in the afternoon, touches at twilight until the ball moved like a language he knew again. He shaved, squared his corners, re-stitched his name to the posture that had once made cadre think twice. The letter still lived in his drawer, creased into a small white gravity. He didn't talk about it. He taped his ankles tighter.

One evening, the mail bag thumped onto the Company table and a thin envelope slid out with REYNOLDS in the return address—the one he'd sent two weeks earlier, now stamped UNDELIVERABLE in red.

He turned it over once. Twice. Then folded it along the old crease and slid it beneath the tray of his footlocker. He didn't rip it. He didn't reread it. He went to the field and ran.

SMI's genius was remedial. It didn't teach men to be whole. It taught them to function when they weren't. The cast forced Ethan to discover momentum without touch; the tours taught Jack to keep circling until mind followed body. Some nights they said nothing at lights-out. Others they traded four sentences over two hours, heavy things laid down carefully between bunks:

"You back?"

"Getting there."

"You mad?"

"Getting past it."

On Saturday, Harris posted the squad list. Jack's name sat in the XI in neat block letters. He didn't whoop. He slid the sheet from the corkboard with two fingers, smoothed the curl, and tacked it back flush.

"You earned it," Ethan said.

"Working on keeping it," Jack answered.

Ethan's cast turned gray at the edges, nicked with chalk and scuffed with drills. He signed it himself, finally—Skunk—just to take ownership of the thing that owned his days. In class he took notes with left-handed chicken scratch and turned in proofs that made Maddox smile without showing teeth. At night, when the barracks settled into that low engine-room hum, he listened to the steady scrape of Jack's boot on the stone as he practiced first touch against the wall. Thock. Thock. Thock. Metronome. Prayer.

One damp Sunday, Harris found them both on the fourth stoop watching rain corner off the parade deck into slick, shining sheets. He didn't say much; coaches at SMI learned to save words for when they mattered.

"You two make each other better," he said finally, like a statement of inventory. "Don't waste it."

He walked on. The rain thickened. Ethan flexed the fingers that could still move inside the cast and counted beats between flashes of lightning and the arriving thunder. Jack bounced the ball twice, trapped it dead on his instep, and let it roll back down.

SMI didn't hand out reconciliations. It gave you time and tasks and let you choose what to do with both. Ethan and Jack did the only thing they knew—show up, shut up, do the work, and make space where men who'd hurt each other could stand shoulder to shoulder again.

By midterm, the white club came off. The hand under it was pale and thin, the fingers hesitating at first like foals learning legs. The trainer pressed a lacrosse ball into Ethan's palm. "Squeeze, rotate, repeat. Hundred a day," he said.

Ethan started right there on the training-room bench, Jack beside him untying tape from his ankles. Squeeze. Rotate. Repeat. The rhythm felt familiar.

Outside, the bell sent a company trotting across wet stone in a blur of gray and brass. Inside, two friends counted reps out loud—just enough to make each other honest.

The cast came off on a Thursday that smelled like bleach and cold rain. The trainer scissored the fiberglass open and peeled it away in pale, crunchy petals, revealing a hand that didn't look like his—shrunken, chalky, the tendons standing like cords under thin skin.

"Grip work," the trainer said, handing him a blue lacrosse ball. "Hundred squeezes, three times a day. Rice bucket in the corner if you want to be an overachiever."

Ethan started right there, left shoulder against the cinderblock, counting aloud while Jack re-laced his boots on the bench. "Twenty-one. Twenty-two."

Jack bumped him with a knee on his way out. "Field in ten."

Ethan wasn't cleared for contact, so he found the places a decent man could stand: at the touchline with a clipboard, tallying sprints and touches; beside the cones, resetting patterns when they blew apart; in the equipment room afterward, coiling bibs into clean rolls and snapping them tight with rubber bands. Harris noticed. He didn't say thanks—coaches at SMI rationed that word—but he started handing Ethan boxes without speaking, which was its own kind of trust.

Saturday's match arrived under a hard blue sky and wind that cut down out of the hills like glass. The last of the oak leaves scraped across the cinders. The stands held a scatter of cadets in gray wool and a few townies with coffee in paper cups. Harris posted the XI in block letters on the board. REYNOLDS—ST. A slash of chalk under CAPTAIN HARRIS. Ethan traced the names with his eyes and then took his place with the reserves in a hoodie, right hand tucked into the pocket like a bird under a wing.

From first whistle, Jack moved like a man who had rebuilt himself one brick at a time. He didn't bully so much as insist, driving center-backs backward on rails, holding up through contact, laying off in one-touch rhythms that made Harris's jaw soften. Twice he rose at the back post and caromed headers off shoulder and skull; twice the keeper punched them away with late, panicked fists.

Midway through the second half, the match still scoreless, a defender clipped him from behind at the top of the box. The ball squirted loose toward the right channel. Jack didn't go down. He kept his feet through the half-foul, rode the second nudge, and drifted the ball a stride wide with his left before lashing it across his body. The shot bent inside the far post like it had a magnet buried there.

For a heartbeat the world went quiet. Then the stands exhaled—boots on bleachers, a handful of voices, the tin clap of wintered hands. Jack didn't sprint to the corner or slide on his knees. He turned once, eyes sweeping the bench, found Ethan, and lifted one palm in a small, square gesture that meant, there.

Harris subbed him off late to an economy-size ovation. In the cinder locker room afterward, steam turning breath to ghosts, Harris cupped the match ball and waited for the clatter to ebb.

"Men," he said, voice even. "That is what response looks like." He tossed the ball to Jack. "For the goal."

Jack caught it against his chest. He could've kept it. He could've stuffed it into the mesh bag and let routine write over the moment. Instead, he threaded through mud-smeared shoulders until he stood in front of Ethan. He held the ball out like a formal presentation, both hands.

"For the tours," he said. "For the boots. For showing up."

It wasn't an apology so much as a ledger balanced in public. Ethan took the ball. It was warm through the leather, the raised seams catching against the new pink of his knuckles. He didn't say you broke my hand or I forgive you. He just nodded once and tucked the ball under his arm.

That night, a few rooms down, a knock started at one door and traveled like a small weather system. A cadet from Second Battalion stood on the threshold holding a folded newspaper. "You see this?" he asked, and the answering hiss moved down the hall.

It was a follow-up article—Caleb Rourke's arraignment, the phrases swallowing their own tails: premeditated, dismembered remains, competency evaluation. The photo was a mugshot: pale, blank, the same hollowed-out stillness he'd brought to summer study and the scratch of his pencil at midnight.

Jack read it propped on his elbows, uniform blouse unbuttoned at the throat, hair still damp from the shower. He didn't look at Ethan when he finished. He set the paper on the desk and slid it aside like an object that might stain.

"I kept thinking he was just quiet," he said finally. "The whole time. Just—quiet."

Ethan pressed the ball into his right palm and felt the ache wake and spread, clean and honest. "We don't know what people carry," he said.

"Yeah." Jack's mouth tightened. "We know what we carry."

They let the room fill with the low-machine hum of barracks at rest: fans, pipes, a far-off laugh from the stoop. Through the open window, the parade deck lay dark and square, its lines ghosted in moon-wet stone.

Later, when lights-out had come and gone, Jack opened his footlocker and pulled the returned letter out from beneath the tray. UNDELIVERABLE glared up in red. He sat on the bunk with it and a pen and stared a long time at the blank back. He didn't write another. He folded it once along the old crease, then slid it into an inner sleeve of his wallet, behind his cadet ID, like a scar tucked under a cuff.

Ethan, on his rack, flexed fingers against the ball. Squeeze. Rotate. Repeat. He pictured tendons knitting, bone laying down mineral across the thin fault lines. He pictured the goal snapping the net, the way Jack's palm had cut the air—a small square, a signal.

"Field at dawn?" Jack said into the dark.

"Yeah," Ethan answered. "Field at dawn."

They went. The morning was all frost and breath, the grass a brittle nap that crackled under boots. Harris wasn't there. The bell wasn't either. They ran stairs until legs burned, then moved to the wall. Jack struck ball—thock, thock, thock— first-time on the half-volley, counting reps under his breath. Ethan worked touch with his left, then his right, the righthand protest softening from pain to heat to the simple animal fact of work.

"Fifty clean on your right," Jack said.

"Forty-eight," Ethan answered. "Start me again."

They did. Sun climbed. Parade deck brightened. On the far stoop a sleepy cadet set a coffee on a railing and watched them like men at sea sighting lights.

By midmorning, when the Corps shook itself awake and class bells started cutting the air into blocks, they were sitting on the fourth stoop with sweat drying into salt at their collars. The match ball rested between them.

"Hand?" Jack asked without looking.

"Better," Ethan said, flexing. It was true. Not all the way. Enough.

Jack's voice dropped into that simple gear he found only when he meant every word. "I'm sorry."

Ethan turned, surprised he'd said it out loud. For a second he considered answering in kind—I know, it's okay, you were wrecked. The sentences lined up, saluted, waited for orders, and then he let them stand down.

"We're good," he said. Not mercy. A status report.

Jack nodded. The ball sat warm in the patch of sun, seams dark like train tracks to somewhere else.

Sophomore year had arrived with absences and letters that didn't land. It would go on with stairs, and ice buckets, and chalk dust on cuffs, with matches under wind and papers under deadlines. Broken hands knit. Broken hearts scarred and thickened until they could carry weight. At SMI, no one was ever entirely whole; the trick was moving like you were anyway.

The bell called first formation across the square. They stood, shoulders bumping for half a breath, then fell into step, two shadows lengthening in parallel across the stone.

Chapter 21 — Detour: Army Green

By the end of sophomore fall, the math didn't pencil. Tuition due in January, bank account whispering zeroes. Ethan ran the numbers again anyway, as if decimals might change their minds. They didn't. If he wanted to finish at Southern Military Institute (SMI), he'd have to leave it first.

Jack stayed in barracks, orbit tightening after Caroline's letter. Ethan packed quiet—two uniforms, a pair of jeans, the battered Jimmy Buffett tape he'd somehow kept through inspections—and slung a duffel over his shoulder. He didn't say goodbye. At SMI, you said see you like it was an order.

The Recruiter

The recruiter's office was strip-mall beige and smelled like burnt coffee and Armor All. A Staff Sergeant with a high-and-tight and a salesman's smile slid a stapled packet across the desk.

"Not bad," he said, tapping the ASVAB sheet. "You can write your ticket, Cole. Aviation, signals, intel—D.C. wants kids like you. Big brain, clean score."

Ethan leaned back, chair creaking. "What's the hardest thing you've got?"

The sergeant blinked once—here we go—then eased into the spiel. "Depends what you mean by hard. You want ugly hard? Nuclear, Biological, Chemical. 54 Bravo. Seven months, two weeks at Fort McClellan. Masks, detectors, decon lines, the works. Most folks don't ask for it."

Ethan didn't hesitate. "That."

The sergeant grinned like a fisherman feeling the set. "You sure? Lotta rubber suits. Lotta time in the gas chamber. You'll hate your laundry."

"I've done worse," Ethan said. He thought of cold showers, sweat parties, and the chapel's stone hush. He thought of the moment the mud closed over his face. "Write it up."

Pens clicked. Boxes got initialed. The sergeant talked bonuses, college fund, GI Bill. Ethan heard tuition and spring and not much else. When the man pushed the contract forward, Ethan signed like a man dropping his name on a bridge he intended to burn behind him.

"Ship date in February," the sergeant said. "You'll be at Fort McClellan, Alabama. One Station Unit Training."

"What's that mean—exactly?"

"Basic and AIT back-to-back with the same drill sergeants," he said, tone almost sympathetic. "No change of scenery. No new faces. Just…more."

Ethan smiled without humor. "Sounds familiar."

He left with a folder, a handshake, and the strange lightness that comes when the decision you've been dreading is finally, irrevocably made.

The Bus

He called his mother from the pay phone outside the PX to say he was shipping. She started to cry, stopped herself, said she was proud, and asked if he had socks. He told Jack in three sentences on the fourth stoop: I'm going green. Back for junior fall. Don't get soft.

Jack's mouth twitched. "Field at dawn when you're back."

"Field at dawn," Ethan promised.

February bit hard. The bus ran south through bare-limbed hardwoods into red clay country, windows fogged from damp breath and cheap heat. The kids around him were a mix of buzzed heads and bravado, laughter too loud for the hour. A few slept with mouths open, chins bouncing. One boy clutched a Bible like a flotation device.

The gates of McClellan rose under floodlights—chain-link, concrete, two MPs who didn't smile. The bus hissed to a stop. Three drill sergeants climbed aboard, brimmed hats low enough to throw their faces into shadow.

"NOBODY LOOKS OUT THE WINDOW," one thundered. "YOU LOOK AT ME."

They looked.

"You are in my Army now," he continued, voice even and terrible. "You move when I say move. You speak when I say speak. You breathe because I ain't told you to stop yet."

The aisle filled with bodies and duffels and panic. Outside: cold, asphalt, a rectangle of yellow paint that became their world.

The Shock

In-processing bled into a kind of waking blackout—hair on the floor, needles in arms, uniforms that didn't quite fit, boots that didn't quite cooperate. Ethan had been yelled at before; SMI had a PhD in volume. But there was a different edge here, a federal weight behind every order.

Night one, they learned what OSUT meant in the bones. No honey-moon of basic then a blessed shuffle to a new company. Just the same three Smokey Bears, day after day after week after month, filing your rough edges down to powder.

"MCCLELLAN WILL MAKE NBC SOLDIERS OR IT WILL BREAK YOU," a drill sergeant barked as they stood lung-deep in a mud trench at dawn. "EITHER WAY, I GET PAID."

"Roger, Drill Sergeant!" the trench chorused.

Ethan did not love the feeling of rubber sealing around his face. The M40 mask sucked to his skin and made his heartbeat loud in his own head. In the chamber, CS gas bit his eyelids and crawled up his nose and reminded him, intimately, that air is a privilege. He walked out eyes streaming, snot on his sleeve, and found himself laughing. SMI had taught him to suffer on command. McClellan taught him to seal the suffering in a can and carry it to the next station.

Day schedule: reveille in the blue-black cold, chow swallowed whole, PT that felt like penance, MOPP drills until sweat pooled in your elbow creases, classes on agents and antidotes, field exercises that smelled like bleach and fear. Night schedule: clean the weapon that never quite gleamed enough, write the list you would forget in the morning, sleep like a felled tree.

Outnumbered

The bay held maybe a hundred and fifty bunks elbow-to-elbow, two long rivers of metal frames and green wool. Less than ten of the faces looking back at him were white. It didn't bother Ethan in theory. In practice, it meant he was a category before he was a name. He did what SMI had taught him—kept his rack tight, his mouth closed, his eyes open.

His bunkmate was a slight kid from Mumbai with precise English and callused fingertips. He said little and moved like noise cost money. That made him interesting to nobody until it made him interesting to everybody.

It started playful—the jostle that should have stayed a joke. By Tuesday, the circle around the kid had three bodies. By Wednesday, it had five and the laughter had a new edge.

"Leave him," Ethan said finally, voice flat from the lower bunk.

The room turned as one organism. The biggest of the five—Eugene, the name sewn above his pocket like a dare— took a step forward and kept stepping until he was close enough to fog Ethan's face with breath.

"What you gonna do about it, college boy?"

Ethan's stomach did a neat little roll. He'd been in this movie. Stand up and maybe it ends fast; sit down and the credits never roll. He stood.

"Not asking twice."

Eugene's palm hit his chest. The bunks rattled. The room laughed.

Something old and simple uncoiled in Ethan's spine.

He moved.

He moved.

Ethan came off the lower bunk like a spring, tucked Eugene's right arm with his left, and snapped a forearm around the big man's neck. A headlock. Ugly, basic, effective. He drove three fast shots into Eugene's cheekbone—pop, pop, pop—knuckles burning on impact.

The bay erupted—boots scraping concrete, metal frames shuddering, a dozen voices spiking into one hot sound. Eugene didn't fold. He cinched Ethan at the waist, lifted, and turned. For an instant Ethan saw the fluorescent tubes above him bloom into white suns—then his shoulders met the polished slab and his skull bounced once, hard. The world narrowed to a ringing tunnel.

He still had the lock.

He tightened, forehead jammed against Eugene's temple, and hammered again—short, mean punches that didn't have to be pretty. Eugene surged, staggered, dropped to a knee, tried to peel the arm loose. Spit hit Ethan's sleeve. Somebody yelled damn! like they were watching a prize fight. Somebody else yelled Drill!

The door detonated inward.

Two hats and a storm of profanity. They pried them apart like mechanics separating seized gears. The drill sergeant's face was an inch from Ethan's, brim low.

"YOU WANT A TITLE BELT, PRIVATE? WE'LL STITCH YOU ONE OUT OF SANDBAGS."

"Roger, Drill Sergeant," Ethan wheezed, chest heaving.

"And YOU," he snapped at Eugene, "IF YOU'RE GONNA PICK A FIGHT, PICK SOMEBODY YOU CAN FINISH."

The smoke session started three minutes later, out on the pad beneath a sky as hard as enamel. Push-ups until knuckles screamed, mountain climbers until hip flexors caught fire, eight-count body builders that made the horizon pulse. When Ethan's arms jellyfished and he face-planted, they flipped him, shoved his heels six inches off the deck, and counted slow enough to rewrite the calendar.

Back inside, there were no handshakes, no apologies, just the new weight of the room. The quiet kid from Mumbai made his rack without looking up. Eugene sat on his bunk and bled into a towel, eyes fixed somewhere middle distance. Heads tipped almost invisibly as Ethan walked past. Not friendship. Not even approval. Respect, the barracks currency.

No one touched the bunkmate again.

Training thickened. Mornings began with frost that skinned the puddles and breath that fogged the formation into a single animal. They learned MOPP levels the way Rats had learned strain—0 through 4, add and shed layers by command, glove discipline like religion. In the classroom they held up M8 paper to the overhead and recited colors—yellow for G-agent, red-brown for H—and traced the plastic pouches of the M256A1 kit like it was a tarot deck that told whether you lived or died.

In the bay, they practiced donning the M40 until it was muscle memory: lift, chin, pull, blow, cover, clear, seal. Outside, they waddled in charcoal suits that trapped heat like a sin, moving litter casualties through sawdust lanes to the decon line—gross rinse, soap, contact time, scrub, rinse again—hands numb, shoulders aching, the wind chewing through the weak seams anyway.

"IF YOU CAN BREATHE, YOU CAN WORK," the drill sergeant barked. "IF YOU CAN'T BREATHE, POKE YOUR BUDDY WITH THE ANTIDOTE AND THEN YOU WORK." They practiced the muscle memory—thumb on safety, jab the thigh with the Mark I—plastic training pens clicking into inert flesh.

In the mask confidence course they crawled through a plywood maze while CS dust skated off their lenses, the mask pumping their own breath back in rhythmic thumps. At the exit, the drill sergeant made them break the seal—lift, name, rank, hometown—eyes slashing, faces leaking, chests clawing, then re-seat and clear. Ethan stumbled out streaming snot and brine, wiped his sleeve across his mouth, and felt a laugh catch—and then, weirdly, hold. SMI had taught him to stand still in humiliation. McClellan was teaching him to function inside it.

They rucked the ridgelines, red clay clutching boot treads, packs chewing divots in traps. They dragged a mannequin named Fred through wire and scrub. They learned to trust the heat in the suit—no matter how loud the body screamed, the mask would keep the bad out if you respected the seal.

At night, when the bay went low and the chatter softened, Ethan wrote numbers. GI Bill estimates, Reserve drill checks, tuition lines. He'd taken the 54B contract into the Reserves— one weekend a month, two weeks in summer—so he could go back to SMI and grind the rest of the degree. The recruiter's pamphlet had made it sound like free money; the reality was arithmetic, ugly but doable if he worked. He penciled margins like he was solving for x in a life he refused to fail.

The bunkmate offered him a small square of halva from a care package, setting it wordlessly on the edge of Ethan's locker. Ethan nodded. That was its own contract.

Eugene kept his lane. In formation his jaw was a purple arch. In the field he lifted anything too heavy without being asked. One night at lights-out he said into the dark, not quite to anyone, "You're all right, College." That was all.

Mail call became oxygen. The drill sergeant stalked the aisle with a fistful of envelopes and a bad mood, pitching names like grenades. "Cole!"—a bent postcard with a soccer ball doodled in the corner and Field at dawn scrawled in Jack's blunt hand. Ethan read it three times, smiled once, slid it under his pillow.

On Sunday chapel he didn't pray in words so much as let the quiet wash through him. On Sunday laundry he scrubbed CS salt out of a liner and whistled two bars of "Changes in Latitudes" low enough the floor sergeant wouldn't hear.

The days stacked, indistinguishable and absolute. He learned to love the certainty: wake, move, work, collapse. SMI had been a machine that stripped the self to rebuild it shiny. McClellan stripped the self and didn't care if it shone, only that it sealed, carried, endured.

Late in the cycle, a storm rolled in off the ridge—sudden, loud rain that hammered tin and turned the decon lane into chocolate soup. They ran the line anyway, masks fogging, hands black with slurry, a drill sergeant walking it like a foreman in a shipyard.

"THIS ISN'T THE TEST," he shouted over the rainfall. "IT'S THE REHEARSAL FOR A TEST YOU'LL NEVER SEE COMING."

Ethan tightened the strap at his temple a quarter-inch. He thought of stone stoops, of drums in the night, of a mud hill on a birthday he spent under fluorescence. He thought of SMI's parade deck and the way silence could break men louder than any order.

He grinned into the mask where no one could see. Two machines, different gears, same lesson.

Keep breathing. Keep moving. Don't let go.

The last field problem ran seventy-two hours and felt like seven weeks. They stepped off at dusk in MOPP 2, charcoal trousers rasping, mask carriers slapping hips, red clay sucking at boot heels. The air smelled like pine and old rain. Sentries flashed cat's-eye chem lights from behind engineer tape while the lane cadre hummed out there somewhere like mosquitoes.

"GAS! GAS! GAS!"

Ethan's body moved before his brain did—lift, chin, pull, blow, cover, clear, seal. He heard his own breath drum the mask like a second heartbeat. He checked his buddy's seal with a palm slap and got the same in return. The drill sergeant watched without expression, then tossed an M8 booklet across the lit table. Yellow stain bloomed where the cadre dabbed. G-agent. Ethan called it out, mechanical and sure, while his hands sorted the M256A1 cards like they were playing for rent.

They ran a decon line in cold rain: gross rinse, soap, contact time, scrub, rinse again. When the litter team fumbled a casualty off the rollers, Ethan caught the elbow, reset the rhythm, pushed them through. No speeches. Just a grunt from the hat—"That's the pace, College"—and the line kept eating bodies.

They bivouacked under ponchos that funneled water into their collars, slept in ten-minute rations of shivering. On day three a kit camo pen exploded in somebody's pocket and striped half the squad green. The drill sergeant didn't laugh. Ethan did—quiet, inside the mask—because he remembered being a Rat with brass polish under his nails and how that had felt like the whole world. This was smaller. Harder. Simpler.

Graduation morning came hard-blue and bright. Bleachers bristled with families and cardboard signs and camera flashes. Ethan's mother couldn't make it; the bus from Richmond would have cost two shifts and she didn't have them to give. He stood in the back row, boots blued, name tape straight, skin a shade darker from Alabama sun, and he felt—oddly—steady.

The commander talked about standards, the chaplain said a prayer, and the hats moved down the line with handshakes that were not quite warm and not quite cold. When the brim stopped in front of Ethan, the drill sergeant lifted his chin with two fingers to meet his eyes.

"You're not big," he said, voice low enough for only one soldier. "But you don't let go. Keep that. You'll do." A small nod. The kind that meant more than a certificate.

Orders followed: report to the U.S. Army Reserve Chemical Company outside Richmond, one weekend a month, two weeks annual training. He signed the line, shoved the copy into a battered folder that already held his GI Bill worksheet and a number circled three times—the tuition gap he still had to bridge to get back to SMI.

They cut them loose on Victory Weekend with a weekend pass that fit in a wallet slot and rules that didn't fit anywhere.

"Off-post authorized. Uniforms not required. Don't be stupid," the first sergeant said, which, translated, meant someone will be.

The bay turned into a barter market for civilian clothes. Ethan bought a pair of jeans from a guy shipping to Benning and a faded Hawaiian shirt from a kid who swore he'd never wear it again. He paid in commissary snacks and two hours of CQ coverage.

He was stuffing the shirt into his ruck when the bunkmate from Mumbai—Pranav—stopped at his locker and set down a folded flyer. JIMMY BUFFETT • SAT NIGHT •

LAKEWOOD AMPHITHEATRE • ATLANTA. The parrothead grin beamed up in neon.

Pranav tilted his head. "Isn't this your singer?"

Ethan had to laugh. "He's… complicated."

He thought of the Chapel at SMI, the RDC line of faces, the verdict that turned a Walkman into a weapon and Buffett into punishment. He thought of lunch hours on his elbows while the chorus mocked him through a pair of foam pads. And he thought of a highway years before that, cars idling in a sunbaked line while he turned a traffic jam into a tailgate with a cooler and a cassette.

"Go," Pranav said simply. "You should go hear him without someone yelling."

Ethan called over to Eugene, who was taping the last corner of his duffel. "Atlanta?"

Eugene wiped a palm across his jaw. The bruise was a memory now. "We don't have a car."

"Buses don't line up with lights-out," Ethan said.

Pranav lifted one shoulder. "There is another American method. Hitchhiking."

Eugene barked a laugh. "Drill'll pin our hides on the wall if we get caught."

Ethan looked down at the flyer again. The lime-green parrot, the cheap print, the block font that promised escape in three chords. He didn't want to run from the memory of Buffett anymore; he wanted to take it back. Claim the music without the shame stuffed into it by a stone chapel and a line of boys with too much power.

He thought of the drill sergeant's one-soldier benediction— You don't let go. He thought of SMI's stoops and Jack's postcard with Field at dawn scribbled in the corner. He thought of how a song could be a handhold if you decided it was.

"Let's go," he said. "We'll make formation. We'll be ghosts."

They scrounged a cardboard square from the dumpster behind the PX and a fat black marker from supply. On the flap Ethan wrote ATLANTA in block letters you could read from a moving truck. He tucked the pass into his wallet behind his Reserve orders, folded the Hawaiian shirt flat, and laced his boots like a man who intended to run if he had to.

They walked out the gate as the sun slid down the pines and turned the base road brass. Traffic hissed by—pickups with toolboxes, sedans with college decals, a semi that blew a column of heat against their shins. Ethan stuck out his thumb and held the sign high.

A minivan blew past. A Jeep hesitated, then didn't. Eugene grinned around a toothpick. "We ain't pretty."

"We're persistent," Ethan said.

Ten minutes. Fifteen. A battered Ford pulled onto the gravel shoulder in a spray of dust. The driver wore a straw hat with a tiny parrot pin on the band and a grin that said the world didn't need to be that complicated.

"You boys Parrotheads or just lost?" he called.

"Both," Ethan said.

The man jerked a thumb toward the back seat. "Hop in. Lakewood's a haul, and the pre-show beach balls don't throw themselves."

They piled in—three soldiers in borrowed civvies smelling of starch and CS, chasing a song that had been a punishment and was about to be a promise. As the Ford pulled back onto the highway, the radio found a station that knew every lyric Ethan had needed for two years and hadn't been allowed to hear.

He leaned his head against the hot window, watched the pines blur to billboard, billboard to skyline, and thought—not of drill sergeants or mask seals or bone sheets—but of a chorus that had once been a collar and could now be a key.

Atlanta ahead. Buffett onstage. Curfew at 2300. The math didn't work.

They went anyway.

Chapter 22 – The Buffett Escape

Ethan didn't smuggle a Walkman into Fort McClellan. He wasn't crazy. But the ghost of one followed him anyway. In the chow line, over the clink of trays and steam-table hiss, a kid behind him mouthed a tune only a couple of souls would clock.

"You a Parrothead?" Ethan asked, low.

The kid's grin tilted. "Born one. Mike."

They shook like it mattered—which, here, it did. In a place that shaved you, starched you, and called you by numbers, finding someone who knew the same songs felt like finding color in a grayscale world.

They kept it quiet. A nod on the PT field. A whispered joke during boot-blousing checks. Then the PX bulletin board sprouted a miracle: JIMMY BUFFETT — SATURDAY — ATLANTA — BOBBY DODD STADIUM.

They stared at the flyer too long.

"We're not going," Mike said.

"Definitely not," Ethan said.

Beat.

"Hypothctically," Mike added, "if two trainees who definitely weren't going… did… how would they?"

They had nothing you'd call a plan. No civvies. No passes. No ride. Just BDUs, shaved heads, and an itch that wouldn't die.

By Friday night, the itch won.

They moved after last formation, 1700 on the dot, walking toward the motor pool like they belonged there, peeling off at the tree line like they didn't. Alabama pine straw whispered under boots; branches tugged sleeves.

"Still time to turn back," Ethan said, because he always said the decent thing even when both of them knew which way they were headed.

Mike pushed through scrub and pointed west. "Interstate."

They popped out by the on-ramp at dusk. Diesel, warm asphalt, the wind off passing trucks tugging their sleeves. They stuck out their thumbs because sometimes the dumbest plan is the only one left.

The first car blew past. The second slowed—brake lights bright as cherries. The driver leaned across and shoved the door open.

"Y'all Army?" he asked.

"Reserve," Ethan said. "Sir."

"You boys got any sense?"

"Some," Mike said.

"That'll have to do. Get in."

They rode quiet at first—the driver with weathered hands and a wedding ring, two kids with regulation haircuts and a secret. The radio found an old-country station; the driver tapped time on the wheel.

"Where you headed?"

"Atlanta," Ethan said. No point lying now.

The man nodded like he'd assumed it. "Stadium run. Good show."

Sunset poured pink into glass towers as they slid into Midtown. Tailgates flared in small bonfires. Bobby Dodd's ramps glowed like a cruise ship on a hill. Their BDUs read like costumes in a river of flowered shirts and straw hats.

Reality cracked at the turnstiles: no tickets.

A scalper fanned a deck of stubs. Mike gestured helplessly at their uniforms, at the whole situation.

"You boys supposed to be here?" the man asked.

Both shook their heads.

He studied them, something softening a hair. He thumbed out two. "Five rows off the stage. Ten bucks total."

"You serious?" Ethan said.

"Go make a memory, Private."

The stubs slid into Ethan's palm like contraband. They were moving—concourse hum, the sweet-sour tang of spilled beer, neon shirts everywhere—before doubt could catch up.

Ethan looked at the field, at the stage so close you could count the scuffs on a steel drum, and felt the old knot in his chest loosen a click. For once, the music might belong to him.

The stadium fell to black like a curtain of warm water. One bright guitar note threaded the hush, then the place detonated— whistles, whoops, a thousand paper parrots bobbing in neon tide. Buffett jogged into the light with that easy, crooked grin and the band slid straight into island time.

In front of them a pack of women on a girls' night turned, clocked the two shaved heads in BDUs, and delighted in the contradiction.

"You legal?" one asked, already fishing out a flask.

"Absolutely," Mike lied without blinking.

"Bless your hearts." A ribbon of tequila found two plastic cups. It burned like polished fire. The second pour came with an orange wedge, which helped exactly one percent.

Onstage, steel pans shivered, the crowd swayed like a boat at anchor, and Ethan felt the knot he'd carried since SMI loosen one click at a time. He wasn't a Rat. He wasn't a trainee. For three songs, then six, then ten, he was just a voice in the weather, shoulder to shoulder with a stranger-turned-friend, singing about warm places where the calendar can't find you.

Between numbers, Mike leaned close. "Worth the trouble?"

"Worth getting smoked twice," Ethan said, and meant it.

The encore landed like a benediction. House lights rose. Reality—exits, ramps, the sudden cool—rushed back in. The women jingled their keys on a flamingo keychain.

"You boys need a ride," one said. Not a question.

"We can manage," Ethan started, reflexively decent.

"You can thank us by not getting arrested," another said, practical as a nurse. "Come on."

They piled into a station wagon that smelled like sunscreen and dryer sheets, windows down to the Georgia night. Talk was easy: best fries on I-20, a cousin who swore he'd seen a gator near Phenix City, a teacher who made everyone memorize state capitals and nobody could remember Pierre. The flask orbited lazily, lighter each pass.

Near Anniston they let the boys out at a bright gas station. "Be good," the driver called, waggling the flamingo.

"Trying," Ethan said, and waved them into the dark.

The trees were less romantic on the return. Pine needles turned to black water underfoot, roots grabbed at laces, and the night had that electric base-hum you only notice when you're not supposed to be out in it. Twice they stopped and listened— no cadence calls, no boots, just a far coyote and the rattle of a flag halyard on metal.

"Left," Mike whispered. "We cut right on the way out."

Left it was. The motor pool rose like a shadowed city. A side door was still wedged with cardboard. They became two neat ghosts moving through bays, across the company area, up the stairs. The corridor smelled like soap and hot dust. Someone snored like a chainsaw two doors down.

At his bunk, Mike grinned in the dark. "We did a bad thing very well."

Ethan nodded, giddy and emptied out. "See you at formation."

He collapsed boots-off, everything else still on. The last thing he felt was the echo of steel pans humming somewhere behind his ears.

Reveille cracked morning open. Cold water, dull mirror, a tired kid staring back with a line of joy at the corners of his mouth. Fall in. Dress right. Cover down. Two shaved heads indistinguishable in a sea of them. No extra PT. No lecture. No one even glanced their way.

At chow, Mike nudged him once with an elbow—the smallest message a man can send and say everything.

Eyes front, Ethan allowed himself a breath of a smile. The grind was back, louder for having been escaped. For one bright night in a city that didn't know their names, the world had opened like a window, and the kid SMI tried to shrink had stretched, just a little, toward the sun.

Reveille still hurt, but it hurt less when your ribs remembered singing.

They formed up on the PT field, breath fogging thin in the Alabama morning. Drill Sergeant Vega paced the line like a metronome with teeth.

"Two-mile formation run," he barked. "Cadence by me."

They took off. Boots drummed, breath synced. Vega's call-and-response hit the usual notes—left, left, left-right-left—until Mike, three files over, slipped in a barely audible counter-beat under his breath. Not words, just a sway of rhythm that sounded suspiciously like steel pans. Ethan didn't look—eyes front—but his stride loosened anyway. The platoon settled into something that felt—if not easy—at least human.

Back in the bays, sweat cooling, Vega prowled their row.

"Why you smilin', Cole?"

Ethan killed it. "No reason, Drill Sergeant."

Vega stared a beat longer like he could sniff a secret. Then he moved on, and the room exhaled.

Saturday meant field sanitation detail. They lugged mops, bleach, and a push squeegee older than all of them. The latrine smelled like hot tin and pine cleaner. Eugene—the big one from the fight—worked the opposite end of the row, saying nothing. He caught Ethan's eye once, gave a single, neutral nod, and went back to scrubbing grout like it owed him money.

At chow, Mike nudged Ethan's elbow. A napkin sat under his tray—PX brown, corner creased. Someone had drawn a quick little doodle on it: a cartoon parrot in sunglasses, two words scrawled beneath in block letters—FINS UP.

Mike didn't ask how it got there. Ethan didn't say. He folded it twice and slid it into the flat space behind his ID in the wallet he wasn't supposed to have.

That evening, the bay sergeant dumped a canvas sack onto a table. "Mail!"

Names ricocheted down the roster. "Cole!" Ethan snagged two envelopes.

The first was from his mother—news about a leaky faucet, a neighbor's new puppy, a twenty-dollar bill tucked in with a note that said, Don't tell me what you spend it on unless it's textbooks. He smiled despite himself.

The second was a single sheet in tight, no-nonsense handwriting he knew from a hundred locker notes and ink-scored play diagrams.

Reynolds.

Ethan read it standing up, heartbeat climbing.

You picked the hard road. Figures. Don't die. SMI's still SMI. I'm getting meaner on purpose. See you when you're done playing with gas masks. —J.

He flipped the page over though there wasn't a second. For a moment the barracks felt like the stoop at SMI—the same iron air, the same gravity—and then the illusion snapped back to cots and footlockers and the sweet burn of floor polish. He tucked the letter into the same pocket as the napkin. Two talismans. Two worlds.

A week later, they hit the NBC dome again—mask drills, suit drills, the gas chamber. This was Ethan's lane now. The cadre's questions got harder; his answers got shorter.

Inside the chamber, CS powder floated in the light like ground glass. Masks on. Hoods sealed. Vega's voice came muffled through his own filter.

"Break seal. Clear. Sound off."

Around him, trainees coughed and panicked. Ethan held the sting for a count, resealed, forcefully exhaled, drew in one clean breath. The burn faded to an edge.

Mike's hands trembled. Ethan leaned until their helmets tapped.

"Slow," he said, voice box tinny against his throat mic. "Break. Seal. Blow. You're good."

Mike followed, eyes wide, then steadied. They rode it out together. Outside, as everyone hacked and cried into streaming sleeves, Vega gave Ethan the smallest nod a man can give without losing rank.

"Fifty-Four," he said—using the MOS, not his name. "You might turn into somethin' yet."

Ethan said, "Yes, Drill Sergeant," because the right answer is sometimes the only one you need.

Sunday's smoke session came out of nowhere—someone had lost a canteen cup, so all of them paid. Mountain climbers bit into wrists already raw from bleach, burpees stole whatever oxygen Saturday had forgotten to wring out. It should've felt pointless.

Ethan counted the reps and pictured the stadium lights coming down like a tide. At twenty, he heard a guitar chime. At forty, steel pans. At sixty, nothing but breath and the slap of palms on concrete. He finished on time.

That night he took the flat pencil from his breast pocket and opened his footlocker. On the inside of the lid, small enough to pass any inspection, he drew three quick lines: a horizon, a tiny sun, and one ridiculous stick-bird in sunglasses. It wasn't art. It was a map. Not to a place—those changed—but to a feeling you could carry when the doors were locked.

Lights out. The bay settled into its chorus of small human noises—snore, sigh, the soft clack of someone's dog tags against a bunk frame when they rolled.

Across the aisle, Mike whispered just loud enough. "Still worth it?"

Ethan stared up at the faint square of darker dark that meant ceiling. His hand found the napkin through his pocket, the paper warm from his skin.

"Yeah," he said. "Worth all of it."

By morning the grind had its teeth in them again— formation, cadence, chow, drill—but the world had shifted a fraction on its axis. Not enough to trip the sergeants' radar. Just enough that when the day pressed down, Ethan knew where to stand to breathe.

The Army would keep its schedule. Ethan would keep a secret sun in his locker and a beat in his stride. And somewhere past graduation, past orders, past whatever came next, a road would angle toward home—whichever one he'd built by then.

Chapter 23 – Back to The Institute

Seven months at Fort McClellan had a way of sanding a man down to his strongest grain. Ethan left Alabama lean, hard, and laminated in Army green—54B, Chemical Warfare Specialist—with a GI Bill brochure folded into his wallet like a promise. Then the bus rolled him back into civilian air, and the promise met a calendar that didn't care.

Southern Military Institute had already slammed the gate on spring enrollment. His class marched on without him, gray coats turning another page he wasn't in. He told himself it wasn't failure. It was timing. But timing can feel like judgment when you're standing still.

Weekends belonged to the Reserve unit. The armory smelled like CLP and floor wax, familiar and oddly comforting. He learned new names stitched above pockets, fell into formations that didn't require shouting to understand, and discovered that competence—quiet, unshowy—could be its own rank. In the gas masks and MOPP suits, he was fluent; in the chow line, he was just another specialist with a tray and a thirst.

Weekdays were everything else.

Mornings at the diner: steam blasting from the dish pit, plates sliding into his hands slick as fish, the line cook swearing in two languages while bacon scorched a permanent perfume into Ethan's hair. He'd clock out smelling like breakfast and walk straight into a lawn crew where the sun hammered his neck and sprinklers stitched rainbows over HOA-perfect grass. On good days there was drywall—third-floor walk-ups, gypsum dust turning his sweat into paste, a foreman who called everyone "buddy" because names were an investment he didn't plan to make.

At night he ran.

Three miles through neighborhoods that felt like sets from a show about normal people. Dogs barked at the fence line; porch lights clicked on; kids practiced foul shots by the echo of their own ball. He liked the part of the route where the sidewalk buckled around an oak's roots—the small audacity of a tree refusing straight lines. Breathing hard beneath a sky the color of dishwater, he tried to hold two truths: he had left to make it possible to return; and he had, in the leaving, fallen out of step with the men who knew his name best.

On his wall, a paper calendar took the punishment. He X'd days like he was walking off a sentence—one box at a time, diagonal slash, then the cross. Some nights the marker squeaked and he had to put the cap back on because the sound got inside his teeth.

Mail thinned, as it does. A postcard from Jack, three sentences: Still here. Getting mine. Hurry up. —J. A form letter from SMI's registrar with deadlines in bold. A note from Dr. Maddox—ink-smudged, precise—You have a mind for the clean line. Don't let time dull it. Ethan propped that one on his dresser until steam from the shower curled the corners.

He stopped by SMI once, early summer, when a job hauling office furniture took him within sight of the stone. Standing across from the parade deck fence, he watched a company drill—rifles snapping, commands ricocheting off walls he knew by feel. A Fourth Classman stumbled, recovered, and no one noticed but Ethan. He wanted to yell, Keep your chin tucked, kid. Shorten your stride on turns. Instead he lifted another desk and kept moving.

At home, Mom asked careful questions. Coach—stepdad, the word still catching in Ethan's mouth sometimes—talked money like a playbook: tuition spread, GI Bill reimbursements, how many shifts made how many credits possible.

"You'll get back there," Coach said, tapping totals with a blunt forefinger. "You're doing the hard part now."

"Feels like the dumb part," Ethan muttered, then hated himself for saying it. Coach let it pass.

On Sundays he'd lay out his SMI gear—boots re-soled, brass bagged, gray folded sharp—then put it all away again because ritual without action can break you. He found himself humming Buffett when the house was quiet, not because he needed escape but because the songs stitched his timelines together: boy in a barracks, kid in a stadium, soldier in a borrowed room trying to aim himself back toward stone.

Sometimes he dreamed the stoops: the echo, the weight of eyes in windows, the way the deck could look like a lake at night. He'd wake to the small noises of the rental—the fridge kicking, a pipe settling—and lie still until his heart agreed to be just a heart again.

Summer bled into a softer heat. The calendar showed fewer clean white squares. Deposit posted. Registration confirmed. Orders squared away with the unit. He found himself touching the GI Bill card in his wallet the way some men touch medallions. Not superstition. Inventory.

On his last night before the return, he ran the route one more time and slowed at the buckled sidewalk. He put a hand on the oak's bark, rough and cool, and laughed at himself for making it a ceremony. Then he went home, shaved, packed the duffel that had become a second spine, and slept without dreaming.

In the morning, the bus hissed at the curb like something alive. He climbed aboard with a ticket he'd earned a mile at a time and watched his reflection ghost in the window as the city slid away.

Back wasn't the same as belonging. He knew that now. But it was the only direction that made sense.

The bus hissed to a stop three blocks from the stone. Ethan shouldered his duffel and walked the rest—part penance, part ritual—until Southern Military Institute rose in its old geometry: gray walls, green deck, brass glint.

Admin Day was a maze. He signed his name a dozen times in a dozen rooms. The registrar stamped forms with the judgment of a judge whose docket never emptied. At Finance, he slid the GI Bill paperwork across a counter nicked by decades of other men's plans.

"This covers tuition," the clerk said, tapping totals. "Room and board's you."

"Me," Ethan said. It sounded like a promise and a dare.

Issue felt like déjà vu: gray folded sharp, belts in bins, caps by size. He'd worn a uniform that summer that could stop chemical death; here he took one that could stop conversation. The quartermaster eyed the way Ethan rolled a belt and gave the smallest nod. Muscle memory travels.

His room assignment landed him with two Thirds he didn't know: Eric from Charleston—tidy, ironic, already a student company clerk—and Hooker from coal country—knuckles scabbed, smile easy, calculus a private war. They shook hands like they'd been warned to be polite.

"You were gone last year?" Eric asked.

"Army," Ethan said.

Hooker grinned. "So you're the old man."

"Twenty," Ethan said.

"Ancient," Hooker deadpanned, and they all laughed, because laughter oils hinges that otherwise stick.

The first mess hall lunch felt like walking into a memory with the colors turned down. No one made him strain. No one took his tray. He sat, lifted a fork, and had the strange sensation of doing something both ordinary and newly miraculous: eating, uninterrupted. Across the room, a Fourth Classman shook so hard his peas made a weather pattern. Ethan kept his eyes front, then—when the kid dropped a napkin and froze—looked away on purpose. Mercy, here, sometimes meant pretending you didn't see.

On the way out, a voice called, uncertain: "Skunk?"

Ethan turned. A First he half-knew squinted, as if trying to superimpose an old photo over the present. "Cole, right?"

"Yeah," Ethan said.

The man smiled, small. "Welcome back."

By late afternoon the parade deck cooked under a slant of sun. Jack appeared where Ethan knew he would—center of a small orbit, brass clean enough to throw back daylight. He dismissed a pair of Fourths, then spotted Ethan and broke from the cluster.

"Buffett," Jack said, grin wide. They hit shoulders like they used to, the collision more careful now.

"You look important," Ethan said.

Jack glanced at his collar, feigned confusion. "This junk? Borrowed." Then lower: "You good?"

"Getting there."

They walked the deck's edge once, two silhouettes pacing the line between past and whatever came next. Jack's stride was command; Ethan's was return. It felt like stepping in and out of the same current.

"You playing?" Jack asked, tilting his head toward the fields.

"Grades first," Ethan said. "Then maybe."

Jack nodded like a captain taking a report. "Find me after taps," he said, already reading the next task in the air. "We'll grab five."

The evening study period hit like rain after drought. Books spread, pencils scratched. Dr. Maddox's syllabus lay on Ethan's desk—proof that some through-lines survive: limits, proofs, measure, the comfort of clean logic. Outside, boots crossed stoops; inside, Ethan built a small fortress of order—shirt drawer by shade, brass kit squared, belt rolled and stowed. Army habits slid into Institute spaces and fit like teeth on a gear.

On his way to the latrine, he passed a Fourth lacing boots wrong—bunny ears where there should have been a straight bar. The kid's hands shook.

"Hold up," Ethan murmured, crouching. He worked the laces through with quick, sure motions, fingers remembering nights by flashlight in other barracks. "There," he said. "Won't bite your ankles now."

The Fourth whispered, "Thank you, sir."

"Not a sir," Ethan said, and kept moving. You don't make a show of mercy here. You just hand it off and walk.

Lights-out found him on his back, hands folded on his chest the way soldiers and penitents do. From the courtyard came the familiar acoustics: a ladder clanking, somebody laughing where they shouldn't, the flag halyard ticking against the pole. He listened for ghosts and heard only the living—their boots, their breathing, their trying.

He wasn't who he'd been when he left. Jack wasn't, either. The school sure as hell wasn't.

But the stone remained. So did the work.

In the dark, Ethan made a quiet inventory: GI Bill posted, classes set, a job at the library starting next week, old nickname fading, new footing forming. He exhaled slow and let the ceiling return to being just a ceiling.

Back wasn't belonging. Not yet.

But he was close enough to touch it.

After taps, Jack found him on the second stoop where shadows softened the stone.

"You said five," Ethan said.

Jack leaned on the rail, gaze on the parade deck. "You're back. That's what matters." A beat. "It won't stitch exactly where it tore."

"I know."

Jack's jaw worked like he wanted to add a rule and couldn't find the words. Instead: "Make yourself useful. That's how this place forgives."

They stood there, two outlines in a draft of night, then Jack clapped his shoulder and peeled off to brief a detail. Command called and Jack answered; it fit him like brass.

Ethan stayed, letting the quiet take a lap around his head. Useful. He could do useful.

The next morning he reported to the work-study desk in the library—cool air, dust motes like slow snow, the sweet-bitter smell of ink and old glue. Mrs. Keating, who had outlasted fifteen Superintendents and six card catalogs, eyed him over bifocals.

"You shelve straight, you show up on time, and you don't talk loud," she said. "That's the contract."

"Yes, ma'am."

In the stacks he found a battered copy of Linear Algebra. Inside, penciled notes ghosted the margins—his own from two years ago, graphite whispers of a boy who thought proof was a kind of spell. He smiled despite himself and turned a page he already knew by heart.

At noon a folded bill lay on the landing—green, deliberate, bait.

Two Fourths slowed, pupils wide. Ethan felt the old heat at the base of his neck, that whisper of paranoia the Institute planted and watered: they're watching. He didn't hesitate. He picked up the twenty, walked to the guard desk, and laid it flat.

"Found on second stoop," he said, voice even.

The cadet on duty—an upperclassman with a scar that pinched one eyebrow—studied him, then wrote a note and slid the bill into a pouch.

"Logged," he said. "Good catch."

It wasn't virtue so much as self-defense, but as he walked away, something inside him unknotted. You choose who you are one small moment at a time; SMI just makes sure the moments are close together.

Afternoons, he drifted to the practice fields. Jack's shot still cracked like a rifle. The coach waved Ethan over and handed him a mesh bag of cones.

"You want to run finishes for the Fourths?"

"Sure."

He set drills, counted reps, corrected a plant foot here, a shoulder there. The kids listened—partly because he wore gray, mostly because he spoke like somebody who'd had mud put in his mouth and kept crawling anyway. When a winger flubbed the same touch three times, Ethan made a joke and then made it muscle memory; both worked.

On the jog back, Jack fell into step beside him. "You miss it?"

"Enough to help," Ethan said. It was the truest answer.

Thursdays became Maddox days. He knocked, and the old man looked up from a chalk-whiteboard already half-conquered.

"Mr. Cole," Maddox said, as if they'd paused mid-conversation last year. "Do not make me regret my optimism."

"I'm here to prove you right," Ethan said, and meant it.

They talked limits that don't exist and series that do, the comfort of absolutes in a place built on conditional love. When Ethan left, his head hurt in the right way.

Nights he found small seams to sew. He showed a Fourth how to iron a sleeve without polishing a crease into the elbow.

He swapped a man's inspection time so Hooker could call his mother before the mines swallowed another bar of service. He learned Eric's schedule without asking and slid a stack of shelved books onto his desk at 2200 so the clerk could sleep twenty more minutes.

None of it made noise. None of it needed to.

On a Sunday he and Jack finally sat with coffee cooling between them in paper cups swiped from the mess line. They traded headlines instead of histories; you don't excavate here unless you have to. When they stood, Jack caught his eye.

"Don't chase the ghost of how it was," he said. "Build how it is."

Ethan nodded. "Working on it."

They stepped into sun, separate vectors tied to the same origin.

Lights-out came easier. In the dark he took inventory again and found new entries: a paycheck taped inside a ledger, a tutoring slot on Maddox's office door with his name penciled in, a kid on Fourth stoop who laced his boots right the first time.

Out on the deck, boots crossed in steady patterns—no haunt, just cadence. He let the sound count him down, then slept.

Back wasn't belonging.

But it was beginning.

Chapter 24 – Jack's New Game

While Ethan was gone, The Institute bent toward Jack.

On the field, it started as chemistry and turned into gravity. Mark Henson on the left—shoelaces always a little loose, first touch glued like a magic trick, the kind of pace that made defenders backpedal before he even looked up. Troy Daniels in the middle—lean, quiet, passes that split seams like a scalpel, a metronome with a mean streak. And Jack, the finisher, the long stride that ate yards, the right foot that could knock paint off a post. The papers called them SMI's Three Kings, and the nickname stuck because every Saturday they made someone kneel.

Game plans were polite suggestions; the three of them turned matches into parades. A one-two at midfield, a shoulder dip, a cut; Mark was through and Troy had already seen it—a ball feathered into space, Jack arriving late and violent, net flinching like it was tired of the abuse. Students who didn't know offsides from olive oil started showing up just to watch the chaos.

After final whistles, the stadium lights ticked themselves to sleep while the three of them jogged a victory lap that looked suspiciously like scouting. Who was impressed. Who was connected. Who'd be useful later. Winning was a scoreline; control was a habit.

Off the field, the habit scaled.

They moved together—into town, into rooms where music was too loud and advice was too quiet, into situations that smelled like bad decisions dressed up as opportunity. Other cadets would have been crushed for the same crimes. Jack, Mark, and Troy didn't get crushed. They got waved through. Charisma is a master key if you hold it with a steady hand.

It helped that The Institute itself was shifting. The Honor Code still hung in the chapel like scripture: A cadet will not lie, cheat, steal, nor tolerate those who do. Everyone recited it. Everyone saluted it. But fear had cooled to calculation. The Court hadn't lost its teeth; it had lost its appetite. Or maybe it just ate more selectively.

Jack noticed first. He always did.

"Give me the rules," he liked to say, "and I'll beat you at your own game."

So he learned the rules like a lawyer and played them like a thief. Lights out was a time, not a boundary. Curfew was a window, not a wall. Specials were a currency; bone sheets became receipts written in the correct hand by the correct friend and filed at the correct hour so the correct officer read them with the correct amount of boredom.

He built a circle without calling it that—no handshakes, no Greek letters, just gravity. If you were in, you knew. If you weren't, you guessed. Mark could charm a guard desk into forgetting to check a roster. Troy could study a professor's tells and call the pop quiz two days early. Jack could walk into a room and turn obligation into loyalty without raising his voice. Favors flowed outward; protection flowed back. After a while the circle wasn't a circle. It was the water the Corps swam in.

Cadets adjusted instinctively. A Fourth Classman with a bad bone sheet found it corrected before dawn. A missed curfew became an attaboy for covering a late-night "detail." Test keys never surfaced wholesale—they dripped: a hint here, a pattern there, just enough to edge a B to an A while innocence stayed plausible. Carelessness got you caught; craft kept you clean. Jack enforced that distinction with a smile and, when necessary, a look that meant don't make me spend capital on your stupidity.

The odd thing was how quiet it all was. No gang signs, no slogans. Just a thousand unspoken agreements braided into a rope strong enough to tow half the Corps through a bad month. Jack didn't use the rope to climb. He used it to pull others— and the more he pulled, the higher he stood.

Weeknights blurred into film sessions and late runs and paperwork nobody else wanted but that somehow put Jack in the room when decisions got made. Weekends split down the middle: ninety minutes of sanctioned violence on a chalked rectangle, then a drive an hour south where curfews and rank dissolved into perfume and neon.

Her name didn't need saying—the homecoming queen from back home, now the gravitational center of a college that felt like the opposite of stone barracks. In her apartment Jack wasn't a cadet; he was a story told in low light. He learned the route with two stoplights and a cop who napped after midnight; he learned what time to leave so the gate guard liked him just enough to wave him through with a yawn. Monday mornings he reappeared pressed and punctual, brass bright, demeanor brighter. Rumor had to sprint to keep up.

People asked what changed in him. The answer was simple: nothing essential. Jack had always loved rules. He just loved them most when they bent.

By late spring, even officers who kept their distance kept their distance more carefully. On the parade deck, heads dipped when he passed and then dipped again when Mark and Troy followed. In the mess line, juniors straightened their covers. On film days, the coach didn't so much assign as announce— Jack's line had already drawn itself.

If there was a gap in the armor, it didn't show. The anger that used to rise like flare-ups now banked low, a pilot light that warmed his voice without burning it. Caroline's letter had broken something; the bend set hard. He used the hurt the way he used everything else: as leverage.

Once, during evening study, a young cadet came whispering with panic in his breath about a chemistry exam he'd already failed in his head. Jack didn't hand over answers. He handed over a plan—sections to skim, problems to nail, a quiet word with a TA who owed him for a ride from the airport in November. The kid passed. The TA remembered. Jack never mentioned either again.

That was the game now. Not soccer, though he still terrified keepers. Not The Institute, though he knew every seam in its stone. Control. Influence. The kind of power that looks like luck if you're not paying attention.

And with Ethan somewhere between Alabama and the idea of coming back, Jack didn't notice the empty space beside him until the day it filled.

Ethan stepped back through the arch like a man revisiting a dream he wasn't sure he wanted to finish. Same stone, same echoing boots, same flag halyard clinking against the pole— only the faces had aged without him.

He checked in, took a room two floors from where he'd once slept, and walked the stoops with that odd mix of déjà vu and displacement, like the song was familiar but the key had changed. Juniors he didn't know were laughing in doorways. Firsts he did know wore rank like armor and responsibility like a second spine.

Jack found him before he could go looking.

"Buffett," he grinned, crossing the courtyard in three long strides. The slap on Ethan's shoulder was friendly, heavy, and maybe a little performative. Brass bright, cover square, Jack looked… established. Anchored. "You back for good or just to make us all feel lazy?"

"For good," Ethan said. The words were true. They didn't feel simple.

They did the tour because that's what old friends do: mess hall, stands, the corner where they used to kill ten minutes before formation. Jack narrated like a genial host. Who'd graduated. Who mattered now. Where not to be on Thursdays because a certain lieutenant liked surprise inspections. Names rolled out of him, each attached to a favor banked or a debt outstanding.

"You'll meet Henson and Daniels tonight," Jack said. "We'll run film, then hit town. Welcome home."

Home. The word fit everywhere and nowhere at once.

Practice was a highlight reel—Jack on half-speed still better than most men at full, Mark knifing inside backs until they stopped guessing, Troy pinging passes through gaps that didn't exist until his foot made them. Ethan lingered by the fence, catching a ball that skidded over the line and rifling it back to a trainer with more accuracy than grace. He hadn't lost the touch; he'd misplaced the context.

After, in the locker room, steam and chatter filled the tile box. Introductions were quick; claps on the back were real enough. But when the jokes slid into code—references to who could "cover a late night" and which professor's "pop" never popped on Fridays—Ethan felt the old language had added slang.

Back in barracks, he found an envelope already waiting: admin stuff for his readmission, a schedule card, a reminder about a chapel brief. Under it, a Post-it in Jack's blocky hand: Film at 1900. Pizza after. Bring your dry sense of humor.

They watched thirty minutes of goals and thirty of mistakes, the coach stopping tape only to point out the latter.

When the lights came up, Jack gave the look that meant our turn now. The coach nodded and left them the room.

"Daniels," Jack said, "walk Henson through the new corner shape. We're changing the second runner."

Troy didn't need telling twice. It took five minutes. Control disguised as leadership feels like competence because it is.

Pizza happened, though "pizza" also meant a cooler under a blanket and the quiet drift of teammates who understood that at The Institute, some rooms were safer than others. Ethan took a warm slice, sat on a trunk at the edge of the circle, and listened.

Stories spilled: away match hijinks, a curfew that wasn't, a Special "fixed" by a wording miracle. Nothing overt. Everything practiced. When someone asked Ethan about Fort McClellan, he kept it light—gas chamber, red clay, drill sergeants who didn't blink. He left out the night in Atlanta and the taste of a concert sung from the middle of a thousand strangers. Some memories are better unshared.

At eleven, the room thinned. Jack walked him out onto the stoop where the night had teeth and the parade deck hoarded its echoes.

"It's different," Ethan said finally.

Jack didn't pretend not to understand. "You were gone a year, man. The place keeps moving. We moved with it."

"And the Code?" Ethan asked. "It feel... softer?"

Jack's mouth twitched. "It feels smarter. People still get hammered for being dumb. People who aren't dumb don't get in the way of the hammer." He let that sit. "You'll catch up."

Ethan nodded like agreement was the same as assent.

The first test came stupid-small, which is how tests like to come. A sophomore from Ethan's new company knocked on his door with panic sweating through his undershirt.

"Cole, right? Hey—uh—Sir—" (rank confusion, honest nerves) "—I screwed an inspection. Sling twist. They want me to bone it. Could you… look over what I wrote?"

He handed over the sheet. Offense: Rifle sling out of alignment. Response: Incorrect.

Ethan could feel the trap in the paper grain. He'd lived it once. He opened his mouth to say Mark it correct and wish to explain, then tasted the memory of tours and a superintendent's pen, the humiliation dragging circles around a courtyard while men on stoops sipped Cokes and commented on his pace.

Jack appeared in the doorway like he'd been summoned by the decision itself. He took the sheet without asking, scanned it, and met the kid's eyes.

"Make it 'Correct,'" Jack said, calm. "Then don't twist your sling."

"But it wasn't—"

Jack's look wasn't cruel; it was instructional. "You can be right or you can be here. Pick."

The sophomore swallowed, nodded, rewrote the line, and left grateful for certainty.

When the hall emptied, Ethan leaned against his locker.

"You just taught him to lie," he said.

"I taught him to survive," Jack said. He said it softly, which made it worse. "No one's marching him out over a sling, but they'll gladly teach him the difference between pride and progress. I saved him a week of tours and a seed of bitterness. He'll shine his gear twice tomorrow."

Ethan didn't argue. He also didn't agree. The line between those two actions is a room you can live in for a long time.

On Saturday, Jack's world bled into another. The drive south hummed—stations fading to static, then snapping back clear. The apartment smelled like perfume and laundry and something frying in a pan. The homecoming queen laughed when she saw Ethan.

"You're the Buffett one," she said, pouring drinks with an easy confidence that implied she'd already decided Ethan was safe.

"Guilty," he said, and meant something else.

They went out with her friends who were all kinetic color and off-campus ease. The bar was too bright, the music too cheerful, the freedom too casual. Jack leaned across a tiny table and yelled over the chorus, introducing Ethan via story: mud hills, moonshine, a highway that had turned into a parking lot party once upon a time. The girls loved that one. Ethan smiled and wanted to go stand under a streetlight and breathe.

Back on the interstate at midnight, Ethan watched the speedometer hover over the line and the gate guard wave them through without looking up. Jack drummed the wheel with two fingers, a restlessness that had nothing to do with nerves.

"You can have both," Jack said suddenly, eyes on the road. "This and the stone. You just can't pretend one isn't real."

Ethan stared out at the black ribbon of highway. In the glass he could see his own face doubled—once in the window, once in the dashboard. He didn't know which one looked like him.

By week's end, he found a rhythm: formations, classes, miles on the track by himself when the field was booked. At night he studied alone because the jokes in Jack's room now had a velocity he couldn't match and a moral algebra he didn't want to solve. They still sat on the stoop some evenings, the easy silence of old friends slipping over them like a blanket. Then someone would call Jack's name from below, and the blanket would lift.

They were brothers still. Just standing on different parts of the same deck, watching the same moon throw different shadows.

Midterms crept in the way weather does—one morning the air different in your lungs and you realize a season changed while you were busy pretending it wouldn't. Ethan took a stack of blue books from a TA in a wool blazer who mispronounced his name and assigned a seat that smelled faintly of chalk and old coffee. Econ. Numbers he could trust. Rules he could follow.

Two nights before the exam, Jack dragged him to "study hall" in a teammate's room—Mark on the windowsill, Troy at the desk, three others flopped across bunks. Pizza boxes curled at the corners. A whiteboard leaned against a radiator, scrawled with supply curves and elasticities.

Jack tossed Ethan a marker. "Walk 'em through marginal cost, Buffett."

Ethan did. The room listened. It felt… normal.

Then Troy set a stapled packet on the desk with a casualness that was more performance than accident. The first page had the professor's masthead at the top and multiple-choice bubbles beneath.

Ethan's hand stopped midair.

"Where'd you get that?" he asked.

"Office bin," Troy said, not bothering with the lie. "Prof prints the wrong set every year and tosses the drafts. He's a recycler. We're recyclers."

Jack watched Ethan, unreadable. "We're calibrating, not cheating," he said lightly. "It's not the test; it's a test. Same pool. We learn the mind, not the answers."

"Same pool," Mark echoed, as if that mattered. "We still have to know it."

Ethan looked down at the packet. He thought of the Chapel's shadows and the drum at midnight; of a slashed-open life marched off the deck; of a sophomore at his door, saved from tours by a single word on a form. The Institute was slippery now. But he could still feel stone under one foot.

"I'm out," he said.

Jack didn't blink. "You're overthinking."

"Maybe. Still out."

Silence tightened. Even the radiator's hiss seemed to wait.

Troy lifted one shoulder. "Suit yourself."

Ethan set the marker on the desk like it might break if he dropped it, nodded once at Jack, and left.

He studied alone in a hallway that smelled like floor wax and winter. He took the exam sober, the way you take a punch you know is coming—chin tucked, eyes up. He didn't ace it. He didn't have to. When the grades posted, he'd done well. Not perfect. Honest.

Jack walked out of class two days later with a 98 and a shrug that said of course. He clapped Ethan's shoulder in the corridor.

"See? Everyone wins," he said.

Ethan forced a half smile. "Everyone?"

"Everyone who matters," Jack said, then softened it with a grin that tried to erase the edge. "Come on. Practice."

The Institute tested them in other ways too. After a home match—three-nil and never close—Coach handed out forms to sign: acknowledgment of the Honor Code for traveling teams. A ritual, really, like bowing before an altar you pass every day.

Ethan signed without thinking. Jack's pen hovered.

It was a flicker, nothing more—the tiniest hitch, the smallest pause—but Ethan saw it. Jack saw Ethan see it. Their eyes met, and Jack's pen moved. Ink on line. Done.

"Stop reading ghosts," Jack said as they left the locker room. "I sign what I live by."

Ethan didn't argue. He could hear steel drums in a stadium three states away and the hiss of a Walkman in a Chapel that made music a punishment. He could hear the drum that sent a boy out of the gates and the cheer that crowned three kings on a field. All of it true. None of it simple.

Rumors follow winning teams the way seagulls follow boats. A week later the Honor Officer for their company "randomly" spot-checked three econ blue books. Mark's was in the stack. So was Troy's.

Jack got there first. Not to threaten, not to plead. To frame.

"Coach ran extra film that night," he said, dropping schedules and sign-in sheets on the officer's desk with the calm of a man who'd already measured the room. "I can vouch for my guys' study time, and for where they were when they weren't here. If there's a pattern, it's that we're prepared."

He didn't lie. Not exactly. He poured the truth into a mold and let it set.

The officer flipped pages, hunting for a reason to care more than he already did. He didn't find one. The blue books went back to a drawer. The drawer clicked shut. The rumor thinned.

Ethan watched it happen from the doorway—how control wears a polite face, how influence sounds like patience. On the way out, Jack bumped his shoulder against Ethan's like the old days.

"See?" he said. "You can be clean in a dirty rain."

"Or you can stay inside," Ethan said.

Jack's smile tilted. "You left the house once, soldier. Didn't mean you quit the war."

They found a way to be friends inside the argument. Some nights they still stood on the stoop and traded nothing-talk until the halyard clinked three lazy beats against the pole and the deck breathed that hollow dark. Other nights Jack vanished south and Ethan laced his shoes and ran tempo laps under stadium lights that hummed like insects.

On a cold Thursday, Ethan stopped by the Chapel alone. No service. Just the old wood and the colored light falling in bars. He didn't pray. He sat in a back pew and let his jaw unclench.

He thought about the kid in Alabama who'd shared a flask and a chorus; about a corporal who'd carried him three miles because that's what you do when a man drops beside you; about a professor who'd saved him from himself with a phone call and a mercy grade. He thought about Jack, who could make a system purr like a well-oiled rifle and who would break his own knuckles before he let a teammate go down alone.

He wasn't sure which kind of strength the place needed more. He wasn't sure which kind he had to give.

When he stood to leave, the stone held the night the same way it always had—heavy and patient. Outside, the flag halyard tapped the pole twice, then once, like it had changed its mind mid-sentence.

Ethan crossed the deck, boots crisp on concrete, and climbed the stairs to his floor. In the corridor, laughter spilled from Jack's room—Troy's sharp cackle, Mark's crow. Ethan paused, then kept walking.

They were still brothers. The game was just two games now.

And for the first time, Ethan understood that surviving The Institute wasn't about choosing one or the other.

It was about not letting either one choose you.

Chapter 25 – The Barber Townee

Mitch rolled in with a smirk and a duffel full of trouble. Star striker, rich-kid smooth, aviators even at dusk. On paper, the kind of cadet Ethan should've disliked. In practice, Mitch was sharp enough and funny enough that the swagger played like a bit instead of a threat.

That first night back at Southern Military Institute, the room turned into a contraband lounge. Greasy pizza, cheap beer, windows cracked to bleed the smell. Jack did what Jack always did—turned stories into theater, hands carving arcs in the air as he reenacted last semester's chaos. Mitch punched his own lines like a stand-up. Ethan added just enough to stay in the lane, more listener than lead. By dawn his eyes felt sanded raw and his hair looked like a mop under a helmet.

He needed the barbershop.

The shop hadn't changed since the seventies: humming fluorescents, talc in the air, oil on the clippers, three bald lifers in stained smocks cycling cadets like cattle.

Chair Four was new.

Blonde. Early twenties. Townee. Bright eyes, easy smile, hands that moved like they'd been taught by someone who cared. She dusted the seat with a flick that said she could do this blindfolded. Softness in a place built from stone.

By chance or fate, Ethan landed in her chair.

Small talk usually felt like a drill he failed on purpose. Not here. He answered without bracing. She teased him for sitting at parade rest. He fired back. Hometowns. why-are-you-here questions. The laugh came out of him before he knew it was his.

He asked if she wanted to hang out that evening.

He heard himself do it. He heard her say yes. He stepped outside blinking into cold air like he'd walked out of a movie and the light hadn't adjusted yet.

Back in the room he blurted it all before the door swung shut.

Jack looked up from a comic. Mitch, shirtless, flipped a smuggled Sports Illustrated.

"Skunk," Mitch said, pitying grin in place, "half the Corps has slept with her."

Heat climbed Ethan's neck. He swallowed. "I don't care," he said. "I liked talking to her. That's enough for me."

Jack's look was half-skeptic, half-smile. Mitch went back to glossy pages. The matter, officially, was a joke. Unofficially, Ethan knew what he was walking into.

They saw each other that night. And the night after. Cheap wine in plastic cups. Townee bars with sticky floors. She talked about leaving this town like it was a dare she'd give herself tomorrow. Ethan liked the way she looked at him—like she'd pulled him out of a crowd and decided this one. He wasn't used to being chosen. In a world that measured you in push-ups and tours and ranks on a collar, being wanted felt… clean.

For a few weeks, it worked. He'd sit in Chair Four on Saturdays and she'd dust his neck like it meant something. He'd sign out, meet her outside the gate, and breathe a different kind of air for a few hours. Back in barracks, Jack would raise an eyebrow and Mitch would make a face, and Ethan would shrug because not everything needed to be a debate.

Then little edges started to show. She loved smoky rooms and loud stories. Ethan loved quiet. She wanted his history; he gave clipped versions like he was still in front of the RDC. She asked about Thanksgiving—Will I meet your folks?—and his throat closed. He was already thinking about how to work extra shifts, how to make the question go away.

But that was later. For now, it was simple. New roommate. New routine. New girl from Chair Four.

And for the first time in a long time, Ethan walked across the parade deck feeling like something in his life hadn't been assigned.

For a while, Chair Four kept feeling like a door propped open to air that didn't smell like Brasso and sweat. Then the hinge squeaked.

She liked smoky townee bars and jukeboxes that stuck on the same three songs; Ethan liked quiet corners and early exits. She leaned across tables, eyes dreamy, wanting stories; he answered like an RDC pop quiz—short, safe, nothing you could use against him later. When she asked, almost shy, if Thanksgiving meant meeting his folks, his throat closed around a half-truth about "work over break." She nodded, but he saw the hurt flash and tried not to look.

By the time they lugged duffels back up after the holiday, the room felt… wrong. Mitch sniffed once like a bloodhound.

"Room smells off," he said.

Ethan smelled it too—cheap perfume under shoe polish. His desk drawer sat a hair open. Before he could process it, a metallic tink pinged the window.

He slid the sash. Two swaying shapes in the courtyard— Chair Four and a friend, both red-cheeked and glossy-eyed under the yellow lamp.

"Skunk!" she sang up, drawing his old nickname out like taffy. "Miiisss meee?"

Mitch leaned into the frame, grinning. "Hey, you in our room over break?"

She squinted, wobbled, then nodded so hard she nearly fell. "Yessss," she slurred. Her friend cackled.

Ethan's stomach dropped. He turned to warn the room—"Jack? Mitch?"—but their bunks were already empty. Door clicked. Gone.

He kept his eyes on the girls. "You should go," he said, trying for firm, landing on pleading. "It's late. You're drunk."

A scrape rumbled above him. Then a slosh.

Ethan looked up just as a white wall of water pitched off the fourth stoop. It hit like a falling room. The two women vanished in the cascade, then reappeared shrieking—mascara in rivers, hair plastered, sundresses clinging.

Ethan didn't have to guess. Only Jack and Mitch would muscle a dumpster into the showers, fill it to the brim, and tip it three stories down.

Silence held for a heartbeat—just dripping and stunned breathing—then snapped. Chair Four's face went hard. She charged for the gate, friend on her flank. The guard detail tried to corral them; one cadet folded after a knee to the groin, another ate a right hook. The courtyard erupted—boots pounding stoops, catcalls, laughter ricocheting off stone. Someone yelled, "Let 'em fight!" Someone else, "Call the cops!"

Sirens answered. Red-blue washed the walls. The two were hauled out spitting and cursing, still trying to swing around uniformed arms as the crowd hooted from the railings.

Ethan stood in the window, wet air cooling his face, shame and disbelief washing over him in waves. He shut the sash on the last echo of laughter and waited for the door to open.

They didn't come back until the sirens were memories and the courtyard had gone slick and quiet again.

Jack kicked the door shut with his heel, laughter still bubbling out of him. Mitch collapsed backward onto his bunk, hands over his face, wheezing.

"Did you see her form?" Mitch gasped. "Lead with the knee—textbook."

"Guard Private Miller's gonna be singing soprano," Jack said, wiping at tears. "Holy hell."

Ethan just stared. "You dumped a dumpster of water on two drunk girls."

Jack's grin faltered a hair. "On two intruders. Who admitted they'd been in our room."

Mitch pointed at Ethan's desk. "Drawer was cracked. Townee perfume in the air. We did you a favor—rinse cycle."

Ethan opened his mouth, closed it, felt the ache in his temples pulse. "You could've gotten them killed."

Jack sobered, just enough for the quiet to take a seat. "We watched the landing. Didn't drop it on them. Just… woke the neighborhood."

A long beat.

"Look," Jack added, softer, "you weren't gonna end it. You were gonna let it rot. We… sped the truth up."

Ethan sank to the bunk. He should've been furious. He was. But braided in the anger was something uglier—relief.

The fallout came quick and bureaucratic. A Townee Incident Report appeared on the Company bulletin, dense with passive voice: unauthorized civilians entered Institute grounds… altercation with guard detail… escorted off premises by local law enforcement. Names were redacted. Warnings were not.

Chair Four got a lifetime ban from post. Her friend caught a disorderly. The police didn't push it further—town had learned long ago that fighting the Institute was like throwing eggs at a cannon. By noon, the story was already mutating on the stoops: Two Amazons stormed First Battalion and broke three jaws. By supper it had a title: The Great Rinse.

Jack and Mitch? They never showed up on any paperwork. Alibis flowered like dandelions. Half the team had "seen them studying" during the window, the other half had "seen them at the library." A freshman swore on his Cadet's Honor he'd watched them pray in the Chapel. The Honor Code bent and didn't squeal.

Ethan got called to the guard office only once. A lieutenant asked him if he knew the women. He said yes. Asked if he'd invited them onto post. He said no. Both were true. The lieutenant stared a beat, then slid a notice across the desk—admonishment to maintain appropriate civilian boundaries. He signed and left without lifting his eyes.

He didn't see Chair Four again.

The next night, Ethan walked to the pay phone outside the PX. The receiver was slick with old conversations; the yellow light made everything look jaundiced. It rang five times. She answered, voice hoarse, still furious.

"I'm sorry," he said, before she could start. "For all of it. For not being honest about what this was. For not stopping last night before it started."

A brittle laugh. "You boys love your games."

"I'm not playing," he said quietly. "We wanted different things. That's my fault for pretending otherwise."

A stretch of static. When she spoke again, the anger had cooled to something clean. "You never looked me in the eyes, you know that? Not really. You kept watching the door."

He closed his eyes, and for once the truth didn't choke him. "I know."

Silence. Then: "Take care of yourself, Skunk."

Click.

He stood there awhile with the dead line humming, then hung the receiver back on its hook like it could break.

What the Corps remembered wasn't the phone call. It was the spectacle. By Friday the story had a rhythm. By Saturday it had choreography. "They say the boys rigged a tub on four stoop." "The townees leveled two guards." "Police brought batons; the girls tried to take them." In the retelling, Ethan's part shrank until he was just a face in a window—witness to somebody else's myth.

He let it happen. He went to class. He showed at formations. He ran in the cold until the burn in his lungs washed the smell of cheap perfume out of his head. At night he studied because numbers still lined up when nothing else would. Slowly, the taut wire inside him loosened.

Across the room, Mitch went on being Mitch—loud, funny, collecting detentions like trading cards and dodging the only ones that mattered. Jack slipped back into the current he'd made, surfing on nods and favors. They were trouble, and they were brothers, and somehow those things could live in the same skin.

One evening, Jack tossed a tennis ball off the wall and caught it without looking. "You hate me?" he asked, so flat it almost sounded like a joke.

Ethan took his time answering. "No."

Jack kept his eyes on the ball. "You hate what I did?"

"Yeah," Ethan said. "And I hate that part of me is glad it's over."

The ball thumped, caught. Jack nodded once. "That's about the size of most things around here."

They sat in the kind of quiet men earn.

By semester's end, The Great Rinse had graduated from rumor to barracks folklore. Rats heard it as a cautionary hymn: don't bring town into the walls. Firsts told it like a comedy. Those in the middle used it as a weather vane—if you laughed, you belonged; if you winced, you remembered being human.

Ethan kept one small rule he wrote for himself that week and never said out loud: no more secrets that make you watch the door. No more rooms that smell wrong when you come back. No more faces you can't meet.

On the last night before leave, the three of them ate contraband pizza again, grease bleeding into paper plates, steam fogging the window. Jack tossed Ethan a beer; Mitch toasted the air.

"To legends," Mitch said.

"To endings," Ethan added.

Jack smirked. "To rinses."

They drank. Outside, the parade deck lay black and perfect, holding the echoes of a hundred stories exactly like theirs— some louder, some quieter, all rewritten by the walls.

Ethan set his empty down and felt, for once, precisely where he stood: not the hero of the tale, not the villain, not the spectator. Just a man learning his own rules inside a place that loved to write them for you.

That would have to be enough.

Chapter 26 – The Last Hurrah

It was supposed to be a simple kind of perfect: one last spring break before Jack graduated, one more story to tell when there weren't any more left to make.

Ethan didn't need convincing. No family trip on the calendar, no girlfriend tugging him home. When Jack leaned over his bunk and said, "Come to Minnesota with us," Ethan answered before the sentence had its period.

"Hell yeah. I'm in."

Jack's grin came easy. He clapped Ethan on the shoulder like a seal of approval. "Good. Time you met my people."

The Ford EXP was technically a two-seater with a hatch, but on the road it transformed into a rolling dive bar. Clothes were an afterthought. Beer was not. Jack drove with one hand, his girlfriend in the passenger seat telling stories wide enough to take both lanes; Ethan sprawled in the back with the coolers, the appointed bartender, popping tabs and passing cans forward like communion.

Miles evaporated. Cigarettes burned down to nubs and turned the cab into a low cloud. They sang to whatever the radio would give them—80s power ballads, tinny country, a scratchy station that faded in and out like a bad memory. Jokes grew taller, truths got fuzzed at the edges, and the dash collected the archaeology of the trip: fast-food wrappers, bottle caps, a map nobody used.

By the time the Explorer rolled into Minnesota, it smelled like laughter and bad decisions. Ethan's head throbbed, his lower back hated him, and he wouldn't have traded the last twenty-four hours for a week of sleep.

Jack's brother was waiting on the curb, taller than Jack by a head and lean with that particular Navy wear-and-tear—eyes that had learned to scan a horizon, shoulders that looked like they remembered burden even when they weren't carrying it. He pulled Jack into a bear hug that rattled bones, then stuck out a hand to Ethan.

"About damn time," he said. "You must be Ethan."

"Guilty," Ethan answered, and did his best not to wince when the handshake tightened to "welcome to the family."

They didn't pretend to ease into it. At ten in the morning, Jack's brother cracked beers like they were checking watches.

"Breakfast of champions," he announced, sliding cans across a table scarred with other people's nights.

By dusk, the room had that soft glow only alcohol and long stories can engineer. The girlfriend laughed with her whole body; Jack kept losing the thread of his own punchlines and somehow made that funnier. Ethan, a couple steps behind and happy there, learned the shorthand families carry: the shorthand of nicknames, legendary screwups, and the quiet pause that means "we don't talk about that part."

Then Jack's brother leaned back and tossed a grenade.

"We're going to the Mall of America."

Jack blinked. The girlfriend blinked. Ethan waited for the twist.

"The mall," Jack said, deadpan. "What are we, twelve?"

"It's the biggest one in the country," his brother said, grinning. "And it's got a whole floor that's nothing but bars."

A beat. Jack's face cracked into a grin.

"Why didn't you lead with that?"

From outside, the Mall of America looked like a grounded starship: concrete, glass, and a scale that made you feel like a toy. Inside, it was its own weather system—bright, loud, air that smelled like pretzels and perfume. And in the middle of it all, towering over strollers and tour groups, a manufactured mountain with a log flume pouring down its face.

"Holy—" Ethan tipped his head all the way back. "They put an amusement park in a mall."

"Tell me we're riding that," Jack said.

"Put it on the list," Ethan answered. "Bars first."

They took the escalator to the fourth floor and stepped into a mile of neon. Every doorway breathed music. The first bar was already a crush of bodies, three-deep at the counter, the kind of crowd that sways as one organism. They muscled into a corner, raised their voices over bass and laughter, and ordered like they intended to make a dent in the national supply.

For an hour, they did exactly what they came to do: drink, brag, and be twenty-something and invincible. Ethan leaned back against a wall that had absorbed a decade of nights like this one and watched the world spin at a manageable speed.

Then Jack's brother squinted toward the back.

"Bathroom," he said, and disappeared into the human river.

He reappeared thirty seconds later, jaw tight. "Line's out the door."

"So wait," Jack said, smirking.

But his brother's face had already gone slack with that fatal combination of too much beer and not enough shame.

What happened next would end the night before it had a chance to begin—and set the stage for whatever came after.

It went sideways fast.

Jack's brother unzipped, let fly right there against the bar's brass rail, and the world snapped into focus. A bartender's shout. Bouncers parting the crowd like linemen. Four hands on four shoulders, then the air outside—quiet, bright, echoing off tile.

"One goes, all go," the biggest bouncer said, door thudding shut behind them.

They stood there, blinking in the giant corridor, the mall still roaring a floor below. Jack's girlfriend started laughing so hard she had to lean on the wall. Jack rubbed a hand over his face, halfway between furious and impressed.

"You're a menace," he told his brother.

"Fair," the brother said, grinning.

They could've called it. Should've. Instead, the log flume's fake mountain loomed into their line of sight, all fiberglass cliffs and blue water under stadium lights. Twelve massive TV screens above the exit cycled through riders' terror-faces like a living flipbook.

Jack's grin returned. "We're riding it."

They wedged into a log, plastic bench slick with spray. The ride slipped into the mountain's dark throat—neon stalactites, fans pushing mist, their laughter bouncing off hollow walls. For a few easy minutes, it was just water and echo and the soothing dumbness of being carried.

Then the chain lift grabbed. The log clanked onto the escalator of slats, angling toward the final drop. Jack's brother stood.

"What the hell are you doing?" Jack barked.

"Shortcut," the brother said—and stepped into the water.

There wasn't time to argue. Ethan and Jack jumped after him, all three scrambling up the wet stairway like kids at a closed pool, palms skidding, sneakers squealing. Behind them, Jack's girlfriend screamed from the log, a one-woman Greek chorus: "Sit down! SIT DOWN!"

Too late. The escalator spat them out at the crest and gravity took over. They pinwheeled through the falls, a tangle of limbs and bad choices, and detonated into the splash pool at the bottom.

Security was waiting. Two guards waded in up to their shins and hauled the trio out by the elbows, dripping and giddy, steering them toward the exit with professional patience and a radio already crackling at a hip.

"Gentlemen," one said, deadpan, "you're done here."

Security walked them the long way—past the food court, under skylights bright as noon—three soggy idiots leaving a trail. A supervisor with a clipboard did the honors at the doors.

"You're trespassed for twenty-four hours," he recited. "If we see you again tonight, you're riding in a squad car."

Jack's brother saluted him with two dripping fingers. "Aye, sir."

Outside, March air bit their skin. Steam came off their clothes. They hustled to the Explorer, climbed in, and laughed until it broke into coughing. Jack's girlfriend sat in the passenger seat, arms crossed, trying to stay mad and failing.

"You two," she said, shaking her head at the brothers. "You deserve each other."

"Tragic but true," Jack said, starting the engine. The heater wheezed to life, good as a blessing.

Back at the house, they peeled off shoes and shirts, left a puddle by the door, and wrapped themselves in towels found in a hall closet printed with cartoon fish. Jack's brother set three beers on the kitchen table and a space heater on the floor. It smelled like dust and hot coils.

"Sorry about the bar," he said after a minute, voice downshifted to honest. "Ship life messes a man up. You get used to doing what you want at three a.m. 'Cause no one stops you in the middle of the Pacific."

Jack clinked cans with him. "We're good."

Ethan took a pull and let the warm fizz sit on his tongue. "You know we're idiots, right?"

"Certified," the brother said, smiling. Then he pointed the can at Ethan. "But you—look out for him when I'm not around." A nod toward Jack. "He runs hot. Whole family flaw."

Jack rolled his eyes. Ethan nodded anyway.

They slept like rocks—three hours on couches, the girlfriend under an afghan in an around them, northern wind working at the eaves.

They hit a diner with a cracked vinyl booth and coffee that could melt a spoon. The waitress called everyone "hon" and slid them a plate the size of a hubcap: eggs, bacon, a pancake that spilled off the rim.

"Y'all the kids who went swimming at the mall?" she asked, deadpan.

Jack choked on coffee. "News travels fast."

"Mall security eats here," she said, topping him off. "Tip your server."

They did.

On the way back, Jack pulled over at a lake rimmed in pale ice. The wind came off it clean and unforgiving. They walked out onto the dock, boards groaning under frost.

"Last spring break," Jack said, breath smoking. "Last everything, soon."

Ethan jammed his hands in his pockets. "You ready for it?"

Jack stared across the flat white. "I'm ready to leave. Not sure I'm ready to be gone."

They stood quiet awhile, the way men do when a feeling's too big for plain talk.

"Hey," Ethan said finally, half-smile, half-truth. "We'll botch something even dumber next time."

Jack laughed. "Count on it."

The drive back was a ribbon of gray—billboards, two-lane blacktop, truck stops with the same three jerky flavors. The girlfriend slept, cheek to window. The brothers traded the wheel. Ethan rode in the back with the coolers again, counting mile markers, picking stations that faded to static and then returned as something new.

Late afternoon, Jack's hand reached back without looking. Ethan slapped it in a lazy high five that said more than talking.

"Thanks for coming," Jack said.

"Wouldn't have missed it," Ethan answered. "Even the… hydration incident."

"Occupational hazard," Jack said, grinning.

They crossed back into familiar geography: red clay thinning to Appalachian folds, then the stubborn hills around The Institute. The Explorer's engine note changed as Jack downshifted at the gate.

Back inside the walls, the place looked smaller and harder at the same time. The parade deck held the last blue of evening. Somewhere a bugle stitched a few clean notes into the air.

They hauled the duffels upstairs. At the second-floor landing, foot traffic forked—First stoop left, lower-class right. Jack paused in the V of the hallway.

"This was it," he said. "Last hurrah."

Ethan nodded. "Hell of one."

They bumped shoulders—man's hug—then split. Jack climbed into light and noise and the easy gravity of a man at his apex. Ethan took the other stairs, his own corridor quieter, the old ache of almost and not-yet settling back into his chest.

In his room, he set the duffel down and sat on the edge of the rack. The mall screens flashed in his head—the three of them frozen mid-drop, ridiculous and alive. He grinned despite himself.

Outside, boots clanged. Somewhere above, Jack's laugh cut through the stone—brief, bright, familiar.

Ethan lay back, hands behind his head, and let the ceiling blur. Spring would bring finals and inspections and goodbyes. After that, the world again.

For now, the last hurrah still rang in his ears like water in the canal. And for a little while longer, that was enough.

Chapter 27 – One Hundred Fifty-Four Specials

By spring, Southern Military Institute didn't feel like a school so much as a stage Jack and Mitch owned. Their network ran like wiring behind the walls—quiet, everywhere. A nod from Mitch made guard teams forget a curfew check ever happened. A shrug from Jack moved a penalty tour off one kid and onto thin air. Upperclassmen called it luck. The Corps knew better.

Ethan rode the wake.

He drank when they drank, laughed when they laughed, skipped classes until the registrar's ink might as well have been a bruise. The difference was simple and fatal: Jack and Mitch could juggle the fire. Ethan just let it burn. He knew it, too. This was his last year at SMI. Not officially—on paper there was always "one more semester"—but the truth had already settled in his bones.

Leaving, though—leaving quietly—felt wrong. SMI took hair and sleep and pride and gave him brothers and scars and a spine that didn't bend. He couldn't just fade out.

So he decided to leave a mark.

The guard room smelled like shoe polish and burnt coffee. Two cadets in sashed belts hunched behind the desk, passing a deck of cards back and forth, bored enough to forget they were supposed to look dangerous.

Ethan stepped in, took a bone sheet, and sat.

Name, company, date. Offense.

The pen scratched. He flipped the page, reached for another sheet. Then another. At five, one guard looked up. At ten, both stood. At fifteen, their card game died in the ashtray.

"What are you doing, Cole?" one asked.

"Civic duty," Ethan said without looking up.

He kept going, the rhythm soothing as rosary beads. Missed formations he never boned. Inspections he'd dodged. Study halls that saw only the back of his head as he walked past. He worked through fall to winter, September to March, letting memory deal the cards. Every scribble felt like tapping a chisel to stone. He wasn't confessing. He was engraving.

Twenty sheets became forty. Forty grew to a stack you could measure with fingers. Passersby slowed, then lingered. Someone snickered. Someone else whispered, "He's out of his mind."

Ethan didn't care. He wrote until his hand cramped and his tongue pressed a small white groove into the corner of his mouth. When at last the math in his head said, Enough, he squared the edges with both palms, slid the mountain of paper across the desk, and gave the guards a pleasant, almost old-fashioned smile.

"Gentlemen," he said. Then he walked out.

Back in the room, Jack was stretched across his bunk reading the sports page like a king on review. Mitch sat on the desk, feet on the chair he was supposed to polish, flipping a coin and catching it without looking.

Ethan heaved the stack onto the dresser. It landed with a sound that made both of them lift their heads.

"What's that?" Mitch asked.

"My legacy," Ethan said, and peeled the top sheet free.

Absent, Breakfast Roll Call, 8/28.

How do you wish to plead?

He checked Correct, but wish to explain and started writing, the grin already tugging.

I was getting busy with the Commandant's daughter. Tried to leave, but she wanted to go again. You wouldn't have left either.

Jack barked a laugh so hard the paper crackled in his hands. Mitch slid off the desk, coin forgotten.

"Do another," Mitch said, eyes bright.

Missed Inspection, 9/12.

Too hungover to find my pants. The Corps deserves better than me in my underwear.

Late to Drill, 10/03.

Truck broke down. Had to push it five miles. Uphill. Both ways.

"Classic," Jack wheezed. "Give me a study hall."

Absent Study Hall, 10/22.

Was doing more important studying—with your mom.

Mitch fell backward onto his bunk, cackling into the pillow. Jack threw a rolled-up sock at Ethan and missed by a mile.

Ethan kept going, a man possessed. Some lines were pure theater; others were razor-true and simply put. Overslept. My fault. Uniform wrong because I ironed it drunk. Skipped because I couldn't stand the room I was supposed to sit in. The absurd and the honest braided together until the pages felt like a summary of the whole experiment—his sins and his smirk in equal measure.

By midnight the pile was a brick. His hand ached. His grin didn't.

He squared the pages, slid them into a neat column like a term paper he finally understood how to write, and tucked the stack under his arm.

"You're really turning that in?" Jack asked, half awe, half pride.

Ethan opened the door. "Already did," he said, and disappeared down the stoop with the second copy.

The guard room was quieter this time. He set the bundle down like an offering. No speech. No wink. Just a crisp nod and the soft click of the door as he left.

In the courtyard, the parade deck held a pale slice of moon. A breeze moved the flag just enough to make the halyard tap the pole—a tiny drum in the dark.

Ethan stood a moment, feeling it. The laughter upstairs. The weight of the walls. The strange, stubborn joy of daring a machine to notice you.

He went to bed with ink on his fingers and sleep came easy.

Tomorrow would have its say.

Breakfast was loud until it wasn't.

Forks scraped, mugs clinked, steam lifted off eggs—and then eight guards blew through the mess hall doors like a storm front. Conversations snapped shut mid-sentence. Ethan didn't even get to swallow his coffee before four pairs of hands hooked under his arms and legs and lifted.

The Corps erupted—whistles, jeers, someone shouting, "Read 'em his rights!" Jack was on his feet grinning like a proud felon's lawyer; Mitch pounded the table and howled. Ethan let himself go limp, a faint smile settled in. If you're going to make a scene, make it clean.

They carried him across the deck, up the stone steps, down the hallway that smelled like brass polish and old wool, and parked him in front of the heavy oak door with the tarnished nameplate:

SUPERINTENDENT HARTLEY

Inside was the same museum of severity Ethan remembered—dark wood, a wall of grim portraits, a glass case with a saber under a bed of blue felt. Hartley stood behind the desk with a slab of bone sheets in front of him, the top one crinkled where someone's fist had hit it.

He didn't sit. He didn't greet. He just lifted the first page and read aloud, voice flat.

"Absent, Breakfast Roll Call, 8/28. Correct, but wish to explain: I was getting busy with the Commandant's daughter…" His jaw worked once. He set that sheet down and picked another. "Missed Inspection, 9/12. Correct, but wish to explain: Too hungover to find my pants…" Another. "Absent Study Hall, 10/22. Correct, but wish to explain: Was doing more important studying—with your mother."

The silence after that line was a living thing.

Hartley looked up at last. Veins stood at his temples the way cables stand in a bridge. "Do you think this is a joke, Mr. Cole?"

"No, sir," Ethan said, steady. "I think it's accurate."

Hartley's stare could have stripped paint. "One hundred and fifty-four violations. If I brought you to the Court on each one, we'd still be reading the charges at graduation."

"Yes, sir."

"Why?"

Ethan could have smirked. He didn't. "Because this place taught me to own what I am. I took everything SMI had to give. I don't have anything left to take. So I wrote it down. All of it."

Hartley let the silence stretch long enough to be its own punishment. When he spoke again, the heat had cooled into iron. "You've made a mockery of Special Reports, Mr. Cole. And of yourself."

"Yes, sir," Ethan said—agreeing to what needed agreeing to.

Hartley tapped the stack, then his desk blotter, then finally the glass case with the saber. "There are two doors here. Administrative withdrawal effective immediately—resignation for conduct—and you walk out. Or we convene proceedings and you leave without the choice."

Ethan didn't have to think. He'd made his decision when the pen first touched paper.

"I'll take the first door, sir."

Hartley studied him a final beat, searching for fear or bravado, finding neither. Only calm. Only done. He pulled a thin form from a drawer, signed his name in a hard line, and slid it across.

"Turn in your gear. Clear your room by sixteen hundred. You are dismissed."

Ethan took the form. "Yes, sir."

He came to attention and saluted. Hartley returned it—automatic, precise. For half a heartbeat something almost human moved in the Superintendent's eyes, the way a man recognizes another man choosing his own ending. Then it was gone.

Ethan turned, opened the heavy door, and stepped into the hall.

Word travels through stone the way water finds cracks. By the time he hit the stoop, cadets were already leaning over railings four floors up. Someone clapped slow. Someone else shouted his name. And then, from the top tier, a voice he hadn't heard in months called down, bright and defiant:

"Skunk!"

It rolled to the second tier, picked up on the third, swelled on the fourth.

"Skunk! Skunk! Skunk!"

The nickname he'd outgrown came back not as a taunt but as a send-off. He didn't look up—didn't dare—but the corners of his mouth turned anyway.

In the courtyard, Jack waited at the bottom of the steps, hands in his pockets, grin cocked sideways.

"You always did like an exit," he said.

"Figured I'd try one big honest thing," Ethan said.

Jack nodded. "Took guts."

"Or stupidity," Ethan said.

"Same coin," Jack said, and stuck out his hand.

They shook. It was a long, quiet shake that said everything they didn't. Then Mitch barreled in from nowhere and wrapped Ethan in a hug that smelled like aftershave and bad decisions.

"Write me from wherever the hell you land," Mitch said into his ear. "Preferably someplace with cheap beer."

Ethan laughed, stepped back, and tucked the withdrawal form into his jacket. The sun was bright on the parade deck, turning the flag's edge into a white blade. Somewhere a halyard tapped a pole—one soft, stubborn beat.

He walked to pack. The day wasn't over, but the season was.

He packed fast because he knew what to keep.

Into the duffel went the Rat Bible—dog-eared, sweat-warped, margins full of dates he'd crammed under a bare bulb. His battered shaving kit. The scuffed belt buckle he'd polished a hundred times for inspections that never loved him back. A single cassette he'd kept since high school with "Buffett—mix" scratched in shaky pen. No Walkman anymore, but the tape felt like a promise.

Everything else he left. The gray wool that never quite fit. The hanger with his name punched into it. The dented footlocker that had carried him from boy to something harder.

He turned in what the Institute owned: rifle, linens, brass. The supply sergeant checked boxes without looking up. At the guard desk he slid his ID across, signed the last line of the last log he'd ever touch, and heard the quiet snap of the card being cut.

On the stoop, people found him—because they always did at the end. A Rat he didn't know shook his hand like it mattered. Two classmates—now Firsts—gave him the short nod you give a man who chose his door and walked through it. The tiny corporal who'd once carried him three miles on a mountain road after the chicken sausage tried to kill him passed by in silence, then doubled back, stuck out a hand, and squeezed. No speech. Just a grip that said, I saw you keep going.

Jack and Mitch waited at the bottom of the steps with a cardboard box of things Ethan would have forgotten: a photo from Rat year where they all looked shaved and ridiculous, the cheap soccer scarf they'd used as a curtain, a tin of polish.

"Leave something for the next kid," Mitch said, dropping the tin in Ethan's palm.

Ethan climbed one flight, set the polish on the fourth-floor rail, and wrote two words on the lid with a Sharpie he borrowed from a guard: Keep going.

He didn't make a speech. He didn't look for Tran Nguyen. He didn't say goodbye to the Chapel or the courtroom or the hill where he'd almost drowned. He took one slow lap of the courtyard with the duffel high on his shoulder, letting the place sit in his bones the way a bruise does—tender and true.

At the archway he stopped.

For a second the old story tried to play—boots across the deck after dark, ghosts straining forever. He listened. The fans hummed. A halyard tapped. Somewhere a door banged. No haunted cadence came for him.

He realized the only boots he could hear were his own.

Jack stepped up beside him. "You good?"

"I'm ready," Ethan said. It surprised him how true it felt.

They hugged—hard, quick, awkward because real things usually are. Mitch saluted him with two fingers and a crooked grin. "Write if you get someplace interesting," he said.

"I plan to," Ethan answered.

He turned, crossed under the arch, and walked down the hill toward town. The air smelled like damp stone and cut grass. Traffic hissed on Main. He didn't have a grand plan. He had a duffel, the GI Bill, a head that could do math in its sleep, and a body that had learned exactly how much it could take before it broke—and how to stand up anyway.

Behind him, the Institute kept doing what it does: forming ranks, calling roll, making more men and losing a few along the way.

Ahead of him was the other thing this place had prepared him for without meaning to: a life where nobody was going to tell him when to eat, when to sleep, or who he was. He'd have to decide that himself.

Ethan Cole—Skunk to some, Rat to others—walked toward the next hill with his own pace in his ears and a small, private smile.

It wasn't victory. It was something better.

It was his.

www.ingramcontent.com/pod-product-compliance
Lightning Source LLC
Chambersburg PA
CBHW020227010826
48973CB00006B/1405